THE ADVENTURES OF DOD

DARK HOOD AND THE LAIR

THOMAS R. WILLIAMS

Zettai Makeru

Publisher's Cataloging-in-Publication Data

Williams, Thomas R. (Thomas Richards), 1971-
The Adventures of Dod : Dark Hood and the Lair / by Thomas R. Williams ;
illustrations by Christine Coleman.

p. : ill. ; cm.

Summary: When Cole finally escapes trouble on Earth and returns to Green, he and his friends must face a horrible beast, a diabolical plot, and an evil villain with an unbreakable, crimson sword.

ISBN: 978-0-9833601-4-8 (pbk.)

[1. Adventure and adventurers—Juvenile fiction. 2. Imaginary places—Juvenile fiction. 3. Magic—Juvenile fiction. 4. Schools—Juvenile fiction. 5. Adventure and adventurers—Fiction. 6. Magic—Fiction. 7. Schools—Fiction. 8. Adventure fiction. 9. Fantasy fiction.] I. Coleman, Christine, 1975- II. Title.

PZ7.W6683 Add 2011
[Fic]   2011935727

Printed in the United States of America

10 9 8 7 6 5 4 3 2 1

For my fans

who have persisted

in seeking the secrets.

TABLE OF CONTENTS

PROLOGUE

As you've been told before, this story is almost too amazing to believe, but it's true! One seemingly insignificant boy did change the future for everyone. It's a tale that is filled with intrigue and mystery, loyal friendships and blackened betrayals.

Cole's first visit to Green left him feeling satisfied that all was well, since The Dread — the very man who had instigated the murder of his grandfather — was on his way to a living-death sentence at Driaxom. However, Cole was naïve to think the forces of evil were contained by the imprisonment of one man, especially considering the lure of powerful hidden secrets.

If you dare continue reading the adventure, beware! Who's a friend and who's a foe? Can you tell? Can Dod tell? Know this, some people will stop at nothing to get what they want!

THE FUGITIVES

"He'll understand, won't he?" whispered a woman, her head wrapped in a scarlet shawl. Her steps were sluggish and labored as she left the safety of her carriage and followed two rag-tag soldiers into the moonlight. "It's not like it was my fault. I took every precaution imaginable. They were just too strong."

The night air was wet and thick, fed by the mist of a murky pool. Tree frogs peeped and chirped from their hiding places in the dense foliage and bullfrogs croaked obstinately from the water's edge.

"And my sons — they're all dead now," continued the woman, pleading her case. "At my age, you'd think at least one of the seven could be answering for me."

The officers didn't respond to her. It wasn't their place to decide what to do. Someone else was in charge of the mess.

"Please, boys," she begged, stopping under the shadow of a giant fir tree. "How does this work? What will he do?" Her eyes met theirs momentarily. Their worn, dirty clothes and scarred, somber faces did little to instill hope of a civil conversation with their boss.

CHAPTER ONE

Up ahead, on the swampy banks of the pond, two ghoulish torches made of skulls flickered sporadically, crackling and hissing as they burnt the unwary bugs that crossed too close. Behind them, a tar-black castle rose four stories from the mud. Moss and vines shrouded the lower half of the building, as though the bog would consume it.

One soldier, a hefty three-hundred-pounder, nodded his head toward the castle's entrance. When the woman continued to hesitate, he grabbed for her arm.

"I'm coming," she barked, prickling up. But before she moved, a giant brown snake, eighteen feet long, crossed the stone path in front of them. Its bulbous, glowing eyes searched the horizon while its forked tongue licked the night air. Three lumps in the snake's otherwise sleek form indicated it had fed on large prey.

No sooner had the serpent's tail left the path than a hearty nudge forced the woman to walk.

"Can't you tell me anything?" she begged, melting with fear. She wrung her hands in torment, whitening her bulgy knuckles.

The smaller of the two soldiers shook his head and looked away.

In front of the castle, a rickety bridge crossed a twenty-foot moat that encircled the building. Muddy, bubbling water filled the ditch as alligators fought over space. They seemed hopeful that someone would fall through the rotten timbers and feed them.

Before entering, the two guards straightened their shoulders, drew their swords, and clanked a dragon's-head knocker.

"Arrival's here, sir," yelled the larger soldier, sucking in his gut.

The giant double doors swung open slowly, revealing a smoky hall. Dozens of poorly dressed warriors sat around four

sprawling banquet tables. They looked like pirates. Up the center
of the room, ten-foot poles held oil lamps that burned dimly,
revealing the remains of dinner — carcasses from a couple of pigs
so picked at that a crow would strain its eyes to find flesh on the
bones that were left.

"Bring her here," yelled a burly man, dressed in dark leather.
He sat at the back of the room on a throne made of bleached bones.

"Murdore — it's good to see you — " began the woman, but
her voice was lost in the vaulted hall. The rats that scurried across
the trusses were louder than she was.

"I very much doubt that!" thundered the man, rising to his
feet. He was the most formidable of the group, and it wasn't just
his size — his face was terrifying, pocked with scars, and his eyes
were threatening, as remorseless as the devil's. The hilt of his
wicked sword had the mark of a gruesome skull.

"Oh, sir — " said the woman, bowing over. Her knees
knocked together as she was hurried through the maze of clutter
to the base of Murdore's throne. She didn't look him in the eyes.

"I thought we had an agreement!" he raged. "Didn't you
sign with your knife?"

"Yes, but — "

"And your kin, too?"

"Yes Murdore, but please — "

"Then we'll follow the law of the billies," declared the man,
raising his fist in the air.

"THE LAW OF THE BILLIES," thundered the men in the
hall, lifting their fists in agreement. Scars and tattoos littered the
sunburned limbs that waved in unison for her demise.

"But please," she begged. "My sons are all dead now — three
from the raids and four more from this — "

"And your kinfolk?" demanded Murdore, his eyes beating down on her angrily. "The whole clan of Tool agreed to take part. If the pact is broken, they must all be punished!"

"THEY MUST ALL BE PUNISHED!" roared the mob.

"But the ones they left behind are all dead — " explained the woman, cowering pathetically.

"Left behind?" barked Murdore. His face darkened and the room took a chill. "I didn't authorize any raids this week. Whose cities are they plundering?"

The woman bent lower to the ground and remained silent. She trembled under her shawl, waiting for the thunder of his judgment.

"WHERE?" demanded Murdore. "Tell me where they went!"

"I-I don't know for sure," she squeaked. "They all packed up and left — except the ones they saved for my help — the ones that died during the break."

"And they thought I wouldn't notice!" scoffed Murdore, snorting through his nose like an angry ape.

"They thought you'd be pleased," pressed the woman, taking her chances. "I told them I didn't think so."

"Pleased?"

"Yes sir. They've joined forces with a few of the strongest men from the closest islands and intend on bringing honor to the noble billies at Bollirse."

"By playing a game?" gasped Murdore. The room filled with grumbled chuckles of disapproval.

"Yes sir," said the woman. "I've heard that they call themselves the Raging Billies. They've gone to play against the teams to the north and west of us, sir, in hopes of progressing to the matches at Carsigo."

"Fools!" raged Murdore. "Humans like us don't play games."

"Right, sir," agreed the woman, beginning to lift her head. "But they had a plan—one brimming with gold."

"Hmmm," grumbled the leader, and the room filled with small chatter. "What say you, men?" he demanded of the motley bunch.

A particularly hairy man, whose bushy brown beard nearly hid his chest, spoke up first, saying, "Gold's not bad, sir."

"AYE!" rumbled the crowd, clicking their mismatched, empty cups against the tables.

"And perhaps a little rum from the mainland couldn't hurt," added another man, whose mouth had more gaps than teeth.

"AYE!" roared the men.

"And Tredder ladies—" blurted a darker-skinned human, whose braids dangled to his waist.

"AYE! AYE! AYE!" thundered the bunch.

"Then the alligators will wait!" boomed Murdore, glancing at the woman. He bent down slowly and looked her in the eyes. "You may live for now—we'll call it a loan. But let me know of their letters. I must be informed of this plan. Perhaps my connections will be pleased."

The double doors boomed open with a crash, and a gust of wind made the frail flames flicker.

"They've been spotted, sir!" yelled a one-armed man who stood at the doorway with a small company of guards. "And they're heading toward the docks. We'd better take action now. What say you?"

"The docks already?" choked Murdore, looking concerned. "Arise men. Get your clans and head to the ships. It's better to overwhelm them with our numbers than to fight this lot. We're squeezed with our orders to keep them locked from the world, but living all the same."

"AYE!" rumbled the crowd.

"Leave your swords and spears at home for this one, men. We must take them alive. Now go!"

"But sir," gasped the one-armed man, scratching at his matted dreadlocks, "shouldn't we bring precautions. I just witnessed—well—"

Murdore's glare seized the man and shushed his tone.

"I-I mean, s-sir," stuttered the man at the door, "a lesser group was in their way—as they were dashing—and now they're all dead—and *they* used their swords!"

"It doesn't matter!" shouted Murdore. "Get your ropes, get your nets, get your sticks, and get your clans—we need to take them alive! The consequences are too great if we don't!"

A rumble of chatter filled the hall with noise. The one-armed man's words were strong enough to sway the otherwise loyal group.

"LISTEN!" boomed Murdore, his face reddening with frustration and anger. "You fools don't realize what would happen if we let them escape—or if we kill them. They're not normal prisoners." He searched the group with his bloodshot eyes and then added, "Do we look like common wardens to you? I say no, men, we're not!"

"AYE!" grunted the pack.

"We've been entrusted with a charge—a tricky one at that—but it pays well!"

"AYE," responded the mob less enthusiastically. A few of them glanced at their worn clothes, while others looked to their empty cups.

"Not enough, of course—"

"AYE!" surged the men, once again fully in agreement.

"But this man—our boss—he's as soft as a nap on a bed

of nails and as kind as the itch for water when you're months from port without rain. His glare alone could kill you—and he'd sooner do that than hear any excuses. He'd feed your young ones to the alligators for sport and then whine that the fun was over too quickly. I'm not lying. And my only stretch is that I've portrayed him on his kindest of days."

The group was silent as Murdore continued to explain what manner of man they served.

"And he rules the lands in secret—all of them! His order is rising as surely as the moon, sneaking past the eyes of the fools who sleep upon their comfy beds of democracy. If we were to cross him—"

Murdore shuddered.

"If we fail him, we're all dead! This whole island—all of our cities and every last member of our clans would be gone. He'd wipe the earth with his dark hand and we'd join the fools in the afterworld—and even there, I'm sure he has his connections."

From the corner of the room an old man, bald and fragile, leaned upon his cane and rose to his feet. His eyes were gone, so he pointed the wrong way when he spoke, saying, "We're billies. We fight. We've raided and been raided. It's just the way things go. If your boss becomes angry, I doubt he'd do any better than the other roaming billies that have attempted to plunder our cities. With weapons in hand, we're a strong bunch of souls!"

"AYE!" agreed the group loudly. Many of them drew their swords and pounded the tables with their hilts.

"And even if he does seek us out," continued the old man, "perhaps he'll punish a different lot—there are so many to choose from—and to mainlanders, we're all the same, just a bunch of ship-scrubbing, bilge-sucking, noble billies."

"Not to this man—" began Murdore when the blind man interrupted.

"Don't forget about the wrath of Durgon! His threats caused such alarm that we hardly dared sail out to catch fish—and what became of *them*? NOTHING!" The man re-situated his weight and staggered forward, adding, "Has your mainlander boss ever been here before?"

"No," scoffed Murdore.

"Then he wouldn't find us, would he?" blared the old man. "We're as far from *anywhere* as *anyone* could possibly be. Their maps don't even show we exist!"

"But this man you so lightly blow off," argued Murdore, filled with rage, "he doesn't go away when he's angry—he stalks and plots and waits, and then, when we least expect it, he strikes! He could hire four other islands of billies to destroy us, or he could get Dreaderious and his poorlings to do the job—or...I wouldn't put it past him to trick Pious into mashing us. This man—this *monster!*—he's impossible to stop."

"Then go recapture our guests, Murdore!" ordered the hunching man, pulling rank. "But don't leave our clans helpless against them. Swords and spears are necessary if you hope to set things right."

Murdore moaned and groaned and fumed as the room silently watched the showdown of sorts.

"As you wish, *father!*" conceded Murdore bitterly. "Rise up with your might, men! Gather your clans and we'll stop them. It's better to get paid in gold than in wrath!"

"AYE! AYE! AYE!" roared the whole room, as the warriors jumped to their feet and stormed out the door, leaving a catastrophic mess. The lady with the scarlet shawl crept for the exit, too, but was stopped short by Murdore. "We'll have you start with this disaster, woman, as the rest of us go to clean up the one your clumsy clan left afoot." He plucked his shield from the wall, threw a gigantic coil of rope over his shoulder, and tapped the hilt of his sword three times for good luck before following after the one-armed guard.

Down by the wharf, thousands of men merged, creating a sea of glittering swords and shields that outshined the moon. A dozen full-sized battle ships were anchored in the bay, a safe distance from the rocky shore, and another three dozen boats of smaller sizes were tied to the pier.

"SEARCH THEM ALL!" yelled Murdore, trying to be heard over the howling wind. A storm was coming. In the distance, black clouds hid the stars, while bursts of lightning streaked the sky. The unsettled water crashed mercilessly against the boats, wave after wave, grinding them into each other and the dock.

Like an army of ants, the men flooded the coastline, searching the piles of wreckage, the supply shacks, and the docked boats. The fugitives were gone. They hadn't stolen any of the smaller vessels, which led the soldiers to assume that they'd opted for the swamps, hoping to steal away from the island after the weather had settled.

But before the throng of men had cleared the first bluff toward the mires, someone noticed that one of their battleships had lifted its anchor, posted its sails, and was heading out to sea.

"I thought you counted boats!" raged Murdore, nearly drawing his sword on his own men.

"We did, sir," reported the leaders. "They're all tethered in place. The blazing brutes must've swam the length and overpowered the men-at-ready aboard the ship."

CHAPTER ONE

"In a storm like this?" barked Murdore angrily. He doubted that the escapees had paddled the distance without a boat, but it didn't matter—with or without a smaller vessel, they had successfully taken control of a battleship and were well on their way to freedom.

"We'll need every able man to load the barges and head to the dashers," ordered Murdore, leading toward the wharf. "Launch the whole fleet! We must overrun them in time!"

But the plan was faulty from the start; the waves were so hard against the billies that their smaller boats struggled to reach the larger ships, and once they did set sail, the pounding rain and howling wind killed their ability to track the fleeing fugitives. By the middle of the night, two of their dashers had been driven by the tempest onto treacherous rocks and had sunk.

Just before dawn, the unthinkable happened. Murdore watched it all through his noculars from a distance. The very ship that they had been pursuing all night was struck by a massive bolt of lightning, splitting the mast down the center and creating a gap in the hull. Within a few minutes, the dasher tipped precariously on its side and sank out of view.

"No!" cried Murdore, blaring his venom at the wind. He cursed the waters and the skies and the powers of evil that had hedged his way, and he kept his course and sought diligently to find any survivors, but his efforts were all in vain.

Weeks later, hidden beneath better clothing than they were typically accustomed to, Murdore, and a valiant billie warrior, and the woman with the scarlet shawl nervously produced a pile of papers and entered High Gate. They had traveled for thousands of miles to bring the unwanted news. It was a frightful chore.

THE FUGITIVES

With somber steps, Murdore led the way. He had brought the woman in hopes that her clan's curious plan would appease his boss, and if not, that her death would cool his rage. And he had brought the daring warrior to be the next in line, if two deaths were required. And he had brought his best shoes for running and his best sword for fighting if three or more bodies were the price of forgiveness.

However, when he timidly sought his boss, he was met with a shocking report—he was told that Sirlonk was imprisoned at High Gate, caught the night before by a nobody named Dod, and that he was about to be escorted to Driaxom for the crimes he had committed as The Dread!

The news changed everything.

With a new lease on life, Murdore sighed. Perhaps things weren't so bad. Perhaps with The Dread gone, the noble billies' little disaster wasn't important anyway. Perhaps the gaping hole in the ranks of evil would be filled by someone who cared less about the loss of a handful of fugitives.

Only time would tell.

SOMETHING'S MISSING

Cole looked out his window and watched the rain come down in torrents. It was unusual for southern Utah to get so much water. He would have taken the time to think that it was odd if his mind hadn't been preoccupied with something that was far more extraordinary.

Thoughts of Green flooded Cole's mind, and at the forefront were his beloved friends, Boot, Buck, Dilly, and Sawny, as well as others who had included him in their circle of camaraderie. He was happy to be home and very glad to see that his world had remained untouched, yet it actually made him feel melancholy to know that his friends were in Green and he wasn't.

"They're waiting for me," muttered Cole to himself, reaching for the medallion around his neck. He pulled on the chain and drew it out of his shirt. Both sides of the golden object were worn, so the faint inscriptions were hard to see. It resembled an ancient coin.

"As long as I keep this on, time will stand still in Green," Cole sighed reassuringly as he slid it back. He looked his bedroom over with new eyes, having been gone for months, and was surprised to see how small and tattered it was when compared to the one he had shared with Boot and Buck. The walls were covered with pictures and posters, hung to hide the holes and cracks in the plaster, and the floor was draped with a worn, secondhand rug that bunched up against the base of his younger brothers' bunk bed. Everything in the room seemed to limp along on its last leg, ready to give out. Even Cole's computer looked ratty, having been obtained as a trade for mowing Miss Emily Holbrook's lawn the prior summer.

At least Dilly can't see this, thought Cole, suddenly grateful for the barrier that separated him from the other Coosings. With the wealth at Twistyard, he couldn't imagine Dilly would understand.

"Water," groaned Alex, mumbling in his sleep. "Help. I can't swim." He appeared to be dreaming about the flashflood that had nearly claimed their lives. Cole approached his sleeping brothers and fought off the urge to embrace them. After having been away for what seemed like a long time, he wanted to wake them up and tell them about his adventures, even if they had only napped a short while. He knew Josh would insist on hearing every detail.

A quiet knock interrupted his thoughts. Cole crossed the room with two steps and greeted Aunt Hilda. He couldn't help giving her a big hug.

"Are you okay?" she asked, stepping back. Her eyes prodded his.

"I'm fine," he said. "I just wanted to tell you thanks for everything." Cole looked down and sheepishly added, "It wouldn't be the same around here without you."

"So, you're thinking about running away, are you?" responded Hilda wryly. "I did when I was fourteen."

"No," laughed Cole. He realized he was acting weird for a teenager who had just barely finished fighting with his mother, and Aunt Hilda had watched the whole thing unfold.

"Nope. Leaving is the opposite of what I'm thinking," said Cole. "And…um…I'm sorry for the way I acted downstairs." Cole searched for the apology that he'd rehearsed in his mind while in Green. "I shouldn't treat you and Mom like that. I'm going to be better. I promise."

Hilda reached out and drew Cole back into her arms, giving him a big squeeze that buried his face in her long, curly brown hair. Cole winced in pain. One of her hands had found the wound on his shoulder, causing it to bleed.

"What's this?" said Hilda, tugging at the neckline of Cole's shirt. "You didn't say anything about getting hurt in the flood this morning." She inspected his gash as well as she could with him squiggling. "I think we need to visit the hospital. This looks pretty serious."

"I'm fine," contended Cole, finally shaking himself loose. "I already had someone look at it. He wrapped it up and…"

Cole's voice faded. He remembered that the medical people in Green had attended to his injury from Sirlonk with strange bandages, but returning to Earth had stripped them off. They were gone. And Aunt Hilda's hug had reopened one corner of the wound.

"Josh doesn't count!" insisted Hilda. "Now hold still and let me get a good look." She reached over and plucked the last tissue from a box on the top of Cole's dresser and wiped the blood away until she could see the cut better. "Huh. That's weird," she stammered, standing on her toes; her trim frame was shorter than Cole's. "It looks like most of it is sealed-up. Just this one spot is oozing. Come downstairs and I'll fix you the way Pap always did."

Cole knew what was coming. Pap cleaned his abrasions with alcohol and then pulled them closed with the sticky part of bandages, after cutting the padded centers out.

The commotion drew Josh and Alex to the main floor. They followed Aunt Hilda, having been awakened by the fuss over Cole's laceration. The two gangly brothers looked like twins. Eleven-year-old Alex curled up on the couch with a blanket and sleepily gazed, while ten-year-old Josh leaned over Cole's shoulder, begging to help.

"What did that?" asked Josh, surprised to see the three-inch wound across Cole's left shoulder. He scratched at his straight brown hair and fidgeted impatiently.

"Don't you mean who?" responded Cole, grinning. His eyes flashed at Josh with excitement. "You'd never believe what happened."

Cole began at the beginning and spent the next three hours retelling his adventures in Green, including all about Twistyard, the Coosings, Bollirse, and his near fatal encounter with The Dread. He would have gone on longer if it hadn't been for Josh's piano lesson that cut the story short.

Hilda listened while she busied herself around the kitchen, tidying up and doing laundry. She never once commented on how outlandish and crazy it all sounded; and when she did finally remark, she simply stated that Cole was becoming more like Pap each day. It was a compliment.

Alex tried to stay interested in the story, from his cozy spot, but eventually gave in to the tug of heavy eyelids. Josh, on the other hand, was so involved in the account that hardly two minutes went by without him asking questions. He frequently interrupted with comments of envy, adding over and over, "You'll bring me there next time, won't you, Cole?"

Part of Cole wished he could bring Josh with him—that is, if he ever figured out how to get back; going to Green and returning to Earth were two moves he hadn't mastered. But another part of Cole was grateful he had an impassible barrier between his safe life on Earth and the precarious circumstances in the other realms.

The following weeks flew by faster than any Cole had ever known. His computer stayed mostly dormant, while other activities took the bulk of his time, which is really saying something considering he was a self-proclaimed computer geek. After having faced The Dread, everything else seemed less daunting, including being teased by Jon. Cole felt like a whole new person, liberated from his fears and driven to succeed.

When Cole was at baseball practice, he was really there. Of course, it didn't hurt that he had a new-found love for Bollirse and his teammates back in Green. Thinking of them and the upcoming Bollirse matches, including the regulation play against Raul Hall, drove him to practice hitting balls like never before. He set up a strange configuration of three old tarps in his backyard and spent hours whacking stuff Josh threw in his direction. Around the block, people joked that Josh would become a star pitcher by the end of the summer if Cole continued at the pace he was going.

And it wasn't just baseball that received attention from Cole. His positive attitude and excitement for life breathed fresh air into everything he did—and he did a lot! He read twice as much as before, researching all sorts of things he had wondered about while in Green, and he joined a local fencing club of mostly older men. He even took part in an emergency-preparedness program that developed his basic skills in first-aid.

His mother, Doralee Richards, was getting used to being asked what had happened to her son. It appeared to the neighbors as though aliens had abducted him and left someone in his place, because he was so different.

But Cole didn't see it that way. He felt like he was finally showing to the world what he had hidden inside for years.

The only thing that bothered him enough to grumble was that his mother continued to occasionally date Coach Smith. Somehow, the closer she became to him, the more he tried to be Cole's father—and nobody could take the place of his father or grandpa.

Every night during the summer, before Cole fell asleep, he attempted to return to Green. He wanted to learn how to zip back and forth, as Pap had done. But his medallion didn't seem to work. All of the time he spent staring and thinking only made him tired—and paranoid that he had accidentally broken the charm.

One particular evening, his efforts began to appear promising. As he lay on his bed in the darkness, he focused on a speck until it grew bigger and bigger.

I'm heading back, thought Cole, bracing himself for the journey. Shortly thereafter, he realized it was a spider descending on him.

Weeks turned to months, and fall came without Cole ever revisiting Twistyard. He began to really miss his friends and wish to be with them, and since the arrival of cooler days brought the rigors of school, his desire to return only increased. Yet nothing proved effective at getting rid of his obligation to attend the ninth grade; fate, it seemed, kept him trapped with no way to avoid the daily lectures or the piles of homework.

At school, things were busy enough that there wasn't time for thinking about Green. Josh was the lone person he continued to speak with about the other realms, since he didn't want people to think he was loco. So it came as a shocker when a girl in his science class asked him about the subject.

"Hey, how do you get there?" she said, staring at Cole with one hand on her hip. She was skinny and tall, the same height as Cole, whose summer of growth had boosted him up to five-foot nine.

"What?" asked Cole, trying to smile. A quick brush with his right hand reassured him that his medallion was hidden beneath his shirt. The circumstance was past bizarre. He had never met the girl before, and until that moment, when they were paired together for an experiment, he had never heard her voice. He didn't even know her name.

"Tell me," said the mystery girl, nodding her head. "What do you do to get there, wherever it is?"

Cole racked his brain to think of how she could have heard of his experience. Josh had promised to keep it a secret and his other family members had quickly dismissed his original tale as just that—a story, nothing more. The only logical explanation was that she was referring to somewhere else. It was an awkward way to say hello.

"I'm Cole Richards," he responded, nervously trying to force a comfortable look. Inside, he was hoping she'd say something that would direct his mind to whatever she was really talking about. When his intro fell flat, he instinctively stuck out his hand to shake. It was a big blooper. The girl raised an eyebrow and left him hanging.

"That's a nice dress you're wearing," Cole quickly said, feeling like he was in a sinking hot-air balloon. He drew back his hand and stuffed it clumsily into his pocket. The girl's gape was intimidating. "Not very many people fancy-up when coming here," he added. "It's refreshing to see you—well—like that." Cole cringed. His words felt wrong and old-fashioned or foreign. He was awkward at introductions, especially to cute or popular girls, and his lab partner was both. Cole vaguely recalled having seen her around with older, high school guys—the football team.

"Fancy-up?" she said, smirking. She twisted her head and her straight brown hair whipped the air, then draped over her shoulder, halfway to her waist. "You're funny."

Before either of them could say anything else, the teacher came walking over and tapped his watch. "Time's a-wasting," he grumbled, scowling. His wrinkly forehead and bushy eyebrows made him look comical, despite his serious intent. "Get going on this or you'll get a bad grade."

Mr. Brewer meant what he said. He wasn't a nice teacher, and from what Cole had observed during the first three weeks of class, he'd happily give both of them lousy scores for incompletion if they missed finishing the smallest part of the experiment. So, with the warning they got, Cole proceeded to work feverishly, explaining out loud what he was doing, while his nameless partner watched, half-interested.

About thirty minutes into the task, Cole noticed that his cohort wasn't even pretending to pay attention anymore. She kept reaching into her expensive backpack, texting. It wouldn't have mattered if Cole had four hands to work with, like Dungo. However, as he had only two, and was approaching the fun part where it became obvious why they were in pairs for the assignment, Cole spoke up and asked for her help.

She ignored him, giggled to herself, and flipped her hair with one hand while grabbing for her phone with the other.

Cole begged, this time with greater urgency. Still no response. Finally, brown goo bubbled over the top of a beaker he couldn't reach, a beaker his partner could have poured into the other two larger ones he was carefully balancing and the experiment would have been complete.

"Oh!" groaned Cole. He was terribly frustrated and wanted to scream when suddenly something strange happened. A flash of unusual images raced through his mind, much the same way they had in Green. They flowed like lightning and were his first experience of that kind since returning to Earth. The message was clear: Back up, NOW!

Cole moved forward, partially spilling one of the beakers' contents on the counter as he attempted hastily to free his hands of the messy liquids before retreating. Unfortunately, the dreaded event happened too fast to avoid. The last thing Cole could remember was feeling something heavy hit the back of his head.

When he awoke, he was lying on a stretcher, being carried to an ambulance.

"What happened?" whispered Cole. He felt dizzy and nauseous. He glanced around at the spinning world. Slowly, two men's faces became clearer.

"Can you see us?" one man asked.

Cole nodded.

"Don't move," insisted the other. "We need to check your neck at the hospital. It might be broken."

"What? I'm fine," argued Cole. He lifted one of his legs and wiggled it in the air, proving he still had mobility.

Regardless, the medical team loaded him into their emergency vehicle and hauled him away.

At the urgent-care facility, doctors ran a series of quick tests to determine the extent of his injuries. Fortunately, the prognosis was good: He was fine, except for a nasty bump on the back of his head.

After the drama of being attended to, a nurse escorted him to one of six cubicle spaces, partitioned off by drab-green curtains, and had him lie down with an ice pack on his goose egg. He wasn't there long before Principal Robinson arrived—huffing and puffing—spouting all sorts of things, explaining how the accident had happened, or at least what some people claimed had happened. Cole listened to the story, while waiting for his mother to arrive.

His lab partner had swung her bag, trying to avoid the messy experiment gone wrong, and in doing so, had bumped others into Mr. Brewer's prized bronze of an elephant perched on top of a pole. The metal statue had taken a detour across the back of Cole's head before making its way to the floor.

Principal Robinson apologized repeatedly for the incident and insisted that Mr. Brewer should have retired when he left Salt Lake for his native town of Cedar. "He's worked his last day in my school!" he grumbled adamantly, tugging at the sleeves of his pinstriped suit coat that didn't quite fit him. "I can guarantee you that much."

"It wasn't really his fault," said Cole, starting to feel sorry for

Mr. Brewer. Despite the teacher's mean streak, Cole didn't want to be responsible for his dismissal.

"Yes it was!" snapped the principal, his portly face turning redder than it already was, matching his flaming hair. "He's got his personal junk all over that room, like a museum. By the way he collects and displays trinkets and gadgets you'd think he was the curator of some dusty auction-house. It's a problem when teachers allow their hobbies and part-time employment to creep into the classroom. He can have all the rubbish he wants in his own residence, and that's where it's going to be, starting tomorrow!"

A sick feeling settled in the pit of Cole's stomach. He felt awful about getting his teacher fired, even if he hadn't liked him. And Cole knew what everyone else didn't: He knew he could have avoided the whole dilemma if he would have immediately backed up, as he had been warned to do.

Principal Robinson continued his apology speech, as though he lacked an off button, when Cole overheard a familiar voice. It was his mother's. She was at the reception desk inquiring about him, and judging by the tone she used, she was drenched with concern. "I'm…uh…Doralee Richards," she said, a bit frail in the lips. "Where's my son? Is he going to be all right?"

Cole stood up, parted the squeaky curtain, and hustled to greet her. His head hurt and his clothes were a mess; nevertheless, he didn't want his mother to worry any more than she already had, so he quickened his steps and played the part of feeling fine.

"Sorry Mom," said Cole, putting one arm on her shoulder as soon as he found her. She smelled like burnt fries and dish soap, suggesting she'd come straight from the Truck-Stop Diner. "You know how schools are these days," continued Cole, forcing a smirk. "If you get a scratch, they rush you in. It's crazy if you ask me."

Doralee trembled and hugged him. Her slight frame looked as though it would give out if she weren't being steadied by Cole.

"They called me at work and said you were seriously injured," sobbed Doralee, her blonde curls jiggling with her shaking shoulders. "They said you had a broken neck!"

"I'm fine—really, Mom," assured Cole, partially lying. His head was throbbing and he needed to sit down.

Principal Robinson began again at the beginning of his apology lecture and continued circling the issues until he felt Doralee was plentifully informed of how regretful he was that the mishap had occurred. The swirl of words found their way past Mr. Brewer's dismissal four times, with each including a pledge that disruptive and dangerous classrooms would not be tolerated by him.

At home, Cole did his best to sleep off the headache, laying down at 4:30 p.m. and not rising until the next morning. He didn't even stir. He slept so soundly that when he awoke on the floor beside his bed, he hadn't the slightest clue of when he had fallen there. And strangely, his right hand hurt more than his head. One knuckle was swollen and tender.

Alex showed concern during breakfast, asking a few questions before inspecting Cole's injuries. Josh, on the other hand, was more interested than concerned and prodded deeper, insisting Cole was holding back the true rendition of what had happened, the one about being wounded while fighting some horrid creature in Green. The conversation continued, with Josh persistently digging for additional information, until Cole nearly missed his bus—which wouldn't have been entirely bad, since the ride to school was more awkward than usual; not only did he sit alone, the chorus of whispers seemed to lead people's eyes in his direction.

As the day went on, from one period to the next, bits and pieces of a peculiar tale emerged—a story that only slightly resembled the things Principal Robinson had told—an account that included Cole swinging his fists and kicking his feet while yelling insane things.

Given the rumors, it wasn't surprising at lunch when nobody wanted to sit by him. Even Coach Smith's son, Bumbling Bobby, who was his usual tag-along lunch-pal, found somewhere else to eat. And that was strange, considering that after Cole had returned from Green and had practiced baseball like an obsessed maniac, his standing on the team had risen near the top while his empathy for Bobby had remained the same.

Tension was mounting, building up to the moment of truth: Sixth period. Stewing over it stole Cole's appetite like a case of the stomach flu, rendering him incapable of even nibbling. He couldn't stop worrying about whether Mr. Brewer would still be there, pending dismissal; and if so, what would he say to Cole? He'd still be mean—and he'd be mad as well! The only thing that made the wait bearable was knowing that at last he could ask his classmates what had really happened and get a reliable answer.

Cole's thoughts pestered him as he pushed his food back and forth, never raising a bite of country-fried steak to his mouth. Even his fudge-frosted brownie was untouched when he gave up trying and left the cafeteria.

With questions nagging, Cole headed to his science class. He hoped to get there early enough to talk with others about what had happened, but late enough to avoid being alone with Mr. Brewer.

Room 125 was the correct door. He took a deep breath and strode in, searching for his seat. The room was completely different. The desks were orderly, placed in straight rows, which hadn't been the case before, and the mounds and mounds of stuff—the awards, piles of paper, scrolls of maps and charts, statuary, tools, boxes, and ancient artifacts—were all gone. The room looked and felt gutted, like a thief had raided the place during the night and had brought a team of men to strip it of everything. Even Cole's favorite inspiration, an African wooden mask, was gone. It had hung precariously above the chalkboard with its scarlet tongue sticking out.

"Find a seat, dear. Take your pick," said a lady that sat in the corner. She looked mid-forties and stylishly dressed. Her straight-backed posture, black hair, and dark brown eyes reminded Cole of Juny Chantolli. Across the top of the board, 'Mrs. Tupper' was written in big letters.

Cole surveyed the empty seats. He was the first student, so he did have his pick.

"Whoa, he's gone!" gasped Jon, entering the room behind Cole. Jon was Cole's baseball nemesis. He had made fun of Cole for years and had gotten a lot of other guys to join in—that is, before the change. Once Cole started performing better at sports and didn't seem bothered by teasing, the ridicule had died down.

"Hey, Jon. This is pretty weird, isn't it?" said Cole, feeling one hundred percent better than he had in the cafeteria. He was relieved that he didn't need to face an angry Mr. Brewer.

"Yeah," said Jon nervously. He looked Cole up and down with his smoky-blue eyes and then moved back out into the hall.

Cole took a seat in the middle, figuring he'd have a better chance of sitting next to someone he could casually ask about the day before, but it didn't work. As other students entered, they too acted irregular, like there was a monster in the room—and Cole was the monster! Nobody wanted to get near him.

To make matters worse, the whole class, for the first time, was completely silent. Even the bubbly girls who always sat on the front row were speechless. It left no leeway for Cole to strike a conversation without being the center of attention.

Mrs. Tupper began by explaining that she was not a substitute, she was their new science teacher. The announcement created a quick moment of whispers followed by a return to silence. She then went over an unusually long list of rules before settling into a monotonous discourse on the value of bees, wasps, and hornets to Earth's sensitive ecosystem.

Except for occasional coughs, the students could have been made of stone. They were hardly the same bundle of people who had attended the previous science class taught by Mr. Brewer. They behaved so dissimilarly that Cole actually spent half of the lecture glancing around, trying to piece together who was different. Finally it hit him. The nameless girl was gone. She and Mr. Brewer were the only deletions—and there were no additions.

After class, Mrs. Tupper asked to speak with Cole for a few minutes, promising to provide him with a note for his gym teacher if he'd stay. She didn't have a seventh period and was looking for answers as to why the students all appeared so averse to being by him.

"I have no idea," confessed Cole, feeling more than confused. He hadn't had so much as one normal 'Hello' or 'How are you doing?' from anyone, which was the exact opposite of what he had expected, given his unfortunate injury the day before. "You probably know more than I do," said Cole, his hesitant voice hinting at the frustration he felt. "Since yesterday's little episode, everybody has been treating me like I have the plague."

"What happened yesterday?" asked Mrs. Tupper, chilling Cole with her gaze. She had obviously already made up her mind that he was the problem, and by her questions, she was clearly attempting to 'help him' discover it for himself.

Cole was shocked. He couldn't believe she had misunderstood the circumstance—he wasn't a troublemaker—and he certainly wasn't dumb enough to think for one second that Mrs. Tupper was unaware of what had transpired the day prior. Principal Robinson had surely filled her in; after all, he would have explained about Mr. Brewer's untimely retirement while hiring her on such short notice.

When staring in amazement didn't work, Cole finally answered her question by saying, "This!" pointing to the large goose egg on the back of his head. He wished she would stop playing dumb and get on with her lecturing if that was her intent.

Mrs. Tupper didn't flinch, so Cole repeated what the principal had recounted to him. Cole even walked over to the counter where he had been mixing his experiment and pointed out where Mr. Brewer's large elephant statue had been.

"You're kidding, right?" said Mrs. Tupper, dumbfounded.

Cole looked into her eyes to see if she was being sarcastic. She wasn't.

"I just don't understand," she continued, sizzling Cole with her stare. "You had an elephant hit your head yesterday, and now everybody hates you?"

It didn't make sense to Cole, either. He felt stupid trying to explain it that way, but it was the truth, as far as he knew.

"And this room had some guy's stuff in it?" asked Mrs. Tupper. She didn't even attempt to hide her doubts; her voice said it all—'You're a liar!'

"It was his classroom!" argued Cole, getting angry.

"Whose?"

"Mr. Brewer's!"

"Your substitute brought a large statue of an elephant?" scoffed Mrs. Tupper. "I doubt that. At least make your story believable, Cole. This conversation is ridiculous."

"He wasn't a substitute!" contended Cole, feeling maligned. "He's been here for two years. He started teaching ninth when I entered seventh."

"Do you honestly think I'm going to believe that?" choked Mrs. Tupper, shaking her head. "Mr. Robinson hired me last spring as the result of a larger couple of grades. Your group has eighty-five more students than last year's, and next year has a dozen or so more than that. When he hired me, he promised to fill the first three weeks with alternates—to help things fit my schedule."

"Mr. Brewer *wasn't* a substitute!" insisted Cole, feeling overwhelmed. He hadn't ever raised his voice to a teacher, much less needed to defend himself against one. "You can ask anyone," begged Cole. "I know for sure he's taught here for two years. He's got a reputation....Anyway, Principal Robinson told me he was firing Mr. Brewer, and it looks like that's what he's done."

The conversation ended abruptly with Mrs. Tupper showing Cole to the door. It left him wishing for more information and wondering where his normal life had gone.

That evening, a few answers finally trickled in. Cole's mother had invited Coach Smith and his son over for a Friday night barbeque, so when Bobby showed up, Cole cornered him about the rumors. It took a bit of persuading before Bobby was convinced that Cole was really himself and not a dangerous person. Some people at school had suggested that the bump on his head had made him go wild.

"They say you went nuts—completely loony—" said Bobby, still looking apprehensive. His eyes kept glancing toward his father, who was standing by the smoking grill, polishing off his third hamburger.

"Hardly," interrupted Cole, feeling the sting of Bobby's words. "It wasn't like that. Once the elephant smacked my head, it was lights out. The next thing I remember was being carried on a stretcher."

"That's not what I heard," divulged Bobby nervously. He kept scratching at his ear. "They say you went down and looked like you were out cold—maybe dead—and then, once your teacher was getting everyone to exit the room, you popped up and started doing freaky things—making noises and hitting people…"

"Hitting who?" barked Cole, shocked by the news. "And why would Mr. Brewer ask everyone to leave the room? Doesn't that sound strange to you?"

"I don't know." said Bobby. "I'm just telling you what I heard. They say a student stayed in the room to help your teacher, and now he's all thrashed. They took him away in an ambulance. That's why people were freaked. It was like a different you…like an evil twin came leaping out…"

Bobby glanced down at Cole's sore hand and backed up.

"They've got it all wrong," complained Cole. "I know they do. I counted heads today in class, and guess what? The only person missing was my lab partner—*a girl!* And the only ambulance was the one that carried me—and me alone! There's no way I 'thrashed' someone."

"But Mr. Brewer was gone, just like they said. He was so beat-up that he couldn't come back."

"Right. I don't think so. I personally heard Principal Robinson say, over and over, that he was going to fire him for bringing his junk to school."

"Really?"

"Yes!" said Cole, disgusted. "Go ahead and ask my mom. It's pathetic to see how quickly things get blown out of proportion. I'm the one who was injured and now everybody thinks I'm bad? Go figure."

"That does sound pretty lame," admitted Bobby, softening.

"Yeah," blared Josh, weaseling his way into the conversation. He had only heard the ending part, yet he figured he probably agreed. "Two-on-two basketball—me and Cole against you and your old man," said Josh, jumping around.

Cole looked over at Coach Smith. All three boys wouldn't stand much of a chance against him, let alone just Cole and Josh.

"Will you tell people I'm not crazy," added Cole, nudging Bobby before they went off to play ball.

Bobby nodded his head and cracked an uncomfortable grin.

Cole could feel something critical was missing, something he should have known, but didn't; however, at least one person in the ninth grade didn't completely hate him.

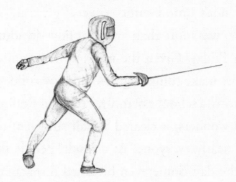

THE BIG MISTAKE

A ll weekend long, Cole obsessed about how to convince the entire ninth grade that he wasn't prone to hurt people. Everyone in his family had advice on what to do. His mother suggested he ignore them and they'd eventually forget about the whole thing. Aunt Hilda told him to get the principal to announce that Mr. Brewer had been fired and that Cole hadn't punched anyone. Alex said he should consider dropping out, since that's what he would be wishing to do if he were caught in Cole's predicament. And Josh, like always, had an interesting twist to his counsel. He told Cole to enjoy the moment, insisting that it was a rare honor to be mistakenly dubbed the number one bully of the school.

Monday morning approached like a snail, and when it finally arrived, it came without Cole ever deciding how to handle his situation. Fortunately, he didn't need to. When he arrived at school, Principal Robinson met him in the front hall and expressed regret profusely for the way everyone had been acting. Apparently, he had just gotten done with hearing an earful of

Aunt Hilda's mind—not a very pleasant experience—and, therefore, was more than aware of how dreadful the rumors had been on Friday. Given the mix-up, he promised that he would personally make things right—and by second period, he had.

During a school assembly, Principal Robinson gave a speech that did wonders; it cleared the air sufficient to raise feelings of guilt in nearly everyone. As a result, people thronged Cole the rest of the day. Some even breathed disparaging remarks about anyone who swayed slightly in the opposite direction, to the extent that his science class associates who had before claimed to have heard screaming, miraculously recanted their testimonies. It was unbelievable.

Mrs. Tupper also made an announcement, but it wasn't to the whole school as Principal Robinson's had been. She informed her sixth period students that she had decided to make Cole her class president for the entire year, which position, in her hierarchy, included participating with her in determining their grades. It was like handing Cole a magical friendship-wand. She also took Cole aside and informed him that Principal Robinson had corrected her misunderstanding; for, even though she had been hired the prior spring, Principal Robinson had decided to keep the excellent substitute, Mrs. Whittwer, and have her continue teaching the science class he had intended on giving to Mrs. Tupper, while using Mrs. Tupper's timely arrival as the solution to his firing of Mr. Brewer.

Monday couldn't have been better—that is, until Cole discovered something truly dreadful. As he lay in his bed at night, he thought it would be a perfect time to take a break from ninth grade and visit his friends in Green. So he began concentrating, determined this time to keep trying until he was transported—even if it took all night. After a while, without any perceivable results, he reached for his luck charm, hoping it would work better if he looked at it. That's when everything went wrong. His medallion was gone!

Cole hopped out of bed and searched frantically. It had to be somewhere. He ran down the hall and checked the bathroom.

"How could I have taken a shower and not noticed it was gone," muttered Cole. "It must have happened after this morning."

The next three hours were spent exploring every inch of the house. Nothing was left unturned, and everyone joined in. They knew how much Cole loved it, even if they didn't understand its importance. He had told them of his adventures in Green, but had never shared that they were in part due to his special gift from Pap. It would have been pointless to add that bit. Only Josh believed that the tales were real, and had Josh known that the necklace was essential, he would have borrowed it for himself.

"I can't believe it's gone," groaned Cole, settling back into bed when their meticulous combing had failed. He smacked his flat pillow with his fists, wishing it was puffier, and tried to get comfortable, despite the nagging anxiety that tore at his insides like a blender. Losing his only ticket to Green was ten times worse than being ostracized by his classmates and deemed a school menace.

"I think you're still lucky," called Josh from his bunk. Alex was already snoring in the bottom half, so Josh had to raise his voice and lean over the edge to be heard from the top. His faded-gray flannel pajamas were oversized hand-me-downs from Cole so they hung on him like Spanish moss. "Besides," he continued, popping his hand in and out of a hole in the sleeve, "I bet you'll find it's in the lost-and-found at school. Maybe it slipped off when you hit your head."

"That's it!" snapped Cole, his face lighting up. "You're right, Josh. The last time I remember having it was before I started that dumb experiment."

Cole's thoughts continued to run a million miles an hour. He began to think of how the nameless girl had been bugging him about Green. It was mysterious that she had known anything concerning the other realms, but as unexplainable as it was, since she had been prodding right before his necklace went missing, she looked pretty guilty.

"I'll talk with her tomorrow," mumbled Cole, deep in thought. He was halfway to getting his medallion back.

"With who? Aren't you going to check the lost-and-found?" asked Josh, playing with his childhood blanket. He wrapped it around his arm and pretended it was a cannon.

"Nope. That's not where it is," responded Cole. "But I think I know who has it."

"The Dread!" exclaimed Josh, bursting with excitement. He tore his wrap from his arm and draped it over his head, pretending to be a cloaked villain. "He's come for your necklace and tracked you down. He probably thinks you'll lose to him now that he's got it….I'll be your luck. Can I help you fight him this time? I've been practicing that move you taught me."

Josh deserted his blanket and hopped off the top bunk without using the ladder, waving his arms in the air like a karate master. It looked silly, not scary—especially when he hit the floor.

"No. The Dread's long gone," assured Cole, trying to hold back a sneeze. "They've locked him in the worst of places. Criminals go in, only corpses come out. And what happens in between is real torture."

"Then who's got it?" begged Josh. "Let me come with you.

I'll bring you twice as much luck as that trinket from Pap ever did. By the time we get it back, you'll want to wear me around your neck, not that thing."

Josh proceeded to do a series of hi-yahs and karate chops to the overflowing dirty-clothes bag that hung from a dresser-drawer knob. Eventually, it conceded to his prowess at martial arts by spilling laundry out its top.

Cole felt like it was pointless to explain to Josh that he didn't plan on fighting someone for the medallion; Josh was already bopping around the room, showing off his stuff, imagining a villain of monstrous proportions, not an ordinary, ninth-grade girl.

"If I run into trouble," said Cole sleepily, "you're the one I want at my side. We could take them."

"Thanks, Cole," erupted Josh. "You won't be sorry. I'll let 'em have it with my fists…"

Cole jumped in to settle him down. "Save your strength, Buddy. Who knows, maybe The Dread has a brother. We'd better get to sleep."

The clock on the wall showed 12:55. Cole had been too concerned about his lost treasure to get tired until he realized where it was. Somehow, knowing who had it made him feel slightly better.

The rest of the week, Cole was the first to arrive for sixth period. Daily, he waited at the entrance to room 125 for the nameless girl, only to be repeatedly disappointed. By Friday, she had been absent five days, going on six. It felt like he would never get a chance to ask her to give his medallion back. And then, while sitting in class, a plan crept into the back of his mind.

"Mrs. Tupper," he said, noticing that sixth period was almost over. "I feel bad about all of the things my lab partner has been missing. She's skipped six days in a row. Would you like me to deliver some homework to her?"

It felt canned. And that's because it was. But fortunately, Mrs. Tupper didn't detect it.

"That would be great," she sighed, flipping through a few stacks of papers. She began to compile the past week's assignments as Cole slipped up beside her. He eagerly peered down the roll, searching for the mystery girl's name.

"Wait a minute," said Mrs. Tupper, looking into the air. "Nobody's been gone for that long. I thought you meant Suzy." She straightened a wrinkle out of her polka-dotted dress, glanced at Cole, and continued, "Do you mean Suzy? She's only been gone three days."

"No," responded Cole, deflated. His hopes had been dashed before she spoke, because his eyes had already noted that every name on the teacher's list of students was familiar. None of them belonged to his strange lab partner.

"There used to be another girl in our class," reflected Cole cautiously. "I didn't realize she had checked out."

"Well, if she's not on my roll, then she won't need this homework, will she?" said Mrs. Tupper. She smiled and began re-situating her piles of papers.

Within minutes, the bell rang and it was time to go. Cole attempted to ask around, to see if anyone remembered the girl's name, but no one even recalled her at all, let alone her name. It was frustrating. It was as though she didn't exist—as though she hadn't been his lab partner—as though she was only in his mind.

After school, when Cole approached the office as Mrs. Tupper's class president, claiming a faulty roll, the office quickly confirmed the same—that there hadn't been anyone else in Cole's sixth period. If the girl had attended, she had done so without proper approval. It was devastating news. It meant she had purposefully been there, stalking him, waiting for the right time to swipe his medallion.

In the weeks that followed, Cole sorrowed over his loss. He kept hoping that he would find and confront the girl. He even stepped far from his comfort level to meet people that he thought might have known her. Still, nothing worked. She was like a ghost.

Fortunately, despite his failed attempts to recover the charm, something inside him whispered he would find it and return to Green.

As fall weather set in, Cole spent more time with his fencing buddies. He learned a lot of new tricks and got a chance to practice them daily. 'The Guys,' as he referred to them, were quite a group of people to be around. The average age in their crowd was over sixty, with only one man being younger than fifty, except Cole. They wouldn't have allowed Cole to join if it weren't for his impressive first day.

Back in early July, he had gone to the fencing club assuming anyone could enroll. He hadn't known that it was a private group of friends, not an open organization. So when one man laughed at him for trying to sign up, Cole had remarked in a respectful way that the man was scared of being beaten. The comment had led to a duel with the man, whose sword skills were amazing, but somewhere in the process of losing, Cole had gained enough friends to sway The Guys into letting him stay.

The club met in an old brick building on Main Street that was solely dedicated to fencing, or at least that's what the sign said. It read in big letters, 'FENCING CLUB,' with a statement below it in italics, '*Dedicated to Excellence in Swordplay, Members Only.*' In truth, though, it was a hang-out joint for a bunch of old men. In one room they had a big screen TV that was always blaring the latest game, and surrounding it, enough couches to comfortably hold two dozen people. The kitchen was set up with three fridges, each brimming with sodas and junk food galore. And the rest of the rooms had fencing equipment and places to practice—equipment that mostly sat unused since The Guys spent a majority of their time talking and eating.

Cole loved to linger at the club. He would go from one guy to the next, having them each teach him about swordplay. And by spreading the role of tutor around, nobody ever felt overly used, even when Cole stayed long hours on Saturdays.

Many of Cole's best friends were in the club. Of course, that's not saying much since he couldn't get back to Green where his real best friends were. One man in particular was endearing. His name was Jack Parry. He reminded Cole of Pap. He was five-foot seven with radiant white hair. At ninety-two years, he was the oldest member of the club and probably the nicest member, too. Nevertheless, Jack was as tough as nails when sword fighting. Over the years, he had proven his place was at the top. Nobody would dare dispute that.

Cole spent a lot of time with Jack, hearing his stories and learning how to duel effectively. It helped fill the void in Cole's life that his father and Pap had left. One of the things he could always count on from Jack was good advice, especially the kind you get from one-liners. He'd frequently say things like "Don't forget, you're not alive until you're really living," and, "If you want something bad enough, you'll fight with all you've got to get it."

As a World War II veteran, Jack knew what it was like to fight hard for something worthwhile—and he told Cole plenty about it.

"Son," Jack said one afternoon. The old man was climbing on his favorite soapbox. "There are only two kinds of people in the world. The kind that do stuff and the kind that always talk about doing stuff. Nobody's in between. Now you strike me as the kind of boy that's destined to be doing."

Jack was responding to a string of comments Cole had just made about how messed-up his life was. The real thing bothering Cole was that he hadn't even seen a glimpse of the nameless girl, let alone reacquired his medallion. With Halloween approaching, he had mostly given up on the idea that the girl was anywhere near Cedar City. Over a month of searching had led to nothing. And to make matters worse, without the necklace, Cole knew time in Green was moving on. Things were happening there—Bollirse games were being played, friendships were being strengthened, all sorts of fun things were being done—and Cole was left out of them all.

"I know," Cole admitted somberly. "I need to do stuff if I want stuff." Cole's attitude was below healthy and Jack's hype wasn't working.

"Well," continued Jack. "If you're a doer, then prove it! If things aren't working out the way you planned—change your plans! Sitting around here moping won't make you any happier."

"But what do you do if you've tried everything?" explained Cole, feeling the conversation was bordering on pointless.

"You can never try everything," said Jack. "There's always something more you can do if you're still interested in pursuing the path you've chosen. And if you think you're done trying, it's not because there's nothing more you can do, it's because you've given up on the path." Jack looked at Cole and then spoke with gentle firmness. "It's okay to change your course a little. Just choose something else worthwhile and get doing."

"I wish it were that simple," complained Cole.

"It is!" snapped Jack. He reached down and pulled up one of his pant legs, past the knee. A wicked matrix of scars ran from mid-thigh to ankle. The muscles on his leg were disfigured and awkward.

"I used to be fast," insisted Jack, searing Cole with his penetrating eyes. "So fast at running that some people joked they'd send me an Olympic gold medal before I could enter just to keep me from humiliating all of the other runners. It was my dream to stand on the highest podium and hear our national anthem. I could smell it, taste it. And then in my prime, this happened!" Jack patted his deformed leg.

"The war cost us a lot more than time. But I didn't sit around blubbering about how hopeless my life was. I learned to do other things—" Jack held up a pair of fencing swords and smiled. "And I've got a whole room filled with junk in my house that proves I'm pretty good…because I'm a doer!"

Jack set the swords down and staggered to a chair before readjusting his pant leg. "What is it, Cole?" he asked. "Is it math, or sports, or what?"

Cole tried to think of how to explain his problem. "I lost something really important to my family—a family heirloom. I brought it to school and someone stole it."

"Then ask around—go get it back."

"I already have," responded Cole. "It's just gone."

"Well it's not gone, it's hidden," said Jack. He didn't try to soften his words like a mother might. "Either forget about it and apologize to your family for losing the thing, or figure out what you haven't done and start doing it."

Jack made the solution sound simple. If Cole hadn't already struggled for a month, he would have been invigorated by Jack's words.

"Was it only valuable to your family?" asked Jack. He was trying to route Cole in a useful direction. "If someone took it, they either did it because they didn't like you, or they're looking for cash. I'd bet they're trying to sell it to someone who's willing to pay. Have you checked around—like pawn shops and antique dealers?"

Cole perked up when Jack mentioned motive. Even if the nameless girl had swiped it, what were her chances of making it to Green? Cole had tried and tried all summer and hadn't successfully returned. After a frustrating month of attempts, maybe she would sell it.

"I hadn't thought of buying it," replied Cole, starting to smile. He felt a burst of hope returning. "Thanks a lot," he said, scurrying toward the door.

"Be a doer," called Jack, giving him a wave goodbye.

Cole was off, rushing home to make some calls. And when the local places didn't turn up any leads, he phoned the surrounding towns, including Salt Lake to the north and Las Vegas to the south. He even sketched a rough draft of the two sides of the coin, as much as he could recall. Most of the inscriptions had been hard to see, but he remembered a very specific marking that would easily identify the coin—a ten-point star in the center on one side.

It took weeks to communicate with the different dealers.

At first, many of them bragged that they had it in stock, until Cole informed them that he was looking for one specific coin, an heirloom that had belonged to his grandfather. Once they knew it was an original, they altered their story and said it would take time to check around.

Days turned to weeks with little change. Cole was busy enough searching that he didn't allow himself to think of defeat. He placed want ads in the local town papers, declaring his willingness to pay top dollar for a special coin, and each time he included his black-and-white sketch. He also posted flyers around the school offering a $400 reward for the return of his medallion, no questions asked. It was pricey for Cole, whose funds were limited to a meager savings obtained by mowing lawns during the summer and shoveling walks during the winter, but as Jack had said, either you're a doer or you're not. And Cole had decided to be a doer.

Thanksgiving arrived with turkey dinner, stuffing, potatoes, rolls, and all the fixings, yet no good news to be grateful for. Still, many people reassured Cole that his coin would surface for the right price, so he continued to make weekly calls, waiting for that day.

Eventually, information did come. It wasn't directly about his coin. It was about Green! On a cold, snowy night in early December, Cole awoke around 3:00 a.m. Sweat drenched his face and clothes. He was shaking all over. What he had just seen was awful.

In his dream he saw Twistyard. It looked the same as when he had left, complete with drat soldiers camped at the base of the wall below Dilly's quarters. He saw Boot, Buck, Dilly, Sawny, Bonboo, and many other people he called friends. They were carrying on with life as though not much had changed. Suddenly, the dream became convoluted. Something black and mysterious lurked in the darkness of the night. It would emerge, take soldiers, then disappear. One here, two there. Twistyard was under attack from a silent and mysterious enemy!

Cole grabbed for his sword. A beast was approaching him. It was horrible. It could nearly look right through him. It was a beast that seemed to peek across space and time. It knew Cole was Dod, and it was searching for him, hungering to catch him, driven by an unusual compulsion. Cole could feel that the beast wouldn't stop until it had destroyed Twistyard and all of his friends.

"It's just a dream. It's just a dream," repeated Cole to himself. His heart was pounding in his ears. "It's just a dream."

"Must have been one heck of a dream!" said Josh, looking at Cole from only a few feet away. His eyes were wide open, and he was shivering. "You were saying all sorts of things and swinging your arms around. It's amazing Alex is still asleep. I sure couldn't snooze through it. Once you yelled 'The Dread!' that was it for me."

"The Dread?" said Cole, confused. "I wasn't dreaming about The Dread. I had a nightmare about something else, something I've never seen before."

"Well, while you were dreaming about that other stuff, you mentioned The Dread…you said, 'I know you—you're The Dread.' And then you mumbled about how much you hate the water."

"See—that proves it was just a crazy nightmare," declared Cole, reassuring himself as well as he could. "We both know I don't hate the water. Do you remember the summer Mom couldn't keep me out of the community pool? I must have gone there at least five times a week. My hair turned blonde from the chlorine."

Cole began to feel better knowing how faulty some parts of the dream had been. It gave him hope that the other parts—the parts about the creature wanting to kill him—were just made up, too. "So, you really heard me say stuff about hating the water?"

"Yup," answered Josh. "I was beginning to think you were going mad—like The Dread's ghost had come to get you, and I couldn't see him. Maybe he was drowning you or something."

"No!" said Cole, fearing his brother's imagination was heading out of control. "It was just a nightmare. Trust me. The Dread's long gone, and ghosts don't really haunt people."

It took a few minutes before Cole was able to convince Josh back to bed, and even longer before either of them was ready to fall asleep. After all, it had been a scary experience for both boys.

The following weeks became known as 'the December of Sleepless Nights.' The Christmas season was ruined by all of the bad dreams Cole had. And despite none of them being as horrid as the first, and most of them not even leaving any images in his mind when he awoke, they all released doom and gloom into the air. It took a toll on everyone else in his family, too.

On the other hand, Cole's obsession with getting back to Green was curbed. Even if the dreams were wrong, the feelings they left were convincing: Twistyard had become a dangerous place, and bad things were happening there. Cole felt sorry for his friends and wished that he could help them. Nevertheless, he wasn't as excited to return to them as he had been before, when he had imagined everything was wonderful and fun.

As the 25th drew near, Coach Smith frequented the house more often than he had before, sometimes with Bobby and other times alone. It was easy to see he was trying to win Doralee's heart, using the holiday season to his advantage. The only thing that slowed his schedule of visits was when he suggested that they exclusively date each other. Cole wished he hadn't heard that part. It meant his mom was heading toward marriage. Fortunately, Doralee refused to consent, stating she thought things were moving too fast as it was and she needed more time.

But with Coach Smith around so often, trying to prove his genuine concern for the whole family, it created some unwanted attention. One such time was when he invited Cole to accompany him to Las Vegas for an all-day adventure, buying cars for Smith's Super Saver Slick Wheels—his used-car lot. He announced it like Cole had just won the lottery. It was scheduled for the upcoming Saturday, December 22. He would leave at 5:00 a.m. and return by midnight.

Cole new something was up when his mother consented without hearing the details and pushed him to go. She actually tried to convince Cole by suggesting that it would be a great opportunity for him to check new pawn shops in search of Pap's medallion. When Cole declined, she insisted he go. She was in on the deal. She knew what Smith was planning, and it didn't only involve cars. Smith had an acquaintance in Las Vegas that was reportedly one of the best psychiatrists in the country. Doralee hoped that Dr. Haslom would know how to help Cole overcome his nightmares.

It was useless to argue, since Cole knew he'd eventually lose to his mother's persistence, so he agreed. And though he doubted it would do any good, it was still worth a shot. At least it would make Doralee feel better.

When the day came, Cole tried to sleep during the drive to Las Vegas. He didn't want to get stuck awkwardly talking with Smith. And the feeling was mutual; when they arrived in Nevada, Smith asked Cole to wait for him in a doughnut shop while he went to conduct business.

After three hours of reading Sir Edward Snake comic books, Cole's food was gone and the restaurant was bustling. Every seat was taken. It made him wish he had plopped himself down at a table for two, not a corner, family-sized booth. Now, with few options, he could continue glutting himself on the luxury of the spacious location, which he had occupied for so long—and in doing so, extend the displeased looks he was receiving from the standing crowd—or he could get up and leave. He chose the latter—and that changed everything!

Out in the crisp air, Christmas was on the breeze. A dusty lot filled with firs and pines beckoned to Cole. It was situated between two small casinos, and it backed onto a fenced construction site. The sign at the entrance read 'X-mas Trees.'

As Cole entered the urban forest, images zipped through his mind. They terrified him. After the horrendous experience he had gone through in his science class, he wasn't sure whether to do what he felt, or run like crazy. It was a moment of moments. He nearly bolted for the safety of the Dealer's Extravaganza down the street, until something inspired him. He could hear Jack Parry in his mind. "There are only two kinds of people. The kind that do stuff and the kind that always talk about doing stuff. Nobody's in between."

Cole clenched his fists and took a deep breath. He instinctively knew his medallion was behind the trees, somewhere on the construction site. It didn't make any logical sense, yet it was real. Men were holding it—or it was near them—or maybe it was in a pile of garbage and the people were incidental to its location. He didn't know very much, but he knew enough; Pap's good luck charm was right there in front of him, close by.

The fence was hung high, leaving a gap at the bottom

that varied from six inches to as much as a foot in one place. Cole dropped to the ground and squeezed under, pushing the chain link until his whole body fit. Once inside, he brushed the dirt from his jacket and looked around. The project area was filled with all sorts of debris. Since it was the Saturday before Christmas, workers had been given the day off, making the location appear deserted. However, Cole knew differently. People were there—he could feel their presence—so he crept around, listening for voices.

Everything was quiet. As he climbed the metal staircase of the half-finished building, the dim light that crept into the concrete shaft made him feel as though the southern, winter sun had disappeared from the cloudy sky and left him alone to search the floors for his treasure. Cole tiptoed around the nine levels. Nothing stirred. Building materials, equipment, and supplies lay strewn around him. Though he looked with his eyes, Cole knew that his best tracking device was the nagging of his insides. They drove him to roam the maze of clutter like a tomb raider, searching the Egyptian catacombs for gold.

Finally, when the hunt proved futile, he returned to the ground level and pressed farther from the tree lot, heading toward the front, street side of the half-completed structure he had invaded. Before reaching the road, he came across a doublewide trailer. It made his heart leap. People were inside, and they were arguing about something.

"I don't care what you want!" someone yelled. His gruff voice was easily heard through a partially-open window.

Cole moved closer and listened.

"It's simple, don't be stupid!" raged someone else. "We've got a once-in-a-lifetime opportunity. Let's take it."

The conversation was intriguing. Cole scampered a few feet away, pried a cement-stained bucket out from under a web of discarded two-by-fours, and perched near the window. Five men were inside. They were disputing what to do. One of them seemed convinced that they should change their original plans, while another insisted that it would be foolish to cross their boss. The three other men seemed concerned, but undecided. All of them were large and rough looking. They were standing around a small card table, bunched up enough that Cole couldn't see what they were pointing at.

Finally, a sixth man—a pirate-looking fellow with a big skull tattoo on his arm—came storming into the room and punched another guy across the face, sending him to the floor. "We can't double-back on Booze or he'll kill us!" barked the tattooed man. "He's been working this out for a long time. And I don't think his contact is neutral, either. We sit tight 'til tonight and play it as planned."

Cole gasped. When the scuffle took place, the men parted sufficient to show the table had only one thing on it: Pap's medallion!

The men continued to argue back and forth. Ultimately, they followed the pirate into an adjoining room. Cole could still hear them. He knew they were close by, but he desperately wanted his medallion back. His heart began to beat faster and faster. He gave a shove to the window and it popped up high enough to squeeze his body through. It was a tight fit. Cole wriggled and squiggled until he plopped to the floor. There was no time to waste. He grabbed the gold coin and turned to exit when he heard one man say "Go get it and I'll show you the mark."

If only the window had been bigger, Cole could have

jumped through it. Unfortunately, it wasn't. And Cole knew he'd get stuck if he tried, so he dove behind a ragged chair instead. There weren't very many places to hide in the tiny room. He knew he was about to get caught. It made him nearly pass out with distress.

"It's gone!" yelled the man.

"What?" bellowed two or three others from the neighboring room. A banging thunder of feet shook the trailer as the men rushed to see.

"It can't be far," said the pirate. "You three—go check outside! We'll tear this place apart until we find it. Whoever did this will pay!"

Cole shuddered. He wanted to cease existing. From his tight position, squashed between the old chair and the wall, the men weren't visible. Still, every word they said was clear. Cole was doomed to face six angry men, and he couldn't think of the slightest thing to say that would calm their wrath. It wouldn't be pretty. He clenched his right fist around the necklace and prepared to defend himself. When they found him, he'd punch and run—that was the plan. Perhaps the element of surprise would catch them off guard enough to escape. It was a long shot—a poor way to make up for his big mistake of climbing into the trailer in the first place—but it was his only shot.

"Right there!" yelled the tattooed man, his voice booming like a farmer ordering his hounds to attack a fox. "Get him!"

As if in slow motion, Cole looked down and noticed the tip of one of his shoes was peeking out from behind the chair. It was his fatal flaw. He stared at it in disbelief, wishing for a lot of things as he braced himself for the unveiling. He wished he were at home with his brothers, decorating the house for

Christmas. He wished he were uncomfortably hanging out with Coach Smith, buying inventory. And most urgently, he wished he could disappear.

It was his third wish that came true! In an instant, his shoe faded from view and was replaced by a wooden canopy bathed in moonlight. Cole was back in Green, lying in bed. The big mistake wasn't his, it was theirs: They had left Pap's medallion on the table unattended!

CHAPTER FOUR

THE UNBELIEVABLE ESCAPE

A wave of relief rushed over Cole when he realized he was in Green, not under attack in a construction trailer. His heart still beat rapidly. In his right fist he held Pap's necklace. Slowly, he loosened his grip and let it slip onto the bed. His respite was brief before a new concern entered his mind.

"I thought time was supposed to go on without me," whispered Cole, noticing the silence of the night. "I haven't worn the medallion for three months."

Everything looked the same as before. It would have made him happy to enter Green where he had left off if things back home hadn't included six angry men who were ready to mash him. Now, with problems on Earth, he wished he could set the necklace down for a while and let time pass by, so when he did finally return, the trailer would be empty.

Cole slid out of bed and hid the gold coin and chain in a joint of the bed frame. Even if time stood still on Earth, Cole didn't want to take a chance on returning before he was ready. "At least in Green," he murmured quietly, "I have friends that can help me fight trouble."

CHAPTER FOUR

A quick glimpse toward Boot and Buck left him puzzled. Their beds were empty. He walked over to inspect them. Their blankets were tucked neatly and folded, and the floor was spotless. Not even Boot's clothes were strewn about. The room was definitely different than the messy quarters he had exited a few months before.

"Maybe time has moved on," mumbled Cole, trying to think things out. He wandered around the dimly lit room in relative silence. One pat to his chest reminded him of the three keys he wore around his neck. While at home, the keys had remained somewhere else, and with his return to Green, the keys had reappeared.

Cole ventured to the bedroom door and opened it up. He could hear noises coming from farther down the hall. They weren't very loud, yet any sound was a welcoming one. At least some of the people in Green Hall were still awake. He walked to the first bedroom, where Pone, Voo, Sham, and many of the other Coosings usually slept. It was empty. Feelings of fear began to creep into Cole's mind. He no longer felt lucky to be back in Green. The dreadful dreams of gloom and doom whirled around in his mind.

Then the girls' door squeaked. *Perhaps Dilly's awake*, thought Cole. *She's a late-night owl.* He tried to push the memories of his awful nightmares aside. *I bet the guys went on an outing together, maybe fishing or something. If I walk down there, Dilly and Sawny will tell me all about it.*

Cole tried to think positively, but he couldn't extinguish the growing alarm that overtook him like a wildfire. Where were his friends? Had they gone to High Gate for safety? And if so, who was left making the noises? And something else struck him as being strange: the hall was dark, void of the glowing stones and candles that had perpetually lit the corridor before. Now, only a few spots were illuminated by moonlight that cheated its way into the inner hall from a couple of open bedroom doors. The whole setting reminded Cole of his experience in Pap's place, the night he had fled for his life.

"My sword," mumbled Cole. It was his only thought that provoked courage. He had fenced so much with The Guys at the club that he actually looked forward to showing Dilly what he could do and felt bolstered by how well he could fare against an enemy.

Cole rushed back to his bed and reached down deep, between his mattress and headboard. It was a tight fit. Fortunately, the sword was still there, waiting inside one of Bonboo's sheaths — the one Sawny had given him from Dilly's cache. He tugged and pulled until the sword and casing emerged. Cole drew the blade out and left the scabbard on his bed.

"Now I'll go speak with Dilly," he said. His voice was no longer a whisper. His hours of practice had boosted him enough to walk with confidence.

As he approached the entry to Green Hall, he noticed the other rooms were vacant. No Coosings or Greenlings were sleeping in any of the beds that they had occupied before. And yet quiet noises continued to come from the girls' wing. They sounded like the squeaking of boards and the shuffling of feet. Someone was awake, walking around. The closer Cole got, the more certain he felt.

"The girls must be alone tonight," said Cole, noticing that Green Hall's giant double doors were closed and the bracing beam was situated across them, completely securing the quarters against assault. He remembered that the Coosings had rarely locked the main entrance, but with the boys away, it made sense.

Cole knocked on the girls' door and instantly knew something was wrong: It swung wide-open!

"Dilly?" cried Cole, his thoughts racing with a surge of adrenaline. He wondered why the front entrance was secured from the inside and yet the girls' door was left unlatched. It was always locked. Concern for Dilly and Sawny jumped to the forefront of his mind. "Are you guys all right in there?" he yelled, trying to decide what to do.

When no one responded, Cole did something he'd never done before, something Boot and Buck had never done before, perhaps something no man had ever done before: He entered the girls' quarters. No sooner did he begin than a crashing sound gave way in front of him and the hall was flooded with light.

"A visitor," groaned an evil voice. It came from a hooded man who entered the passage with a leap. He wore a long, black cloak that completely covered his clothing, and on top of it, a necklace with three brightly glowing stones. His face was shrouded by a veil that hung just below his eyes. Cole's first impression was that the mystery man was The Dread; the way he drew his sword looked familiar. But the blade was different than anything Cole had ever seen. It was crimson red and luminescent.

In his retreat toward Green Hall's entrance, Cole was forced to wield his weapon. The hooded man was lightning fast, jabbing for the kill. He wasted no time with small talk or fancy moves. It was clear that he meant to end things quickly. Fortunately, the pajamas Cole was wearing were from Boot, since his others that fit him better had been horribly muddied from his ride to Higga's house during his last visit to Green, so the larger ones dangled enough to lure a misplaced stab that sliced the cloth but zipped past Cole's abdomen without drawing blood.

CLASH, CLANK. CLASH, CLANK, CLANK.

Cole and the hooded man darted back and forth, slicing and stabbing. It was an amazing display of swordsmanship on the part of both contenders. Cole fought for his life, remembering all sorts of tricks The Guys had taught him. He moved better than ever before. It was as though his skills were enhanced by entering Green and heightened by the rush of a nighttime surprise and the imminent threat of death.

Something stank. As Cole fought with the man, odors poured out of his cloak like vapors from rotting flesh, or some other putrid source. It was appalling. The duel continued, with Cole moving backward, mostly on defense. Occasionally he drove forward, yet in the end he lost more ground than he gained. The hooded man was remarkable with a sword. It was terrifying for Cole. He knew if the fight went on much longer, the outcome would be fatal.

In a bold move, Cole threw Pap's sword. He was acting on an impression that led him to believe it was his only way to escape. He didn't directly hurl it at the man, but at the base of his cloak, right where it brushed against a floorboard. Since it appeared to miss its mark, the hooded man didn't even try to block it. He let out a gleeful cackle and plunged for Cole.

At the same time, Cole bolted for Green Hall's entrance. He pushed up on the barricade and flung the doors open.

It worked. Pap's sword held the assailant momentarily, pinning his cloak to the wall until he ripped it free. The trick slowed the mysterious man only a matter of seconds, but that was all Cole needed.

CHAPTER FOUR

Out in the hall, Cole stumbled and fell to the floor in front of three dozen drat soldiers, armed and ready, with candles burning brightly. They had been gathering for some time after discovering Green Hall's doors were locked. To their knowledge, nobody was supposed to be inside.

"We've got you surrounded, Dod!" blurted Jibb. "Don't move or we'll run you through!"

The mention of Cole's other name brought back fond memories. It was the first time he had been called Dod in months. It felt nice, even if the circumstance was precarious.

"Get *him!*" yelled Dod, "not me!"

Dod pointed at the dimly lit hallway, and to everyone's surprise, Mr. Nasty Breath came darting around the corner, expecting to finish Dod off. The drat soldiers who had surrounded Dod's retreat now turned about-face and began to fight with the cloaked man, seven against one. And when it looked as though they were gaining ground, something astonishing happened: A second hooded man, smaller than the other and wearing a drab-gray cloak, jumped from the girls' hall and began helping the first.

Together, the two intruders were ferocious. They inflicted injuries on the drat soldiers until the seven men in the front fell back, and no sooner did that happen then the doors swung closed and a clumping noise indicated that they had once again reemployed the barricade.

"Quick!" ordered Dod. "Go to the window-side! Don't let them get away!" Dod looked around, perplexed. None of the soldiers responded. They stood still, quietly waiting. The only ones that moved at all were the four injured men, who were inspecting their wounds.

"I'm in command!" barked Jibb, glaring angrily. He approached Dod with his sword drawn and pointed it at his throat. "Why should we believe you aren't one of them?"

"I'm not," responded Dod, answering the question poorly. He didn't want to talk about anything until more action was being taken to apprehend the intruders. "At least send a few men outside to hedge their escape. We can discuss me later. Please, Jibb. Don't let them get away."

"Not so fast," answered Jibb. "I know you. You're full of tricks. The moment I turn my back, you'll disappear for another three months."

"You can watch me all you want," begged Dod, "just send somebody…anybody!" He wanted the villains caught before they caused more trouble. Not to mention, obviously they were followers of The Dread.

"Now I'm asking nicely," said Jibb, pulling back his sword a few inches. He picked at his white beard with his free hand. "Tell us the brain-load. Tell us everything. Why were you in there?"

Dod looked around and felt lonely, surrounded by drats with their beards and uppity noses. They rigidly followed Jibb's every command and didn't look the slightest bit sympathetic.

"I don't know what's going on," explained Dod honestly. "I arrived here tonight and attempted to sleep in my bed. Is that a crime?" Dod scanned the soldiers with his pleading eyes. "I have no idea why those men are in there, or who they are—though the taller one resembles The Dread, don't you think? Perhaps they came here seeking revenge against me for my part in sending Sirlonk to Driaxom—or maybe they hated Pap and I'm as close to jungo as they can get—I really don't know. The only thing I'm sure of is that they're trouble. And since we're sitting here, doing nothing, they're probably climbing out a window and making their escape."

"Hardly," scoffed Jibb conceitedly. He drew back his sword and put it away. "I've got four times as many men out there, with bows drawn for the kill, waiting to pluck them out. The only surprise will be if they live to answer my questions."

Jibb turned to his men and gave a cheer that they all responded to. When he was done, he smiled at Dod and added, "We've captured Dark Hood and his little helper. There's no way they'll elude us this time. And if they do live, they can show The Dread all the loyalty they want—side-by-side with him in Driaxom!"

The change in Jibb's attitude toward Dod was welcomed. One moment he was interrogating him with a blade to his throat and the next he was smiling. It was odd.

Dod rose to his feet. "So, am I okay?" asked Dod. He wanted to know whether he was still suspected of being a traitor.

"I suppose you're innocent," answered Jibb, looking down his nose at him even though Dod was a little taller. "We sure thought you were Dark Hood until just now. It's good you've decided to grace us with your presence. The past three months have been hard, with all the attacks and deserters. But seeing you and Dark Hood at the same time seems to indicate you're not him. And since you've been injured—" Jibb pointed at Dod's torn, borrowed pajamas.

"I'm fine thanks to you and your men," said Dod, feeling better to be back in acceptable standing. "Without you rescuing me, I'd be dead right now." Dod stuck out his hand to shake. At that moment, he noticed his Coosing ring was back, shining brightly. It, like the three keys around his neck, had been gone while at home on Earth.

Jibb didn't reach for Dod's hand, which was normal considering they didn't customarily shake hands in Green, but he appeared to notice Dod's sincerity. "Where have you been?" asked Jibb.

"I had a few things that needed immediate attention—family business," choked Dod. He hated making excuses. "After The Dread was captured, it seemed reasonable to leave for a while—"

"Let us know next time!" ordered Jibb, once again grunting like a commander. "Without a note, we've all been blaming you for the problems around here. We thought you took over where The Dread left off, stepping in as Dark Hood. It'll shock the crowds tomorrow to see you're not him."

"Didn't Bonboo say anything?" asked Dod. He wondered how Bonboo would have allowed that sort of rumor to circulate when he knew better of Dod.

"He must have forgotten to mention it to us," said Jibb. "I never got your message. But it doesn't surprise me...poor Bonboo. He's had a rough recovery. I'm just glad he's doing better. We feared the worst for him."

Dod felt bad that Bonboo's health had troubled him, yet it bothered Dod even more to hear that his reputation had been slandered, especially considering he had left Green as a hero for stopping The Dread.

It wasn't until Jibb became preoccupied with his men, sending messengers around to the soldiers outside and giving orders, that Dod remembered his big question: Where was everyone?

Unfortunately, before an opportunity opened up for additional conversation, Dod was escorted by three towering drats to Youk's quarters for the night. Saluci greeted him at the door. It was Dod's first time meeting her. She had been gone on charity business for the duration of his last visit to Green.

Dod took one look at Saluci and could see why Youk had married her. She was beautiful and polite, quickly welcoming him in despite his late-night arrival. Her clothing was ornately beaded and her brown hair looked freshly set. She walked and talked like a person of noble blood, but not condescendingly as Sirlonk and Juny had done.

"I was nearly ready to call for bed," she said, showing Dod to a guestroom. "Youk's been out all day on important business. That man works much too hard. Of course, if he did any less, he wouldn't be the wonderful person I fell in love with. Anyway, I expect him soon."

Saluci went on and on about Youk and his great accomplishments. They were truly amazing. Hearing Saluci's descriptions of the battles he had planned was much different than the watered-down, humbler versions Youk had given. Dod remembered sitting in Youk's gathering room, listening to his tales. Recalling the incident also brought back vivid memories of scaling Youk's wall up to Pap's place. Dod poked his head out of the room, looking back toward Saluci's patio doors, while still listening to her ramble on about her husband.

"I don't imagine he'll be here to bother you tonight," said Saluci, catching Dod off guard. He thought at first she was still talking about Youk, for his accomplishments had occupied most of her conversation up to that moment, but she wasn't. She pointed at a second bed in the guestroom, a bed that was covered by two open suitcases brimming with junk.

"He's out watching again," she continued, "as he has for the past few nights in a row. He's quite a dedicated man. I've got to hand him the day; I'd have concluded my work weeks ago if I were him. He's everything Youk said—as thorough as they come—"

Saluci's words ended abruptly when someone down the hall began screaming. Dod shivered. The cries sounded like the ranting of a tormented soul.

"That's my baby," said Saluci, heading for the door. "He's having another nightmare. I can't wait 'til he grows out of them. He terrifies the toenails right off my feet. If you can't sleep, there are pluggings for your ears in the top drawer of the yip-cabinet."

As she passed Dod to walk down the hall, he begged one last question: "Where is everyone tonight? Green Hall was empty."

Saluci gave Dod a strange look before responding. It was the kind of look that people generally give when someone has asked a dumb question.

"The Games," she answered. She hurried down the long corridor to the end and then disappeared around the corner.

Dod slept poorly. It wasn't because of the crying boy, or the duel he'd endured with Dark Hood, or even the visitor who'd shared his guestroom for the second half of the night. It was his torment over being at Twistyard while his friends were at The Games. Dod knew plenty about The Games. It was a nickname given to the Bollirse semi-final championship series. The matches were played to determine who would represent the Western Hemisphere of Green in the final showdown for The Golden Swot. And after Dod had spent so much time practicing—all summer in Cedar City—he was sick at the thought that they were going on without him.

"I wonder if Green won this year against Raul?" whispered Dod to himself, shifting around in bed. "Probably not. Raul always wins."

Dod attempted to make himself feel better about being left behind. He convinced himself that Green Hall was just at The Games to support their teammates from Twistyard's Raul Hall. Nevertheless, his nighttime of mumblings didn't change what he heard in the morning.

"Hey, aren't you Dod?" asked a brown-haired, blue-eyed boy. He looked like a tall six or seven-year-old, and he was as skinny as a stick—clearly Youk's son.

"Yes," said Dod, squinting. He hadn't been tired for most of the night, but now that it was morning, his eyelids felt heavy.

"Why are you here?" prodded the boy. "I thought you were meeting Dilly and the others at Carsigo for The Games."

"What?" asked Dod. He felt a glimpse of hope.

"Two weeks ago, before she left, Dilly told me that she planned on meeting up with you at Carsigo. She said there was no way you'd miss the matches there."

"Really?"

"So why are you here?" the boy continued. He poked at Dod with a beautifully carved swot. "The tournament can't be over, and it would be poor sportsmanship to leave before congratulating the winning team."

The boy looked Dod up and down curiously. Finally, his face lost a bit of enthusiasm as he concluded, "You didn't go, did you?"

"I wanted to," defended Dod. He sat up and looked squarely at the boy, pushing sleep from his eyes. "If I could've gone, I would've—it's hard to explain."

"I know, I know," said the boy, twirling around in a circle with his swot. "You were working, doing secret mission stuff, huh?"

"Yup, you guessed it," answered Dod. "Who told you?"

"Dilly. She knows pretty much everything. And my dad does secret stuff all the time—stuff we can't talk about."

Dod looked around the room and noticed that the other bed was filled. A short, stocky man lay sprawled out, wearing thick, silky pajamas. He had a large bruise on one arm and a fresh scab across his forehead.

"Who's he?" asked Dod, pointing at the other guest.

"The Messy Man," answered the boy. "He's always sleeping and making messes. I know. I sometimes have to clean them up."

"Sammywoo," called Saluci from another room. "Breakfast is almost over and your sisters are getting anxious to make it to their lessons on time. Don't make them late again."

The boy bolted out of the room. Dod got up and prepared to follow. He didn't have any clothes to change into, so he wiped the sand out of his eyes and ran his fingers through his hair twice. As he walked across the floor, trying not to step on anything important-looking, he agreed with Sammywoo that the other guest was a slob. It looked like he had randomly thrown his things from his bed, creating clutter everywhere.

"Man, that kid's right," said Dod, surveying the disaster that was twice as bad as it had been the night before.

"Right about what?" asked a girl, surprising Dod at the doorway. They nearly collided. Embarrassment flushed Dod's face bright-red. He had been caught talking to himself.

"I'm Dod," he said, awkwardly waving. The girl responded by giving the Coosings' sign of friendship—she stuck out her hand, all four fingers apart and her thumb tucked under. But she didn't wear a Coosing ring.

"My name's Valerie," said the girl. She was trying hard to hold back a chuckle. She looked like the spitting image of

Saluci, well proportioned and beautiful. Her curly brown hair flowed over her shoulders and gracefully adorned the top of her attractive clothes.

"And mine's Dari," said a face that popped up from behind Valerie. The second girl was taller, about the same height as Dod, and bean-pole skinny like Youk and Sammywoo. She had bright-blonde, straight silky hair that stopped abruptly at her shoulders and clear-blue eyes. She was an anomaly among young tredders, for not very many of them varied far from having shades of brown or black hair. Neither of them looked much older than Dod, but they were tredders, so instead of fifteenish, they were likely fiftyish.

Dod noticed the girls' smiles and thought about how lucky they were to be tredders; they got to have decades of teenage-like years before entering adulthood in their late fifties or early sixties. Of course, the more Dod thought about it, he couldn't complain—he had a medallion that allowed time to stand still for him.

"Are you hungry?" asked Valerie.

"Dumb question," responded Dari, blaring in Valerie's ear. "He hasn't eaten this morning. Obviously he's hungry." She bumped her gentler sister aside and said, "Give him some room."

"Thanks," said Dod to both girls. "I am very hungry."

Breakfast was scrambled eggs, ham, and musash, a wheat and sweet potato pancake. As he ate, Valerie politely informed him about the latest news that she regarded as important. She spent a lot of time explaining her significant role in the upcoming Dance Delight, set to take place in a few weeks. It was a fancy occasion where boys and girls would don formal wear and then spend a pleasant evening of dancing and eating. It sounded fun. The best part was that Dod didn't need to specifically invite any one person, since it was assumed that he would be well-mannered and dance with a number of girls.

On the other hand, Dari interrupted plentifully, filling Dod in on the woes Twistyard had suffered over the past three months while he had been away. She mentioned Dark Hood, stating that he had caused serious trouble from High Gate to the Carsalean Sea, wreaking havoc on many people, and that to his credit, over two dozen drat soldiers had gone missing from Twistyard, assumed to be dead—or worse, turned traitor. Her comments dominated over her sister's in capturing Dod's attention.

When Dari brought up the possibility of defectors, Dod had to jump in. "Last night they thought I was on the wrong side, too—"

"That makes logical sense," said Dari. "Some drats have been claiming for months that you were Dark Hood. They supposedly found proof of it."

"Ohhhh!" groaned Dod, once again feeling slandered by Jibb and his fellow soldiers.

"But don't fret about it," added Dari. "I don't think very many people believed them. I mean—boingy-boing—you single-handedly caught The Dread. Why would you suddenly turn foul on us? How stupid can they be? And to think they're trying to help us? It's ridiculous."

"Careful now," boomed a powerful voice. It was Youk. He had entered the kitchen without anyone noticing. He wore a dark suit, not typical of Youk, who had always worn white before, and he had a flattish cap instead of his large feathered hat. Dod couldn't take his eyes off the scabbard that Youk wore at his waist. It held the longest sword Dod had ever seen.

"Dad. You're back," called Sammywoo, jumping around at Youk's feet and waving his swot in the air. "Are we going today? You promised we'd see the last match."

Youk patted his son on the head and reassured him that he would keep his promise, one way or another, and then returned his full attention back to his daughter Dari. "The drat soldiers are doing their best, my dear. You can't blame them for suspecting someone like Dod, here." He reached over and rapped Dod firmly on the shoulder. It was forceful enough to prove Youk's skinny six-foot frame had plenty of muscle. "They're checking all of the possibilities. Many clues lead to Twistyard. Dark Hood is likely amongst us, just as The Dread was."

"Well, I'm not The Dread!" said Dod. He meant to say Dark Hood.

"We all know that," said Valerie, rolling her eyes. "The proofus-print has been displayed for weeks in the Hall of The Greats, right under your picture. I've seen it a dozen times or more. Sirlonk and Dungo are gone for good. They've been processed at Driaxom according to justice. You'd think Dark Hood would catch on that he's in a lousy business."

"They have a picture of me?" gasped Dod, embarrassed. He was surprised to find out that Bonboo had insisted on hanging a painting of him on the wall, in company with The Greats.

"That's where I was leading," continued Youk. "You came from nowhere, claiming to be Pap's grandson, and then disappeared right after The Dread was defeated—about the same time Dark Hood emerged. And your picture is sitting on the wall, day and night, reminding the soldiers that you beat them to the catch. Now, with all of that to think about, how can you blemish them for pointing a jealous finger in your noble direction? It's common nature."

Saluci entered the room and drew all of Youk's attention. "You're back, my dear," she said, rushing around the table to hug him. "I worried about you all night when you didn't come home."

"Yes," responded Youk. He hugged his wife but didn't give any explanations. "I love you, too, my thimble hat."

The room turned quiet. Nobody said anything for at least a minute. It was awkward. Even Sammywoo didn't speak.

Someone broke the silence by rapping at the door. Two loud thumps—it sounded like bad news. The hushed moment had built up enough tension to expect something dreadful. Youk went to the front hall and returned with Tridacello on his heels.

"So, they didn't catch him after all," said Youk with surprise, reentering the kitchen. He turned to his family and added, "Everyone, I'm sorry to say it. We were attacked last night. Dark Hood broke into Green Hall, and it's been confirmed that he's not working alone. He had an accomplice—and they got away, so be on alert."

"It's unbelievable!" complained Tridacello. He reached up and rubbed his sunburned head, pushing the remaining white hair into place. "All night I stood with sixty drat bowmen and twenty more swordsmen, waiting by the base of those windows, and Jibb kept a watch at the entrance to Green Hall. I can't imagine how they escaped without us noticing. The windows remained closed. We had them trapped. Yet somehow, when we climbed up the wall and broke in this morning, they were gone. Fifty drat soldiers did the most complete search I've ever seen. It was like they vanished."

Tridacello nodded at Dod when he noticed him sitting at the table. "You've returned here in time for more trouble, I'm afraid."

"I know," responded Dod frankly. "Dark Hood is wickedly good with a sword. I clashed with him last night."

"That's right. You're the one Jibb mentioned. It makes more sense now. We found Pap's sword stuck to the wall in the girls' quarters, holding a piece of black cloth."

"Sorry I didn't get the rest of him," joked Dod.

"That's quite understandable," admitted Tridacello matter-of-factly. "Dark Hood is the best I've fought. I think he's sneakier than Sirlonk, or at least more daring. About four weeks ago, he bested a dozen guards by himself at the Histo Relics Building and stole the Farmer's Sackload."

"You're kidding!" exploded Saluci. She looked ill, as did Valerie. "He has Bonboo's best collection of pure-sight diamonds? Oh no! I'd face Dark Hood by myself just to get my hands on The Sparkle, let alone everything else in the Farmer's Sackload. Youk, my dear and faithful, why didn't you tell me of this? Did Dark Hood really take them?"

Youk looked guilty. As a master of deception, he poorly executed a defense of innocence against his wife. Still, he didn't have time to plead his case before his friend continued on.

"He took them, all right!" explained Tridacello, shaking his head with disgust. "I tracked him along the shoreline of Lake Mauj, a short distance up from Zerny and Jibb's place. It was night and the moon was full. Tinja and Strat were both with me. We finally stopped him by the rocky outcropping and all three of us fought with him, clanking and jabbing our best. I even tried my zip-rope whip. He cut the metal line like it was nothing. In over fifty years of using a zip-rope whip, that's the first time someone's blade has sliced through it—and plenty have tried."

Dari and Valerie sat nervously on the edge of their seats as

Tridacello finished his tale. "And then in a flash, he dove off the rocks into Lake Mauj. He disappeared into the water with his blood-red sword and his pack full of loot. After that, he never surfaced, not even for air—"

"Not that you saw," added Youk with skepticism.

"We would have seen him rise if he had," argued Tridacello. "The night was extremely calm—a flea would have turned our heads. He didn't rise!"

"Regardless," said Youk, not wanting to fight with Tridacello, "it's no wonder we have had so many drat soldiers disappear since then. He's probably buying their loyalty, raising an army right under our noses. Dreaderious has done it for years. Of course, it's different for him—his help is farther away, where it's much cheaper."

"Or he's killing them one by one as a night stalker," squeaked Dari. Her bolder voice had left her.

"No, honey," insisted Youk. Saluci was giving him the '*Don't-terrify-my-kids-any-more*' look, which prompted him to smooth things over. "I'm sure we haven't had any casualties. He's injured a fair number of our men, but they've all survived. Dod faced him last night—and look, is he dead?"

Youk pointed at the rip in Dod's pajamas. The girls both gasped and stared at the hole in horror, imagining how close the villain had come to running Dod through with his unstoppable sword. It didn't help Youk's case any, so he quickly continued.

"If Dark Hood were killing people, he wouldn't take the time to carry them off. That's a pretty big burden for a man who's busy fighting other soldiers. He'd leave them for us to bury. I'm sure he's just buying the weaker sorts, the desperate traitor types from among our troops. He'll have a hard time fighting with that caliber of an army, if they stick around at all. Don't be afraid. We'll stop him."

The conversation ended hastily when a small crowd of The Greats came and asked Youk and Tridacello to join them for a meeting. Dark Hood had made another unbelievable escape, and nobody could explain it.

LUCKY ENOUGH

"**D**id I miss something?" called a scratchy voice from down the hall, becoming louder as it neared the kitchen. It was the Messy Man. He stood five-foot three, short enough to show most everyone the bald patch on top of his head, which was circled by coarse black hair that stuck straight out. His build was stocky and muscular, with mounds of hair on his arms and feet. He had a rough-looking face, chiseled chin, and bushy eyebrows. He would have passed as a tough guy if it weren't for the sloppy food stains down his front and a well-used sock, protruding out of the side rim of his collar.

Everyone sitting around the table said nothing, but smiled when they saw his disheveled appearance. It was a welcome change after the frightening conversation about Dark Hood's attacks.

"What did I miss?" he repeated, scratching one leg. "Not more bad news, is it? After hearing of Polomious's death last week and Rootber's death the week before, if another representative from my part of Green dies, I'm leaving this place to go run for office."

He continued to read their faces and knew something was amiss with his wardrobe, particularly after Sammywoo hopped up and down, pointing his swot at the man's shoulder. Slowly the man turned and inspected himself in a large window that faintly reflected his image.

"Very funny," he said, spinning back around. He made a goofy face and danced on one foot while singing, "I'm in the circus, a gobly-goofus, a morning-sleeper, a bombling-beeber."

He twitted at himself as he bobbed around, seeming to have a jolly time, until he noticed Dod.

"I'm Rot Fieldmaker," he said, bowing his head toward Dod in jest. "Though you can call me whatever you'd like. It won't hurt."

"This is Dod," said Saluci, jumping in to give formal introductions. "He's the one that—"

"I know, we all know," sang Rot. "Dod, Dod, Dod. We all know Dod. He poked and jabbed and also stabbed. We all know Dod."

Saluci rolled her eyes and shook her head apologetically toward Dod. "This," said Saluci, pointing with her whole arm, "is Mr. Rot. Youk invited him to join us for a spell in order to study the decline of our rare varieties of singing doves. They've dropped dramatically over the past few years and much worse recently. The hills used to be filled with their beautiful songs. Now, even with our rooftop gardens as a sanctuary for nesting, and the added breeding programs in place, their numbers are continuing to dwindle."

"That's very true," chimed Rot happily, starting into another round of singing. "They're here today and gone away, the doves can't sing or walk or play, and who can solve the mystery, he's standing here, his name is me."

"Have you met Bowlure?" asked Dod, chuckling.

"I have," said Rot. "We're thinking about starting our own trio."

"And who would the third voice be?" chimed Dari, flicking her short blonde hair. She was beginning to lighten up and was the last one in the room to smile after hearing the troubling news about Dark Hood.

"We were hoping you'd volunteer," he responded.

"Then I guess you'd better keep watching birds," she said half-jokingly. "But find someplace else to stay. You've been here too long already."

"That's not true," said Saluci, embarrassed that her daughter had jabbed at the truth. "Mr. Rot may continue here if he'd like. He's very particular about things being done properly—that's a good quality."

"Your daughter's right," confessed Rot, moving alongside of Valerie. He smelled of garlic and mud. It was strong enough that Valerie retreated, leaving him her seat. He quickly filled it and began to pick at the remains of Sammywoo's half-eaten breakfast.

Dari, too, got up and vacated the table, a safe distance from his smell. Dod followed.

"Have you had anyone take a look at that?" asked Saluci, changing the subject entirely. She pointed at Rot's fresh scab across his forehead, while sliding the last of the musash onto his commandeered plate.

"No, I'm fine," he said. "Sometimes you fall in the night. It's easy to do when you're stalking birds. I take my job very seriously—all kidding aside. I think I may be onto a big breakthrough. We'll see—"

"Dark Hood came back," blurted Sammywoo, "just like you said."

"I knew he would," mumbled Rot with a full mouth.

"Dod sworded him," added Sammywoo, swinging his swot back and forth like a weapon.

"That's enough talking," interrupted Saluci. "You kids need to hurry. I promised Mr. Clair you wouldn't be late any more. It's a real favor to have him here right now, and with the way things have been, a little preparation could make us all sleep better."

When Saluci mentioned sleep, she looked right at Sammywoo. He had erupted into sobbing and screaming at least half-a-dozen more times during the night after his episode that had ended Dod's greetings. It was nothing short of astonishing that Saluci was able to be up and well after having had such a dreadful bout of caretaking.

The girls tugged at Sammywoo and headed for the front door. Dod followed them until Valerie informed him that it was hardly proper to be walking about the halls at Twistyard in pajamas. She suggested that if he wished to join them for their lessons, he could do so after preparing more appropriately for the day. They would be in the little ribble-barn.

"But I didn't bring any other clothes," complained Dod, feeling like it was becoming a common problem. It brought back memories of spending his first few days in Green wearing the same outfit before begging old clothes from his friends. He had intended on digging into Pap's closets, but hadn't found the time.

"Oh, stuff it," said Dari, giving Valerie a shove. "You take Sammywoo and tell Clair I'll be down in a minute." She brought Dod back to the guestroom and started opening closet doors. There were five of them along one wall, each bulging with their contents. "Do you see anything that might fit?" she asked.

Most of the stuff was not clothing. All sorts of toys and books and gadgets dripped from sagging shelves. Dari stooped down and picked up a number of items that had escaped the moment she opened the doors.

"Maybe that," suggested Dod, pointing to a cream-colored pair of pants that were different than the others—they were folded nicely.

"Fabuloo," chirped Dari, grabbing the pants and tossing them at Dod. She dug deeper in the wall of clutter and plucked out a matching shirt.

Dod didn't need to ask Dari to leave the room for him to put them on. He didn't even need to tell her to turn around. They were way too big. By the time Dod caught them in the air, they had spread out full, showing that they hung from his chest to the floor.

"Maybe not so fabuloo," teased Dari, chuckling.

"I need my own clothes!" complained Dod, feeling dumb that the pants were much bigger than anything he could wear.

"*Well-o*, my little *friend-o*," continued Dari, putting her hand on her brow. She was having fun teasing Dod, pronouncing each word carefully.

"Little? I'm as tall as you."

"Like *that-o* means *anything-o*."

"I'm taller than Mr. Messy Man," said Dod, tripping over Rot's stuff that nearly filled the floor.

"But his *mom-o* was a *bobwit-o*, was *yours-o*?"

"He's a bobwit? I thought they didn't crack much above four feet."

"His *dad-o* was like *you-o*, a human."

The conversation drew memories of places and people Dod couldn't clearly identify, but he instantly remembered a lot about the subject. A large number of humans and bobwits and tredders were intermingled. They weren't all human or all bobwit or all tredder.

Many people, such as the nobles possessing royal bloodlines, were predominantly of one race, yet not completely. And based on the close similarities of the different races of people, it didn't matter. Of course it did affect their height, and life cycles, and other traits that were characteristically found in the blood of one group or the other. However, from one location to another, there were already many differences within the races, as in the most notable example where a grand society of humans, called The Mauj, substantially outlived all of the other humans and other races, living up to five hundred years; though at the present, tredders had an upper hand on longevity over the existing races.

The big exception to intermarrying was with drats. Although physically very similar, humans and bobwits and tredders weren't typically attracted to women with beards, and drats weren't usually fond of those without them.

"So, do you have any human blood in you?" asked Dod, returning the teasing. He vaguely remembered hearing that Youk did.

"One of my great, great-grandfathers on my dad's side was a human," said Dari, scowling playfully at Dod. "But don't talk about it in front of my mother. My dad's still a good pick for Chief Noble Tredder when Bonboo dies—human blood or not. Besides, you're a human and you're not that disgraceful, and the best of The Greats was human, too."

"Yup, Pap was incredible, wasn't he," said Dod.

"He was good, but boingy-boing, Humberrone was unbelievable!—no offense to your grandpa."

It bothered Dod that whenever the conversation turned to

Humberrone, Pap was left far below on the scale of greatness. As far as Dod was concerned, Pap was the best. And Dod did take offense when anyone suggested Pap wasn't.

"You must not have known Pap very well," responded Dod. "For if you knew him as I knew him, you'd realize Humberrone paled by comparison."

"Uh—not even *close-o*, my little *friend-o*," answered Dari. She knew that the subject got under his skin, so she laid it on thicker by reverting back to adding 'oh.'

"Whatever," said Dod, irritated. "I guess I'll go find some clothes in my closet, the kind that fit people, not seven-foot creatures like Bowlure."

Dod walked out of the room and made his way to the front hall, though he didn't leave before Dari caught up with him.

"You *might-o* at least put something on over *that-o* before walking out *there-oooo*," said Dari, pointing at Dod's torn shirt. She smiled wide.

Dod looked down and blushed. Somewhere between breakfast and that moment he had snagged the hole and ripped it much bigger, nearly all the way up.

"Perhaps a *coat-o* or cloak for my little *friend-o*?" She opened a closet that held dozens of different coats and hats. It was a room filled with attire. "You can borrow one from my *dad-o*," she continued.

Dod glanced around for anything less elegant to take. He hated the thoughts of risking harm to a part of Youk's fancy wardrobe, especially when remembering how Youk had displayed his bloody zarrick near Dod's face after the Brown Sugar incident had ruffled his feathers. But what Dod found when he flipped through the clothes was unexpected. Behind a cluster of dark jackets and coats, Dod saw two swords. They were mostly concealed by a leather satchel, with the tips of the hilts showing. The rapier Youk had been wearing wasn't the only weapon he kept.

"How about *this-o*?" asked Dari, pulling down a beautiful, white cloak. She held it up to him and then paused. "Yup. Fabuloo. My father's outgrown this, so it's yours."

"I couldn't," said Dod, stepping out of the closet.

"MOM," called Dari. "Can Dod have Dad's old cloak—the white one he doesn't fit anymore?"

"Sure, let's see it on him," said Saluci, appearing from around the corner. She nodded with approval when she saw Dod wearing it.

"Thank you," said Dod, feeling bad that he had gotten worked up over nothing. He called back over his shoulder as he left, "I'll catch up at the little ribble-barn after I'm *ready-o*."

In front of Green Hall, Dod ran into a squad of soldiers guarding the entrance. When he tried to explain that his clothes were inside, they didn't seem to care. Nobody was allowed in.

Rather than attempt a struggle with drat loyalists, Dod resorted to Pap's place. He remembered the way—across the hall, through a small conference room, to the left of a wooden stage, through a locked door that was hidden by curtains, up a twenty-five story shaft, down a short hall, through another locked door, and into his house.

Pap's place was comfortable during the day. Sunlight streamed through a wall of windows that adorned the back side of the entry room. It created a pleasant ambiance. Dod looked around at the cluttered shelves filled with gadgets and statuary, and the drawers and cupboards packed with useful contraptions, and remembered filling Boot's bag the first time he had visited alone.

"I dumped all of Boot's buster candles on the floor behind that chair," recalled Dod, talking to himself. "And that's where I found the palsarflex, behind everything else on that shelf. Maybe he's got another one."

Dod eagerly climbed on the back of the same chair he had used before and balanced his weight as he searched for a palsarflex. There was none. The one he had taken before was safely stowed in a closet, along with the rest of Boot's things. Dod didn't mind that Boot had a tendency of claiming stuff; he shared with Dod and that was good enough.

While climbing down, the chair tipped and Dod fell to the floor. He gasped. From his ground-level position, he could see that the candles were no longer in a pile behind the chair. It made his heart pound faster. Who had taken them?

"My sword," mumbled Dod, rising to his feet. He carefully worked his way down Pap's cluttered hallway, heading for the office. Dod had discovered Pap's sword collection when visiting before and knew right where to find one—or so he thought. When he reached the room, it was spotless—not robbed, just cleaned. Someone had put away all of the effects and had thoroughly dusted.

The swords were not scattered on the floor as they had previously been. Instead, they hung neatly in rows on a wall, displaying their various sizes and shapes. All of the other items that had littered the office were now stowed in drawers and re-situated in what appeared to be their proper places. The only thing that was amiss was the empty shelf above Pap's desk, where his special books had been.

CHAPTER FIVE

"Pap?" whispered Dod. "Pap's here. He's come back somehow. Maybe he didn't die after all. It was faked, like Bonboo's assassination."

Dod walked over to the neatly arranged collection on the wall and picked a sword. He drew it out of its casing and admired the shiny blade. It was beautiful with intricate designs. It had the appearance of being made of gold, yet it clearly wasn't, for the metal felt as tough as hardened steel. Pap's insignia was engraved on the hilt and on the scabbard.

"Pap," yelled Dod, returning to the hall. Once he knew that the office had been cleaned, he noticed that the hall had been tidied, too. It was still encumbered with all sorts of statuary and other possessions, but it wasn't dirty.

Dod continued searching each room for Pap, or anyone else. There were plenty of signs that Pap had returned; the older food in the kitchen had been discarded and a basket full of fresh fruit had been placed on the counter, and someone had freshly laundered Pap's bedding and fixed the back patio door.

When the house turned up empty, Dod went outside, hoping to find Pap. But the chirping of birds and buzzing of bees was as much as he found for company. Nobody was around. It was baffling. The flowers, bushes, and trees were well manicured, and the vegetable patch had orderly rows of produce ready to pick—vegetables which appeared to have been planted after Pap's poisoning at High Gate. And a shovel with fresh dirt was propped up against a fruit tree, beside a basket of ripe apples. Everything indicated that someone had been living there for months, attending to the duties of maintenance.

"PAP!" yelled Dod. He rushed around the gardens, searching for anyone. Nobody responded. Still, the proof was abundant, and it gave him hope.

Dod hurried back inside and loaded a bag of clothes from Pap's closet. He also selected a handsome outfit and put it on, adding the finishing touch—Pap's golden sword at his waist. He scribbled a note and left it on the yip-cabinet, next to the bed. His note stated that he was in Green and that he wanted to meet with Pap. It said a lot of things and then ended with an apology if the real person staying there was Bonboo. Dod couldn't think of anyone else who would know of the secret house and care enough to fix it up.

About the time Dod entered the busy corridor in front of Green Hall, it struck him how foolish he had been in leaving a note for someone who was dead. He knew Pap was gone. He had worn a stuffy black suit and listened to sappy talks about how wonderful his grandpa had been. He had even slipped a bag of small stones from the creek into Pap's casket, right beside his lifeless body, promising him he'd keep throwing. It represented the summers Pap had spent with him fishing and camping.

Being near people in the hall brought Dod back to the realities of life: Pap was gone and Bonboo had instructed someone reliable to take care of the hideout. After all, it would be a shame to let it spoil, and Dod hadn't been doing his share of the work to keep it looking nice.

It was only a few moments before thoughts of Pap were far from Dod's mind. And it wasn't just that he realized Pap couldn't have returned, it was the patrol of soldiers who stopped him that drove the nostalgia away. They had noticed him carrying a sword at his waist—everyone was staring at it. The fancy scabbard drew attention from passers-by. The guards indicated that he wasn't authorized to be equipped as he was and that they had orders to strip him of his weapon and take him in for questioning.

CHAPTER FIVE

Dod felt like fighting. The drat soldiers were out to get him, he knew it. They were biased by the lies that Jibb and others had spread, saying he was Dark Hood. And even though he had been proven innocent the night before, obviously some people were still thinking he was involved. The thought raced through his mind, *You can have my sword if you can take it from me.* It was his connection to Pap and his tool that inspired courage within him. Wearing the fancy sword made him feel like he was destined to defeat Dark Hood as he had The Dread. Not to mention, Youk and Tridacello had been wearing swords.

Nevertheless, Dod backed down and began to comply. He looked around and noticed that except for the militia, everyone else was weaponless, suggesting Twistyard in general had maintained its original policies with only a few exceptions. Dod slowly unhitched the casing of his rapier.

"Ludicrous!" yelled an old woman. She stormed up to Dod and stood inches from him, hunching over and occasionally using a cane to steady her weight. She was at least four hundred pounds, which was heavy, even considering her six-foot-plus stature. Her brown and graying curls stayed close to her head as she swayed.

"Stand back," she said, waving her cane in the faces of the soldiers. "You're telling me he's a threat? Stand back! I'll fight you myself if you don't stop picking on this boy. He's Pap's grandson! That's credentials sufficient to walk with a sword. I've seen his face on the wall in the Hall of The Greats—go look at it! He's the one who stopped The Dread. If you wish to take his sword, you must be working for Dark Hood yourselves. Traitors! You're all traitors!"

She continued to wave her cane, nearly striking the noses

of some drat soldiers who didn't obey her requests. The strident ramblings of the lady attracted the attention of everyone walking by. People began to point and say, "Look, he's the one who defeated The Dread!" and "It's Dod. He's back to help us!"

Most of the people in the hall were Pots—young visitors who hoped to eventually become one of the fifty Lings, or fifteen Coosings who represented each realm. They came from all over Green, Raul, and Soosh. There were other guests, too, such as dignitaries; yet none of the hundred or more guests who began to cluster near Dod had met him before. The people who knew Dod best were preoccupied at The Games.

The guards felt pressure from the crowd. Some people pushed their way through, wanting to pat Dod on the shoulder, while others began to warmly contend with the soldiers. It was clear that the woman's words had been powerful at swaying the masses, and the masses were equally good at convincing the drat legion.

"I suppose if you're Dod," said the commanding officer, approaching him carefully and pretending to inspect Pap's insignia on the scabbard, "we'll extend you The Greats' exemption. Our apologies."

All of the soldiers had known he was Dod. They made it their business to keep an eye out for anyone they suspected of treachery, and they had suspected him. Regardless, they pretended it was an act of mistaken identity.

"Ludicrous," mumbled the lady, still shaking her cane at the guards. She scowled and watched as they walked down the hall. Her wrinkly face of baggy skin added to the look of discontent. It vaguely reminded Dod of a Halloween mask he had worn one year for a neighborhood spook alley.

"My name's Ingrid," she finally said to Dod. She grabbed his arm and insisted he walk her to the kitchen.

"Thanks for helping me back there," sighed Dod. He was relieved that the guards hadn't hauled him off to who knows where, especially with Bonboo out of town. "They don't like me," he continued. "I've tried to be nice to them. It just doesn't do any good."

"They're jealous," grumbled the lady, leaning heavily on Dod. "I think they should pack up and leave. But who cares what I think? I'm just an old lady, and not a very popular one at that. 'Course, it is my first visit to this place. I haven't even met Bonmoob yet. I hear he's old like me, having all sorts of trouble with his baggage and bones."

The more Ingrid leaned, the more Dod realized she smelled like Rot—garlic and mud. It was revolting. It made him wish to get away.

"I care what you think," answered Dod, trying not to breathe through his nose. "And I agree with you perfectly. The drat soldiers aren't doing their jobs very well. They're harassing people…and spreading lies, too. They thought I was Dark Hood. Can you imagine that?"

Dod vented to the lady as he would have to Aunt Hilda back at home. He was grateful for her help and also her listening ear. She seemed to have the same views about the soldiers. It felt safe to complain to her.

"I know. It's a shame," said Ingrid, shaking her head until the rolls of skin below her chin wiggled. "You should talk with Bonmoob if he ever comes back. You're cozy with him, aren't you? Better get a word in before he checks out."

"Bonboo was doing well when I left," said Dod. "What happened to him?"

"He got sick and went to see my cousin Higga. He stayed there with that loyal drat friend of his at his bedside for weeks, and only got worse by the visit. And then relatives came storming in and scooped him up—took him off someplace. I think that's the real reason Higga left. It wasn't just the lure of research. She was offended—and rightly so! It wasn't her fault. She didn't poison him."

Dod was interested to know more about the unusual events surrounding poor Bonboo's treatments. He began to ask when he was cut off by Mercy, the moment they rounded the corner into the kitchen.

"Dod! It's great to see you made it back. We were all getting worried about you. Don't scare us like that. If you've got things to do, at least come and tell me goodbye, or leave a note. And the post works, you know. We could have used a few letters. I've got to hear everything. Let's start with the morning you left. Where did you go next?"

"I went home—" began Dod.

"Good for you," interjected Mercy. She didn't wait for Dod to say any more before continuing on with her own list of things she wanted to tell him. She spent ten minutes blaring without so much as a break for air, all the while making food and interjecting directives to the other helpers in the kitchen. It was classic Mercy.

Ingrid sat down on a chair in the corner and breathed heavily, listening. Dod was relieved to get farther from Ingrid's smell. He had felt like Mercy was an older woman—she did have graying brown hair and a rounder condition—nevertheless, having Ingrid in the room lent perspective. Mercy was comparatively at the top of her game.

"I see you're staying with Youk," continued Mercy, pointing

at the white cloak that draped over Dod's arm. "That's a smart choice. Green Hall was besquashed last night. Good thing you weren't there! Dark Hood showed up—who knows why—and then poofed away like a baked ice-cake."

Dod was willing to keep Mercy in the shade about having faced Dark Hood, to shorten the conversation, but Ingrid wasn't. She spoke up and told the story, adding heroic details that painted Dod as a real champion. It was baffling how she knew more about it than Mercy.

"I'm glad to hear," said Mercy, patting Dod on the shoulder as she passed by with a tray of delectable cookies. "Dark Hood is trouble, no doubt. It's a good thing Bonboo can perceive his tricks, as he did with The Dread. There's no need for us to play into the hands of corrupt individuals. Bonboo's been a wonderful Chief Noble Tredder. When he passes, I'm sure Youk will do a good job, too—assuming his name's in the box."

"You think Bonmoob would choose him over Pious?" gasped Ingrid, shocked. "Pious has been winning so many battles against Dreaderious that we hardly consider ourselves at war anymore. The seas are finally safe again. And if it weren't his name, I'd expect to see Commendus written down. He's proven himself plenty while leading our democracy. Maybe it's time to combine the two positions."

"Not wise," responded Mercy. "I'd predict Voracio over either of them. As a matter of fact, I think he's more suitable than Youk. He's one of The Greats, equal to Youk, and comes from the best tredder blood-line!"

"Whose?" snapped Ingrid, getting angry. Dod stepped out from between the two snarling women. Ingrid had risen to her feet and was leaning on her thick, wooden cane.

"BONBOO'S!" boomed Mercy. She stepped closer to Ingrid, showing she wasn't afraid of her. "Voracio is his grandson, which counts for a lot. He dropped everything and rushed here to be with us, to attend to things properly. And with Dark Hood lurking about, I'd say he's proven himself invaluable."

Ingrid nearly pounded Mercy over the head with her cane. It looked more like a club when she raised it up. Fortunately, before anything happened, she began to choke and cough. It brought her back to a hunching position, relying on her cane to stand. She murmured a few things and then hobbled away without striking.

"Good to be out with that!" celebrated Mercy, fanning the air. "And to think she actually wants to cook in my kitchen! That nasty garlic clings to her—I don't want any part of it. She can keep stewing with the soldiers outside. If people like it, they can go out there to eat it."

Mercy handed Dod a pile of cookies and insisted he come back later for more. She promised to have even better ones—chouyummy delights.

In the courtyard, Dod found that things were relatively similar to the way he remembered them. The biggest difference was that the drat soldiers had extended the borders of their camp, with their numbers reaching five hundred or more.

In the center of the tent city was a communal pavilion, constructed directly below Dilly's window. It appeared to be the place where the soldiers ate their meals and spent their extra time. Dod wondered how Dark Hood and his associate had escaped through one of Green Hall's windows. They all seemed to be improbable routes with the guards' camp littering the ground below them.

CHAPTER FIVE

"No more sneaking out at night," said Dod to himself. He made his way across the field of lawn and then along the tree-lined path to the little ribble-barn.

"Nice of you to come now that we're basically done," said Dari, faking a cross look. She picked at her short blonde hair until she drew a tree beetle out of it and then looked up at the oak they were sitting under.

"Like you're one to be talking," chided Valerie, positioned stiffly next to Dari on a bench in front of the barn. "You barely beat him by a few minutes."

"Hardly," barked Dari, flipping the beetle into her sister's curly hair. Valerie jumped to her feet and hopped around, screaming, until the bug fell out.

Dod walked over and offered the girls and Sammywoo cookies from his stash. He set his bag and new cloak down before planting himself next to Sammywoo.

"What a challenging lesson," teased Dod. It appeared that their course was in sitting.

"Mr. Clair's gone to fetch his assistants," said Sammywoo. "He's going to show us what it's really like."

Within a few minutes, three men came storming from the barn, yelling horrible threats. Two of the men faced the other, swinging their swords menacingly. The man who stood alone was remarkable with his blade. He held them back, blow for blow, and finally forced them to retreat until they were trapped against the barn. With no escape, they threw their swords to the ground and begged for mercy.

"See kids, that's the way it's done," said the man who still held his sword. He was tall, six-foot four or better, with midnight-black curly hair and a muscle-bound frame. He looked late twenties, but was clearly over one hundred as a tredder.

Youk's kids clapped and clapped while Dod stared. He hadn't been prepared for the show, so during the realistic fighting, Dod had reached for his own sword. The only thing that had kept him from drawing it was the look on Sammywoo's face — the boy hadn't appeared threatened at all.

"Wow!" said Dod, standing to meet the men. "That was well planned. You had me convinced you were fighting for real."

"You don't know Clair, do you?" blurted the shorter of the two assistants, who was only an inch taller than Dod. "It wasn't planned — it was intense practice. And had we not begged at the end, I suppose we'd need patching right now."

Dod laughed like he didn't believe the man, so the man lifted his sleeves, revealing a series of scars that ran up both arms.

"Most of these came from him," said the man, pointing at Clair.

"You're exaggerating," chuckled Clair, brushing off the statement as a compliment. He spoke with a deep, manly voice as he swaggered over to Dod. "You've been gone long enough to find yourself displaced, haven't you?"

"I don't know what you mean," answered Dod.

"Well, look around — we're doing just fine without you. And since Pious has commissioned me here, I'll take care of things. You can work somewhere else…somewhere you're wanted."

"I'm Dod," said Dod, feeling confused and embarrassed. He assumed Clair had mistaken him for a different person.

Clair laughed and his assistants joined in. The taller of the two had light brown hair and stood about six-foot two, the shorter had black hair like Clair.

CHAPTER FIVE

"Wearing a fancy sword doesn't make you *great*," growled Clair, glancing at Dod's intricately decorated sheath. "You were lucky with Sirlonk—and you're fortunate that I'm going to pretend I believe that, or I'd show you what I do to traitors!" Clair turned to the girls and smiled politely. "Lessons for today are over," he said in a civil voice.

The three men took their swords and disappeared into the barn the way they had come.

"I think he hates you," declared Dari to Dod, being the only one that dared say anything after such an embarrassing episode.

It was hard for Dod to disagree.

The remainder of the day was over, despite it being only lunchtime. Dod faked ill and requested a break from the other events. He didn't need anyone else wanting to assault him on his first day back. And in truth, he was horribly tired. It was like he had jetlag. He had tossed and turned his way through the prior night, which was really the rest of his Saturday on Earth, and now at noon was ready to sleep.

Saluci met him at the door and bid him a quick recovery before he faded off to sleep in the cluttered guest bedroom.

CHAPTER SIX

ONE MINUTE TOO LATE

"Wakeup! Wakeup!" chanted Sammywoo, poking at Dod with his fancy swot. "Wakeup! You need to eat breakfast."

Dod rubbed his face and looked around. The room was still cluttered with stuff and smellier than before. Rot was snoring in his bed.

"I have a surprise for you. Quick, get up," begged the little boy, his blue eyes filled with anticipation. He couldn't wait to see Dod's reaction.

"What is it?" asked Dod, clearing his throat.

The boy shook his head, smiling. "I can't show you until you're done eating. Quick! Get up!"

Dod rose to his feet and rummaged through his bag. "I'll be there in a minute, little buddy," said Dod. "How about you save me a place at the table. Can we sit together?"

"I've already eaten. Quick! Hurry!"

Dod rushed his preparations to please the boy and made his way to the kitchen. In truth, he was excited to see what the boy was so enthusiastic about. An afternoon and full night of sleep had bolstered his spirits back to soaring heights, making Dod ready for the day, even if it presented more mean people and slanderous remarks. But, remembering the day before, Dod wrapped Pap's beautiful sword in Youk's white cloak and carried it instead of wearing it.

The breakfast table was quiet; Dari, Valerie, and Rot were still asleep, awaiting the sun to rise, and Sammywoo had accompanied Youk out the door to their patio-garden, where they reportedly were 'preparing the surprise.' Saluci served a feast of delicious foods and insisted Dod eat them to ensure better health. She told a Humberrone story that suggested the very meal Dod was gobbling had the capacity to guarantee good luck. It was nice of her to say it, even if it wasn't true.

"Humberrone was fortunate," admitted Dod, devouring a pile of brown cubes that tasted like steak. "He seems to have done enough impossible things to have landed at the top of everyone's hero list—hasn't he? And in fifty years—it's quite amazing. So, what happened to him?"

Dod had been told bits and pieces from other people about Humberrone's mysterious death, but Saluci seemed to have an inside track. She claimed to have been in love with him at one point, when he was younger and less popular. It was about the same time she had begun dating Youk.

Shortly thereafter, Humberrone and Youk had experienced a 'falling away,' and Youk had found himself on the outs from Twistyard for a long time. Saluci didn't say what either of them had done or why Youk had been asked to stay away, but she went with Youk, not Humberrone. Dod liked hearing that. For once someone who knew Humberrone well also knew a dirty little secret about how he had wronged Youk. It was proof to Dod that Pap was better than Humberrone, for Pap had been nice to everyone Dod knew.

"I'm not sure," said Saluci hesitantly, finally answering Dod's question about what had happened to Humberrone. "I've heard…well…I don't know exactly. He died about fifteen years ago. The…let's see…whole thing was an immense tragedy."

Dod could tell Saluci was retaining a juicy story, something she felt would be imprudent to share. It drove Dod nuts. He desperately wanted the details—whatever they were, whatever she was holding back—but Saluci's resolve to keep the information to herself was beyond the influence of persuasion.

"Are you done?" called Sammywoo, bursting through the door. "Hurry up. We won't make it in time." Sammywoo disappeared back out into the patio garden. It was an acre filled with bushes, trees, flowers, and statuary. At the edge of the garden, a beautiful, waist-high rail protected viewers from falling twenty stories to the courtyard below.

Dod shoveled the rest of his breakfast into his mouth and made haste to the door. He was more than ready for his grand surprise, though not prepared for what he saw. It was astonishing. Hidden behind a ten-foot wall of shrubs and bushes, Youk and two other men held the reins to a giant flutter. It was more than twice as big as the flutters Dod recalled from his experience with Tridacello, Dungo, and Bowlure. It was enormous, with charcoal-black wings that appeared to be covered with rubber-like skin and feathers. Its length from beak to tail was only slightly longer than a regular flutter, about twenty-five feet; however, its body-mass was more than double, and its gigantic wings spanned as far out on each side as the creature was long. Dod could imagine the beast carrying three or four men easily without causing it to falter—that is, if the men dared to ride it.

"You probably thought they were extinct, didn't you?" said Youk, beaming with delight. "It's amazing what you can accomplish if you're one of the Zoots. My wife is both clever and magnificent."

Saluci had followed Dod to the gathering. She waved her hand, as if to say, 'stop teasing.' Still, she glowed with pride in her family name.

"Yup," said one man, who helped Youk contain the creature's riggings. He had long gray hair, tied back in a braid. His face was wrinkled and sunburned. "The Zoots are about the only ones I know of who could pull off something like this. I confess, Youk, you've won again. I never would have expected Horsely to return this morning with an answer like *this*." The man patted the lower neck of the giant flutter. "That note must have said something special!"

Dod knew Horsely. He was the lead man who controlled the beast. Horsely was a young tredder, mid-seventies, strong and handsome, a little less than six feet, with black hair and blue eyes. He looked like he could have been Boot's older brother, though he walked slower, with a limp, and read lips because he was deaf. He had been a Green Coosing with Boot, years before, and had fought with The Dread. Unfortunately for him, the remains of that confrontation still lingered.

Horsely occasionally labored in the barns alongside his aging uncle, Stallio, who wore the braid. They handled Zerny's special requests regarding animals, having both been personally trained by Miz as maylers. Since Stallio and his wife had no children, Horsely lived with them on a small farm outside of the Twistyard complex, combining their efforts to keep it going.

It was technically Bonboo's land; they were sharecroppers and horsemen, working a hold along the shore of Lake Mauj.

"I know, I know," answered Youk happily, tipping his white hat at Saluci. "My wife pulled it off. She asked a favor and got a stupendous reply. It just shows that I'm not the only one who recognizes how important she is." He then turned toward Horsely and added, slowing his speech, "You did a good job delivering the message. Were you scared when they responded with this big guy?"

Horsely laughed. "I was nearly born on the back of one of these! And since my accident, riding anything beats walking. Besides, I was assured that this one is well educated." He reached up with both hands and covered the nose-holes of the flutter, forcing its giant head down at his command. It was an act that clearly showed he wasn't afraid, even though he could have been—the menacing beak was colossal and would have had no trouble snipping his hands off, had the bird not been properly trained.

Dod stared. Thoughts ran through his mind of the night he had fled from Pap's place. Sawny had mentioned seeing two giant flutters leave the rooftop gardens. It made chills roll down his spine. He glanced above the forty-foot wall to the enormous fish statue Sawny had seen the riders pass. The stone sculpture was smaller than the beast that stood in front of Dod. This was a creature that even Bowlure could ride.

"Surprise!" said Sammywoo, giggling. "We're going to The Games, just like my dad promised. The last match is today, and if we hurry, we'll make the start." Sammywoo wore a white three-piece suit that matched his father's, completed by an elegant, feathered hat.

"But I thought Carsigo was days away, up the Carsalean Seashore."

"It is by horse," said Stallio, looking straight at Dod. He reached over and slapped the side of the flutter. "Good thing this is no horse. It can fly right over the top of Janice Pass and cut straight across the Gulf of Blue, landing at Carsigo before lunch if you hurry."

"Go get your stuff," commanded Youk. "I won't be able to bring you home tonight. You'll need to ride back with Boot and Buck."

Dod rushed inside and returned with his bag of things over his shoulder, his sword and cloak stowed within. Horsely and Youk were already mounted with Sammywoo squished tightly between, while Stallio stood by holding the reins. Dod nervously climbed up a five-step lift to his seat. The flutter shook and clawed at the ground as Dod clamped his bag to a rack and buckled himself in.

"Fly her safely," said Stallio, talking to Horsely. He handed him the last of the leather straps, which attached to a metal bar below the flutter's beak. The harness jolted and readjusted the moment Stallio was no longer forcing the beast to stay in place. Dod looked forward and noticed Youk's hat had strings that connected tightly to his shoulder clips. He was prepared for rough action.

"Please be careful and have a fun ride," called Saluci, looking worried yet jealous; an adventurous spirit lurked somewhere within her, hidden behind a sophisticated exterior.

Dod recalled being told that he had ridden flutters, yet the experience was entirely new. He couldn't remember the slightest detail. And the moment they left the ground, Dod had a greater respect for the original Dod, the one who had died on the cliffs, presumably at the hands of Dungo. According to Bowlure, the boy had flown well at the trials.

Riding a flutter was not like riding a horse. It took greater skill, pulling various leather bands at the correct times to get the creature to go as desired. The birds were cantankerous and willful by nature, and the one they were riding was extraordinarily so. It started off in the wrong direction, heading straight for High Gate, and even jerked around until Horsely lost one of his bags. And despite Horsely's best attempts, it took fifteen minutes before the bird was persuaded to turn around. Slowly the flutter gave in and allowed Horsely to steer.

Thirty minutes into the ride, as they were passing Twistyard, finally heading in the right direction, Dod realized he needed to go to his room in Green Hall—he needed to wear his medallion. If Earth-time had continued while the necklace was hidden, then the men in the trailer would be long gone—it would be early Monday morning. If he waited days until a more convenient opportunity, he would miss Christmas and worry his mother to death. Not to mention, a bad feeling came over Dod as he thought about leaving it in his bed frame.

"I forgot something," yelled Dod, nudging Youk.

"Me too," he responded, turning around. "Flying's for the birds." Youk laughed at his joke. He clearly enjoyed riding, even if the flutter hadn't conformed to their plans from the start. And Sammywoo was having the time of his life, calling out all sorts of phrases about how wonderful the day was and how he'd never forget it.

"I need something from Green Hall," pleaded Dod. He spoke loud enough that Sammywoo poked Horsely until he turned around, too.

"That's impractical," blurted Youk. "We're already flying and finally making our way toward Carsigo! Whatever it is can wait 'til you get back." His attitude had changed in a flash and wasn't very favorable.

"Besides," he continued, "the drats are still carrying on their investigation—" Youk's words trailed for a moment while he thought of the right ones to say. "Well, it would impede the process if you rummaged. They'd be furious at us—mad at me! Green Hall is off limits to everyone! When you return with Boot and Buck, I'm sure they'll have it reopened."

"Please!" begged Dod. "Help me get into Green Hall. I'd owe you the biggest favor. It means more to me than I can explain. It would only take a moment. I promise."

Youk adamantly refused.

But it didn't matter: Horsely was deaf and couldn't hear Youk's voice, he could only read lips; and the ones facing him were Dod's.

In a flash, Horsely spun the flutter around and made it dive toward Twistyard. Youk yelled in vain. The giant bird continued its course, ending in the most precarious of positions, clinging to the rock wall below Dod's bedroom window. It wasn't until the bird stopped flying that Dod noticed talons along the wingtips; they, in addition to its clawed-feet, helped the flutter to secure itself to the wall.

The ride had been varying degrees of horizontal, like racing on a horse up and down hills, but while stuck to the wall, they were completely vertical. It was uncomfortable. Their buckles and straps were put to the test, holding them from falling to the courtyard below.

Horsely reached in a bag at his side and produced a rope with a hook on the end. He threw the line until the clip snagged on the window trim, and then he dropped the rest of the rope down, dangling it next to Dod.

"Hurry," called Horsely to Dod. "This thing might change its mind any minute."

Dod grabbed the rope and unbuckled himself. He climbed past Youk, who was fuming and struggling to contort his body into a backrest for his son.

"I hope you're happy!" blurted Youk. "Now all the drats down below will make issue of this and I'll be answering jabs for ages. You and your barnyard pal have lost your freshy-minds. This is absurd!"

Dod raced up the rope, disregarding Youk's bitterness. He only slowed temporarily at the window, to pop it open, and then entered and exited in record time. The whole ordeal, from the moment he started climbing to the moment he finished re-buckling was a minute or less. It was so fast, only a couple of soldiers down below had gathered to point. Nevertheless, it was long enough to guarantee Youk's white suit had been noticed.

"Thank you," mouthed Dod to Horsely, who had spun around to make sure he was properly secured.

Horsely raised his chin and eyebrows in acknowledgement, smiling. He didn't seem bothered or intimidated by Youk's display of anger. He appeared glad to show off his ability with the flutter, making up for the detour test flight they'd taken in the wrong direction.

When Youk turned to see what Dod was whispering, Horsely mouthed, "You owe me." Dod knew he did. Even though he had only briefly been around Horsely in the past, he felt strangely drawn to him. There were times when Horsely had demonstrated unusual levels of loyalty to others like Boot and Buck, suggesting he would do anything for his closest friends. It made Dod want to be on his short list of them.

CHAPTER SIX

After stowing the rope back in his bag, Horsely drew out a large and unusual pair of goggles. The lenses were at least three times the size of regular ones, parting in the center for his nose and dipping all the way to his mouth at the bottoms. They were held tight against his cheeks by a band that wrapped around his head. He looked like a fly-faced, crazy man.

"Now we'll make this bird soar," said Horsely.

When the beast launched off the wall, everything shook. They plunged backwards, falling upside-down before correcting. It was terrifying and exciting at the same time. It started off better than any amusement ride Dod had ever been on, but eventually became breezy and uncomfortable. The flutter rose to greater heights and flew much faster than it had before. Horsely's large glasses protected his eyes against the wind. Youk had none, so he gradually slumped behind Horsely, sharing the shielded spot with his son, and Dod followed suit behind Youk.

Around noon, when the sun beamed its hottest, Dod awoke from an awkward slumber. He had been cramped over long enough, avoiding the breeze, that his stomach ached. Horsely was shouting about something down below. In the distance, positioned at the southernmost tip of the shoreline enclosing the Gulf of Blue, a monstrous arena rumbled with noise. It was filled to capacity with over three hundred thousand screaming fans that could be heard from miles away. To the northeast of the sprawling city, a giant mountain range continued east as far as the eye could see, following the coastline, a few miles inland.

"It looks like they've already started," said Horsely, pointing at the stadium. "They're early." He nudged the flutter to dive.

"Finally, Carsigo," mumbled Youk, trying to straighten his

back. Sammywoo cheered and squealed with excitement. He didn't seem the slightest bit bothered by the morning's ride.

Horsely guided the bird to circle the beachfront community, eventually gliding right over the top of the crowded Bollirse match. There were countless numbers of people. It was the biggest gathering Dod had ever seen. Below the sea of admirers, a comparatively small field was set for the challenge, with thirteen-foot poles topped by cone-like bots. It made Dod's heart pound faster with excitement. His friends from Green Hall were making their way down a rope ladder onto the field—the match hadn't begun yet.

"That's unusual," said Youk. "The Green Coosings have actually done it. They're competing in the semifinal game. If they win this, they'll play next month for The Golden Swot. Who would have thought they'd make it this far?"

"They're gonna win!" yelled Sammywoo. "Just as Dilly said. And then they'll claim it all. Can we go to the championship game?"

Youk was amused, but not delirious with anticipation like Dod and Sammywoo. "One at a time, my boy. Let's find a spot and see how it goes."

Horsely directed the flutter over the arena twice before landing in a grassy pasture, a few blocks away. It was disappointing. Dod had wanted to hop off and join his friends in the scrimmage. In his mind he had imagined the whole crowd rising to their feet, pointing their fingers and chanting his name as he slid down a rope onto the field. After all, the people had shown interest when Dod flew above them. However, Horsely and Youk had insisted it was too dangerous to drop a line for him while in flight.

Once inside the stadium, Dod quickly realized he was too

late—an announcer had just barely proclaimed the start—and nobody seemed to care that he wasn't playing. It was the giant flutter that had attracted the crowd's gaze. Many spectators had never seen one before.

"Sorry," groaned Sammywoo, reading Dod's disheartened face. "A minute earlier and you could have played with them." He held his fathers hand as they pushed their way to the lower front.

Some of The Greats from Twistyard were seated in a group at the very edge of the pit, enjoying premier spots with perfect views. At last there were faces Dod recognized. And right in the middle of them was Bonboo, encouraging Green Hall's players with reassuring words, looking perfectly healthy.

"Dod!" called Bonboo. His white hair glistened in the afternoon sun and his big smile doubled the wrinkles on his face. He squinted his soft, brown eyes in the sunlight to see better. "You're back. I'm so glad. I've been worried." Bonboo glanced at Youk and then added. "Come, Dod. I insist you sit beside me."

Youk glowered. He was very perturbed. There was only space for one more person, or two if it was Youk with Sammywoo on his lap, but since Dod took it, Youk had to fumble back through the countless hosts to where other Twistyard members were standing higher up. Dod watched him pass Eluxa to squeeze in between Sawb and Doochi, amidst the Coosings from Raul.

"How did you ever come by a giant flutter?" asked Bonboo, putting one arm around Dod. He leaned in to be heard over the noise.

Dod turned back around, though his mind was still focused on Youk's journey to the nosebleed regions. Dod felt awful about repeatedly making Youk mad. He wished he could patch things over.

"Perhaps Youk could sit here instead of me," suggested Dod. He didn't answer Bonboo's question.

"No!" persisted Bonboo. He looked at Dod, unrelenting. "I'm pleased to have *you* next to me. Now I must know, how did you obtain a giant flutter?"

"I didn't," said Dod. "Youk got it...or I suppose Saluci helped. The Zoots provided it somehow."

"Hmmm," droned Bonboo, drifting into thought. His response indicated there were stories to tell and puzzles to solve—things Dod wanted to hear, but it was impossible with the game in progress.

"Come on! That's absurd!" yelled a man that had risen to his feet. He shifted most of his weight onto one leg, gently caring for his other that was wrapped from his knee to his hip with a strange bandage. He had been seated next to Bonboo until Dod displaced him. The man was furious. His tredder ring turned purple with blood, and part of it stuck out from under his elegant, yellow shirt. He threw his giant arms in the air, shaking them at a bad call, and then lost his balance and resorted to grabbing Dod's shoulder. He leaned on Dod and continued to rage as though the referees would hear him and change their judgment.

Dod looked to see what was happening. Boot was being escorted to a ladder. His swot was broken in half. It made Dod sick. He knew how badly Boot loved the game.

The Bollirse field had thirty poles on each side, with cone-shaped bots on the tops of most of them; three or four had been knocked down during the first few minutes of play. Buck was leading a group to attack—payback for what had just happened. A volley of globes filled the air in the direction of their opponents, the Raging Billies.

Dod knew plenty about billies. Much like pirates on Earth, billies roamed the seas and inhabited islands, pillaging and plundering each other's cities. Occasionally their warfare crept onto the mainland, but those were the rare exceptions. The general rule was a state of truce between billies and other groups.

The Raging Billies had tough-looking players, composed mostly of twenty to forty-year-olds—their bodies tanned and tattooed, their hair long and tied back, and their muscles rippling. They were real warriors that delighted in killing, but restrained themselves enough to play within the accepted bounds of the game of Bollirse. When they hit a globe, they hit it hard, and when they blocked with their shields, you could imagine they had spent plenty of time blocking swords. They seemed unbeatable.

"No!" roared the man at Dod's side. "No! That's not fair!" He was still leaning on Dod, trying to stand. Tinja, the Hatu expert from Twistyard, was seated directly behind the man and became annoyed when he wouldn't sit down.

"Please, Voracio, you're blocking everyone's view," said Tinja politely. Dod turned and stared.

"Voracio?" whispered Dod to himself. *No wonder Youk was doubly insulted that I took his spot*, he thought. *He was probably annoyed to see 'him.'* Dod looked Voracio up and down. He remembered Mercy saying Voracio was Bonboo's grandson, one of The Greats that had been helping Twistyard fight Dark Hood. Dod couldn't understand why Mercy had thought that *he* was the most likely candidate for the position of Chief Noble Tredder—preferred over Youk.

Voracio looked and acted nothing like Bonboo. He was a foot taller, six-foot six, with dark black hair and a burly figure.

He wore expensive, showy clothes that touted his position and bandages over his pant leg to remind people of his injury from heroic actions. He was nothing short of a braggadocio.

On the field, Buck was in the middle of a disaster. He had surged forward, persisting with his band to hit globes at the billies and their bots until, like Boot, his swot broke. The game paused while Buck was escorted to Green Hall's ladder. Apparently, there was an old, official rule on the books that stated if your swot or shield experienced a significant malfunction, you were out. It had been established to stop a disastrous trend wherein some teams had purposely broken their own equipment. They had done it, from time to time, to claim their circumstance was unfair, which in turn had led to brutal fights and fatalities after the games.

Voracio went mad. He almost fell over the edge into the pit. His language was not statesmanlike, and many of the things he yelled were threats at the refs for perpetuating an outdated regulation and at the Raging Billies for rigging the mess.

"Sit down or go to the back," insisted Tinja, firmly tapping Voracio on the shoulder. It nearly led to fists. Voracio swung around, heated and ready to brawl. It wouldn't have been much of a contest; Tinja was Twistyard's martial arts specialist, and since weapons weren't allowed in the stadium, his six-foot one, muscle-bound frame would have likely tamed Voracio.

Dod observed Tinja. He stood his ground calmly. His eyes flashed with confidence, his stubbly-shaved head suggested his no-nonsense personality, and his worn clothing fit perfectly with the crowd of commoners.

"Please!" intervened Bonboo, leaning over Dod to scold his grown grandson. "Act your age!"

CHAPTER SIX

Dod agreed. Voracio hardly seemed mature, let alone Chief Noble Tredder material. His displays were not only juvenile, they were reckless.

Down below, Pone continued with the assault where Buck left off. He played well, aggressively pursuing, and all the while motivating Green Hall to fight harder. Dilly had been in the back, as usual on defense, yet with Buck's early exit, she was in charge. It made Dod smile to watch. He knew she was pleased with her opportunity to lead so early in the game, even if the circumstance that had brought it about was a misfortune.

"Hold your ground!" shouted Dilly.

With Voracio finally quieted, Dod could hear some of the things his friends were saying. He wished he could join them. It was torturous to watch. From his vantage, he could see the Raging Billies setting a trap. They moved as a larger group, appearing to stay together, when in fact they were depositing three of their best players behind strategic poles, sneakily hidden. It was a perfect illusion. When they faked a retreat, Pone fell for it, rushing in with his clan. They all focused on the mob in front and, as a result, went down together. Pone, Voo, Sham and Toos were struck by globes launched from the concealed billies.

Next, Dilly ordered her team to regroup. With six gone, she had twelve players left, while her opponents hadn't lost any. The billies stormed the mid-field and jumped the short wall that separated the two halves. They advanced slowly, lined in a row, with their shields in front. It didn't look good for Green Hall. And to make matters worse, the leader of the billies had a wicked arm. He walked directly behind four of his men and systematically popped the bots off the posts like a star pitcher, always hitting his mark.

It was too much to watch. It looked like a pending massacre. Suddenly, someone took a bold position. One of Green Hall's players climbed the rear-center post and put the bot on his head. He then carefully stood on top of the log, holding a swot—no shield. It was crazy. From Dod's view he looked like Boot, but Dod knew he wasn't because Boot was squatting with the other ousted Coosings and Greenling in the holding yard.

The Bootish boy taunted the army of billies, challenging them to hit the bot off his head.

"It's a distraction, right?" said Dod to Bonboo.

"I suppose," he answered. Neither Bonboo nor Dod had very much faith in Green Hall's ability to survive the approaching mob.

"You've lost your freshy-mind," roared Voracio, rising to his feet again, shaking his fists. Bonboo quickly poked with his cane and beckoned for him to lend an ear. Voracio consented. He practically squished Dod to the ground when he dumped his weight on him to reach Bonboo. He was like a three-hundred-pound rock.

Whatever was whispered was unusually powerful. Voracio stood back up and glared at Bonboo. He was beyond furious, but he quietly limped out of his seat and disappeared into the crowded stadium.

"Come on, shippies," hollered the boy with the bot on his head. "Is that the best you can do?" he teased, luring their attention.

Meanwhile, Dilly led a group of six up the front, hurling globes at the enemy forces. She and the others hid behind posts, one person per log, slowing the advance of the Raging Billies.

"Shippies, shippies, wobbly-legged flippies."

The Bootish boy was amazing. As he drew the billies

rage, their captain began zipping shots at him. He no longer attempted to hit the other bots as he had before, he just wanted one thing: To shut the boy up. However, his efforts were counterproductive. Dilly held him and his men by the mid-wall, so when they launched globes at the boy, their shots were long, easily deflected. And eight of the fastest globes were returned with incredible force. The perched boy was a homerun hitter, and three billies went down as a result.

Eventually, Dilly's six began to run out of ammunition. The billies sensed it and pressed hard, all at once. It was awful. Four more Coosings went up the ladder, leaving Dilly, Sawny, and five others huddled around the post upon which the Bootish boy was perched. The ground around him was littered with globes that he had gently deflected. Sawny filled her jung to the top and then did the wildest thing Dod had ever seen her do—she ran solo, around the approaching troops, up against the side wall and into their undefended territory. She was extremely fast. She didn't seem like her bookworm self.

Dod was so amazed that he turned to Bonboo and had him confirm that it was Sawny.

"I can't believe it either," said Bonboo, showing concern for his great-granddaughter. She was pursued by six formidable opponents, eager to make her pay.

"Oh, Sawny," groaned Dod. He couldn't help voicing his nervousness for her wellbeing. The men didn't appear to be playing anymore. "Just give up! It's not worth getting hurt!" yelled Dod. He didn't intend on shouting; nevertheless, the thoughts in his mind provoked him. They were faint memories of experiences with billies—their mean temperaments, their cruelty, their lack of fairness, their bloodthirsty natures.

Dod's heart began to pound faster. He wanted to jump down the twenty-five feet and run to Sawny's aid with a battle-striker in his hand—a swot hardly seemed enough. But before Sawny was overcome by her assailants, the Bootish boy earned a place in Dod's book of heroes: He hit a real homerun! When the billies' best player fired a fast globe at him, he sent it long and hard, right into the back of the first man who swung at Sawny. The globe struck with such force that the man was knocked to the ground, tripping two more who followed close behind. It opened up a larger gap between Sawny and her attackers, and one of them was out.

The crowd went wild. It was the kind of moment that would live on forever in the minds of everyone present. It reminded Dod of his own less-significant moment when the crowd at Twistyard had cheered him on against Raul Hall.

The man who'd been hit made a big enough fuss over his injury that the game paused for longer than usual, while the referees helped him up the Raging Billies' ladder. It was good for Sawny. She caught her breath and was ready to run when the whistle finally blew.

Now more determined than ever, the billies' captain fired another mean globe at the perched boy, this time low, by his feet. It didn't work. The boy swung and it lobbed high into the air, bombing into the middle of Sawny's aggressors. It nearly clipped another man. The billies' defense squad slowed their pursuit, necessarily keeping half of their attention on their rear, skyward.

The crowd went wild again. It was obvious Twistyard had more fans in the audience than the noble billies. Dilly and her contingent pushed forward, claiming ground. It seemed almost equal. Every globe that went near the Bootish boy's direction was sent flying to Sawny's aid.

"That's the way," said Dod, perking up. Sawny was in less danger, and with space between her and the billies, she began taking out their bots—at least those not already downed by the Bootish boy.

Amazingly, the billies didn't cease supplying globes to the bot-topped boy, despite his uncanny accuracy in attacking their home turf. His taunting had made the billies react out of emotion, not logic, especially their leader. They truly wanted him down.

The billies surged against Dilly's crew and took two of them out. One limped as she exited.

The billies were throwing harder, and the game neared a critical point as four were sent to the edges of Green Hall's domain to knock bots. With such small numbers, Dilly couldn't defend the perimeter and keep the billies far enough from the perching boy to give him a fighting chance.

It wasn't long before Dilly, Sawny, and the Bootish boy were all that stood between the Raging Billies and their victory. One bot remained for Green Hall—the one on the boy's head.

Ten billies against three Coosings wasn't great odds, but with only two of the billies in the back to rush Sawny, she plunked away and directed fire from the perched boy until only four of their bots remained.

Suddenly, the game ended. A globe hit Dilly's arm and she fell to the ground, yet instead of waiting for the referees to escort her out, three billies rushed her, swinging their swots and firing globes at close range. The boy on the pole couldn't let it happen—even if the misconduct led to penalties, they weren't worth letting Dilly get seriously injured. He did the honorable thing and jumped to her aid. And no sooner did he leave his post than a billie dislodged the winning bot.

Horns blew from every angle of the field announcing the Raging Billies' victory, but the three men continued to move in on Dilly and were joined by their leader and the rest of the billies that stood by. A brawl broke out. The numbers were terribly unfair—Dilly and the Bootish boy against eight massive men. Swots were flying around like swords.

Dilly and the boy fought hard, backing up until they were against the wall. And then the tables turned. Someone slid down Green Hall's rope ladder and rushed to their aid. He carried a swot and swung it better than anyone Dod had ever watched. The billies had started the fight—and he ended it! His swot knocked three men to the ground, unconscious. The others retreated, frightened.

It all happened so fast that Dod was amazed anyone had reacted in time to save his friends from a vicious beating. But as he watched, he recognized the man by the way he stood. It was Strat, The Great Bollirse Instructor. He had rescued Dilly and the Bootish boy.

CHAPTER SEVEN

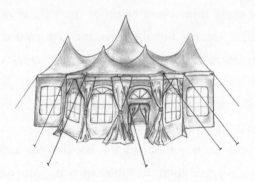

PREPAREDNESS DRILL

After the Bollirse game, fans filled the air with complaints. Soldiers stormed the stadium by the hundreds, ensuring disagreements wouldn't create pandemonium. It settled things down, but also clogged the walkways. Everyone had to be patient.

Bonboo stood up and stretched. "They played better at the end than I would have thought," he said. His face beamed with relief that his two great-granddaughters were finally safe.

"I'd say," agreed Dod, watching Sawny climb out of the pit. "Dilly got her chance to lead and came close to winning the match. It's too bad things went wrong."

"With billies, you expect it!" interjected Tinja, joining the conversation. His eyes flashed with prejudice against the noble billies. "I was surprised they waited 'til the end to act out. With the mischief they've been causing Pious, it's amazing they were allowed to compete at all. If it were up to me, Green Hall would get the win. I'd send a message that violence on the field wouldn't be tolerated."

"It was deplorable how they brawled," said Bonboo. "But

you know the league—the Bollirse Rules Board will stick to what's written in the books. The Raging Billies will be representing the Western Hemisphere of Green in next month's match. They won it."

"Then they'll need to change its location," blurted Tinja, his face reddening. "High Gate is hardly reasonable considering their natures—the team alone would be hazardous, not to mention their fans. I don't think our democracy would stand if Dreaderious used the billies and this opportunity to sack The City. Even with guards escorting people to and from Champion Stadium, as they have done in the past, it wouldn't be enough. What if the billies bolted through and successfully took out the triblot barrier—hordes of soldiers could be waiting in the forests. And I doubt anyone would be able to detect a civil spectator from the disreputable among the billies—they're all criminals! Not a one of them would pass into High Gate if I stood watch."

"Don't condemn the group for the actions of a few," answered Bonboo scoldingly. "You're being too hard on them. Besides, it's not our decision to make. I'll talk with Commendus and advise him once I've determined my own mind. Hosting the match in that arena is a tradition that goes back a long time. This year is the one-hundred-and-fiftieth anniversary, so with a momentous celebration already planned, I doubt Commendus would listen even if I weighed against it. He'd block the billies' fans from entering and pull half of Pious's troops to stand guard before he'd move it."

"And chance giving High Gate and the whole democracy to the likes of them?" questioned Tinja rhetorically. "I'd hope not!"

"You give High Gate more credit than it deserves," said Bonboo calmly. "There are more than two dozen cities here in Green that each top a million people, if you count their suburbs—Terraboom alone has three or four. They're just as important to our freedom as High Gate, so even if the Grand City was attacked, it wouldn't be the end of everything. You young ones don't remember the days of Doss when fighting really did cover the land. What we deal with now is comparatively small—a mere annoyance—and I include the troubles Dark Hood is causing."

"What other cities?" barked Tinja incredulously. He caught Bonboo's eyes and then bowed his head, showing he recognized that he had stepped beyond his bounds. "Respectfully, sir," he added in a proper voice, "High Gate is a gem among the common stones. Aside from Twistyard, it's the last place in Green that boasts that nearly all of its inhabitants are tredders. The rest of Green's capitals are mixed in nature, with a drat majority in most, and human-bobwit numbers exceeding tredders in nearly all. If High Gate experienced trouble, don't you think revolts would emerge simultaneously?"

"Your question only emphasizes what I've been saying for many years," concluded Bonboo. "We need to financially help more drats and bobwits and humans to become sufficiently educated to be elected as representatives—noble billies included. The current high ratio of tredder leaders in the other cities is disappointing. If billies were more involved in our government, it's likely that Pious wouldn't be struggling with them right now. Democracy is a public matter—it ought to be somewhat proportional or it's not truly democracy. I believe that most citizens want the best for everyone—regardless of their blood."

Tinja's brow furrowed with disagreement. He, like many other tredders, felt that they were a superior race, and as such held a monopoly on exceptional people. In truth though, money, education, health, and longevity gave them a substantial advantage over the others.

"Did you see that?" squealed Sammywoo, redirecting the conversation. He popped out from behind Tinja. Youk was left far behind, struggling to follow after his son. He was much bigger, so the crowds posed more of a challenge to him.

"I told you they'd win," said Sammywoo, looking up at Dod.

Bonboo smiled and patted the boy on his head. "The Raging Billies won today. Maybe next year Twistyard will do better."

"That's not what my dad said," interjected Sammywoo, climbing on the back of Dod's seat. He fidgeted around, getting his energy out. "My dad said the billies pulled an illegal move at the end, forcing Bowy to give up his place. If it weren't for that, Sawny would have finished them off."

"Really?" said Dod, intrigued. He hoped somehow his friends could still claim the victory. The match had been unfair from the beginning, with Boot and Buck disqualified by bad luck.

"Just wait," continued the boy, swinging his swot around. "My dad's set on fixing the problem. He's going with my great-unc to talk to the refs."

Dod looked up and noticed Youk had merged with the main flow of traffic and was no longer coming toward them, and at his side, he was accompanied by Neadrou.

"Yup," rambled the boy. "My dad loves Bowy. He'll fix things."

"Bowy?" said Dod, turning back toward Sammywoo. "Was Boot and Buck's brother the one that—"

"Didn't you recognize him?" blurted Sammywoo. "He's superior to you. My dad said it turned out better with us late…it got Bowy in the game. He's still sort of a Green Coosing."

"Oh," groaned Dod. He felt replaced.

Bonboo sensed Dod's disappointment. "Green Hall probably would have won the day if you had been down there," he said, patting Dod on the shoulder. "They've been sick with worry this whole tournament, watching for you to arrive. And I must admit, I've lost sleep, too, and had my wonders over the past few months. How's home?"

Wonders about what? thought Dod. He couldn't say anything important with crowds around. "It was nice to visit my family," he hesitantly replied. "I got things taken care of for now—"

Images flashed through Dod's mind. Bowy was in danger. It was unclear how, or by whom, though not amazingly hard to guess why. After the show he had put on and the taunting he had done, it was remarkable he hadn't already been bloodied by the eight billies that had attacked him on the field.

"I've got to go and congratulate them," said Dod, pointing to his friends in the distance. They were huddled in a group under a tree by one of the exits. Their bright-orange shirts made them easy to spot.

As Dod wiggled into the masses, Bonboo called out that he fully expected to speak with him later. He had important things to discuss.

Dod agreed and then disappeared. He made his way, ducking and dodging, shamelessly squirming past others that were patiently waiting for their turns to move. It was embarrassing but necessary: Bowy's life was at stake. Dod knew he needed to warn him.

By the time he reached the big maple, his friends were no longer there. They had exited. Two bobwits swung in the lower limbs. Aside from being only four feet, they looked perfectly human. One man, with blaring-red hair and brown freckles, poked fun at the other for betting his horse on the match. They were both in favor of Green Hall, for their shirts had slogans that declared themselves as such.

"Excuse me," said Dod, looking up at them. "Did you see where the players went—the ones wearing orange shirts?"

The bobwits pointed toward a wooded area and then added that fans weren't allowed to follow.

Dod turned to go when a holoo crawled out of a backpack that one of the bobwits was wearing. "I told you the Raging Billies would win," teased the little man. "I like Coosings and Twistyard, but billies are mean to the core. I've seen plenty of them."

The holoo was less than two feet, yet still proportionately developed like a grown human. He resembled a large, male Barbie doll, complete with dashing clothes and well-groomed hair. He was more handsome than either of his bobwit friends, just much smaller.

"So, if I say you were right, can we call it even?" asked one of the bobwits. He had wagered with the holoo.

"Nice try," laughed the holoo.

"But my horse is awfully big for a tiny like you," said the bobwit. "I doubt it'll obey your pulling."

"Boosap!" said the man. "I train flutters for Pious. Your horse will be easy."

Dod waved and left the conversation. He was glad to have seen a holoo. They were a rare breed of human, every bit as smart and capable as the bobwits and other humans, and maybe more courageous than either of them. It baffled Dod to think of such small people daring to ride flutters, let alone tame them.

Outside the stadium, soldiers were directing the mobs—billies to the seashore and all others, inland. The only exception was Green Hall's Bollirse team. His friends had continued straight forward, into a thicket of trees that was heavily guarded. Men were posted every fifteen feet along a tall, stone wall that completely surrounded the courtyard they had entered, and a battalion was situated at the opening. When Dod attempted to pass through as his friends had done, dozens of soldiers insisted he couldn't. He explained that his teammates were expecting him, but his words fell on deaf ears.

"To the right, sir," is what he was repeatedly told.

When reasoning failed, Dod worked his way around the blockade, hoping he could find a second access, or at least a less guarded portion of the fence. It took time to circle the enclosure. Mobs of people were gathering in clumps all along the way to discuss the game and regroup with friends. The troops held their places, with pockets of extra men under the shady trees, prepared with weapons of all shapes and sizes. They were ready for action, turning the location of Twistyard's camp into an impenetrable compound.

"It's a fort," groaned Dod to himself, noticing the watchtowers. "Or maybe a prison."

Dod decided to give up until another warning rushed his mind. Bowy was about to be killed. Dod knew it! There was no doubt about it and no time to spare. Even a few minutes would possibly be too late.

"What can I do?" he mumbled. And then it hit him. He did have proof of his Twistyard ties.

"I'm a Green Coosing," he breathlessly declared to the guards at the front. He had jogged all the way around and now stood where he had begun. He held up his ring for them to see. "I'm one of the players. I'm just not wearing my orange shirt right now. My name is Dod. Ask Boot, or Buck, or Dilly, or any of them and they'll confirm it for you."

The soldiers looked skeptically at his ring. They recognized him as the boy who had attempted to enter twenty-five minutes before.

"It's a fake!" declared the man in charge. He was a large tredder, built extremely well.

"Please, it's not," begged Dod.

"Yes it is, and if you don't hurry away, I'll send you to the cribs for stealing and impersonating. It's your last warning. Be gone, boy."

Dod's heart sank into his stomach. He couldn't think of anything to do. He had tried and failed. People were beginning to stare at him. His feet felt like they were laden with rocks. Bowy's life hung in Dod's helpless hands.

"Can you deliver a message for me?" asked Dod, returning to the commanding officer. "I've got to speak with Bowy."

"I warned you," boomed the giant tredder, shaking his head. Two guards grabbed Dod, one on each arm. They hadn't waited very long.

"All right, I'll leave!" said Dod, attempting to shake the soldiers loose. He didn't want to be hauled off. The holding cages would be filled with discontent crazies, the kind of people Dod wasn't particularly craving to spend time with—especially the fighting billies.

"Too late," said the man in charge. "Take him."

"General Faller!" called a familiar voice. Someone from the crowd was attempting to speak with the tredder who had just consigned Dod to incarceration. "Do they have you working this mess?"

"Yes, and I've about had my fill," responded Faller. "Pious can send me to any of the fronts...anything but this again."

Dod struggled to turn his head as he was being carried away. He recognized the voice. It was Saluci's uncle.

"Neadrou! Neadrou!" yelled Dod, fussing to be heard. "Tell them I'm a Green Coosing. Help me, Neadrou!"

"Do you know this boy?" asked General Faller, pointing at Dod.

"Know him…let's see—" Neadrou approached his associate and looked at Dod. "Turn him around so I can examine his face better."

The guards spun Dod and brought him back. Dod smiled with satisfaction. At last the thick-headed men would be told what he had been telling them for half-an-hour.

"Nope. I don't know him."

The words were as sharp as knives. Neadrou didn't even crack a smile. His eyes revealed something beyond recognition, but it wasn't friendly.

"He looks dangerous," added Neadrou, stepping away. "I'm glad you've caught him. Good show to you, my friend Faller. I'll sleep well tonight knowing you're on guard. Thank you…and thank your men."

Dod was dumbfounded. He didn't say anything. He expected Neadrou to recant and laugh, and then everything would be better, but without another word, Neadrou proceeded to the entrance. The two guards that held Dod captive pulled at him.

"You heard my friend," said General Faller to the soldiers. "Take him away and put him with the billies. This one's trouble. If his intent was to hurt our Twistyard guests, it won't be criminal to let the system play out."

Dod knew what he meant. Faller spoke of allowing the locked-up billies to take their frustrations out on him. It was awful. And to make matters worse, Neadrou's intent had to be villainous. He was likely the traitor—the one headed to harm Bowy—possibly Dark Hood, or one of his helpers.

"I know of your plan to kill Bowy!" screamed Dod. He fought back, struggling with all of his might to free himself. "You're a traitor, Neadrou! You're a lying coward and a traitor!"

It suddenly dawned on Dod that perhaps Youk had brought him to The Games for the sole purpose of disposing of him. Youk was part of the plan. It fit together perfectly. No wonder the Zoots had helped Youk get the giant flutter. They hadn't run Dod through with their swords in Green Hall, the night he had arrived, and now, in the middle of the post-game confusion, they were going to finish the job.

Dod kicked with his feet and squiggled his arms to no avail. The two guards had wrapped a rope tightly around his wrists, behind his back, and they held his arms firmly. It was no use. Dod stared at a rock on the ground and did his best to escape the only remaining way he knew how—or at least he knew of: He tried to zip back to Earth.

I wish I could escape this mess, thought Dod, closing his eyes. *I wish I could make all of this craziness go away.*

His wish was granted. When he opened his eyes, he didn't see a rock or a dirt-covered road anymore; and he didn't see swarms of people. He only saw one thing, really close to his face—it was Sammywoo.

"Dod?" he said. "Where are you going?"

"These men don't know I'm a Green Coosing," gasped Dod, lifting his head so his eyes could actually focus on Sammywoo.

"He's a Coosing!" said Sammywoo, sticking his arms out sideways, blocking the men from dragging Dod away. They would have to knock Sammywoo over to do it.

"Oh—*that* Dod," said Neadrou, reemerging from amidst the soldiers. "Yes…Faller, my friend. I've made a slight mistake. This boy is from Twistyard. And now that I think of it, I met him at Commendus's palace once before. He's quite a hero. You should let him go."

"A Hero?" asked Faller, looking confused at Dod. "He's a human boy."

"I know," said Neadrou. "He doesn't look like much, but behind his mask of incompetence lies a dragon. He'd likely destroy the billies and then your men if you did lock him up. You'd never guess what he did."

The soldiers all waited to hear as the two guards that held him began to untie his wrists.

"He's the one who caught The Dread."

Gasps and whispers filled the air. General Faller approached Dod and personally finished freeing him.

"Next time," said Faller, "wear the proper sign so we don't confuse you with everyone else." He handed Dod a horse pin. "Don't lose it. With all of the confusion, you can understand how we…well…how my men made this mistake."

Dod accepted his half-apology and rushed into the fortress, followed by Sammywoo. Neadrou remembered something he had forgotten and shouted to Dod that he would appreciate his help in placing Sammywoo under Dilly's watchful care until Youk's return.

It didn't take Dod long to locate his friends. They were standing around a giant table of food under a pavilion. Boot was laughing at a prank he had just pulled on Buck, and Dilly was shaming him for being insensitive.

"Dod!" said Dilly, noticing him first. She rushed over and greeted him with a big hug. Sawny followed close behind. The two sisters looked so much alike in their orange uniforms that it was fortunate Dilly's curly hair was deep brown and Sawny's was lighter, or he might have confused them. It took time to readjust his mind to their slight differences. Normally, their clothes would have announced them—Dilly was more fashion conscious and extravagant, while Sawny dressed stylishly simple.

"Why didn't you join us?" complained Dilly. "We could have used one of your fancy saves today."

"He's moved on," said Boot jokingly. "It's hard for him to worry about trivial things like Bollirse when he's busy riding giant flutters and fighting battles."

Boots words revealed some jealously. And the way Buck wouldn't look straight at Dod indicated he, too, was bothered.

"I'm sorry, guys, but it's not what it looks like," said Dod. He felt sick to his stomach. "I had to visit my family. They were having problems. And I didn't mean to be gone long, it just…I had bad things happen, and Dark Hood nearly killed me. And I'm so glad to see you…all of you! And the giant flutter was Youk and Saluci's doing—you know, the Zoots pulled it off to get us here—or actually, it was to get Sammywoo here. I just lucked out and hitched a miserable ride on the back. I wanted to see you play."

Dod looked at the ground and felt like crying. He didn't explain his whereabouts very well, and in truth, he couldn't. They didn't know he was from Earth, or anything about Earth, or anything about his medallion, so they wouldn't have understood how his stolen necklace had caused him to leave Green without saying goodbye. Only Bonboo knew the truth about him and Pap.

"I wanted to join you in the big game," said Dod. His voice

quivered and cracked. "I really did. I've been practicing. Sorry I let you guys down."

"You saw Dark Hood?" blurted Pone, his mouth full of fruit. He gave Dod a pat on the shoulder and added, "Nice, bro. He must be everywhere these days. He's been causing all sorts of trouble at Twistyard since you left."

"Yeah," added Voo, grabbing for a large wedge of watermelon. "Some of the soldiers even started spreading the word that you'd turned on us—became, you know…him!"

"*I* always knew you had a good reason for leaving," said Boot, approaching Dod. "Welcome back!" He flashed the Coosings' sign with his right hand.

"Thanks Boot," said Dod, trying to swallow the lump in his throat. He lunged forward and gave Boot a hung. It reminded Dod how big and strong Boot was. His six-foot-plus frame was solid muscle. "You've been working out," said Dod, attempting to chuckle as he stepped back before the hugging thing became too weird.

"Working out what?" said Boot, confused. He smiled at Dod with his blue eyes beaming and his wavy black hair moving slightly in the breeze.

"You were right!" said Sammywoo, storming up to Dilly. He danced around her in circles. "Dod did plan on being here for the match. He begged my dad to drop him from a line onto the field. Can you believe that? Horsely said he would have burst his brains on a post."

When Dod saw Sammywoo, he instantly remembered his need to rush. He had completely forgotten about the images.

"Where's Bowy?" asked Dod. "He's in danger!"

"No he's not," responded Dilly. "My dad's over there talking with him." She pointed at a tall, raven-haired, middle-aged tredder, who had his arm around Bowy. The two of them were walking into a giant tent.

Buck finished brushing cake crumbs off his clothes as he entered the conversation. He finally looked Dod in the eyes. "How do *you* know Bowy? He's been at home since his injury—years ago."

"I don't know him," admitted Dod. "I've never met him, and the only time I've seen him was today when he played on the field. I just know he's in trouble. I've got to talk with him."

Dod took big strides as he walked to the tent, leaving his friends back at the pavilion. He wasn't sure what to say. And when he arrived at the door, it was awkward opening it without knowing either of the people. Nevertheless, with his heart pounding in his ears, he flung the flaps and entered.

The structure had multiple rooms on the inside, with privacy walls made of heavy burlap. The roof and exterior were constructed of thicker layers of the same material.

"Bowy?" whispered Dod, walking around the first corner. Nobody was in the second section, or the third. Bedding and bags littered the floor. Dod proceeded carefully, stepping around the debris. Something wasn't right. Dod wished he had his sword. Maybe Youk had been waiting and had ambushed Dilly's father and Bowy. After Dod's most recent experience with Neadrou, he didn't trust either of them.

The tent was quiet. Unless there was a back door, the men had to be in the last quarter. Dod drew near the entrance cautiously. He heard commotion, like the sound of two people scuffling. It was terrifying. Dod searched the ground for anything he could use as a weapon. The closest thing was a wimpy, leather belt; it didn't even have a big buckle.

Dod jumped into action, forcing himself to enter the next room. He found Dilly's father holding Bowy in a headlock with a six-inch blade to his chest. It looked like Dod had arrived in time to see him die, and nothing more. Dod swung the belt over his head.

"Release him!" shouted Dod. "If you kill him, I'm a witness. I'll personally see you're sent to Driaxom."

It was all Dod could think of to convince the man to stop his evil designs. Perhaps the threat of torturous imprisonment would sway him to spare Bowy.

"What?" said Bowy, choking. He reached up and pushed the tredder's arm off his neck. "Oh, you thought he was attacking me for real—No! He was teaching me a move—an escape trick. Set your belt down and I'll demonstrate."

Bowy got back into position and then flung his body sideways, forcing the blade parallel to his torso, while maneuvering his arms to free his neck. It worked. Dilly's father landed on the ground and the knife bounced across a pile of blankets at his side.

"See. It's a clever one, isn't it?" said Bowy cheerfully. He stuck his hand out and helped Dilly's dad up. "Thanks for the advice and the move. I'll keep alert."

Dilly's father approached Dod and sternly glared at him. He flipped the knife up in the air with his foot, caught it, and bent the blade over. "It's a fake," he said, cracking a contagious grin. "I'm Chikada Tillius. Are you, by any chance, the great Dod we've been hearing a bucket-load of swoosh about?"

Dod liked Chikada's soft brown eyes and pleasant temperament. They reminded him of Bonboo. And the more Dod looked at the man, the more he saw a family resemblance. His mannerisms, and the way he spoke and smiled, were just like his grandfather. Without question, Chikada appeared and acted more like Bonboo than anyone Dod had ever met—certainly more than Voracio.

"I am Dod, but the stories you've heard are probably exaggerated," said Dod, sighing with relief. It was nice to know Dilly's father was not a traitor.

"I doubt that," snapped Bowy. "You do look like the type that would wear your shoes to bed." He laughed and confessed that Buck had divulged the information.

Dod enjoyed talking with Bowy and Chikada, but a feeling of danger still prevailed. It sucked the fun out of the moment. Dod looked around the room for a hiding spot. Perhaps an angry billie was waiting to pounce. He casually walked over to a pile of blankets that looked suspiciously large and kicked them with one foot.

"Are you looking for gizzlers?" asked Bowy. "Don't bother, we all painstakingly searched the place last week when we arrived—to please Princess Dilly—and since then, the guards have kept the front watch around the clock. Besides, our efforts were empty."

The mention of gizzlers reminded Dod of the snakelike creatures. Along some parts of the shoreline, poisonous gizzlers, with bright-red skin and sharp fangs, inhabited the waters. They frequented the land by day, bedding in cool, shady locations, and went searching for rodents and fish at night.

"Right, and you're sure?" asked Dod, using them as an excuse to poke for trouble. He hadn't found anything. Nobody was hiding in the one lump that was big enough to conceal someone.

"And if you're wondering about the smell," said Chikada, "I heard it'll go away soon. While we were at the game, they sprayed waterproofing on the exterior. It looks like rain tonight."

Dod solved the puzzle. The smell was familiar. He couldn't recall encountering it before, yet he knew it was flammable.

"It's a trap!" said Dod to the others.

They stared at him and laughed uncontrollably. Bonboo's grandson patted Dod on the shoulder. "The look on your face is, uh…diligent," he finally said, regaining his composure.

"No, I'm serious. This tent is a trap! We've got to get out!"

"I know," said Bowy, trying to act serious, his voice hopelessly revealing he wasn't. "After that game, this place is bound to ensnare me for a couple of hours." He lay down and sprawled out on a thick, patchwork quilt.

"You don't believe me, do you?" said Dod. "You think I'm kidding. That smell is a bonfire about to ignite."

"Oh, I see," said Chikada. He gave Dod a fatherly look of approval. "If you practice today, you'll be prepared tomorrow."

Chikada was convinced Dod was attempting an emergency drill of sorts, honing his skills for the time when they would be needed. He didn't believe Dod was serious.

"Right!" said Dod in a commanding voice, nodding to Chikada. "We've got a man down. Let's get him out of this burning tent before it blows."

Dod played along with the idea in order to accomplish his main design of coaxing them out before anything real happened.

"Grab the other end," ordered Dod, collecting one side of Bowy's blanket in his hands. Chikada obeyed and scooped up the remaining edge, capturing Bowy in the middle. The boy swung back and forth like he was in a hammock.

"You're heavy," said Dod, grunting as he struggled to walk backwards with his load.

"Yup, I've just about caught up with Boot," answered Bowy proudly. He grinned, enjoying the ride.

"You're supposed to be injured," prodded Chikada, looking at Bowy. He then turned to Dod and made a suggestion. "Don't you think he looks too happy? Maybe we should drag him for a while and see if he keeps smiling." Chikada dipped his side onto the floor for a moment and let it bump into a few things before he lifted it back up."

When Dod and Chikada came hauling Bowy out of the tent in a blanket, Dilly and the others rushed to see what was wrong. They met halfway.

"I should have believed you!" blurted Dilly before she was close enough to see Bowy. "You knew something was going to happen. Was it a gizzler?"

"A gizzler!" squealed Sawny. She and a few Greenlings scampered back to the food table and climbed up. They weren't going to take any chances on a gizzler getting them.

Bowy heard her and knew how to act. "Ohhhh," he groaned. "If only you'd have warned me sooner, Dod, I wouldn't have been bitten. Please, carry me to the table."

"Sucking the venom doesn't work," chimed Sawny, not sure if she wanted Bowy close to her. "I've read plenty about it. If they've hit you, your only hope is to rub salt in the wound. Sometimes it draws the poison. But we don't have any at this table—go over there." Sawny pointed to another pavilion that hosted many of The Greats from Twistyard. She looked squeamish.

"Besides," she continued, "I think Treep is with *them*. He knows more than I do about poisons."

"It's useless," groaned Bowy, still being carried to the food table. "I'm dying. I need that last piece of chouyummy cake. I want to enjoy the taste of death."

Dilly caught on and gave Bowy a shove, rolling him out of his cocoon. "You nearly scared me stiff," she said. "I can't stand gizzlers."

Chikada began to explain that their actions were part of Dod's emergency-preparedness activity. He had only just begun when he was interrupted.

BOOM!

The tent they had just exited exploded into flames, burning so hot that everyone standing around the table could feel the warmth from eighty feet away. It continued to sizzle and flare, determined to leave nothing but ashes.

"Did you see that?" gasped Boot, staring at the inferno. "A flaming arrow came flying out of nowhere and hit the tent…and then whoosh, the whole thing lit up."

"I know," added Buck. "I saw it, too. It looked like it came from the sky, way up there." He pointed at the low drifting clouds. Stormy weather was approaching from the sea, drenched with fog.

Tredder guards poured in from all over and the Twistyard contingent of guests gathered together for safety. Chikada and many of The Greats strapped on their swords and other weapons. Dod wanted his sword, but it was inside his bag, with the luggage.

Bonboo approached Dod. "Where did you land the flutter?" he asked urgently. Dod tried to explain. It was difficult.

"Horsely's probably still with the bird," he finally said. "And maybe Youk's there, too. They couldn't bring it in here. It's enormous."

Bonboo directed fifteen soldiers, along with Chikada and a few other Greats, to accompany Dod to the giant flutter. He suspected it would be gone. Dod really hoped he was wrong. His things were stowed on it.

Outside of the fortress, people still meandered the streets and many more were camped in tents and wagons all over the surrounding fields. They were pointing at the plumes of smoke and discussing what they thought had happened. Hundreds of soldiers gathered around the walls of the encampment, preparing for further attacks.

Dod traced his steps back to the place where Horsely had landed. The flutter was gone. But in the distance, there appeared to be a sizable object underneath six giant oaks. When he and the others jogged over, they found Horsely resting on a blanket, taking a nap, and the monstrous bird securely leashed.

Horsely awoke and was shocked to find out that the camp had been attacked. He gladly offered to fly around in search of the enemy, since the two flutters that Pious had supplied for the soldiers were currently patrolling the waters for any signs of disgruntled billies and hadn't returned.

Dod climbed aboard and rode with Horsely, while Chikada and the others headed back to camp. Together, Dod and Horsely ventured into the clouds and dipped below to survey the busy landscape. It was impossible to tell who might have caused the problem. Throngs of people still crowded the streets.

It didn't take long for Dod to suggest they land. The flight was rougher than before, with strengthening stormy winds rolling in from the sea. Horsely consented, laughing all the way. He loved the adventure and found it wonderful to have an excuse to fly the magnificent creature in dangerous conditions.

Back on the ground, Horsely tethered the giant flutter before helping Dod unload the bags.

"So, where will you go now?" asked Dod, wondering what Horsely had planned.

"It's not up to me," he responded. "I'm waiting for Youk. It's his...well, the Zoots' bird. Rain or no rain, I'm staying put 'til he returns."

Dod picked up his bag and turned to go when he thought to ask something that had been bugging him. "What's been happening between the billies and Dreaderious?" he questioned, looking at Horsely. The man hadn't been expecting Dod to say anything more, since Dod had already begun to leave, so he didn't read his lips.

Dod approached Horsely and asked again. This time he got an answer.

"Some of the billies have joined Dreaderious," he said. "I think they're sick of fighting each other, while people like us get rich off the good land. Supposedly, the ones that have caused Pious problems are seeking revenge. They claim his men sank some of their ships and destroyed a whole island—completely unprovoked." Horsely shook his head and added, "I don't think it's true, but that's what they believe...and that's why they're helping Dreaderious fight him."

"Oh," said Dod. "Are they all joining?"

"Not yet. Only a handful of billies are sailing his orders. Besides, you know them—they've never united under their own kind. I doubt Dreaderious will have any better luck."

Dod thanked Horsely and turned to leave when he was handed another bag. It was Sammywoo's.

"You should bring this to him if you can," said Horsely. "Whether he's staying or going, at least he'll have his stuff."

PREPAREDNESS DRILL

Dod hefted the two bags as he walked away. They were lighter than he would have expected. And then it hit him—Pap's sword. He dug deep and unrolled his white cloak, frantic to disprove his impression. Unfortunately, the beautiful golden sword was gone!

CHAPTER EIGHT

THREE SURPRISES

When Dod realized his sword had been stolen, he feared Horsely had taken it. The man was intrepid and adventurous, not to mention dangerous. A prize of Pap's blade would be nearly irresistible. If he had remained with the giant beast all afternoon, he would obviously know what had happened.

Dod carefully surveyed his surroundings, still fumbling with his bag. The bluish-green cowgrass was matted down by the giant flutter and knee-high everywhere else. The closest person was out of hearing range, for Horsely had wisely placed the rare bird in a private field, half-concealed by hanging branches that swayed with the billowing storm. A gust of air blew past Horsely's quilt and folded it over, revealing a glint of yellow. Horsely noticed and flashed a cautious glance at Dod.

"Oh!" Horsely said, faking a chuckle, "I've got something for you." The air filled with tension. "Come and get it."

Dod wasn't sure whether he dared. Something in him screamed to run, screamed that Horsely was as evil and fraudulent as Sirlonk himself had been, but Pap's sword was right there for the taking.

"Could you toss it to me?" asked Dod, staring Horsely in the eyes. It was a showdown of sorts, a tricky chess match. Dod had faster legs and could run for help if Horsely played poorly, and Horsely had the confidence of a monstrous flutter if Dod didn't respond well. Their eyes met long enough to say volumes. Neither of them budged.

"Funny story," said Horsely, carefully uncovering the scabbard. He drew the blade out. "While I relocated our winged ride, he hit a branch and spilled your things. I knew this might attract unwanted attention if the guards came around searching bags, so I hid it—I know you've had poor luck with them lately, haven't you?"

He was right about that—at Twistyard with Jibb, and later in the hall when Ingrid had rescued him, and then again with Neadrou and General Faller. The guards were causing him all kinds of trouble, disbelieving everything he said.

"Thanks," replied Dod hesitantly. He couldn't tell whether Horsely had done him a favor, or meant to harm him, or whether he had actually sided with the guards and had taken the sword as a precaution for his own life, fearing Dod was as bad as they had rumored. It was hazy.

Horsely rose to his feet, clutching the casing in one hand and rapier in the other. His black hair blew in the wind, cascading across his forehead. He was a warrior, ready for battle—a seasoned general, commanding his men to attack. And then he took a step haltingly toward Dod, and then another. He was just Horsely, an injured, has-been Green Coosing.

Once the weapon was safely wrapped and stowed, Dod felt

dumb for questioning Horsely's integrity. The man had only done good things, including flying him to Green Hall's final game of the season and helping him reacquire his medallion despite harsh opposition from Youk. He had proven his friendship and deserved a bit of trust.

If anything, thought Dod guiltily, *it is he who has plenty of reason to doubt my motives, not the other way around.*

Horsely gave the Coosings' hand sign of friendship as Dod adjusted the two bags on his back. "Don't forget now—you owe me!" said Horsely, staring at Dod. "We're friends, right? And if you see Youk, remind him I'm still out here waiting, okay?"

"Sure thing," said Dod, feeling sorry for Horsely. He was left to tend the flutter, while Dod was headed back to camp, where shelter from the approaching rain was waiting, and friends would surround him, and guards were on alert to protect him, and tasty food was spread out like a celebration banquet.

At the entrance, hundreds of soldiers marched back and forth with all sorts of weapons. They carried bows and arrows, double-tipped spears, straps of half-blades, and a few men held Tridacello's favorite—zip-rope whips. The bonfire had alerted them.

Overhead, a flutter fought the wild breeze, ridden by one warrior. It was amazing to see how much smaller the bird was when compared to the giant one he had just left. It was agile and braved the storm like a hawk, patrolling the perimeter in search of anything questionable.

Dod fumbled to find his horse pin. He didn't even want to look like he planned on entering until he was ready to flash the proper sign, but before he could locate it, General Faller broke from the crowd and approached him.

"Let me help you with that," said Faller, attempting to take

Dod's bag off his shoulder. It made Dod uncomfortable since it contained Pap's fancy sword.

"I'm fine—just give me a minute," stammered Dod nervously.

"Don't be ridiculous," barked Faller. "After the way my men treated you this afternoon, allow me to be your baggage-boy." He grabbed the luggage from Dod's shoulders and pointed the way. "Move to the side," he boomed. "Dod's coming through!"

The soldiers obeyed and stood in rows, tipping their chins as General Faller and Dod passed. It was amazing to see how much respect they had for their leader, or so Dod thought. However, it turned out, their admiration was for Dod. Chikada and Bowy had shared with the soldiers how Dod had saved them from a sizzling fate by his unexplainable foresight; in addition, the swirling stories about Dod's single-handed capture of The Dread were embellished enough to gag a mule. Even the notion of him being aided by a swapper couldn't explicate his ability to sense pending danger, for swappers were capable of enlightening people in the present with past occurrences, not glimpses of the future.

It was humorous to Dod that the soldiers had so suddenly and completely changed their mind about him, but he wasn't going to argue with them.

Inside the fortress, it hardly seemed like a battle zone. People were laughing and enjoying themselves. Heavy tarp walls had been lowered from the pavilion roofs, forming rooms to gather in away from the storm. And aside from the Green Coosing guys losing their gear, nothing was lost by the attack.

"Here comes the hero," chirped Sawny, looking up from her book. She was seated on a log in the corner, not participating in the ruckus. Dod hustled inside to avoid his things getting soaked. The rain had just begun to fall.

"Nice—you have clothes!" shouted Buck, sitting up straight. "Do you happen to have an extra pair of pajamas—or anything else not orange?"

"Baby!" added Dilly, poking Buck with her shoe. "You should be thanking him. He saved *your* brother."

"And *your* father," countered Buck.

"Yes, he did," answered Dilly, smiling. She had changed into a classy outfit, drenched with pink-and-white lace. Buck, on the other hand, was still wearing his team uniform.

Dod looked around and felt at home. Everyone was happy to see him. The Coosings and Greenlings rushed close to ask questions and hear the story retold. Dod downplayed his role, suggesting it was more luck than anything.

With over sixty people in the room, and the whirl of excitement surrounding the attack, it took time before Dod noticed Bowy and Boot were not among them. He nudged Pone and discovered that they had been invited to join The Greats for dinner. It was disappointing. Dod still wanted to talk with Bowy. He hadn't gotten a chance to tell him how impressed he had been with his Bollirse moves, and though Dod attempted three times to bring up the game with everyone else, it was too fresh and painful to discuss, particularly in front of Buck.

It rained all night. Since the boys' bedding tent had been destroyed, and the other tents were filled to capacity, Dod and the Green Coosing guys slept on tables in the eating area. And notwithstanding it being uncomfortable, Dod was so tired from his long day that he quickly drifted off and didn't stir until people were already gathering for breakfast. He hadn't even noticed whether Boot and Bowy had come in or not.

"Wake up, Dod," said a memorable voice. Dod smiled,

cracked his eyes, and peered at Sammywoo. The boy was once again using his swot to prod Dod from bed. "It's time to eat, and you're hogging the table."

Dod was surprised to see Sammywoo was not with Youk or Neadrou, he was wedged between Dilly and Sawny.

"Do you sleep with that thing?" asked Dod, pointing at Sammywoo's swot.

"Yes!" blurted Sawny. "And he steals like a pro all night. I didn't have so much as a kerchief's worth of covering by morning. You'd think he could stick to his own blanket."

"It was hot anyway," yawned Dilly. She looked tired. "I had a hard time resting."

"In your woolies!" added Sawny. "Not all of us anticipated the storm. Of course, I only packed one case—not four!" She crossed her eyes and waved her hands for emphasis, portraying Dilly as a stuck-up princess. It was all in jest.

"If you slept any with him nearby, you did well," said Dod, climbing out from under a torn quilt. His past two nights as Youk's guest had been dreadful. Sammywoo had screamed over and over, experiencing multiple bad dreams.

"Why is that?" asked Dilly. "He was the perfect little angel and gentlemen." Dilly squeezed him with one arm.

"Didn't you…uh…have trouble with his shouting?" prodded Dod.

"Quiet as a mouse," said Dilly. "What would he have been shouting about?" She looked confused for a moment and then sparked with recognition. "Oh, I see—no, he's not scared of gizzlers. Thoughts of them slithering around only kept me awake, not him. He's too young to realize they swarm the shores during a good downpour like that."

"That's a myth!" spouted Sawny, annoyed. She had obviously already explained it to Dilly a million times before. "They stay in the water and hunt fish when it rains at night—rats and mice hide. If someone's seen a swarm of gizzlers during a storm like that, they were heading to sea, not land."

"So, he didn't have any nightmares?" asked Dod. He was shocked that they hadn't mentioned it. Dod had experienced Sammywoo's bloodcurdling cries from down the hall and, therefore, preferred the hard table he had just slept on over going back to Youk's guestroom. He couldn't even imagine spending a night next to Sammywoo.

"Nope, he's my bud," said Dilly. "He did just fine with Youk gone."

"Dilly let me wear her footlet," added Sammywoo, pulling his left pant leg up so Dod could see a red-and-blue braid of twine around his ankle. "She promised it would keep me safe from the voices."

"Oh," said Dod. He wondered how Dilly did it. She was like a magical fairy or powerful magician with unbelievable skills—children loved her.

"Youk was unexpectedly pulled away yesterday," said Dilly. "And when Neadrou had to leave, Bonboo brought Sammywoo to me."

"I begged," giggled Sammywoo. "Bonboo snores like a wolf."

"Now how would you know that?" asked Sawny playfully, trying to compete with her sister for his affection. She wasn't as natural around children as Dilly was.

"I saw him with my dad lots," said Sammywoo, fidgeting. "You know, it was dark and he was sleeping all the time, making those noises—and we had to sneak, even though I didn't want to—and he scared me like a bad dream—and my dad tried this stuff, but it didn't make him stop or anything—and I told him to leave, but we stayed anyway, so I cried. It wasn't the fun kind of stuff, you know, like they said to me, if I did it....Don't you think?"

Sammywoo looked straight at Sawny, his big blue eyes twinkled with pride in having told her his story that explained all about how he had learned Bonboo was a snorer. Dilly loved the moment. She joined Sammywoo in staring mercilessly at Sawny, as they waited for her to respond to his question.

"Ooookay," said Sawny, feeling self-conscious. She knew she didn't speak kid-talk well enough to know what Sammywoo meant. It knocked her out of her comfort zone.

"Where's your dad?" asked Dod, looking at Sammywoo. He broke back into the conversation, which was welcomed by Sawny.

"Just like he said—I guess," said Sammywoo. The answer was unclear.

"Do you remember?" inquired Dod, trying a second time. When Sammywoo didn't seem to know, Dod continued to prod. "When we were first leaving Twistyard, he told me he had to go to other places and wouldn't be able to give me a ride back on the flutter. Do you know what other places—"

"I don't think that's what happened," interrupted Dilly. "Youk was specifically called away on important business, right after the game. It seemed to be a high-priority mission—the kind of assignment you drop everything else to go and do. If I could have, I would have followed him. You know how I live for adventure—"

Dilly momentarily slowed her speech while she waved to Boot and Bowy, who had just arrived.

"Anyway," continued Dilly, "I saw him leave toward the sea, racing on a black horse. It was when we were making our way here, after gathering together by the gate. Whatever his original plans may have been, yesterday's meeting in the Glitz Room changed them. I'd imagine Commendus himself was there, securely watching the match from behind the black glass. Afterwards, he must have had an emergency for Youk to attend to. Who knows, if he had been more successful, maybe you wouldn't have slept on a table last night."

"If it was necessary to move quickly," grumbled Dod, still confused, "then why didn't he ride the giant flutter with Horsely? Besides, he told Sammywoo he was going to challenge the referees—get them to declare Green Hall as the winners—didn't he Sammywoo?"

"Yup. My dad said you won, Dilly. He promised to fix it for Bowy."

"Regardless of his intentions to fight the impossible for us," answered Dilly, beginning to get perturbed—hearing Dod mention the match clearly stirred feelings of anger, frustration, and regret—"whoever he met changed his plans, and the new ones didn't include Horsely, or you, or me, and didn't include coming back last night."

Dod wished he hadn't brought it up with Dilly. She was more edgy and irritable than usual, likely due to a bad night's rest on top of the painful Bollirse loss. In truth, though, Dod wondered about Youk and Neadrou's loyalties. And he had felt sorry for poor Horsely all night, knowing that he was out in the rain with the giant flutter, faithfully waiting for Youk to return. It didn't seem nice.

"There he is!" said Boot, approaching Dod. He and Bowy came up and squished him from both sides.

"Hey, bros," called a groggy voice from under the last occupied blanket. Buck peered out.

"That can't be comfortable," laughed Boot, pulling Buck's quilt down, exposing him to the morning. "Tables are for eating, not sleeping."

"Easy for you to say, silver-tongued snake," grumbled Buck, searching for his shoes. He was still wearing his orange uniform. "How is it that Dod did the saving and you got the comfy tent... and the new clothes?" Buck griped at his brothers who were sporting fine apparel they had obtained from The Greats, nothing less than the best—three-piece riding suits, complete with matching hats and boots.

"Thanks again," said Bowy, turning to Dod. "I can't believe you saved my life yesterday! I thought you were kidding. How did you know?"

"He does stuff like that," said Buck from under the table he had slept on. He had found one of his shoes and was searching for the other. "You ought to come back to Twistyard with us. It's more fun being a Coosing now that Dod's around...and he's Pap's grandson, too. Bonboo gave him Pap's stuff. It's jazzy."

"Here you go, Buck," said Boot, holding up his shoe.

Buck crawled out and took it, swung around to a sitting position, and then threw it in the air, screaming like a frenzied baboon and shaking uncontrollably. The shoe flew up and hit a support beam before coming back down, but it didn't come down alone: A bright red object squiggled out and landed on Sawny.

"Gizzler!" she shrieked, dancing spastically. Even after the snake was cast out of her hair, she continued moving, instinctively reacting. She couldn't help it. Terror had taken hold on her—mind, body, and soul.

But it wasn't over yet. The gizzler had caught Sawny's hand

in an unfortunate swing and had launched onto Dilly, sending her into convulsions that made Sawny look sedated. It was an ugly mess, the two sisters dancing for their lives, doing the most horrendous moves.

In the end, Dilly successfully flipped the snake with a frantic hand. It flew back at Buck and landed in a bucket that had been catching drips. Boot was roaring hysterically. He was the only one who seemed to think it was funny…until he reached in the pail and drew out a common water snake; red dripped off, revealing its true color—brown! When people realized it was a joke, they broke out into laughter, having watched the ultimate dance competition between the two sisters.

"That's it!" snarled Dilly, scowling with twice the venom a real gizzler would have had. She took Sawny and Sammywoo by the hand and stormed off, highly incensed.

"She's going to get you one of these days," said Bowy, showing sympathy for the girls. "You better watch your back. Besides, if you prank her wrong, she'll plunk you with her sword and watch you bleed out, only to discover later that you were kidding. All the same, you'd deserve it."

"That one barely topped your pull," responded Boot, still chuckling. "After Dod told her you were in grave danger, and she didn't believe him, it was premium to have you fake a gizzler strike. She's more afraid of them than anything." Boot shook his head and added wistfully, "I'll miss this beach."

"You always take it past the top, Boot," said Buck, finally putting his shoes on. No wonder Bowy won't come back with us—he knows what I go through; he remembers it too well."

"That's not it," responded Bowy somberly. "You're both well aware of why I can't." His mood had changed drastically. He didn't say anything more. Instead, he patted his brothers and Dod on the shoulders and then left the pavilion in search of the girls.

Breakfast was quieter without Dilly and Sawny. Boot and Buck carried the bulk of the conversation, with contributions from Dod as well as Pone, Voo, and Sham. They ate outdoors, sitting on logs around a fire pit. The morning was gorgeous. After raining all night, the sky had turned turquoise-blue and the wind had completely dissipated. It was a perfect day to begin their long journey home.

Pone, Voo, and Sham were inseparable triplets, even though they came from three different families. They strongly resembled Boot and Buck. They all had dark hair, with Pone's jet-black, Voo's nearly-black, and Sham's dark-brown; and they all wore the same hairstyle, wavy on top and stubble-short on the sides and back; and they all were around six feet, nearly as big as Boot, just not as well muscled out.

Dod couldn't help feeling fortunate to be joined with them as a Coosing. Each of them had done great things to earn his place in the prestigious group. Despite their playful natures and youthful tendencies, they were more capable of serious business than most seasoned individuals at the height of their prime. Truly, Twistyard had gleaned the best from Green and had put them together as Coosings. It seemed likely to Dod that their pictures would eventually be hung on the wall in the Hall of The Greats.

Of The Triplets, Pone in particular was prone to silliness like Boot, but was still a warrior and thinker. He had fought side-by-side with Pap and had personally dueled one of The Dread's most notorious assassins, Rumbly, while on assignment in Raul. Pone didn't talk about it very much, yet Dod had heard the story from

Dilly. Pone had been sent to stay with Sawb's father, Terro, as a goodwill messenger from Twistyard and also to secretly be eyes and ears for Bonboo.

It was an internship of sorts with Terro's chief of staff. He had spent months studying Raul's Democracy in hopes of bringing ideas back to Green on how the two governments could get along better. Then one night, chaos struck a wing of Terro's manor. Three key ambassadors were assassinated and five more injured by Rumbly's cruel blade. With no time to wait for Terro's men to give chase, and with little thought for his own safety, Pone had taken a sword from the lifeless hand of his most cherished mentor and had pursued Rumbly by himself.

In the end, Rumbly had escaped into the night after a brief encounter with Pone, but not without first receiving a wound that marked him; it was a slice across his cheekbone, making him identifiable to Pap and Bowlure, who later sent Rumbly to Driaxom. It was that act of heroism, along with many others, that had led to Pone's induction into the Green Coosings.

Voo and Sham had less exciting stories; nevertheless, they too had both served special missions for Twistyard as Greenlings. Together, they had aided Pious in negotiating peace with some cities in the distant Northern Lands, across the Carsalean Sea and Moop Ocean. Because of their kindness to the locals and persistence in educating people about the truth, they had successfully persuaded the people to stop providing men and support for Dreaderious.

It had taken years of dedicated service to accomplish Youk's masterful plan for reducing Dreaderious's northern recruits, but Voo and Sham, with the aid of a few others, had done it, and by so doing, had earned their Coosing rings.

Buck's biggest credential was that he was Boot's brother, and Boot's was his longevity at Twistyard, but they both had done impressive things. At one point, Boot had even saved Dilly's life by defending her against four armed men, using nothing but a stick to fight off their swords while she ran to safety.

Boot loved his friends and would quickly give his life, if required, to save them. They all knew it deep down inside, so despite his habitual teasing, they accepted him as their leader.

By the end of breakfast, Boot's kinder self felt sorry about torturing Dilly and Sawny. It gnawed at him. He kept looking over at where they were sitting, enjoying their breakfasts with Bowy, Chikada, and Sammywoo. Finally, an idea lit up Boot's face. It was his way to fix things.

"Excuse me," said Boot loudly, climbing on top of a large rock. "I'd like to speak with all of the Greenlings and Green Coosings. I have a very important announcement." He waved his arms and indicated for messengers to retrieve the stragglers.

Dod nudged Buck for answers as the group waited for everyone to assemble, but Buck was as oblivious as he was about the news.

"As you all know," Boot began, "we had a number of unfortunate things happen the other day at the game."

"Yeah, you lost!" yelled Sawb from the back of the crowd. He bopped knuckles with Doochi and they both laughed.

Many of the Raul Coosings and Raulings had come running to hear Boot's important declaration, not to mention have a good time rubbing it in about their loss. It was no secret that Raul Hall felt jilted over not getting to represent Twistyard, and they were angry at Green Hall for ruining their six-year winning streak.

"Hey, Sawb, you weren't invited," responded Boot in an unusually bold voice, pointing his finger at him. "What I have to say is for us only."

"Oh, you thought we were here to listen to you?" jabbed Sawb. At six-foot four, he had no trouble seeing over the crowd, and his two henchmen, Joak and Kwit, were securely at his sides, nearly as tall. "Doochi and I were actually having our own little rendezvous back here, trying to determine why you're still leading Green Hall—I mean, it's no secret morale has been down: Julius quit on you, Dod's been keeping his distance, and even your own brother Bowy won't come back. That's pretty pathetic."

Boot held his tongue. He wanted to rattle off a string of mean things at Sawb, and he had plenty to say; Raul Hall had lost to them in Bollirse, twice; The Dread had been disgracefully identified as Sawb's uncle Sirlonk; and Sawb's own father, Terro, had promised to make The Games at Carsigo and then pay for everyone in Raul Hall to take a magnificent two-week cruise up and down the coast on Green's premier luxury ship, The Golden Anchor, but he hadn't even shown up for a visit, much less brought money to buy Sawb's friends.

Nevertheless, with so many options available, Boot chose to be mature. "I'd appreciate you showing some respect, Sawb," said Boot, holding back his anger. "We would like a few moments to talk alone. Perhaps you could have your gathering by your own pavilion."

"No thanks, we're already here," said Sawb coolly. He was agitated and looking for a fight. "Why don't we duel for dubs, you against me?"

Eluxa cheered obnoxiously, as she sat perched on the shoulders of another girl. "Go, Sawb, go," she chanted, waving her hands in the air like a cheerleader.

"Maybe back at Twistyard," answered Boot. "We have things to do and places to go. Pious is waiting for us."

"Oh, that's right," whined Sawb contemptuously. "You're dropping off some of your Greenlings as goodwill sprats." He turned to the Raulings and Raul Coosings that flocked behind him and laughed as he added, mockingly, "Perhaps Pious will provide them with tinker and wands and dust…and don't forget about the lacy slippers."

"You seem to know a lot about sprats," yelled Pone, sticking up for Boot. He had heard enough out of Sawb, who mocked anyone attempting to practice diplomacy over weaponry.

"And you, Pone, know even more—being stuck with two of them." Sawb referred to Voo and Sham. "At least in Raul we honor men that deserve to be honored, men that wield a sword well, or prove themselves faithful in battle; and as for hand-wavers and baby-squeezers, we keep them in their own place. That's why being a Raul Coosing means something."

Sawb's followers cheered him on. They loved to feel superior to everyone in Green.

Boot slowly climbed down from his perch and walked through the crowd to Sawb. Dod and The Triplets followed, with Buck tagging along further behind. It was a moment Dod had never seen before: Boot was standing up to Sawb, face to face.

"I asked nicely," growled Boot. He was only inches from him. When they were close together, it was apparent how large Sawb was, nearly four inches above Boot, and pound for pound as solid. Joak and Kwit stood a hair shorter than Sawb, but stockier.

"What does nice have to do with anything?" snapped Sawb, glaring angrily. "You're sounding as pathetic as your mother!" He put his hands up and imitated a helpless old woman, "Let's all be nice. Forgive and forget. It was just an accident."

"Ooooooo," taunted Eluxa, flipping her long black hair out of her face. "Be a man already, Boot," she added, slipping him a wink.

Boot clenched his fists. He had been holding back a whirlwind and was nearing his capacity to contain it.

"Go ahead," challenged Sawb.

Eluxa grinned. She was hungry to watch Boot get creamed, so she kicked at the girl who carried her, insisting that they move closer to the action.

But before blows could erupt, the crowd parted and Bonboo came walking over, escorted by Dilly and Sawny.

Eluxa scowled at Dilly.

"Is something wrong?" asked Bonboo, studying Boot and Sawb.

"No," said Sawb, smiling politely at Bonboo. "I was just coming over to congratulate Boot on his victory against the Raging Billies—or so I've heard from Sammywoo." Sawb looked at Boot and grinned sarcastically, "Green Hall brought *honor* to Twistyard this year, didn't they."

"I think they did," said Bonboo, patting Boot on the shoulder. "Life presents challenges to everyone; it's what we do with them that makes us great. How we act is ultimately more important than what we get in return."

"Well said," admitted Sawb. "Will you be safe on your journey or would you like Raul Hall to escort you, wherever you've decided to go?"

"I'm fine, thank you," said Bonboo. "I appreciate your concern."

"Then we'll be off," said Sawb. He turned and the crowd

from Raul followed. And then he spun around and added, "Once again, it's so good to see you up and well. My father sends his regards and best wishes. He had hoped to come to The Games but was detained by a most egregious matter."

"Boosap!" coughed Buck under his breath. Sawb flashed a last crusty before strutting away.

"Now boys," said Bonboo in a fatherly tone, "I know it's hard to be around them. However, they're our guests here in Green. What we teach them by the way we treat them will last long into the future. It may be the only legacy we offer to Raul. Those fellows, as rough as they are, will likely grow into positions of authority in their homeland. And so, for the sake of good people elsewhere, let's be one step better here."

Bonboo poked his cane past Boot and tapped Dod on the arm. "May I have a word with you?"

Dod was hesitant. He wanted to go with Bonboo, but he also wanted to hear what Boot had to say. It was a tough decision.

"All right," he sighed, taking Bonboo by the arm. They walked past the ashes of the burnt tent and into a thicket of younger trees, where stone benches dotted the little forest. It was a quieter place, filled with foliage.

"I know you'd like to run back with your friends," said Bonboo, taking a seat. "I'll be brief. You've returned to a dangerous Green. The Dread has covert followers—no one knows how many—and now that we sent him away, they're determined to exercise revenge."

"I know," said Dod, nodding his head. "When I first arrived, I was greeted by Dark Hood. He nearly ended my life."

"Really?" gasped Bonboo. "Was it in the forest or by Lake Mauj?"

"Neither," said Dod. "It was in Green Hall."

"Oh!" groaned Bonboo. "He's becoming more brazen. I'm surprised he dared enter the castle with all of the guards we've had storming the halls. Jibb and Zerny have been busy."

"Especially Jibb," responded Dod, shaking his head in disgust. "He seemed surprised to find I was fighting for Twistyard, not against."

"Yes, that poor misguided man," answered Bonboo. "They're doing their best. It's been very hard for them lately, with so many soldiers disappearing. I've tried to dissuade them from pointless accusations—did you see your picture?"

"No. I haven't had a chance," said Dod, flicking a horsefly off his arm. It had just taken a chomp of him and left a bright-red mark.

"In my absence, I had them post the painting to remind them of your loyalty," said Bonboo. He looked Dod in the eyes and teared-up. "We need you, Dod. Please stay and help us. I don't fully understand everything you can do, but you're Pap's grandson! Perhaps your gifts will aid us in finding the traitors before they blast our peace. I wish I didn't need to tell you this—I really do—"

Bonboo looked behind him nervously and studied the back-drop before continuing. "You can't trust anyone, Dod! I mean it! Someone poisoned me at Twistyard and then nearly finished me off in my guarded quarters at the hospital in Lower Janice—and that too, with Higga on duty. My grandson Chikada came to visit and sensed my recovery was being tampered with. He took me away and saved my life."

"Oh, that's what happened," said Dod. "I thought Voracio—"

"No, not Voracio," choked Bonboo. "He came right after

you left. I think he's hoping to make an impression—I'm getting older, you know."

Bonboo gazed into the air longingly and added, "I've outlived my wife and kids, Dod—and most of my grandkids."

"I'm sorry," said Dod.

"It's all right," responded Bonboo, perking back up. "Anyway, it's a good thing Voracio came when he did, even with his crazy temperament. While I've been gone, he's done plenty around Twistyard. He even chased after Dark Hood by himself and dueled with him. That foolish man's got a nasty limp to remind him of how lucky he was to have escaped on horseback. If he would have been on foot, I fear we'd have found him dead on the shores of Lake Mauj. Man to man, Dark Hood is unbeatable with his peculiar crimson sword. It'll take careful planning and a well placed legion to apprehend him. Be alert and stay alive. He's got you pegged!"

"Me?" squeaked Dod. He felt miserable. He knew Dark Hood was likely aware of him—they'd already met—but hearing Bonboo say it so bluntly made Dod ill.

"I'm sorry if I've scared you," added Bonboo, looking concerned. "I'd say The Greats are mostly trustworthy and, of course, your friends are probably fine. Just watch out for the fringes and don't go anywhere by yourself."

Bonboo rose to his feet and started to lead Dod back to Green Hall's assembly when he paused. "One more thing for now, Dod: The new word is Tillius. And don't bother Higga since I've given her a break. Commendus has the map, and you have the key, and Dilly knows what to do with them. If I should die, please get the truth. The secrets are good and bad, and both are needful."

"Can't you tell me?" begged Dod. "They're about Dark Hood and The Dread, aren't they?"

"I wish it were that simple of a problem—I really do. And knowing what I know only weighs me down. I keep hoping to live long enough to solve the puzzles and stop the—"

Bonboo's voice faded.

"Stop what? Who?" begged Dod.

"Perhaps you won't need the secrets anyway," said Bonboo. "If we could just catch Dark Hood—" His face told the truth that his words tried to hide: The secrets were essential.

"Are you kidding?" groaned Dod, boring into Bonboo with his eyes, his gut aching to know what Bonboo was hiding.

"Be safe," said Bonboo. "Besides, I've just decided to go along with Voracio's advice—I'm heading back to Twistyard. It's my home, Dod, and if someone thinks they drove me off for good, they're going to be sorely disappointed. We have justice on our side. Truth will prevail."

Bonboo waved his cane in the air, invigorated by his inner courage. Dod wanted to continue talking with Bonboo, regardless of whatever Boot was doing or saying—there were still too many unanswered questions—but before he could prod any more, Sawny came rushing up to them, beaming brightly.

"I'm a Coosing now!" she squealed enthusiastically, showing off her new ring. "Boot said he was impressed by my actions during yesterday's match and insisted I fill Julius's place. Isn't that splendid?"

"I'm proud of you," said Bonboo, wrapping her in a hug. "You and your sister remind me of your mother when she was a Coosing. She had such energy and spunk...why, I knew right off the swot that anyone lucky enough to catch her would be lucky indeed; and I'm not embarrassed to say that I pointed my grandson Chikada in the right direction."

Dod followed them back to the celebration and then remembered one last question as Bonboo was rushing off. "Who's taking care of Pap's place?" he asked, raising his voice to be heard above the crowd. The answer shocked him.

"We already agreed you would, right? You've got the only key."

THE REDY-ALERT-BAND

Dod was overjoyed to discover he was still in charge of Pap's place. It meant one thing: Pap had to be alive, somehow, someway.

"Did you hear the news?" asked Buck, bumping Dod, who was deep in thought. The crowd of Greenlings and Green Coosings buzzed with excitement.

"What?" mumbled Dod. His focus was far away from the bustling conversations that filled the air. He was searching for his grandpa. If he could have transported himself to anywhere at that moment, it would have been right back to Twistyard, up the old quick-rappel and into Pap's freshly-cleaned house.

"Boot just announced that Sawny is the new Coosing," said Buck. "Isn't that the tops? After the match the other day, it's no wonder he chose her. She surprised me. I didn't think she had it in her."

"Yeah—she was unbelievable," agreed Dod, still distracted.

"Let's hurry and be on our way," bellowed Boot, pushing the throng toward the tents that still stood. "If you're lucky enough to have gear, get it ready. We'll be heading to the barns in ten."

Dod lingered and was approached by Boot. "Your things are together, right?" asked Boot, looking dapper in his showy outfit. The Greats hadn't held back anything when clothing Boot and Bowy after the fire had destroyed their temporary quarters.

"Yes, my stuff's over there," said Dod, pointing at his bag. He walked over and plopped himself down on it. The solid lump in the middle reassured him that Pap's sword was safely inside.

"Good. Good. We're almost there," sighed Boot excitedly. He hurried off to help nudge the laggers.

Dod sat alone and watched everyone scurrying around. It reminded him of the last morning of a weeklong Scout camp: people were frantically cleaning up and packing, getting prepared to leave.

Three younger Greenling boys came walking toward Dod, toting piles of bags. "Over here?" one of them yelled, looking back.

"By Dod," shouted Dilly, some distance away. She was heading their direction, carrying a fancy pink purse.

Five suitcases plopped onto the grass at Dod's feet. "Hey, nice work last night," said the smallest boy. He looked eleven or twelve.

"I thought Sawny said you had four," teased Dod when Dilly was within reasonable hearing range.

"I do. One of them is Sawny's," said Dilly cheerfully. Her spirits were drastically different from the perturbed girl that Dod had encountered earlier. She walked over and joined Dod on his bag.

"What's in this?" she asked, looking at Dod. Her eyes revealed what she suspected.

"My safety!" answered Dod.

"Good for you. I wish I had one on me. It's dreadfully lonely without my stash. And after last night, a sword is only practical. You'll need to talk with Bonboo about that for me—seeing how you're becoming cozier with my great-grandpa than I am." Dilly shoved Dod on the shoulder playfully.

"About your stash—"

"What about it?" snapped Dilly nervously.

"I'm sure it's not so…private anymore."

"Why not?" asked Dilly. "They're hidden under tons of blankets and stowed in the farthest back corner beneath my bed—no more clanking."

"We'll—" said Dod hesitantly, "after Dark Hood nearly ran me through in Green Hall, Jibb and his crew blocked it off. The soldiers are doing a scrupulous search of the place, trying to figure out why he was there and how he escaped. They wouldn't even let me back in to get clothes—and I was wearing pajamas!"

"You're kidding, right?" said Dilly.

"*Nope-o.* I'm *not-o.*"

"You've been chirping with Dari, haven't you?" said Dilly disapprovingly.

"How could you tell?"

"It's rubbing off," scoffed Dilly. "Don't do that again."

Dilly slid to the side of his bag, acting like Dod had a contagious disease. "You need to watch yourself," she continued, doling out her advice. "Dari and Valerie are sweet one minute and then brutal the next. You never know which flavor you're going to get. They've got real emotional issues."

"Oh," said Dod, sighing loudly. He found it amusing that Dilly couldn't see how similar she was to them—mood swings included.

"So, are you serious about Jibb going through my stuff?" asked Dilly. Her eyes looked hopeful. "Zerny wouldn't let him: He knows better."

"Zerny?" said Dod. "He wasn't at Twistyard. He was supposedly with Bonboo."

"No—that was weeks ago," replied Dilly. "Zerny returned to Twistyard after my dad scooped gramps and took him home to Terraboom."

"Perhaps," said Dod, thinking back. "Either way, Zerny wasn't at Twistyard when I was there. And I vaguely recall hearing someone say he hadn't been there for a while."

"Oh, I know why!" said Dilly, turning to look at Dod. "He was visiting 'the spot.' He does it every year about this time. How long were you at Twistyard before you came here?"

"A couple of days."

"Yup," said Dilly. "He's gone to pay his respects. Years ago, Zerny drove a wagon with his wife and six kids inside. They were heading to visit his family in Durboo. Somewhere along the road, a yappy dog spooked the horses and they bolted. With Zerny steering, he thought for sure he could persuade the horses to stop before anything bad happened, but he was wrong. The horses ran straight into a large tree, throwing him from the carriage and killing Zerny's wife and kids. Jibb was staying at Twistyard at the time as a Greenling, so he survived."

"Wow. I never heard that story," said Dod, feeling bad that he had always judged Zerny based on their first encounter. In light of the new information, Zerny's suspicious actions made more sense. He had probably done exactly what he had regretted not doing for his wife and kids—he had unhitched the wagon from the horses.

Dod looked over and noticed five boys approaching, carrying something wrapped in leather. From the distance, they appeared young and rough looking, and since one of them had whitish-blonde hair and none of them was taller than Dod, he thought they were humans.

"Dod, I'm glad we caught you," said Jim.

The boys were Soosh Coosings. They were drastically different than their Raul counterparts. Their worn-out clothing and messy hair made it easy to distinguish them, and not one of them was as old as most of the Raulings, let alone Raul Coosings. It was clear they had plenty of growing to do as tredders. Still, they had been chosen from Soosh and sent to be part of the program.

"We've got the slots full again," said Jim, beaming. "Tinja came with me to Soosh and convinced people it was safe to send more. He reminded them of Pap's commitment to Twistyard, not to mention Humberrone's ties."

"Fifteen Coosings and fifty Sooshlings," blurted another boy, who was standing next to Jim. He had the customary black hair and big brown eyes. "I'm Hal, Toolor's younger brother," he said, saluting Dod with the Coosings' hand sign.

Dod didn't recognize Hal, but he remembered hearing about Toolor. It was a sad tale. Toolor had been a Coosing for years and had fallen in love with another Coosing from Soosh. He was on his way home with his sweetheart to be married when they were both poisoned at High Gate alongside of Pap.

"It's nice to meet you," said Dod, standing up. "I'm sorry about your brother and his bride."

"Me too!" snapped Hal, his eyes flashing with hatred for The Dread. "He was the best…well, as good as any of their brothers." Hal pointed at the other three boys who stood next to Jim. "All

of us lost family that night. It's pitiful how they've let Sirlonk
live. If he would have been captured in Soosh, we'd have dealt
him plenty for his deeds—it's the right of the offended families."

"A living-death sentence at Driaxom is no afternoon
picnic," said Dilly, trying to console the boy. "Sirlonk will suffer
immeasurably and then die, cold and alone."

"I guess that's good for Green, eh?" choked Hal. It was clear
that he and the other three boys felt ripped off. Jim, on the other
hand, looked sad but not mad.

"We miss them, too," said Dilly sincerely.

Jim shifted his foot, kicking the grass, and then looked side
to side. "We didn't come here to make you feel bad; we actually
intended on the opposite." He handed Dod the leather ball he
had been holding. "Here you go. We figured this might come in
handy where you're headed for the night."

"Thanks," said Dod, beginning to unwrap it.

"We all appreciate what you've done," said Jim earnestly,
"and I speak for the folks back in Soosh. The Dread's hands are
red with blood from our people, and not just the ten Coosings
and twenty Sooshlings that died with Pap. He killed hundreds
of thousands by tricking the noble tredder families into fighting
each other. If Humberrone hadn't stopped him twenty-two years
ago, I probably wouldn't be here."

Dod struggled and then finally untied the last string,
releasing the gift. "Wow! This is really something special," said
Dod, completely clueless.

"You don't know what it is," piped the boy who was standing
furthest from Dod. His fingernails were black with mud and
his clothes were filthy. Dod couldn't help thinking that the boy
reminded him of Josh when camping.

"Yes I do," said Dod. "It's wonderful. I'll wear it tonight and remember how lucky I am to have such crafty friends."

The present was a brownish-yellow bracelet made of braided, shiny leather.

"We didn't make it!" said the band of boys in unison, beginning to laugh.

"We got it from my uncle," confessed Jim. "You remember him—Shelderhig."

"Oh yes," replied Dod, trying to recover. "How's Doctor Shelderhig these days? Did he catch the snakes?"

"Nope," responded Jim, shaking his head. "They keep wriggling away. He can't seem to trap them. It's driving him mad."

"He hasn't?" groaned Dilly. "Boot told me he solved that problem long ago. If I'd have known the diasserpentouses were still there, I'd have adjusted our itinerary!"

"Not likely," argued Dod boldly. "You love Commendus's pampering."

"I know, but really—" Dilly looked horribly conflicted.

"Then stay close to Dod," said Jim, beaming with a secret. "That's my unc's ingenious creation—his Redy-Alert-Band. It starts to turn pink if you're anywhere near a snake and bright red if you're within fifty feet. The chemicals in the air from the snake's skin react with that thing and it lights up. He's calmed Commendus's nerves considerably with it. The man's wearing loads of them, just in case. 'Course, with Mama and Popslither in his pond, I can't say I blame him."

"Wow! This detects diasserpentouses?" said Dod. "That's amazing!" He turned the band over and noticed its carefully woven pattern.

"Not just the big fangers," added Jim eagerly. "It'll turn red just as fast from a tiny pond snake—"

"Or even a gizzler?" interrupted Dilly excitedly.

"Yup. Tonight as you rough it with the soldiers, you'll have constant proof of your safety."

Dod tied the Redy-Alert-Band around his wrist and gave each of the boys a pat on the shoulder. Even though they were much older than Dod—in their late twenties—they looked like large twelve-year-olds.

"Thanks again," said Dod. "Stay away from Dark Hood."

"I don't think so," piped Hal, turning away. "We're going to find him!"

"C'mon," urged Jim, pointing toward the camp's exit. "Tinja's waiting."

No sooner had they left than Dilly began begging and pleading to wear Dod's bracelet. "You know how terrified I am of gizzlers," she said, grabbing Dod's arm and holding the precious wristband close enough to kiss. "This would be my salvation. I mean it! Pleeeease."

"It depends," teased Dod, enjoying the moment. "If there are more of those horrid red snakes around Pious's camp, I wouldn't be able to sleep without this." He knew he would eventually give in. When Dilly wanted something desperately, there was no stopping her.

"Pleeeeease!" continued Dilly, getting louder, twinkling her best puppy-dog eyes. "At least let me try it on. I want to know what it feels like to wear the… *Redy-Alert-Band*!"

Dilly liked the name. It musically rolled off her tongue, and before long, she was chanting it as she stole the present from Dod's wrist.

"What do you think?" chirped Dilly to Sawny who arrived

after the crime was over. Dilly turned her hand around, displaying all angles of the bracelet.

"It's pretty," she said, grinning ear-to-ear. Sawny held out her own hand, waving her fingers. "Doesn't my new jewelry look good, too?"

"I think it does," said Dilly, still preoccupied with looking at her pilfered loot. It was the answer to her prayers.

The two sisters gossiped back and forth about things they'd heard and all sorts of miscellaneous fluff. It wasn't terribly interesting to Dod, but he tried to be nice, occasionally nodding his head. He did enjoy the atmosphere. It was great to hear Dilly and Sawny happily chatting.

Suddenly, out of the blue, Dod knew what Sawny was about to say. It was strange. He had an image in his mind of her with one hand in the air, spouting on about how pathetic Sawb was.

As soon as Dod thought it, Sawny did it. The event was the most quickly-realized glimpse he had ever experienced, almost like he had watched it on television and then rewound it and watched it again. He could have accurately predicted the exact verbiage she would use and the look she would give.

"That was sweet!" said Dod, mumbling to himself.

"What?" gasped Sawny. "I think you're psychotic. Sawb spouted anything *but* candy talk."

"He was being sarcastic," said Dilly. "Dod knows it was cruel. Sawb was dredging the bottom today, wasn't he?"

"I'd say!" said Sawny. "Mentioning Boot's father like that was completely heartless and unforgivable. Only a rock with no emotion whatsoever would concoct the things he said."

"His father?" asked Dod, looking confused.

"Yes," said Sawny. "You know—his calamity."

Dod didn't know, and it showed on his face.

"Shortly before Boot came to Twistyard," said Dilly, pushing hair out of her face. "Well, about thirty-three years ago, Boot's father was caught in the middle of a horrendous mistake—a mistake our uncle Voracio made. At the time, Voracio was in charge of mock-war training, preparing men to fight Dreadluceous—Dreaderious's father. Voracio had been given charge of training thousands of soldiers. He had them shooting arrows, launching rocks, fighting with swords, and doing all the tasks you can imagine a general would expect."

Dod listened intently. As Dilly spoke, he remembered the event. Details poured into his mind. It was like Dilly's voice had unlocked a file of memories.

"Boot's father was there, running an errand," said Dilly. "He wasn't part of the exercises. But on his way, he noticed a handful of Coosings heading out to fill their quivers with arrows. They hadn't waited for anyone to okay the range—they just went, assuming the shooting was over. It turned into a big problem. The brush and scrubby trees were thick enough on the edges that the soldiers couldn't see the Coosings.

"When Boot's father noticed the men preparing to fire, he ran to stop them, taking the quickest route, which was straight across the field. It put him in the middle of trouble when the storm of arrows rained down. He and five Coosings were killed. One of them lived long enough to tell what had happened before he died in my uncle's arms."

"It makes me sick to imagine it," said Dod. He meant it. He knew what had occurred, for he could see bits and pieces of it in his mind. They weren't clear, but Boot's father was unquestionably a hero among men, genuinely kind and good, always seeking to help others, willing to risk his own life for a handful of strangers—and that's exactly what he had done.

"And of course Voracio was beside himself," said Dilly, continuing the story. "He fretted needlessly, feeling the blame for a nasty misunderstanding. There's no way he could have known to tell his men to hold their fire, and Boot's mom understood that. She openly pardoned everyone involved and went on to plead with the parents of the Coosings to forgive and forget. Her kindness prevailed with some of the families—the three from Green. But it struck a bitter chord with the relatives of the two boys from Raul—they were Sirlonk's sons. Tonnis is all he has left."

"Oh!" groaned Dod. "They were Sirlonk's sons."

"Yes!" said Dilly emphatically. Her eyes helped stress how strange the coincidence was. "And so, we were shocked when Tonnis followed his brothers' footsteps and became a Rauling, and even more so when Juny and Sirlonk came to stay. Of course, now that we know Sirlonk was The Dread, it makes more sense that he wanted to live here while plaguing the area."

"Poor Juny," lamented Sawny. She shook her head and her eyes became moist with sincere compassion. "She's lost a lot: first her two sons to a ghastly mishap, and then her husband and homeland to a poor choice of companionship. I'm glad Bonboo has let her stay at Twistyard. Anywhere else, her life would be in danger from jungo-hungry crazies. Even after Green's investigation of her and Tonnis, Raul is still requesting to interrogate them at Terro's palace, but it wouldn't be fair. We know how they feel about revenge—the whole family pays! Their justice system would most likely do an injustice."

"I know!" agreed Dilly. "Just look at what's happened to Tonnis: Sawb's demoted him to a Rauling and reinstated Doochi as a Coosing."

"They treated him poorly before they knew," added Sawny. "Now with this, I bet his life is hot ashes. No wonder he didn't accompany them here to The Games—more time to breathe back in Raul Hall by himself."

"And don't forget about Juny's burden," reminded Dilly. "She's got Ingrid staying with her, watching her day and night for any signs of trouble. That woman is a project. Voracio could have at least picked someone with more sympathy."

"Or better breath," said Dod.

"You've met her, haven't you?" said Dilly, smiling. "Anyway, you can see how it was cruel beyond measure for Sawb to mock Boot's mother—she's a hero, stronger and tougher and greater than the kind that swings a sword—"

"Are you talking about me again?" interrupted Boot, pouncing from behind. The girls gasped.

"Yes!" joked Dod. "They were just explaining how strong you are."

"It's true," replied Boot, posing with his muscles rippling. "Sawb's one lucky pebble-head that I've also got huge amounts of patience. Any other steel-back would have cleared Sawb's face for future planting."

"I guess Bonboo's rubbing off," said Sawny. "Is that gray I see?"

"Careful, now," interjected Boot, hopping onto a skinny stump with one foot. He ran his fingers through his wavy hair, while jiggling to balance. "I'm still content to have this stuff firmly rooted. Black is fine by me—wisdom can knock later, when I'm settled with half-a-dozen squealers."

"Booties," said Sawny teasingly.

"Why stop at half?" taunted Dilly.

"Are you proposing to me?" laughed Boot, struggling to stay perched.

"Eew gross!" blurted Sammywoo, approaching the group,

waving his hands in front of his face. "Your dancing is going to make me vomit. Stop! Please stop!"

"Who, me?" said Boot, spinning around. His attempts to steady himself on the stump did appear to be a discombobulated groove of sorts.

Sammywoo smiled big and gave Dilly an awkward wink. It was obvious that the line had originated from his know-it-all friend and had been rehearsed plenty in front of her. Dilly glowed with pride in her prodigy.

"You!" said Boot, raising one eyebrow at Dilly. "I've found the source." He lowered his voice, like a sports announcer, and added distinctly, "You will live a short life of regret for your treasonous acts—Guilty! You're hereby condemned to bathe in gizzlers."

"It's not going to happen," laughed Dilly, holding up her wrist. "Dod gave me this."

"Hmmm," said Boot. He fell off the log and stumbled his way to the ground before crawling over to inspect the bracelet. Everyone roared at Boot's uncoordinated dismount. Dod had tears rolling down his face from laughter, and Dilly and Sawny were nearly as far gone.

"It'll save you for sure," choked Boot, trying to contain his own laughter: He had pulled at the Redy-Alert-Band and was lucky enough to have Dilly's knot slip, leaving the bracelet dangling precariously.

"Hey," said Dilly, jerking her arm back. She readjusted the band and then tied it on securely. "Dod's a lifesaver! I don't think I'd be able to sleep tonight without this. It's a Redy-Alert-Band, made by our dear friend Dr. Shelderhig. If a gizzler comes within fifty feet of me, this thing will turn red. He's...a genius!"

"Didn't I tell you that before?" said Sawny.

"Yeah, but playing with plants and tinkering with beetle droppings isn't as cool as saving my life. If you'd have informed me that he invents essential treasures like this one, I'd have sided with you sooner. The bracelet is on for good—they can bury me with it!"

"I hope so," added Boot. "That knot you just tied is a snarl."

"One-handed," gloated Dilly.

Greenlings and Coosings began to gather, carrying bags of supplies and gear. It toned down the show Dilly was willing to put on, but Boot continued to be himself, making his rounds in the crowd, joking and laughing boisterously. He was flying high on an adrenaline rush from his face-off with Sawb.

Preparing to leave had taken longer than ten minutes, so when Dod finally stood up, his legs tingled uncomfortably.

"Can you carry one of mine, too?" asked Dilly, handing Dod another bag. Sawny rolled her eyes and pointed at a larger one that was still on the ground.

"I'll take that one for you," said Dod, trusting Sawny's judgment. He was glad to find that it was much lighter than the one Dilly had tried to hand him.

"Strat! Over here!" hollered Dilly, waving her arms. The famous Bollirse teacher cut through the crowd, followed by another man.

"Are you heading to the barns?" asked Dilly. "I could really use a hand."

Strat smiled and held out both of his: They were blistering and bloody on his palms. "What do you need me to carry?" he responded.

"Oh! What happened to you!" gasped Dilly, shocked. "Those cuts look terribly painful."

"It's nothing," said Strat, shrugging his shoulders. He had a medium build and was on the short side of average height. His hair was dark, with sparse stubble on his lip and chin only. Strat's clothes were about as Dod remembered them, very plain and well worn.

Strat's companion, however, was the opposite. He looked like Commendus, dressed in fancy duds and stacked like an enormous body-builder. The one feature he had that was truly original was his red beard; it was well-trimmed, yet stuck out because of the oil-black hair on his head.

"Perhaps your friend could carry a bag or two for me," said Dilly, turning to the mystery man. It was amazing: Dilly didn't recognize him.

"You were right, Strat," said the man. "She must not know me."

"This is my friend Bly," said Strat. "Years ago, you crossed him at High Gate—"

"Yes, Bly," Dilly straightened her clothes and brushed the grass off her pants. "It's a pleasure to meet you again."

"It wasn't last time!" joked Bly, chuckling pleasantly. He reached down and grabbed one of Dilly's bags from the ground. Strat plucked the other and then pulled one out of Sawny's arms, positioning the two bags on his shoulders, steadying them with his fingertips to avoid using his sore palms.

"Do you still feel dissatisfied because my legs are free of Ankle Weed?" continued Bly. He was enjoying Dilly's agony.

"I was too young to know what I was saying," said Dilly, turning beet red. "I should have listened to my father—people write things all the time and get the story dead wrong, don't they?"

"So it's all right that I'm not rotting away my miserable life in the…now what did you say?" Bly looked into the air and pushed his memory. "Yes, not rotting away my miserable life in the befittingly grimy and putrid recesses of the lowliest quarters of Driaxom."

"Did I really say that?" asked Dilly "It doesn't sound like me."

"You most certainly did—and in front of the Council, no less. My heart nearly stopped. Your tender age tilted everyone in the room, making my attempt at a fair investigation all the more difficult. It took me four years to clear myself and I'm still working on cleaning my name."

"Ohhh!" moaned Dilly, trying to gain his forgiveness by pulling the pity card. She walked with her head down, somberly. "Now I know I've got an enemy, and it's too bad, you're just the type I'd likely strike a friendship with—smart and talented, not to mention the most celebrated inventor of our time."

"No, Dilly, I'm not your enemy," said Bly. "But if I had a sprig of Ankle Weed burrowing into my leg, waiting to send me mad, you can be sure we'd have a hard time getting along. Of course, with Driaxom's no visitor policy, I suppose you wouldn't have known my feelings anyway, much less cared two sniffs."

"Right," mumbled Dilly hesitantly.

"Besides, I just donated to your cause. If I resented your family, the gold would stay mine, or be given somewhere else. So in all of this, learn a lesson: It's the sensational stories that spread, not the truth."

"He's right about that," said Strat, who had quietly carried Dilly's two heaviest bags. They were nearing the barns, approaching a crowd of soldiers and stall boys. "I'd imagine all sorts of foolish articles will post about me—how I hate noble billies. They'll claim the most absurd things. And in truth, I get along well with them. My family lived on the Southern Islands of the Carsalean Sea for all of my younger years. I consider myself at home with billies." He glanced around and added, "If only I felt the same toward horses. We didn't have them on the islands where I lived."

Dod felt sorry for Strat, remembering how sick he had been while riding to High Gate. Twistyard was far away, which consigned Strat to feeling nauseous for three or four days, depending on his route.

In front of the barns, two people were arguing. Tinja was mounted on the back of a horse, scolding General Faller, whose men were close by, getting agitated.

"...then who provided the spray?" demanded Tinja, red in the face with frustration.

"I already explained," said Faller, equally angry. "My men made a mistake and applied the coating, following the directions they were given."

"Your men slopped it on—fine! I understand that part!" ranted Tinja. He rarely lost his cool, but looked nearly ready to show the general his skills in martial arts. "Where I'm hazy," he continued, "is how you obtained a solution that wasn't rain-proofing."

"All I can say is that my men made a mistake," responded Faller, repeating himself like a prerecorded message.

"Okay, regardless of the mishap," said Tinja, taking a deep breath. "Are you deploying troops to punish the billies? They need to learn that on land we have rules! It's not acceptable for them to come here and do whatever they want. Punish them—punish them all!"

After spewing his heavily biased remarks, Tinja didn't linger long enough to hear Faller's reply before riding off to join with

Jim's lot from Soosh; they were waiting for him on a neighboring hill, their horses lulling around eating grass.

"And to think I'm the one they're going to pin as hating the billies," said Strat, watching Tinja ride away.

"There's a story behind that rage," said Bly, helping Strat set Dilly's bags in a pile on the ground. "Someone he loved must have been hurt by them. It reminds me of the fighting in my homeland of Soosh. I'm glad to be here right now. For years it was the noble tredder families, seeking revenge for this and that. Now there's a constant brew between the remaining tredders and the drats, priming to go to war anytime over disputes that began thousands of years ago—not to mention the tribal humans and their hatred for everyone, killing each other by the thousands. Can't people get along?"

"Is it that bad?" asked Sawny, poking her head between Strat and Bly.

"It's not wonderful," assured Bly, leaving it at that. He didn't want to give Sawny the gory details. "Raul and Green are certainly in much better shape."

The stall boys retrieved horses based on numbers they were given, supplying each of the Greenlings and Coosings with the same horse they had arrived on. Dod felt bad. He knew he needed to ride double with someone, yet looking at the bags being loaded onto the backs of Dilly's Song and Boot's Grubber made him nervous that there wouldn't be any room for him.

"Here you go," said one stall boy, handing Dod the reins to Shooter. "It was an honor attending to this horse." General Faller stood in the backdrop and nodded at Dod, acknowledging he had summoned the lad to fetch Dod's horse.

Dod was shocked. His friends had anticipated his arrival

enough to have brought his horse on the three-day journey from Twistyard. It proved they expected him to join them, or so he thought. Dilly soon shattered that theory with the truth. She had borrowed Shooter to carry her luggage, not wanting Song to strain himself. And since Dod had arrived, she did the next best thing for the return trip: She constrained Boot and Sawny to each add an extra bag to the back of their horses, making it even, two-a-piece. Dod, on the other hand, was spared the additional burden because Dilly still remembered his unfortunate experience up Coyote Trail and, therefore, took precautionary action to protect her things.

Within a few minutes, everyone was riding away from Carsigo. They had said their goodbyes and warm wishes. Most of the visitors from Twistyard were headed the same direction Tinja had gone, taking the shortest route home—northeast on the southern shoreline of the peninsula, wrapping around to Harbin, southeast across the flatlands to Canteen, southwest up the winding road to Janice Pass, and then down to Lower Janice and Twistyard.

But Green Hall stuck together, accompanied by Chikada, heading on a different road which led them farther north. They planned to follow the coastline northeast on the northern side of the Hook Mountain Range, in order to stop at Fort Castle, where Pious was waiting. From there, a three-day ride east and south would take them along the eastern side of the mountains, up to the back door of High Gate and down to Twistyard.

On a map, the two routes looked comparable, with the latter adding an extra day for travel to Fort Castle; nevertheless, Dilly sadly reassured Dod that the way they were headed was more difficult because of the time they would spend torturously trotting across the edge of the Ankle Weed Desert.

While journeying to the military base, Dod found himself positioned behind Boot and Sawny and between Buck and Dilly. They all tirelessly talked with one another. Dod's central location in their company made it easy to ride, such that he could have fallen asleep and Shooter would have continued along just fine.

As they exited Carsigo, Dod noticed Horsely and the giant flutter were gone. It only made sense that Horsely wouldn't wait forever. Yet seeing the empty field by the six giant oaks bothered Dod; it poked at the back of his mind like an elusive sliver on the sole of his foot.

Dod replayed his most recent events, searching for clues—anything that would reveal the source of the feelings—and though he found plenty of concerns, none of them was the big pest, the unknown something that made him uneasy. Eventually his head hurt from contemplating, so he abandoned his attempts and enjoyed the ride.

Finally, as evening approached, the wearied clan crested a hill and saw Fort Castle in the distance, nestled up next to a fingerlike alcove of the Carsalean Sea. The protected bay was dotted with hundreds of ships, docked at Green's biggest naval base. A large valley of bushes and short, windblown trees sprawled before the traveling caravan, separating them from the military base at Fort Castle and the metropolis beyond it. The terrain looked dreary compared to the lush fields that occupied the gentle hillsides to the north and east of the city; but rightfully so—it was a servicemen training ground, spotted with broken arrows and ruined military gear.

As Dod surveyed the view, scenes from Dilly's story about Voracio flooded his mind. He could see more clearly than before the fallen Coosings and Boot's father. The more he saw, the more his own conclusion of what had happened began to drift away from Dilly's report.

In Dod's images, Voracio seemed to recognize that there were people on the field when he ordered his men to fire. But it didn't make sense. Why would he have done it? The Coosings were his men—sent from his grandfather's house to train for a season.

Regardless, it was spine-tingling to consider that perhaps Voracio hadn't fallen into a bloody accident—he had purposefully caused it!

"Is this where Boot's dad died?" asked Dod, leaning toward Dilly. He kept his voice low enough that she was the only one who heard.

"What?" said Dilly, caught off guard.

When Dod repeated the question, pointing to the meadows below, Dilly shocked him.

"No," said Dilly. "We passed the spot first thing—on the outskirts of Carsigo—where Boot and Bowy went early this morning to leave flowers. The place is beautiful now—blanketed with grassy fields. I'd have had a hard time recognizing it myself if it weren't for the six trees they left to commemorate the deaths." Dod knew which ones she meant. And just like that, he had found the mental pest that had plagued him all morning: Voracio's notorious mistake was suspicious.

The rest of the way to Fort Castle, Dod asked questions about Dilly's uncle. He wanted to know as much as he could before accusing him of treacherous behavior. Surprisingly, Dod found Dilly, too, had mixed feelings about Voracio. She said she felt anxious around him and hadn't been particularly excited when he had arrived at Twistyard, despite the fact that he was her father's oldest and only living brother.

Still, by the end of the conversation, Dod decided to wait before telling anyone about his impressions, since Dilly had recently gained a greater appreciation for Voracio. One dark night, a month prior, Dilly had personally aided a medical team in sewing Voracio's leg back together after he had received a nasty gash from chasing after Dark Hood. The experience had cemented in Dilly's mind Voracio's loyalty to Twistyard, regardless of his quirky behaviors.

Dod, on the other hand, remained uncertain about the man. Voracio's actions at the Bollirse match had revealed he was prone to anger, and the glimpses Dod had seen of him suggested he had plenty of skeletons in his closet.

TADS AND SWAPPERS

At the Fort Castle military base, Dod was amazed to find countless thousands of troops living in giant tents and barracks. From the distant hillside, it had looked like a quiet village attached to the outskirts of the main city, but close up it was clearly a state-of-the-art training center, complete with dozens of buildings which were dedicated to honing critical skills. Upon attempting to enter, a battalion of tredder soldiers stopped and inspected the group, coordinating their names and information with a record they held. Dod was in the directory, cited as being a Green Coosing and Pap's grandson. His file also contained a list of miscellaneous information about him, including his looks, reported talents, and typical whereabouts.

The sheet that held Dod's data had a bright-red star on the top, right in the center, yet all of his fellow Coosings' and Greenlings' pages didn't. Even Chikada's paperwork lacked special notations.

When Boot observed Dod looking over the shoulder of the man with the papers, he couldn't stop himself from teasing.

"I'm in there," said Boot, grinning. "Don't worry, Dod, you won't have to spend another night separated from your best friend."

Dod returned the smile. It was nice to be loved. He backed up and asked Boot about the star, assuming it meant 'Watch out for this guy, you can't trust him!' After all, everywhere Dod went, the soldiers had had a way of making him feel unwelcome, at least at first.

"A red star..." said Boot. He looked into the night sky and concocted a tale to fit the question. "It's a mark they rarely use. I'm embarrassed to be the one to tell you, but seeing how most people don't know much about the military's secret codes and such, I'll do my best. They apply the symbol to remind everyone about your condition—"

Dod had a hard time discerning if Boot was trying to explain something real about Dod's file or whether he was still searching for a believable answer; the night had caught up with them enough that Boot's face was hard to see unless he turned toward the soldiers' candles.

"That's true," said Sawny.

"It is?" stammered Boot.

"Yes. You know the mark."

"Oh!" said Boot. He turned back to the light and his face glowed with recognition. He had been bluffing before. "*That* red star. They think you're a tad! Are you?"

"I don't know," Dod replied uncertainly. He remembered Bonboo saying his situation was completely separate from swappers. And in truth, he had never had any mentoring from a swapper that he knew of, but the thought of him potentially being aided in the future by a swapper was not entirely ruled-out. "How can you tell?" he finally asked. "I'm clueless about tads—so if I am one, it's news to me."

Sawny jumped into the conversation, well versed about tads from books she had read. "They're people who have a potential to be aided by a swapper—or at death, become a swapper. The golden family chains are predominantly found in tredders, though reportedly there are two human chains still in existence in Soosh, with a few of their relatives here in Green. Years ago, there were just as many among drats and bobwits—but they're all gone now—"

"Gone?" mumbled Dod.

"Yes. Not everyone in a family with a golden chain is capable of being helped by a swapper, and over time, if the tads die off without new ones in their posterity, the chain disappears. I once read that some scholars suspect drat chains were originally from intermarriages with tredders and humans, and since in modern times that practice has become extremely infrequent, drat tads have vanished."

"He wants to know the distinguishing signs," said Boot, reading Dod's impatience.

"Right," said Sawny. "To be honest, I think it would be highly unlikely…" Sawny drifted off into thought for a moment and then asked, "Where did you say your ancestors came from?"

"All over," responded Dod, feeling uncomfortable. Given the truth, he couldn't think of a better response.

"Pap was aided by a swapper, wasn't he?" blurted Pone, butting into the conversation. "I thought he fought against Dreadluceous with the help of one—it was while he was an active part of the military, long before he ever came to Twistyard, right?"

Half-a-dozen others squished closer, not wanting to miss the answer.

"Well, that's a good question," stammered Dod. "I don't know for sure. He never talked about that kind of stuff with me."

"You're kidding—" gasped Pone.

"Then he wasn't!" said Voo, poking his head over Pone's shoulder. "I once heard of a family that had twelve kids, and every one of them knew all about their great-grandfather and his days as a tad, regardless of the fact that he never was chosen by a swapper for anything. And each of those poor nuggets did their best to show the signs, wanting to be like old gramps—hopeless though, none of them turned out to be a tad."

"What signs?" begged Dod.

"You're killing him, Sawny!" blurted Boot.

"Well, you're a human," said Sawny, patting Dod on the shoulder. "Logically speaking, unless your progenitors were from Soosh, I don't think you could be a tad—regardless of what Tridacello and Bowlure say."

Dod sensed that Sawny was thinking he had set his heart on being told he was a tad, since the chart had shown a pretty star, so he quickly clarified his position. "It doesn't matter to me, either way. Tad or not, I'm still the same person. I was just curious since some people seem to think I am."

Sawny sighed, as did Dilly from behind Dod.

"Good," said Dilly. "I think they made a mistake on your chart. People assume all sorts of things when they hear what you did to The Dread—or what people say you did to him. I heard one friend at The Games mention the story to another. He said you easily bested The Dread with your sword, no trouble at all. The way he spun the yarn, I would have thought you were

Humberrone. It's amazing to see what a little gossip can do to the truth."

"Sorry guys," confessed Dod apologetically. "You know me better. I was lucky. The Dread would have cut me up in little pieces if it hadn't been for—"

"And last night?" added Sawny, breaking in. "You're special, Dod. We all know you are. The way you sense things is incredible. But as for being a tad, I don't think your ear lobes hang down low enough—and you don't look well-muscled."

"Right," said Dod tentatively, glancing at his arms.

"However," continued Sawny, "ear lobes and physical strength are the most visible signs—of course, it's not like picking a turnip. In rare cases, tads have been known to not possess the outward marks. In the end, tads usually outperform most of their peers in feats of strength, agility, and skill, and that's without being aided by a swapper. It's no wonder the military is keeping track of possible candidates. They're constantly seeking recruits—people they can persuade into their Red Devils' squad."

"Oh," sighed Pone. "You have to be a tad to get in?"

"You wouldn't want to join anyway," chided Dilly. "How many of them can you think of that lived to grow old?"

"Pap did!" snapped Pone. "Wasn't he a Red Devil in his early years? I think I once read he was, and his three sons, too."

"Nope. And I would know," said Dilly affirmatively. "Pap and I were close. Not to mention, don't you think Dod would have a clue about the matter if his own father, or uncles, were ever a part of that group? Pap never once mentioned it to me. It's like the crazy tales Bowlure puffed-and-fluffed about Dod; the truth stretches and before long, it's just a bunch of cobwebs. You heard it yourself—Dod doesn't know very much about swappers.

And to talk to Bowlure, you'd think Dod was an expert. It's a slippery slope."

Dod felt uncomfortable hearing Dilly had spoken with Bowlure about the issue. The original Dod had been aided by a swapper, and Bowlure had overheard him. It was awkward. Poor Bowlure had probably told the truth as it was, but Dod wasn't about to start trying to explain how he had arrived in Green from a distant planet and stolen the other boy's identity. His friends wouldn't have believed him anyway.

"She's got a point, there," chimed Sham, jabbing at Pone. He slipped into the discussion with perfect timing, alerting the group that the guards were now directing everyone to remount and ride single-file, following a crew of soldiers to the guest quarters.

"Finally!" said Buck excitedly. "I'm starving."

"I'm not," responded Boot proudly. "But I'd happily eat if the food's as good as lunch was."

"Not more honey-roasted chicken," groaned Buck, climbing onto his horse.

"If it is, can I have yours again?" added Boot. He reveled in having devoured his brother's unwanted food. It made him feel manly.

As the group rode through the compound, Dod noticed the soldiers. They were all tredders. He learned that drats and humans shared quarters on the other side of the base. Even though the men were all part of the same army, there was certainly a pecking order in the troops, with tredders at the top, and drats, bobwits, and humans somewhere below them. The likes of the tredder soldiers that Dod saw left no question as to their capability, for they were strong-looking warriors, the type that could each single-handedly best three or four of the drat soldiers that had been left at Twistyard. Dod surveyed the crowds and couldn't help thinking Dreaderious and Dark Hood, along with all of the other trouble causers, were hopelessly fighting a losing battle.

Down by the seashore, Pious greeted Chikada warmly with a big wave, calling out to his friend. He climbed down from a large platform and welcomed Green Hall, saying he was honored that a number of Greenlings had chosen to help him attempt a goodwill mission of sorts. The crowds surrounding the stage parted to let Pious through.

The whole area was as bright as day, lit by giant stacks that hung thirty feet in the air. They made the stars completely disappear.

Pious was much smaller than Dod had expected. He was beanpole thin like Youk, and shorter—stark contrast to the massive, six-and-a-half-foot average, bulldozerish soldiers that stood around him, with some nearing seven feet. His customary tredder-black hair was sprinkled with specks of gray. His uniform was plain, void of medals he had earned, and at his side he wore a standard-issue military sword. As he approached, Chikada dismounted and greeted Pious with a hardy round of shoulder slapping. The two men appeared to be dear friends.

"We've kept dinner warm," Pious called out to his guests. "Come and eat while you watch the show. Your timing is perfect. I'll have men attend to your horses and baggage."

No sooner did Pious wave his hand above his head than dozens of drat soldiers approached, marching in lines. They aided Green Hall in dismounting, and they took their horses and gear.

Chikada, grabbing a sleepy Sammywoo by the hand, followed Pious, who led the group through the crowded courtyard to a series of stone tables positioned perfectly to see the stage. Dod stole a seat between Boot and Buck, only a few feet away from Pious and Chikada. Excitement filled the air. Over five thousand men stood around, waiting to be entertained.

"Just you wait," said Pious, nudging Chikada and Sammywoo, "I think this is the best group we've ever had. Our numbers may be lower than before, but they're the cream of the crop."

"So what are you down to?" asked Chikada. "Three hundred?"

"Ah, those were the days," answered Pious, sighing heavily. "There just aren't many of them left. I suspect we've got most of Green's, and a majority of Raul's, too. Dreadluceous successfully depleted the population during his campaign, and what he's left, Dreaderious is finishing off. Any young ones that pop up outside of our protection disappear quickly. I suspect he pays well."

"It's barbaric!" interrupted Dilly. She was seated directly next to her father with Sammywoo on her lap. "How can anyone be so heartless as to kill a child? They're not dangerous."

"Less tads, less swappers," said Pious sadly. "We're down to forty-six, and only three of them are aided by swappers. It's tragic. I suppose we may live to see the day when they'll all be a thing of the past."

"But your men are well protected," said Chikada.

"We try our best to keep them safe, but you know their fighting spirits. Asking a Red Devil to sit polished like a jewel under glass is as pointless as trying to spark ice cubes for kindling. Good thing our enemies aren't as sophisticated anymore. I think we've got it covered—swappers or not."

"And if Doss returns?"

CHAPTER TEN

Dilly and Sawny both gasped, and Boot and Buck stared with their jaws hanging open. It was easy to tell that they, along with Dod, were the only ones paying attention to the conversation, for no one else seemed interested.

"Could he?" asked Dilly, poking at her father. "I thought he was killed a long time ago. Even Bonboo was young when they defeated him. How could he come back?"

"He can't!" said Pious. "It's impossible. And Doss was an anomaly. There is absolutely no chance of seeing another person like that."

Chikada smiled and patted his daughters on their heads. "I'm talking hypothetically with Pious," he said gently. "We all know Doss is gone. Don't worry about him." He turned back toward Pious and resumed his position. "But if somehow someone like Doss emerged—someone with the capacity to jump realms without even using the portals—someone with his abilities to orchestrate chaos—what then?"

"We'd be fine," said Pious, less enthusiastically. "Swappers don't have it all. I can still hold my own with Urch and Lag, and I can nearly beat Goosh." Pious patted his sword. "Just because someone is aided by a swapper doesn't mean they're that much better."

The conversation ended abruptly when the stage lit up with action. Men dressed in black leather came swinging through the air at the end of ropes, with bright-red spider insignias on their shoulders. When they let go, each swooped onto the stage with a unique sequence of flips, somersaults, and other difficult moves. The scene resembled an intense gymnastics tournament.

Next, six flutters darted overhead. They circled the crowd and dove, whizzing by at remarkable speeds. Dod had never seen anything like it. Eventually, the men riding the flutters dismounted without landing the birds, ending up amidst their associates on the stage. The flutters then disappeared into the night sky.

Other men, dressed the same, approached from all four sides, waving swords in the air and rushing to the center. Each showed off his agility, jumping effortlessly onto the platform, six feet up.

Finally, the crowd went wild as three dots appeared overhead. The swirling objects descended until the lit courtyard revealed they were men, riding the night sky using mini-parachutes. Their landings were rough, but all three of them hit their marks.

Once the Red Devils' squad was all together, pandemonium erupted on the stage. The men fought with each other, showing off their skills. Swords clanked in the most amazing display of warfare. It reminded Dod of Clair's 'intense practice.' Dilly nearly fell off her chair. She was impressed and jealous at the same time. Her eyes couldn't hide how she felt. The Red Devils were remarkable swordsmen—and they were good at pretty much everything else it seemed.

But before the show was over, someone approached Pious discretely, bending to avoid blocking people's view of the fun, and told him that a courier had just arrived from Twistyard with an urgent communication from The Greats. He also indicated that he and his men were leery of the messenger's truthfulness, since she didn't fit the usual note-bearing qualities, and she didn't appear anywhere on their records, and she didn't have travel papers—despite having reportedly just disembarked from a docked transport in their bay.

Pious glanced at Chikada and then back to his soldier. "Just a minute," he said. "We're in the middle of the show and they haven't eaten—"

"It's all right," interrupted Chikada, sensing what they were thinking. He glanced down at his daughters and added, "They've seen enough fighting—especially this one." He pointed at Dilly. "Besides, she knows everyone at Twistyard. We'd be happy to take a look at your messenger."

Chikada stood up and hefted Sammywoo, who had fallen asleep on Dilly's lap. Sawny didn't protest in the slightest, but Dilly looked horribly torn. When they got up to leave, Dod followed. He was dying to know how anyone had left Twistyard after he had and yet had made it to Fort Castle so quickly.

"We really appreciate your help," insisted Pious. "This is such an inconvenience for you—and after a full day of riding, too. You must be starving."

"We're fine," responded Chikada.

Dilly seemed reluctant to leave. Her head was kinked over her shoulder as she walked so she could catch a few last glimpses of the clanking swords before rounding a building that would block her view.

"I'm right here," teased Dod, stepping in her line of sight.

"So I see," affirmed Dilly, stopping to take one final, envious look at the Red Devils. "They're incredible, aren't they?"

"About as good as you," replied Dod.

"Whatever," laughed Dilly, gawking at the men on the stage.

"No. Seriously," said Dod, keeping a straight face. He knew the Red Devils were better, but Dilly was on her way to being every bit as good. The only thing she lacked was a few more years of practice.

"They're tons smoother," confessed Dilly sadly.

"Nope!" stressed Dod. "It's their outfits, Dilly—the black leather and red spiders make them look official, like they mean business. Besides, when you get a crowd of them smacking things and rolling around, the commotion makes you believe they're better than they really are. It's more of an optical illusion. We Coosings could match their show if we dressed the part and hopped around with spar swords."

"You think so?" asked Dilly. She was still staring at them, pausing with her hand on the corner of the stone building that her father had rounded a minute before.

"I'm sure of it," said Dod. He peeked around the bend and couldn't see Chikada, and the lighting was much dimmer than back at the tables. "We'd better hurry," he added. "Your dad's gone."

Dilly and Dod rushed down the street in search of Pious. Dilly thought she could see the group turning at another bend, but when she reached the intersection, it was clear they hadn't. Three tredder soldiers, decked in their casual military uniforms, were walking down the shaded alley—not Pious and Chikada. The men were fighting over who got the pleasure of handling something they referred to as 'the feeding.'

"I did it last time," insisted one man, whose long hair was pulled back into a stubby tail. "She nearly bit my arm off. It's ripe for one of you to try."

"I—I just can't," stammered the smaller of the remaining two men. He cowered a few feet away from his partners, slowing his steps. "I'll clean the mess up after she's gone—take care of it all by myself—and I'll do your bunking duties for a month, too—for both of you. Just don't make me feed her."

Dod turned toward Dilly and they both crouched behind a square garbage box.

"Fine," grumbled the first man. "*You* attend to her tonight," he said, pointing at the other soldier. "C'mon, we'll help you get the fish."

The three men faded with the shadows as they trotted away toward the docks, eventually disappearing into the foggy, night air.

"Should we follow them?" whispered Dilly, restraining herself as well as she could. Her eyes were wide with excitement.

"I doubt your dad was with *them*," joked Dod.

"You think?" said Dilly. "Of course he wasn't. My dad wouldn't be out feeding some creature in the night—some creature that could snip our arms off or pluck our eyes out. Pious must have a secret weapon. Let's go take a look." Dilly stood up and started toward the darkness.

Dod lagged. His feet felt tingly and heavy with dread, the way they got when he sensed trouble was coming. "I think we should go back," he suggested nervously. "If we can't find your dad, we should return to the party. This place is hardly Twistyard. If we get caught lurking, there's no telling what the consequences would be."

"*Baby!*" teased Dilly.

"I'm serious," insisted Dod.

"Me too—*baby!*" taunted Dilly.

"Besides," argued Dod, "your dad will be disappointed if we get in trouble."

"Waa, waa. I need my diaper changed," mocked Dilly, suggesting Dod was a thumb-sucking infant.

"Okay," said Dod, giving in. "We can follow, but keep in mind that I told you this was a bad idea."

"Fine," responded Dilly, glowing with glee. "Is that my dad down there?" She raised her hand in jest. "Sawny, wait up for us."

Dilly smirked at Dod and pretended to be hurrying to catch

up with her father. The charade didn't calm Dod's nerves; his feet still felt heavy. The closer they got to the docks, the more fog cloaked the night air with a muggy, haunting blackness, and the occasional candles at the intersections seemed to cast less light on the adjoining, vacant streets.

Eventually Dod and Dilly came to a dead end of sorts. The road they had rushed down bent right and left but not straight. A waist-high rope blocked wanderers from stumbling forward off the drop at the junction. Below the ledge, Fort Castle Bay lay twinkling with partially visible lights from the ships that were shrouded by the water's nighttime fog. The sight was eerie and beautiful at the same time.

"Now where?" whispered Dod. The sounds and smells of the bay's occupants drifted in the air—the distant voices of laughter and conversation, the aroma of exotic foods on the grill, and the muffled sloshing of ships repositioning. Even though the water was hidden, the haze above it glittered like a sea of fireflies.

"Over there," said Dilly. She chose the right and prodded Dod to hurry beside her. Together they dashed along the seafront, following the cobblestone lane that slowly dipped downward. Minutes passed without seeing so much as a glimpse of the three soldiers they had set out to track or anyone else. The doublewide road was disturbingly empty considering it was still early enough that most adults were likely awake. The tattered buildings that lined the street on one side appeared to be warehouses or industrial structures, their evening silence adding testimony to their possible purposes.

"Do you want to head back now?" huffed Dod, beginning to feel winded. He looked at Dilly with concerned glances. "We've lost them, I think."

"Waa." responded Dilly playfully. "We're nearly to the water."

Another minute of jogging led the duo right to the edge of the wharf. Closest to them a rickety, wooden building rose five stories from the sea, precariously perched on crooked logs; it had shattered windows and a dilapidated roof. Further down the dock, nicer buildings seemed to skulk in the haze, watching the tethered boats bob gently. Larger ships were faintly visible, a distance off shore, and lights from additional vessels glimmered through the fog.

"Creepy, Dilly," muttered Dod. "Have you had your fill yet?" He stood motionless, breathing, staring at what looked like a prize-winning candidate for a haunted house.

"Nope," sighed Dilly. "Stick to the shadows. They've got to be around here." She slid up against a gigantic barrel, one of many that dotted the otherwise flat planks. Each pot-like structure contained a tree.

"Why would Pious have soldiers come to a place like this at night?" asked Dod. "You'd think he would have them feed their whatever-it-is during the day."

"I know," said Dilly quietly. "They're hiding it. I'm telling you, Dod, Pious is keeping a secret weapon—"

Noises from the other side of the crumbling building caught Dilly's attention and stopped their conversation. She pressed toward the opposite face, heading in the direction of a ripped hole in the wood slats. "It's got to be the soldiers," whispered Dilly smugly.

Dod's heart began to beat faster, yet he continued to follow. "Please Dilly!" he begged, tugging at her arm. "Let's get out of here. It doesn't matter what it is."

But Dilly refused to heed his words. She tiptoed across

the porch, out over the water, and felt the building sway with the sloshing waves. The clanking and creaking continued, now coming from within the hazardous structure. When they reached the gap in the outer wall, they discovered it was a tight fit. Dilly went first, pushing the broken boards out of her way as she entered. Dod followed, smelling the rotten wood beneath him. He didn't speak for fear of being discovered, but he still repeatedly pulled at Dilly.

Old, deteriorating ropes, fishnets, and ship gear lay strewn on the floor and draped over fallen beams and piles of debris. Many parts of the upper levels had collapsed, creating the junkyard they stood in and the open vaults above them. It was amazing that the outer walls were still intact, considering the wretched state of the inside.

A hazy light stole its way out of a distant room and past the rubble to Dod and Dilly. Rats scurried back and forth, in and out of the rubbish. Some of them were as big as small cats. Vapor from their droppings drenched the wet air with a pungency that overpowered the rotten wood.

Dilly no longer looked adventurous. She delicately waded a distance into the mess, plugging her nose, and then conceded with a nod to Dod that they could leave and forget the matter. Her curiosity wasn't strong enough to get her to journey across the battlefield of vermin-infested terrain to the other side of the hall where the men would be visible.

No sooner did they turn to leave than their retreat was foiled.

"I've been collecting it over here," said a voice that grew louder as people entered the main chamber. One man carried a torch that hissed and sputtered. The flickering glow stirred the army of rats to motion, sending them away from the approaching people. Hundreds of critters scurried about, squeaking. With the added light, the whole floor seemed to move.

Dod and Dilly scampered through knee-deep, nasty piles of decomposing junk and ducked behind a larger mound of waste. It was too late to make a run for the breach in the back wall without exposing themselves.

As Dilly had predicted, it was the three soldiers. They entered the room with an additional man—someone who wasn't wearing a uniform. Together, the small group made their way to a corner of the hall and began shoveling something into bags.

"Will this be enough fish?" asked one of Pious's men.

"It'll tide her over," responded the visitor. "We'll move her tomorrow."

Dod stared through the maze of clutter, past the cobwebs and wriggling frenzy of rats, and tried to see the new face. The man's voice sounded vaguely familiar. It piqued his interest.

Suddenly, Dilly froze stiff as stone and her breathing quickened. When Dod looked at her, he saw terror in her eyes. She pointed frantically at her bracelet. It had tilted its way into a brighter pocket of light, revealing that the color was no longer a shade of yellow—it was shiny red! "Gizzlers," she muttered softly but hysterically. "Gizzlers! Gizzlers!"

"Maybe not," whispered Dod. He didn't want to get caught, and he was increasingly feeling like the actions of the soldiers were not entirely approved by Pious.

The ground below them moaned and the building shook rhythmically, responding to a series of larger waves.

"Gizzlers!" continued Dilly, getting louder.

Dod nudged her to keep quiet. "Please," he begged, "Shush."

A large rat hopped from a nearby beam and landed on Dod's

back. Dod gasped and shook it off. A knot lodged in his throat from fright, making it hard for him to breathe the noxious air.

"Gizzlers!" repeated Dilly, feverishly rubbing her bracelet. She began to shiver uncontrollably.

"And then what?" barked one of Pious's men in an agitated voice. "We have the numbers, don't we?"

Dod only glanced momentarily in their direction. Most of the conversation was muffled anyway—not that it mattered; he and Dilly had their heads too full of their own problems to care about the argument that was beginning across the sea of approaching rats.

Something large moved in the darkness near the floor. It crossed Dilly's feet and rubbed at her leg.

"GIZZLER!" screamed Dilly, jumping up and down. She let out such a cry that everyone at Fort Castle likely heard her.

The commotion instantly alerted the suspicious men, who dropped their shovels and drew their swords. Dod pushed at Dilly, who was busily surpassing her morning's dance. He tried to get her to the hole in the wall, but his efforts were useless. She was completely incapable of wading through the mounds of refuse to the exit.

Finally, in desperation, feeling the four men approaching, Dod swung Dilly over his shoulder and bolted for freedom. It didn't matter that she was nearly his same size—he was in survival mode, fleeing from the soldiers like a rabbit dashing from a pack of baying hounds.

After flying over the junk, Dod rammed Dilly through the slot, head first, and then followed vigorously behind. Outside, the porch was dotted with rats and gizzlers, escaping the building through cracks in the wall. Some of the poisonous red snakes were over twelve feet long.

Dod hopped to his feet and forced Dilly to run. He had a bad feeling about the men. In his gut, Dod knew their intent wasn't to bring prisoners before Pious, it was to silence anyone with knowledge of their activities.

By the time Dilly and Dod reached the cobblestone road, one of the soldiers had made it out and was pursuing. His dedication to catching them proved he had plenty to hide.

For a few minutes, things seemed hopeless for Dod and Dilly; neither of them had a sword, and the running man was stronger and faster—he was gaining on them. He'd have easily finished things if he hadn't first been slowed by the mounds of junk and the narrow slit. Fortunately, before he caught up, a carriage approached, surrounded by fifteen horsemen, and magically, the chase ended.

MORE THAN A DARE

"Ludicrous!" blared someone from within the guarded carriage. "I'll tell you this much—it's ludicrous!"

Dod and Dilly bent over, gulping for air. They had narrowly escaped the blade of the rogue soldier, who was now nowhere to be found. Like the shadows that had fled with the approaching torches, he too had disappeared.

"Hold your place!" ordered the front horseman, drawing his sword. "What are you doing on shore? This is a military base." His eyes glared at Dod more than Dilly.

"We know," huffed Dilly, bedraggled. "We're...uh—" She strained to catch her breath enough to speak.

"I'll need to take you in," he continued, glancing down at a series of patches and medals on his uniform. "It's not lawful to enter this facility without approval."

"We know," wheezed Dilly, making a second attempt. "We're with the Coosings—"

"See—" added Dod, equally spent. He staggered as he moved forward to show off his Coosing ring.

"We were with Pious—" continued Dilly, but she was rudely snipped off.

"Don't mock my intelligence!" boomed the man incredulously. "You just came from the docks! You can't sweet talk your way out of trouble around here, little missy!"

"What?" gasped Dilly, looking shocked. She had likely never been doubted before. "I-I'm Bonboo's great-granddaughter," she professed indignantly, rising to a proper position. "We've already had our papers checked."

"And I'm Commendus," mocked the officer.

"Ludicrous!" wailed a disgruntled voice from somewhere behind the locked doors of the windowless carriage. "Are you going to let me out, or not?" A muffled banging sound ensued.

One heavy soldier, his stomach bulging over his belt, nudged his horse closer to the wagon and thumped his meaty hands against the side, saying, "We're not there yet, smelly hag. But we've got some company for ya."

The lead officer nodded and two robust tredders slipped off of their steeds and guided Dilly and Dod to the wagon.

"We can circle them back to the holding yards," ordered the man in charge, "just as soon as we've discovered the truth about *her*." He pointed at the carriage with his sword.

Shockingly, when the clanking and fussing was over, the door opened and revealed none other than Ingrid sitting within.

"Ingrid?" sputtered Dilly, climbing aboard. "W-when did you arrive?"

"See boys," bellowed the old woman, glaring angrily at the battalion of tredders. She shook her cane at them and boomed, "This girl knows my name! I told you I'm well branded at Twistyard! My cousin's Higga, the famous doctor! Now let me speak with Pious!"

The ranting wasn't addressed directly; rather, the door was slammed in her face and locked.

"Ludicrous!" muttered Ingrid to Dod and Dilly. She occupied two seats with her four hundred pounds and stunk like rotten garlic. She wore a tentish, long-sleeved red-and-white dress that came nearly to her ankles and eight tacky necklaces, each dripping with cheap, cut-glass jewels. "Here I've dressed up and traveled all this way to meet Pious and they treat me like this. It's Ludicrous! I'm sure Bonmoob wouldn't allow this sort of treatment to a lady."

"You're right," sighed Dilly sadly. She glanced down at her soiled shoes, rat-pee pants, and scraped arm, and then somberly looked at Dod. "Sorry about not listening to you—"

"We're alive, aren't we?" responded Dod. He began to smile through his exhaustion, glad that they hadn't been bitten by a gizzler or stabbed to death by a rogue soldier.

"But they didn't believe me," groaned Dilly dejectedly, still partially in shock from her blood-curdling experience with gizzlers. "Why didn't they believe me?"

"Join the crowd," said Dod. "It'll be okay."

"Hardly," groaned Dilly, noticing her foot peeking through a hole in her suede shoe. "My buckle's ripped off."

Ingrid began to laugh. She roared until her heavy frame shook and the mounds of fat under her chin wobbled side to side. "What happened to you, girl?" she choked in a rough voice, not sounding like much of a lady. "You've lost more than your buckle! With your hair like that, I'd say you've lost your mind."

Dilly reached to primp her curls and drew back a giant, rat-dung-laden cobweb from her hair, complete with a quarter-sized spider within it.

Ingrid laughed hysterically until it forced her into a bout of garbled coughs. Unwell, she hunched over, leaning on her thick cane, and barked into a ragged handkerchief.

The carriage ride was brief. By the time Ingrid had regained her composure, the door swung open and Ingrid was invited to leave.

"What about them?" she asked, glancing over her shoulder at Dod and Dilly as she poured her weight onto a trembling soldier, who aided her in exiting.

"Pious wants to see just you," said the lead tredder.

"But they're from Twistyard," protested Ingrid. "Let them go!"

"My men will decide where they're from," snapped the officer.

"You ridiculous buffoon!" boomed Ingrid, inadvertently spitting on the face of the poor man who stood by. "Do you know who *she* is?" she said, swinging her cane recklessly at Dilly. "She's Bonmoob's great-granddaughter! And as for that one," she pointed at Dod, "he's Pap's grandson—the lucky soul who captured The Dread! How dumb can you possibly be?"

The man in charge looked doubtfully at Dod and Dilly, who both appeared pathetic and dirty, and then waved his hand. "I suppose we'll take them, too," he said. "Pious has experts—they'll know if these drops are from Twistyard or not."

No sooner had Dilly emerged from the carriage than Chikada came bursting out of Pious's opulent dwelling.

"What happened to you?" gasped Chikada, racing to his daughter. He knew something had gone wrong when he saw how her clothes and hair were awry.

"Gizzlers—" muttered Dilly, holding back tears and shivering.

"We lost sight of you," added Dod, not nearly as traumatized. "And once you were gone, we ended up at the docks—searching. That first shack—the rickety old one—is filled with gizzlers."

"Dreadful," said Pious from his front porch. "I've been meaning to have my men remove that thing—"

"And you thought we were in it?" asked Chikada, looking at his daughter.

Dilly sobered. "We heard noises, Dad."

"I do make noises," sighed Chikada, trying to help his daughter smile. "Next time, honey, if you get lost like that, just go back with the others—all right?"

Dod grinned. It was the second time Dilly had been given the same sound advice.

At the entry, Pious directed Dilly and Dod toward the bathroom, suggesting they could take turns cleaning up. But fearing they hadn't understood how thoroughly he meant, he also added, "I'll send men with Sawny to collect your bags so you'll have something to wear when we—uh—burn those."

"Good idea, Pious!" rambled Ingrid, huffing as she broke her way into the conversation. "They stink like rats!" She struggled to catch up, thumping the wooden floor with her cane.

"*We'll* meet over there," responded Pious, pointing back toward the entry.

"Fine enough, but can't you let an old lady like myself use your facility first. I'm likely to leak any minute. Your men rudely dragged me away from the shipyard, claiming I was trouble for not having papers—can you believe that—*me* trouble? And I told them the darn things blew right out of my hands while at sea—not much I could do. The shippies had me plopped on the outer deck for the whole day—and all alone with the wind blowing in my face, too. Ludicrous! What rudeness! You would think at my age I'd be treated better. They should have seated me within the cabin! Of course I lost my papers!"

Pious noticed her smell and changed plans—he decided to expedite things with Ingrid to avoid filling his house with her odors. "Dilly, can you vouch for this woman?"

"She's Higga's cousin," said Dilly. "Her name's Ingrid. She's currently staying at Twistyard and doing her share of service—Voracio has her splitting quarters with Juny Chantolli."

"No telling what side that woman's on!" barked Ingrid, becoming more agitated.

"She's a victim," said Chikada, joining the conversation. "Juny's innocent of Sirlonk's crimes. She's been carefully researched."

"Not careful enough for me!" grumbled Ingrid. "Only time will truly tell. With how brilliantly planned The Dread's schemes were, nothing would surprise me. This Dark Hood fellow pales horribly in comparison—"

"I'm told you have an urgent message from Twistyard," said Pious, his eyes beginning to water as Ingrid leaned upon him.

"Right—I have it here," the old woman said, reaching into her dog-eared purse. She drew a folded leather wad that would have occupied the bulk of her handbag. "Shortly after Dod left for The Games with Youk, aboard his *opulent* ride, Tridacello obtained *this*—right from Dark Hood."

"Then they've captured him!" blurted Pious happily. "That's fantastic!"

"No!" snapped Ingrid "With drat guards, they haven't a chance. Perhaps if you sent a thousand of your best—"

"And the message," rushed Pious, sticking out his hand. A tear rolled down his cheek, proving the strong man had weak eyes around caustic smells.

Pious opened the leather and discovered it was a map of Green, dotted with stars.

"The Greats think Dark Hood is planning attacks on these places," said Ingrid. "He must be working with Dreaderious—"

"Unbelievable!" muttered Pious.

"That's a lot," added Dod, squeezing between Dilly and Chikada to see. There were over a hundred targets, and they were scattered across the whole world.

"Well," continued Ingrid. "The Greats thought you ought to be aware. They nearly lost two soldiers getting this—the men are recovering from a real dashing. And Dark Hood didn't have his helper, either. But at least he was driven off."

"So how did they get it?" asked Dilly, pointing at the map.

"It fell out of his cloak as he retreated," responded Ingrid.

"Then you're sure he was seen after we left Twistyard?" asked Dod, feeling the story wasn't adding up."

"Yes!" said Ingrid, grabbing at Dod's arm. She shifted her wait off of Pious, who then retreated a few paces. "Dark Hood tried to break into the Histo Relics Building yesterday morning, while it was still dark. No telling what he wanted. But guards spotted the old rascal and gave him chase."

Dod wiped spit off his cheek. Her Ps and Bs were wet.

"And Tridacello?" asked Dilly.

"He's fine," said Ingrid. "The wounded soldiers turned this over to him, and he sent me off within the hour by carriage to Fisher. If he'd have gotten it a few minutes earlier, he could have handed it over to Youk and I'd have been saved an unpleasant two days. I arrived, seaside, late last night and then spent all of today in the wind, coming here—well, I'm glubbed!"

Dod hated keeping Ingrid any longer, but he had to know when Dark Hood had struck. "So how can you tell whether

Dark Hood fought the soldiers before we left, or after?" asked Dod, cringing as he waited for the answer.

"Because!" boomed Ingrid, spraying Dod's cheek again. "I'm not stupid! Youk must have departed Twistyard near the middle of the night to get you to The Games in time to suit up and play."

"Oh," groaned Dod. "I guess Dark Hood probably attacked while we were still there," he concluded sadly.

"You didn't play?" gasped Ingrid, looking shocked. "Why in the world would Youk pull a flutter favor if it weren't to save Green Hall from losing at Bollirse?"

Dod pointed at Sammywoo, who was sound asleep on Chikada's shoulder. Sawny had been seated holding the boy, but had left with soldiers to retrieve luggage.

"For him?" chortled Ingrid in disbelief. "Parents do the strangest things for their wee ones! It's good I never had kids. I like being logical."

Pious waved his hand and instructed men to situate Ingrid in nice quarters by herself, so she could be shown proper respect. Ingrid returned the kindness with a shower of platitudes and warm wishes.

Later, after Dilly and Dod had scrubbed the night's mishap out of their hair, Pious's wife fed them dinner and invited the group to stay in her private guestrooms. Dilly, Sawny, and Sammywoo slept in one, and Chikada and Dod slept in the other, across the hall. The accommodations were perfect. And surprisingly, Sammywoo didn't so much as peep the whole night. The only thing that troubled Dod's sleep was calculating how to make sure Dilly and Sawny wouldn't notice the large painting of Red Devils on Pious's study wall. Dod had examined it, while waiting for Dilly to finish in the bathroom, and had observed that Pappileehonogoso's face was in the bunch—the old Pap, not Dod's grandpa Pap.

In the morning, Dod took a seat next to Sammywoo. Pious's kitchen table was heaping with piles of ham, fried eggs, French toast, and chilled fruit. A knock at the front door drew Pious away for a minute before he returned, wearing a curious look.

"Your daughter was right about gizzlers and the Old Pier House," said Pious, plopping back down next to Chikada. He glanced at Dilly and nodded. "My men made a sad find. I ordered them to prep the wreck for a burning this morning, so they drew perimeters and made a thorough search, only to discover Chance Hissop was dead inside, knee deep in garbage. The poor man was always timid, to put it kindly. I think his squad must have pushed him with a nighttime dare, not realizing how many poisonous serpents were hiding amongst the wreckage. It's an awful tragedy."

"And it could have been you!" blurted Sawny, catching Dilly's eyes. She knew better than anyone that Dilly's love for adventure had likely placed her in the deathtrap.

"I know," said Dilly, feeling fortunate. "My life was saved by this." She held up her wrist, showing off the yellowish Redy-Alert-Band. "Dod gave it to me. It turns red when snakes are around."

"Fascinating," said Pious in a subdued voice. "Poor Chance should've been wearing it." He turned to Chikada and added, "You probably knew the man's grandpa—Hal Hissop. He fought years ago, down south—"

"Hal's grandson!" moaned Chikada. "That's a shame. Their family's seen too much misfortune already."

CHAPTER ELEVEN

When breakfast was over, Dod helped the girls heft their bags out the front door and onto the horses that were waiting. Nearly all of Green Hall was ready to ride. They were parked in the street, wishing well the Greenlings that planned to go abroad as goodwill ambassadors.

"Looks like your dreams came true," said Boot, greeting Dilly with a grin. "You slept indoors where you didn't have to worry about gizzlers. The rest of us had to keep one eye open all night, since Pone found a dead snake by our tents. It was a five-footer if it was an inch. The sight of it set us all on edge. I'd imagine you'd need therapy if you'd have seen it. Gizzlers are limp-neck scary looking in real life."

"Tell me about it!" laughed Dilly.

"You don't want to know," added Buck ominously. "The beast we saw was probably the biggest one anyone's seen."

"I doubt that," said Dod. He, like Dilly, was beginning to chuckle.

"No really," chimed Pone, his mouth full of biscuits. "I don't know if they get much bigger than that ripe thing. Its fangs were huge."

"They do!" said Sawny, breaking the squabble. "A grown gizzler can pass ten feet if it's had plenty to eat—"

"Or twelve—" blurted Dod. "We saw a bunch of them last night and two or three were far beyond ten.

"What?" coughed Boot. "We? 'We' meaning who?"

"Dilly and I," said Dod. "It's a long story."

Dilly beamed smugly as she climbed aboard Song. "We'll tell you later," she said, raising her eyebrows.

As the clan from Twistyard exited Fort Castle, smoke from the Old Pier House billowed high into the air, tarnishing the perfect azure sky. It was hard for Dod and his fellows to leave friends behind. Eight Greenlings boarded ships for faraway lands, and Chikada lingered at Fort Castle, having been convinced by Pious to stay for a few more days before heading home to Terraboom. Bowy wasn't in the group, either, though Dod learned while traveling that Bowy had parted ways at Carsigo, determined to take his horse on a northbound ship rather than ride the extra days he would have spent clomping alone from Two Tree to Ridgeland. Dilly's father had given him money for the sea fare.

Ingrid, however, stayed no longer at Fort Castle than she needed to, and fearing she'd be forced once again to face the wind and waves from the outer decks, she begged a three-seat buckboard and two horses from Pious—loaners from Twistyard that needed to be returned anyway—and joined the procession toward High Gate.

Unfortunately, one hour at the reins exhausted Ingrid, so Boot pressed upon the boys from Green Hall and had them all draw straws for the 'honor' of driving Ingrid's wagon. Toos magically came up with the shortest stick and found himself squished next to Ingrid, helping her along while his horse trotted behind them, tethered to the back rail.

Buck sighed heavily when he drew a safe pick. Even though Boot had made it clear that they all had an equal chance of being encumbered with the task, Buck knew Boot well enough to suspect some sort of trickery—and seeing the way Boot smiled and teased Toos before Toos drew poorly only cemented Buck's assumptions.

The day's ride was long and difficult. From Fort Castle to Two Tree, the road wound back and forth, gaining thousands of feet in elevation. And from Two Tree to Last Chance, the sheer distance they had to travel before sundown required a fast pace, which stirred the dust as they galloped.

By the time Dod and his friends laid down for the night, their muscles were sore and they could taste grit.

The day after was different, but still difficult. Well before sunup, the group had to race from Last Chance to High Gate's eastern entrance before the noon dropping of the triblot barrier. Aside from waking up early, most of Green Hall didn't mind putting some hours in before daylight, since much of the terrain was the westernmost tip of the Ankle Weed Desert.

For miles, there wasn't a tree or blade of grass in sight to the east. The sand was a brownish, puke-green color, which grew hot as the sun beat down on it. Despite regular rainfall, the poisonous ground kept plants from growing. The only thing that thrived in the desolate land was Driaxom—the worst prison in Green. Convicts from all over the globe were confined there if their offenses were grave enough to justify a living-death sentence. One lonely, worn-down sign noted the turnoff for Driaxom. It looked like a road to nowhere; it shot straight out into the bleak, flat landscape and disappeared with the mirages on the horizon.

As they passed it, Dod felt uncomfortable. Part of him wanted to ride across the forbidden landscape and see Sirlonk—Dod wanted his own two eyes to prove to his mind that The Dread was imprisoned. He couldn't help wondering how Sirlonk was enjoying his stay, and he hoped that somehow the rough circumstance would prod the cruel man into telling what he knew about the growing tide of evil. But they were pointless thoughts. Driaxom traditionally didn't allow visitors, and if Sirlonk was cursed with an Ankle Weed—doomed to go crazy—he'd surely feel no need to speak up.

Once near High Gate, the group hustled to get in before it was too late. The east entrance was bigger and more traveled than the other accesses—and it wasn't only bogged down with land-faring traffic; supply boats that had already been checked and papered at Lake Charms were allowed to progress along the Blue River into High Gate's harbor. Thousands of people passed through daily. However, when crowds exceeded the usual number, many people were turned away by the second string of ringing bells and were forced to remain outside of High Gate until the next day.

"It looks like we're lucky this time," remarked Sawny, noticing that the line was moving fast enough that they'd make the cut.

"Stay together everyone," called Dilly, almost like a mother. She nudged Song to circle the group as she counted heads. "We're missing two," declared Dilly, putting the problem on Boot's shoulders. "And *you've* got to hurry and find them. I'll be cross for a week if we blow our engagement with Commendus tonight!"

"I'm sure they're around here somewhere," said Boot calmly. "Maybe you miscounted."

"No!" insisted Dilly, craning her head to see faces. "We've lost—let's see—Coosings are all here...and the Greenling girls are all here—so it's two Greenling boys."

"Figures," said Boot. "I bet I know where they are. Hold tight in line and I'll round them up. I wouldn't want your evening to be ruined."

Boot started his horse into the crowd when he stopped and hollered back, "Hey Dod, come give me a hand."

Together, Boot and Dod passed through a sea of people.

Hundreds of them were riding in bright-red carriages—Green's equivalent of taxis and buses.

Down by the river at the water's edge, Boot went straight to the two Greenlings, who sat on their horses admiring something.

"How did you know they'd be over here?" asked Dod. A canopy of trees hid their position from the thoroughfare up the embankment.

"They're trying to get a good look at the line in the water," said Boot. "If you're at the right angle, it's pretty clear where the triblot field covers. The water's a little greener than everywhere else—see?"

"Oh," said Dod, not terribly interested.

"The triblot field cuts to the bottom of the river," continued Boot. "It's over eighty feet deep in some places. Years ago, a band of renegades were kicked out of High Gate for treasonous activity and were forbidden to reenter. So look over there—" Boot pointed at a twenty-foot-long submarine that was suspended from metal cables, attached to the side of a mid-water guard tower.

"The rascals thought they could stroll in undetected. And as you can guess, they all died. I bet it was awful. Now the sub hangs up there to remind people that that sort of action is really stupid. The only way through a triblot field is to wait 'til it's lowered."

"Unless you fly over it and drop in," said a Greenling named Hermit. He glanced at Boot with mischievous eyes and smiled, knowing he and his friend had been caught wandering off.

"Wouldn't work," said Boot. "That's been tried before, too. A flutter can hardly fly high enough to get above the bubble. But one once nearly did. The crazy Red Devil riding it thought he'd be the first to prove that you can pass through the field alive if you're falling. He figured he'd drop below the line, then pop his gear and coast to the ground with a royal headache."

"Wow," sighed Hermit, imagining the sight.

"But he underestimated the power of the triblot field," said Boot. "He never even got a chance to dismount. The poor flutter flew so high that the winds pushed him into the upper reaches of the triblot's grasp, and by the time they had fallen low enough to pass the danger line, they were dead—or at least unconscious. I guess it was hard for anyone to make heads or tails of their deaths since their remains were scattered across the roof of Champion Stadium."

"Eew," gagged Hermit.

"It just goes to show," added Boot, holding his best stern face, "You should stick to the rules and follow orders or you'll end up pigeon feed."

"Right," mumbled Hermit, tapping at his horse's reins. "Sorry about coming down here without telling you."

"It's okay," said Boot. "Just let me know next time. You could have been left behind, and then I'd have been stuck eating your share of the banquet Commendus is hosting for us tonight."

The two boys glanced at Boot admiringly.

When the foursome reached the Green Hall crowd, they were just in time to begin entering the wide lane to High Gate. Dilly was terribly anxious since she had seen the five-minute warning rag. The soldiers positioned at the entrance to High Gate had waved a white sheet-like piece of fabric to coordinate with the soldiers who were stationed at the guardhouse outside of the triblot barrier.

"You nearly missed it!" scolded Dilly.

Boot didn't respond. He was preoccupied with watching a large family of noble tredders who had just exited High Gate and were waiting for a private transport. They circled around something and were calling out to each other.

"Boot!" continued Dilly, "We're going."

"Right," said Boot, bringing up the rear. Alongside of him, a band of six soldiers rode; they had been assigned to escort the last people of the day into High Gate. A much larger battalion of soldiers held a line by the outer guardhouse, preventing anyone else from entering.

In the distance, bells began ringing, making their way around the city. Boot kept looking over his shoulder; concern shrouded his face—he was horribly conflicted. When he reached the halfway mark, he spun his horse around and yelled, "Ya! Ya!" coaxing Grubber to bolt. Dilly and Dod, who were also in the rear, turned in shock. Boot was racing away from High Gate, leaving himself with no time to return!

WORTH DYING FOR

"Where does he think he's going?" asked Dilly, staring over her shoulder. She couldn't believe Boot was riding away from them. With the bells ringing and the guards watching, he was headed for trouble. Commotion and excitement of any kind were not tolerated around the entries to High Gate, especially when the triblot startup or dropdown sequence was underway.

"I don't know." said Dod. He had a sick feeling in his stomach.

The six soldiers who had trotted beside Boot kept their place in the farthest rear, pushing the group to move faster. They didn't even look back at Boot, knowing that the militia who waited by the guardhouse would discipline him severely.

Boot's horse ran like it was in the Kentucky Derby and only slowed a little as it reached the wall of standing soldiers. Out of necessity, the men parted, but weren't happy about it. They signaled to other guards, who were already mounted on horses a short distance away. It looked ugly for Boot.

Finally, Grubber stopped at the edge of the noblemen

Boot had been eyeing. Lickety-split, Boot slid off his horse and disappeared into the middle of the crowd and then pushed his way back out, fighting past two large tredders who tried to prevent him from leaving. He flew into his saddle like a bank robber running from the cops and bolted for the entry road to High Gate.

By the time he reached the wall of soldiers, it had been fortified with fifteen mounted guards, and right behind him, nipping on his heels, he had five more.

The Green Hall crowd had already made it to High Gate before Boot met up with the battalion, so from a distance they watched helplessly, all the while hearing the ringing of the bells.

"What's he doing?" moaned Buck.

"I don't know," said Sawny nervously, "but he's headed to jail—"

"Or worse," cried Dilly. "It looks like they're drawing their swords."

But Boot didn't slow down—he sped up!

At full press, Grubber charged into the line of steeds. Since he was a larger breed, his body pushed the other horses aside, causing a breach in the wall, and despite a few swords that waved in the air, Boot slid past, ducking his head as he flew toward the closed road to High Gate.

No one followed. The triblot field would be up in minutes, or possibly seconds, and anyone crossing over at that time would be torturously killed by the brain-splitting waves.

"He's crazy!" cried Buck, squinting anxiously. "All the riding we've done has driven him mad. Why's he doing it?"

"Tell me when it's over," whined Sawny, covering her eyes with her hands. She couldn't help counting how close the bells were to their completion. The invisible barrier would be fully operational in seconds.

"He'll make it," said Dilly in a hollow sort of voice. She hesitated a few seconds, holding back tears, and added, "He better! Come on, Boot!"

All of Green Hall was rooting for Boot to live, even though it was a foregone conclusion that if he did, he was in a heaping load of trouble. Hundreds of soldiers stood ready to apprehend him.

"Ten...nine...eight..." counted Sawny quietly. She knew the system well enough to call it.

Dod couldn't take his eyes off Boot, but was next to Sawny, so he heard the numbers—and he knew they didn't add up. "Please be wrong," mumbled Dod. "Please be wrong." He was hoping that for once Sawny had judged poorly.

Boot raced his fastest, leaving clouds of dust behind him.

"Seven...six...five..."

"I can't watch," confessed Dilly, joining her sister in turning away; she reached behind Sawny, who rode double with Sammywoo, and covered the boy's eyes as she buried her own head close to theirs. Boot was still a fair distance out.

"Four...three...two..." whispered Sawny. She didn't say one. Even if she had, nobody would have heard her.

"AWE! NO! NO!" roared the crowd. They knew the instant the triblot field went into place by Grubber's spastic movements, and Boot wrenched at his ears and head in agony.

"Boot!" screamed Dilly, turning back to see him. She was sobbing. Sawny wouldn't look, and after a few seconds, most of Green Hall had turned their heads away, too, overcome with grief. Their jovial leader was dying a horrendous death, and his distant cries were enough to nearly tear their hearts from their chests.

Toos, who faithfully sat squished next to Ingrid on the buckboard, couldn't take the emotions he felt and began vomiting over the side.

No! thought Dod. *There must be something—some trick I can do that will save him.* But his mind remained as empty as the road in front of Boot.

Grubber continued running, though he zigzagged hopelessly, casting his head about as if he were being whipped across the face and knifed in the rear.

Eventually, Boot slumped over and his lifeless body bounced up and down, beginning to slide out of the saddle. He would have immediately fallen off if it weren't for his arms that were wrapped up in the reins.

"BOOT!" screamed Dilly, pushing her horse past the others. She went dangerously close to the triblot field and began yelling to Grubber, who had started to stray in a sideways direction. "COME ON, BOY! OVER HERE, GRUBBER!"

Hearing her call, he staggered toward her and marched out of the triblot field. The horse nearly collapsed at Dilly's side. He leaned against Song for support.

Dod and Buck rushed to help Boot off his horse, followed by a crowd of Coosings. They untangled his arms from the reins and set his body on the ground.

Dilly slid her head up to Boot's chest and listened, while gently rubbing his cheek with her hand.

"Please, please, please be alive," whispered Sawny, approaching through the crowd. Unfortunately, her fears were justified.

"He's dead!" wailed Dilly, shaking with grief. "He's dead!"

Pone slid her aside and eagerly bent down to Boot's chest, listening for any signs of life. Ten seconds passed, then fifteen, then twenty. Finally, Pone raised his head and shook it sadly. A tear rolled down his face. "Boot's dead," he said somberly. "He's really dead."

The howls and cries that instantly followed filled the air with such sorrow that the waiting soldiers retreated, ashamed to watch any more. Buck, overcome with the moment, collapsed to his knees and grabbed Boot's hand. "You can't die, Boot," he sobbed. "You just can't die. I can't live without you, Boot. You're the best brother anyone could ever ask for."

Dilly wept uncontrollably at Boot's side, stroking his hair and mumbling things through her tears that were meant for only Boot to hear.

Dod had a huge lump in his throat that he couldn't swallow. Boot was his best friend, and now he was dead. It wasn't fair, it wasn't right. The moment didn't fit. It was so horrid that Dod pinched his skin, wishing he could wake up and hear Boot slipping a snake into his bed or a bag of rocks into his shoes. But Dod didn't wake up—he was already awake. The surreal moment was reality—a horrible, awful, nasty, bitter reality.

Sawny wiped at her tears and struggled to breathe. "Why?" she whispered. "Why, Boot. Why?"

Sammywoo momentarily left Sawny's hand to solemnly set his beloved swot next to Boot. It was the first time he'd let go of it since leaving Twistyard days before.

Dod wished in his heart to flee away, to disappear, to not have to listen to his friends' agony any more; his own grief was nearly past what he could bear as it was. And so he thought of home, and then he was filled with hope.

Without hesitation, Dod dropped to his knees and desperately began to do something he had learned over the summer: It was CPR! His movements were awkward and sloppy compared to the paramedics who had taught the course, but Dod did them with more conviction than anything he had ever done before.

Fifteen chest compressions per two breaths, thought Dod. He counted them in his mind as he worked to save Boot's life. Up and down, up and down, over and over he went. The task was exhausting. Within a minute his arms were burning, and after three he was seeing stars. But he didn't stop. He couldn't. He desperately wanted Boot to live.

Come on, Boot! begged Dod in his mind. Tears of sorrow and frustration streamed down his cheeks. *Come back to us! You have to! We all need you, Boot!*

Knowing nothing of CPR, the Green Hall crowd would have pulled Dod away if it weren't for the heroic saves he'd already done. Given his track record, however, no one attempted to stop him. They continued sobbing along with him and tried to hold out for a miracle.

Eventually, Dod's strength gave out. He had worked so hard that his body couldn't physically do it any more. He collapsed beside his lifeless friend and fought to stay conscious. The guilt he felt over failing to bring Boot back was almost unbearable.

Suddenly, a raspy gasp leaked from Boot's lips. Was it just air escaping or was he really breathing? The circle of mourners around Boot and Dod went silent, praying desperately that he'd do it again.

And then it happened—another raspy gasp, and then another, and then another. Boot was breathing. His shallow, wispy, hardly-noticeable breaths were the most wonderful sounds that his friends had ever heard.

"Boot! You're alive!" sobbed Dilly, hurrying to hug him. She was elated. She continued crying, though her tears of sorrow had turned to tears of emotional unrest mixed with joy.

Buck lingered with his hope and wore a worried, weepy face.

Boot didn't respond right away, but he kept breathing, and with each gulp of air, he got stronger. Slowly, his pale face began to regain its normal color. Then he coughed and choked and drowsily opened his eyes.

"Don't ever try that—okay, Buck," said Boot groggily in a faint, scratchy voice. He blinked and strained to see his younger brother.

"You too," responded Buck, plunging in to hug him. He was overjoyed. "I thought we'd lost you," whispered Buck.

"You thought…or you h-hoped?" mumbled Boot, struggling to speak. His wit was coming back faster than his voice.

Dod continued to rest on the ground, trying to regain his own head. He felt like he had just completed a race and had pushed himself harder than ever before. It made him dizzy and nauseous.

"Dod, how did you do that?" asked Sawny, big-lipped with restrained emotion. She was drawn to know more, for she'd never read of anything like it, much less seen a demonstration.

Dod shrugged his shoulders. The rollercoaster of events had taken every ounce of his strength—both physically and emotionally.

Boot felt the shrug and turned toward Dod. "What happened to *him*?" he asked wearily.

"He just saved your life!" responded Dilly, stepping over Boot to congratulate Dod with a pat on the shoulder. "And it's a good thing he did—well—otherwise—who would help me carry my bags?" Her playful tone and stuttered words were strained, but regardless of how hard it was, Dilly pushed herself to act normal. She didn't want Boot finding out how she felt about him—and she wished everyone else would forget what they'd heard.

But Boot didn't buy it. He noticed her tear-streaked cheeks and bright-red eyebrows and knew Dilly cared more for him than just as a baggage boy, though he wasn't going to call her on it.

"I'll do my best, my lady," he teased and then spun into a bout of coughs.

"Perhaps when you're feeling better, kind sir," responded Dilly. She walked over to her horse and fetched a canteen of juice. "Here," she said to Boot. "Maybe this will help."

When he reached for the drink, their hands met momentarily. Dilly's heart raced and she blushed.

"What were you doing back there anyway?" she asked, looking through the triblot field at the distant guardhouse. She turned the conversation over to him, hoping he wouldn't notice her flushed cheeks. After nearly losing Boot, it was hard for her to hide the way she felt.

"Oh!" said Boot, perking up. "Buck, can you grab my bag for me?"

Dod sat up and eagerly waited. What had Boot risked his life to get? And who were the people he had confronted?

When Buck set the bag at Boot's side, most of the Green Hall crowd came scurrying back and formed a tight circle. Once they realized Boot was well enough to explain what had happened, they were all dying to hear the tale. Even Ingrid wanted a front-row spot, so she hobbled from her wagon and pushed people out of her way with her cane.

"I guess you're all wondering—" started Boot, looking around at the mob.

"Yes we are!" boomed Ingrid, unable to contain herself. "We're all glad you're not dead anymore—and all that fluffy stuff—but what you did back there was ludicrous, boy! Just plain ludicrous!"

"I'm sorry," responded Boot. "I'm sorry to all of you. I just couldn't let it happen—not when I knew I could do something about it."

"About what?" jarred Ingrid.

"He's getting to it," said Dilly, glancing impatiently at her.

"Well, as we were nearly ready to go," said Boot, fidgeting with his belongings, "I saw a large group of nobles, waiting to be driven somewhere, and I overheard their conversation." He dug his hand into the biggest pocket of his bag and out popped a black ferret. It smelled the air, looked around, and ducked back in.

"So what?" blared Ingrid. She wanted the point.

"The people had decided to kill this little guy," said Boot. "They claimed it bit one of their boys."

"Well if it bites—" gasped Ingrid, raising her cane and stepping back as the ferret peeked out. Donshi and some of the other Greenling girls squealed.

"The boy probably deserved it—arrogant wippling!" argued Boot.

"So you went all the way back just get that furry thing?" asked Dilly. She crinkled her brow in disbelief.

"They were swinging sticks at him!" said Boot. "Another two minutes and he'd have been crow food to the side of the road."

"But if he bit someone," grumbled Ingrid, "he ought to be

mashed!" She pressed her cane against the ground and twisted it, crushing a beetle into the dust.

"No!" said Boot, getting moist in the corner of his eyes. There was more going on in his head than talk of a ferret. "Everyone deserves a second chance," he insisted, looking at his bag sadly. "Everyone."

"I suppose," said Dilly hesitantly.

"But didn't you hear the bells?" asked Sawny, trying to understand Boot's logic. "The guards were already across the way—they don't block the road to be mean, they block it to be merciful."

"I know," sighed Boot. "I knew I was pushing it really close, and I even considered heading to Trot's house on Lake Charms for the night—"

"You should've!" exploded Dilly, lecturing Boot like a mother. "You just can't take chances like that anymore! When your life's on the line, Ingrid's right: It's crazy to race the clock. Not to mention, the guards nearly swiped you with their swords before you even hit the road. They follow rules—they don't break them!"

"But Dilly—"

"No Boot!" insisted Dilly, beginning to turn away from him. She was angry that he didn't get it. He had died and been given a miraculous second chance at life and yet he still thought that he had a good excuse for his stupidity.

"But Dilly," said Boot, struggling to get his weakened legs to lift him up. His eyes were sincere. "You said you'd be angry if we didn't all make it to the banquet at Commendus's tonight. I didn't want to ruin your special dinner by running off."

Dilly paused, speechless. The ferret was the reason he had

left the group, and she was the reason he had risked his life to come back.

"Ludicrous!" blared Ingrid. "You're a fool, Boot—and nothing more!"

The black ferret poked its head out of the bag again and seemed to scowl at Ingrid. Boot glanced down and smiled. "He's a smart critter," he bragged. "I can tell." He carefully lowered himself back to a resting position on the ground and reached for the ferret, which appeared to be tiptoeing away from the bag.

"I think I'll call him Sneaker," said Boot proudly, lifting the squiggling creature into the air. "Look at how cuddly he is."

"And ferocious!" argued Ingrid disapprovingly. "It's just waiting for its chance to go for your throat." Her eyes widened as Boot set the ferret down. Though rather than attack, it slunk back into Boot's bag.

"Perhaps it will strike later," said Ingrid, swinging her heavy weight as she reached for Toos. "My wagon. Help me to my wagon."

No sooner had she been seated than a storm of soldiers passed her and rushed to Boot.

"See! I told you he was faking it!" said one weasel-eyed tredder, wearing the lowest rank on his uniform. "I've dealt with that one before. He's full of mischief. The last time I saw him, he was causing problems for some of our esteemed guests from Raul—Terro's son was in the group."

"Oh—Terro," said the commanding officer with respect. He turned to Boot and yelled, "UP! NOW!"

Buck bent down and began to help his brother to his feet when two guards pushed him back. "The charade's over!" barked one of them. "We know he's fine."

But Boot wasn't fine. Without Buck's arm to steady him, he tumbled to the ground.

"COME ON!" ordered the commander, glaring angrily. "We won't be mocked any more by your nonsense. You're off to confinement. Thirty-day minimum—and that's if we find you're not toting other offenses, though I'm sure the nobles across the way will have an enlightened perspective. What did you steal? Their pocketcases? Jewelry? Speak up, boy! We'll know the truth tomorrow. The soldiers are writing this up as we speak—see?" He pointed to the distant guardhouse, where a cluster of men were busily doing something.

"He didn't take anything they wanted!" said Dilly, stepping beside him. "And he didn't fake anything, either!"

The commander waved his hand and men pulled Boot to his feet, dragging him into the mob of guards.

"Careful, please!" begged Dilly, scampering beside the soldiers. "He's not well. He needs help, not prison."

Her pleadings didn't even tilt their eyes.

"My great-grandfather will hear of this!" she roared desperately.

"I hope so!" gloated the commander, pointing at Dilly with a crooked finger. "Let's keep her overnight, just in case she's involved."

Clammy hands seized Dilly, rudely twisting her arms into painful positions.

"My great-grandfather is Bonboo!" she cried, struggling to free herself.

"Then he'll be glad when we bring this matter to his attention," snapped the hotheaded commander. "A man like him needs to watch his relatives closely. He'll thank me—I'm sure of it."

"She's not involved," begged Boot. "Let her go. I'm the one that messed up. Take me but leave her. She's got an important meeting tonight with Commendus."

"Unlikely," growled the guard who held Dilly.

"She really does," choked Sawny, bravely coming to her sister's aid. Sammywoo, who clung to Sawny's leg, swung his swot at them menacingly, though yards away.

"And if you're taking them," added Dod, bolting into the squad of soldiers, "you're going to need to haul me off, as well, because I'm not leaving *his* side." He pointed at Boot.

"Fine," said the commander. "We'll take him, too—and ANYONE ELSE who thinks they need to open their mouths. This matter is CLOSED!"

"Ludicrous!" blared Ingrid, who had left her wagon to approach the commanding officer. She poked at his behind with her thick cane. "Let them go! You're making a big mistake, here," she grumbled, huffing and puffing.

"MA'AM!" gasped the commander, spinning around to confront her. He was furious. His nostrils widened and his eyes turned to slits as he waved his men to take her.

"Who's the general in charge?" squawked Ingrid, leaning on her staff. "I insist you fetch him!"

The first guard who reached for her was clocked across the head, sending him to the ground, and the second got it worse—a whack between the legs, forcing him to double over in pain.

"And you call yourselves soldiers?" mocked Ingrid.

Seeing the commotion, a band of horsemen moved in, with a medal-laden officer at the front.

"General Oosh," said the red-faced commander, hopping to salute. "We have the situation contained, sir."

"So I see," he remarked, looking at the two downed men.

"If you're in charge," said Ingrid with a raspy voice, "I'll speak with you alone." She motioned for him to follow her to a bench.

The general dismounted and spent five minutes sitting beside Ingrid, nodding his head over and over while the other soldiers continued to keep their positions, holding Boot, Dilly, and Dod.

Eventually, General Oosh stood up and helped Ingrid to her feet. Together, they approached the waiting throng.

"There's been a misunderstanding today," he said carefully. "I'm told that *that* boy just saved this woman's priceless pet—a family heirloom of sorts."

"What?" gasped the crowd.

"Yes," he continued. "She's heading back to Raul today to join her nephew, Terro, and the whole Chantolli family in celebrating this special creature's two hundredth birthday. Had that boy not done heroics—" he turned to Ingrid and she nodded, "then all of Green would have faced the anger of the Chantolli family. There's no telling how their financial holdings here in Green would have been used—"

"Because of the pain—" added Ingrid, nudging him.

"Right," sighed the general uncomfortably. "Due to their grief, the Chantollis would have been driven to dire actions, such as unwisely using their money and power here in Green."

Dod stared in shock, as did everyone else. The soldiers looked at each other in confusion, as if they weren't sure whether to let go of their prisoners, or continue holding on; they awaited the punch line, for the general's words seemed like a joke.

"Are you asking us to release them?" stuttered one of the guards.

"Nearly," responded General Oosh. "But before you do,

there's one little thing I'd like to ask." He turned toward Ingrid and said, "I'm sure you're an honest woman who has somehow misplaced your identification, and as an honest woman, your descriptions are naturally without reproach; however, the one proof I ask of you is that you kindly introduce me to this gentle, shy pet. Please show him to me—show me this animal that you've fed from your very lips and I'll let them all go."

"Well," scoffed Ingrid, shaking her head nervously. "He's very shy! I already told you! Nobody can see or hold him!"

"That's too bad," said the general. "Then I guess you'll understand if we let the process move forward."

"No!" barked Ingrid. "Terro will be upset if you make me late."

"Then I won't," said General Oosh. "I'll have guards escort you to the portal right now."

"That's not necessary—" continued Ingrid.

"Then show me your pet!" demanded Oosh. His patience had worn thin. He was finished being delicate and had made up his mind that she was certainly not Terro's relative.

"If you insist," grumbled Ingrid, hobbling toward Boot's bag. "But I'll keep you to your word about letting my friends go."

Everyone was shocked when Ingrid drew Sneaker from the pocket—the soldiers because they had been led to believe that there was no pet and everyone else because they knew how terrified Ingrid was of the ferret.

"See?" she said, doing her best to hide her fear. "Now let us go. Commendus awaits them, and Terro awaits me."

General Oosh was speechless. The guards released their prisoners and watched them mount their horses and ride away, with Ingrid squished beside Toos on the buckboard, holding her family's pride.

CHAPTER TWELVE

"I told you he'd bite!" growled Ingrid as soon as they rounded the first bend. She threw Sneaker at Boot, who rode double with Buck for support. The ferret gladly retreated into Boot's shirt, while Ingrid fumed, blood dripping down her hand.

"Thanks," said Boot. "I didn't know you had it in you."

"We're even," grumbled Ingrid. "Enough with the second chances!"

BUGS

Commendus's estate looked more beautiful than before; flowers of every color burst the edges of his gardens, flooding the air with the sweet smells of nature; and his lawns were greener and thicker; and his forests even appeared better trimmed.

"He's stepped things up a notch," commented Boot, as the crowd from Twistyard passed the guards at the entrance.

"He's showing off to someone," said Buck, smirking.

"You promised!" huffed Dilly. "You both gave your word that you wouldn't bring it up—"

"To Commendus," clarified Boot. "We promised we wouldn't speak a word of it to Commendus."

"Aah!" groaned Dilly. "Why do I tell you guys anything? If other people hear you joking about his possible interest in seeking a fiancé, it may get back to him—and then—well—he'd throw us out!"

"He's good at that, isn't he?" teased Boot.

"Please," said Dilly. "That's just the kind of comment he doesn't want to hear."

"Because the truth hurts," poked Boot, peeking inside his shirt at Sneaker, who was sound asleep.

"No," snorted Dilly. "Because he was heartbroken! He was madly in love with Yarni and she chose to leave him—"

"Or she was kicked out," added Dod, trying to enter the conversation.

"You too?" groaned Dilly, glancing at Dod before shaking her head at Boot and Buck. "You guys are impossible. Commendus did everything he could to make her happy, and in the end, it wasn't enough. She packed up and disappeared. It doesn't get much worse than that."

"Inter-realm relationships are hard," said Sawny, nudging her horse into the mix. "I never understood what Commendus saw in her. You have to admit, they were complete opposites. She was from the backwoods of Soosh, and he was from all of this. And she was a young human—I think only twenty-five—and he was a middle-aged tredder, still bound to outlive her. And if that didn't separate them enough, she hated the social scene. I think I only met her once during their eight-year marriage."

"I spoke with her twice," said Dilly, swatting bugs that flew near her face. "She was like a shy version of Eluxa."

"So you didn't like her, huh?" added Dod smugly.

"I didn't say that," argued Dilly.

"In a way, you did," said Dod, rubbing his aching back. He was ready to be done riding horses for the day.

"He's right," added Boot, flipping a marble-sized biting fly from his arm. "We all know how much you love Eluxa. If Yarni struck you as being similar, it couldn't mean you were impressed."

Dilly fidgeted in her saddle.

"Was she hot like Eluxa?" asked Pone, overhearing parts

of the conversation. He looked back at Dilly and smiled, while running his hand across the stubble-short hair on the side of his head, forcing the gnats to stop drinking his sweat.

"No!" said Dilly. "I mean yes! I mean no, Eluxa's not attractive and yes, Yarni was. And even though I may not have enjoyed her company as much as his previous wife's, I didn't hate her."

"What about the two wives before her?" joked Boot. He enjoyed disparaging Commendus because it crinkled Dilly's collar.

"Wow!" said Pone, still riding with his head kinked back. "I didn't realize he was looking for the big number *five!*" He crunched into an apple, taking such a big bite that he nearly couldn't chew.

"It's not what you think," contended Dilly, trying hopelessly to stick up for Commendus. She couldn't help being impressed with his style, especially when it came to gift-giving. And since he'd been a friend to her family for ages, she had many fond memories of him—enough to look beyond the appearance of scandal in his past marriages.

"He's kinda lucky," added Pone, looking envious. His mouth was still stuffed to overflowing.

Sawny's ears turned red.

"Well he is!" choked Pone defensively, swallowing hard. He had to speak up when he noticed how both sisters were scowling at him. "He's old enough to know what he wants, rich enough to buy what he wants, and powerful enough to win whomever he wants. He's got the tri-trumpous!"

"And what are you saying?" blurted Sawny irritably. "You'd like to be just like him when you're his age?"

Pone paused, recognizing a trap.

"With all of the women he's burned through, you'd think he'd have more than one child," continued Sawny. "Besides, numbers don't lie—he's the one with the problem. Any woman blind enough to consider being with him is dumb enough to deserve him."

"He's worked hard at the impossible," said Dilly, turning on her sister. "And he's a wonderful leader. Not to mention, he is hosting us for the evening, as he so often unselfishly does. It's just—well—the poor man's been unlucky at love."

"Not according to Pone," mumbled Sawny bitterly, only partially opening her mouth because of a passing swarm of flies.

"That's not what I meant," said Pone.

"But it's what you said," teased Boot. "You're guilty and we all know it."

Dilly glanced at her bracelet and gasped. They were approaching the strip where the pond nearly met the road, and Dilly's Redy-Alert-Band was turning light pink.

"The diasserpentous," gasped Dilly nervously, kicking at Song to leave the lane for the bushes on the opposite side as the water.

"It looks yellow to me," said Boot, yanking Buck's hand that held the reins to the horse they were on. He insisted they ride beside Dilly, even if it meant clomping through foliage, which was filled with bugs.

"Don't worry," said Sawny calmly, forcing her horse to the edge of the road, but not going so far as Dilly and Boot, who had left it altogether. "It's not likely that the snakes would strike at a group this large—and if they did, they'd nip at Boot's poor horse, not us."

Grubber trailed behind Ingrid's wagon on a rope, nearly stepping in the water as he pulled toward the lake for a drink.

BuGS

"Grubber!" yelled Boot. "Get away from there!" He whistled and the horse trotted back onto the road, falling obediently in line.

"Yellow, huh?" teased Dilly.

Boot rolled his eyes.

Suddenly, Dod felt like he was drowning. He coughed and choked and gasped for air. His mind was cluttered with glimpses of water—someone was trapped, trying to surface but couldn't.

"Water," mumbled Dod, wondering why the images were coming.

"It's beautiful, isn't it," marveled Sawny, staring at Commendus's newest substantial addition to his manor. It was a gigantic rock waterfall, towering a hundred feet in the air. It was positioned on the pond's shore, occupying the edge that was nearest to the castle. Torrents of water flowed out of the top, splashing and sloshing against rocks, like a raging river.

"It's trouble," said Dod, shivering. His mind raced to know what to do.

"Actually," spouted Sawny, "the moving water is not as favorable to a diasserpentous as the calmer parts of the lake, so that fountain is probably Commendus's attempt to keep the snakes away from his palace—and I can't say I blame him—at least…not for *that!*"

"He means well," said Dilly, looking less distracted as her band turned full yellow. "Come on, Sawny, don't make an issue of it."

"Of *it?*" questioned Boot. "Go ahead, Sawny, make an issue. We're listening." He wanted to hear what was causing the sisters to fight.

"They'll find out anyway," said Sawny, ready to spill the news. It bugged her bad enough that she wanted to vent.

"No they won't!" insisted Dilly. "I've taken care of things, and it's normal—"

"It's not normal!" gagged Sawny. "And it's just not okay!"

"I already told you," Dilly glared. "It's not an issue."

"So you say," grumbled Sawny.

Buck and Boot were all ears. Dod, on the other hand, wanted to know what they were talking about, but had a hard time focusing on anything other than the unsettled feelings he was getting from the lake.

"Here goes—"

"No!" begged Dilly.

"Commendus wanted Dilly to consider spending more time at his palace—a lot more time!"

"He proposed?" gasped Boot, looking horrified.

"Ugh," moaned Dilly.

"Not exactly," said Sawny. "But he likes her! And he's too old for her, and she's way too young for him—not to mention his pathetic track record with past wives! He should hang up his hat and call it quits with the ladies, or at least consider dating women his own age!"

"That's how you knew!" blurted Buck, eyeing Dilly. "Commendus approached you—he really is shopping for a fifth wife. I thought you were jumping to another one of your wild gossip guesses when you told us he was already looking around. He's not wasting any time mourning the loss of his marriage, is he? Yarni's only been gone a few months."

"I can't believe his audacity," mumbled Boot. The rough hairs on the back of his neck bristled up.

"I'm sure he's got a full tank of fish to choose from!" said Dilly. "He just hoped I'd join the rest of them in spending my days here—waiting to occasionally date him."

"Oh!" groaned Boot, huffing loudly.

"But of course I declined," added Dilly. "Sawny's right: He's crazy to even think it. He's old enough to be my father. And besides, I enjoy being a Coosing, and I have years to go before I need to think about courting for a serious relationship."

When the road parted, Dod felt driven to approach the new fountain instead of rushing to the barns. He didn't want to, especially with the unusual number of bugs in the air, but he felt he had to.

"Who wants to check that out?" asked Dod, pointing to the mountain of rocks. He hoped he wouldn't be alone.

"Didn't you say it was trouble?" joked Sawny, instantly happier than she had been all day; after hearing Dilly admit that Commendus's offer was wacky, a huge weight was lifted from her shoulders.

"I like trouble," said Pone with his mouth full of nuts. He was the first to tip his horse toward the bend they had missed.

"Me too," chirped Sawny.

"But the diasserpentouses!" blared Dilly.

"They won't even pink your bracelet," assured Sawny. "I'm serious. The rushing water's not their favorite. With over fifty acres of territory, and as deep as that lake goes, they wouldn't hang out anywhere near the splashing thunder."

As Pone led the way, the rest of the Twistyard crowd turned and followed. Even Ingrid's wagon eventually caught up.

The new fountain was a masterpiece. Each rock had been carefully cemented in place to look completely natural. And there were planter boxes that supported a wide variety of species common to the Hook Mountains. Flowers, grasses, bushes, and small trees grew in the right spots to convey an atmosphere of serenity, a scene of beauty, a glimpse of the rustic world that lay miles away to the north and west. It was in stark contrast to the bustling metropolis that bordered Commendus's estate.

From across the lake Dod had focused on the booming whitewater, but from the castle side, the fountain was a well-planned garden, with plants tapering down the rock face. Since the structure was boomerang-shaped on a corner of the pond, the rocks had been wisely situated to send the noise outward toward the open water, not inward toward the castle. Workers were finishing with the final touches, painting three benches to appear like they were made of stone.

"Now why would Bonmoob block his waterview with a thing like that?" asked Ingrid, being the last to arrive and the first to speak up. "Those benches won't work at all!"

"This is Commendus's estate," said Dilly, approaching Ingrid. She kept glancing at her bracelet.

"What? The head of our democracy lives here?" gasped Ingrid. "You weren't kidding earlier, were you?"

"No," assured Dilly. "We'll be staying here tonight."

"But girl! I haven't a thing to wear—and my jewelry—" she frantically dug into her ragged purse, "Where did I put my necklaces?"

"It's okay," said Sawny, "Commendus is a pro at dishing out clothing. You'll be wearing something wonderful before you meet him."

"But he could be watching!" replied the old woman nervously, tugging at her messy curls. "I'd be mortified!" She looked so worn from her days of travel that her hair flopped about her head in clusters of matted curls, like an unkempt wig, and a few bugs stuck to her cheap makeup. The flies liked Ingrid more than anyone else, and Toos nearly as much. The stinky smells that poured from them were delicious to creeping things of all varieties.

"Can we get to the barns?" asked Toos desperately. His hand waved in the air constantly, swatting traffic that buzzed around him. "This whole place is a mess of wildlife," he said. "What happened to the refinement? I've been sucked and nipped and poked and stung more in the past fifteen minutes, while coming up this fancy drive, than on all of my fishing trips combined. I can't take another minute of it!"

"Easy, Short Straw," teased Boot, referring to Toos's unlucky chore of riding next to Ingrid. Boot couldn't contain his laughter when he saw how disheveled Toos appeared. His regular, banker-slick hair and dapper clothes had been degraded to little more than a filthy-boy look.

"It's actually better right here," claimed Dilly. "I haven't had to swat in three minutes." She glanced behind her to make sure Sammywoo was still okay. Pone had helped to situate a makeshift recliner of sorts for the boy out of Dilly's bags, so he was pleasantly sleeping.

Toos continued his waving, less than eight feet away.

"The bugs don't stop for a snack when they can feast," said Sawny, pointing at Ingrid and Toos.

Dod dismounted and walked along the wall, heading to the water. He had to see the front, close up.

"Be careful," called one worker, an older tredder whose eyebrows were so big that they blocked part of his vision. He jogged over and joined Dod. "There are two beasts in this lake, the likes of which you can't imagine. You shouldn't go anywhere near the water's edge without one of *these*." He held up his Redy-Alert-Band.

"Okay," said Dod. "Then walk with me."

Together, they journeyed the hundreds of feet through thick bushes and tall grass to where the wall came to an end. All the while, the worker kept eyeing his bracelet as he explained what trouble the snakes had caused.

"So after they ate most of the fish," he said, "these rotten bugs started to show up in large numbers. And without predators for their larva, they multiply constantly. The waters are teeming with batches of them."

"Eew," groaned Dod, slapping a nickel-sized Long-Nose Fly. It looked like a huge mosquito.

"And that's not all," continued the older man. "Ducks and geese are disappearing by the hundreds. Everyone in High Gate is complaining. Since the triblot field is up most of the time, birds stay in the city, lake-hopping, so their numbers are closely regulated."

The conversation ended abruptly when they hit the shoreline. It was like entering a blaring stadium of fans as they turned the corner and heard the thunderous water, crashing against the pond.

Dod felt uncomfortable. He knew there was something strange about the spot, but what? Perhaps it was the snakes—how had they gotten there? Or perhaps something awful had taken place near the falls.

"Shall we go?" asked the worker.

Dod read his lips and nodded. The impressions were too vague to take action.

When they reentered the cluster of people, the worker exploded with frustration. "NO! NO!" yelled the man. He rushed at three young painters, who had covered each other with shades of brown. "I leave you for ten minutes and you act like this!" he growled. "You can't misbehave *here*! Now go and clean up in the pump room! Hurry! Commendus must not see you!"

The three boys sulked as they snailed toward the foliage where Dod had just come from and disappeared.

"My sons are idiots!" the man said to all who watched. "I'm sorry you had to see them go strutting the fool."

"That's okay," said Boot. "I thought they were funny. Thanks for the show."

"Perhaps they need more discipline," barked Ingrid, staring the man down as Toos urged the horses to head for the barns.

Inside the palace, Dr. Shelderhig was the first to say hello. He greeted them warmly and wore a smile that stretched to the back of his head, hiding his eyes behind a mask of wrinkles.

"You've made it," he said, pushing a clump of gray hair from his brow. "I'm so glad to see you all." He was dressed in a sharp, dark suit, not typical of his usual clothes.

"And who's your friend?" asked Dilly, getting straight to the point. She could tell that the older, stout woman beside the good doctor was likely the instigator of his happiness.

"This is Newmi," he said blissfully. "She's an expert of sorts, giving all of us here at the palace some important tips on a subject that—well—needs to be carefully dealt with right now. We'd die without her."

"He's too kind," said the woman gruffly. She wasn't exactly feminine, and her voice matched her rough appearance. She easily looked as old as Dr. Shelderhig, but as a human, she was much younger.

"Introduce me," huffed Ingrid, approaching Dilly's side.

"This is Ingrid," said Dilly. "She's Higga's cousin and she's come to stay at Twistyard for a while."

"I'm watching Juny," she blurted eagerly, tipping her head to appear important. She leaned with only one arm on her cane so as to appear casual about its use. "Bonmoob trusts me to the difficult task of tracking her traitorous connections."

"Bonboo?" corrected Dr. Shelderhig.

"Right," said Ingrid. "And my cousin has me checking in on her place while she's gone, and I'm running top secret messages for The Greats as well. I suppose you'd be correct in suggesting that I'm indispensable."

Dilly and Sawny tried hard not to laugh.

"So—how is it that you stay sane while running the affairs of the world?" asked Ingrid.

"Excuse me?" choked Dr. Shelderhig. "I suppose I do my best," he stuttered.

"Well, I for one think you do a fabulous job," she said readily. "And your rocks out front look marvelous. When the paint dries, I'd love to sit on one of your well-positioned benches and enjoy—"

"This is Dr. Shelderhig Grick," said Dilly, quickly getting to the rest of the introductions before things became too awkward. "He's visiting Commendus while he continues his research."

"Oh," groaned Ingrid, blinking with surprise. "Nice to meet you both." She went silent once she realized that Dr. Shelderhig wasn't Commendus.

"What kind of expert are you, Newmi?" asked Dilly. "If you've impressed Dr. Shelderhig, I'm sure you'd impress us."

"Um—I don't know that I'd consider myself an expert at anything," explained Newmi, grabbing at her graying braid uncomfortably.

"That's nonsense!" chuckled Dr. Shelderhig. "She knows

more about noble billies and their crafty ways than anyone I've ever met—and with their growing unrest—and the, um—well, and the coming tournament—" his eyes read Dilly's disappointment and he ran through a string of apologies. "I think it's great that you went so far, and I'm terribly sorry that the Raging Billies came up winners. I'd have pushed my full weight and a tad more on your victory if I'd have watched you play the big match. What a shock that they slid in a sneaky win."

"It's okay," said Dilly. "We nearly had them."

"They're impossible to beat, aren't they?" said Newmi, sparking with a burst of excitement.

At the mention of the Bollirse loss, most of the Twistyard crowd filed away.

"Commendus said you played well," added Dr. Shelderhig kindly.

Ingrid tugged at Dilly's shirt. She wanted to leave but not without her guide.

"I've noticed your snakes are still swimming," said Dod.

"Yes, they are," groaned Dr. Shelderhig. "It baffles me how smart they are. The bait I use is so strong that I've nearly been nipped a time or two when setting the traps, yet I can't seem to catch them." He strode briskly to a closet nearby and plucked out a bucket of what looked like brownish clay. "This stuff drives them mad," he said. "If only I could get the kinks straightened out of my snares—they keep breaking."

"I'm sure you will," sighed Dod, glancing at the entrance they had just come through. The door opened and a small mob of rough-looking workers came in and asked for directions to the bathroom.

"There's one for you to use in the biggest barn, to the side of the tack room," responded Dr. Shelderhig uncomfortably.

CHAPTER THIRTEEN

"Oh—I see—right," mumbled the group. Their eyes panned the opulent mudroom of sorts before sauntering back out the way they had come.

"Really!" exclaimed the doctor. "If Con hires any more help like that, I'm going to lend Commendus my views! He needs to teach his son how to lead, not flail and limp."

"Is Con living here again?" gasped Dilly with surprise.

"Yes. Once Yarni left, Commendus pulled many of his loved ones to the palace. I think it's part of the way he's dealing with everything."

"So—Con's done with his escapades, huh?"

"Yes, that's what I've heard," said Dr. Shelderhig. "He's decided to pause his military campaign—at least for a while."

"Wow!" said Sawny, echoing her sister's amazement. "That's a change, isn't it? I'd have never guessed that Commendus would let him back. Maybe he is softening in his *older age*." She glanced at her sister and smiled.

"It's better for Con to be here than at Twistyard!" said Dilly without hesitation. "His days with us were a real disaster! The only thing that came natural to him was fighting!"

Boot had quietly leaned on Buck for support, since he was horribly drained, but hearing of Con made him rub his jaw as though it still ached from the time Con had displaced it. And Buck shuddered, nearly enough to awaken Sammywoo, whom he held in his strong arms; the young boy's head was on Buck's shoulder and his swot was cramped between them.

"Perhaps the snakes will eat him," huffed Dilly meanly.

"I think they, too, fear him," said Dr. Shelderhig with reluctance, but only after looking around the room as though searching for Con's towering shadow.

"At least I don't need to worry about snakes," said Dilly proudly, holding up her Redy-Alert-Band. "Thanks for the bracelet! It's been a life saver."

Dr. Shelderhig and Newmi both pulled up their long sleeves and showed that they, too, were wearing matching bands. "I've had a number of interesting breakthroughs," the doctor said eagerly, looking past Dilly to Sawny. "You should come by in the morning and see them."

"I will," promised Sawny, happy to have been directly addressed. She felt a little displaced by Dr. Shelderhig's new friend.

No sooner had they parted ways and headed for the guest quarters than Con came strolling down the magnificent hall, decked head to toe in fancy clothes and wearing a beautiful sword at his waist. He looked like a mixture of Commendus and Sawb, but bigger than either of them. His nearly seven-foot frame bulged with muscles. The only men Dod could imagine beating Con in an arm wrestle would be Dungo and Bowlure. Anyone else wouldn't stand a chance.

"I thought I'd find you trailing your ducklings," called Con, approaching Dilly with a curiously suave look on his face. He acted as though nobody else stood by, and he held a brilliant flower that was as big as a grapefruit. Its petals were stunning shades of pink and maroon—they were so delicate that they resembled lace.

"Here," he said, handing Dilly the flower. "I'm glad you've come for a visit." He then waved his elegantly-ringed hand around, pointing at the spacious, two and three-story vaulted rooms that connected to the main hall and chuckled, "Please, make yourself at home, Dilly. And stay as long as you'd like. *You're* welcome here anytime."

"More than you, I'd imagine," blurted Boot, glaring up at him.

Con glowered coolly and approached with a clenched fist when Ingrid poked in his direction with her cane, blocking his advance. "Is this Commendus?" she asked, turning to Dilly.

"No," said Dilly frankly. "This is his *wonderful son*, Con."

Hearing Dilly's compliment, Con stepped back and returned to civility. "Please ask for me if you need anything, Dilly—and I mean *anything*." He then slid in a disgustingly slimy wink and strode off toward the barns.

"That was gross," said Sawny, watching Con turn a distant corner. "I think I'm gonna need three showers to wash the grime off. Did you just see that? Commendus must have been tugging at you to stay here for *him*." Sawny looked at Dilly and laughed. "He's hoping you'll fall madly in love with his loony son—not him."

"Now *that* is a romance that would never work!" said Dilly curtly, handing the flower to Ingrid. "I know he's only half from Raul, but that's the half I see. Dating him at all would be like going on a picnic with Sawb! No thanks. I'd sooner tote an alligator—and at that, the conversation would likely be better."

"He didn't seem so bad to me," said Ingrid, smelling her prize. "If I'd have had men like that calling when I was younger—well—I'd have considered it. Maybe the boy has changed since last you were acquainted."

"Yup," groaned Buck. "About three or four inches—stay away from him, Boot. He's a bear full of trouble."

At dinner, everyone wore fancy clothes that Commendus had kindly provided. Ingrid loved her silky black dress and bright-white pearl necklace. She couldn't believe she was allowed to keep the presents. And she finally got her chance to meet

Commendus. He was the last one to enter the banquet hall, though when he came he wasn't alone.

"Dilly," Commendus said, stopping at her table first. "I hope you'll reconsider my offer about a room here in the palace—especially now that you've had time to see my surprise."

Dilly blinked. The only surprise she could think of was the one hanging off of Commendus—she was a middle-aged, brunette bombshell.

"Well," continued Commendus, fiddling with one of his four Redy-Alert-Bands, "I couldn't say anything to you before about Con's arrival. The war's a fickle thing to take part in, and I didn't want you to get your hopes up too high."

Dilly continued to blink. She wasn't sure which thing to be more shocked about: Commendus's plan to throw her at his pathetic son, Con, or the elegant and infamous woman at his side, Saluci's cousin Sabbella.

"Tri-trumpous," coughed Pone from a few chairs down. His voice was muffled by a strip of beef filet mignon. The extra clanking of silverware that followed was a subtle high-five of sorts from Voo and Sham who both agreed.

"Well, Dilly," remarked Commendus, glancing away from Dilly's table, "I would have thought that you'd be sitting over there." His eyes pointed at Con's table full of girls. He had at least fifteen who seemed to hang on his every word.

"I'm fine, thank you," said Dilly. "Besides, there's only one chair left and I'm happy to be joined by my buddy." She gave Sammywoo a sideways squeeze.

"And Dod," chimed Commendus, waltzing toward Dod the moment he recognized him. "It's so nice to have you visit again." He turned to the woman on his arm and explained how Dod was the one who had captured The Dread on his last visit to the palace. "Perhaps you'll catch Dark Hood for us tonight," added Commendus, chuckling.

"Only if you've invited him for dinner," responded Boot bracingly, insinuating that Commendus had been good friends with Sirlonk. Boot was mad at Commendus for trying to pressure Dilly. They traded quick, awkward glances before Sabbella spoke up.

"How's your great-grandfather, girls? Is he doing better?"

"He's fine, thank you," said Sawny, smiling as sweetly as she could. "And how's your family? We saw your father, Neadrou, briefly at The Games. He seems well."

Dod got chills. Knowing that Sabbella's father was Neadrou changed everything. Her smile and eyes looked less nice and more cunning by the second.

"As you can all see," said Commendus, stepping back. "I'm a fortunate man indeed. Sabbella of the Zoots has agreed to marry me."

His words would have received more attention if they weren't instantly followed by a loud announcement that came from guards who stormed in: "The Capitol's on fire, sir! We think it's the billies again—tarjuice and flaming arrows."

"Stay calm," ordered Commendus, looking more annoyed than concerned. "We'll handle it just fine—stay indoors."

But by morning, everyone could see that things hadn't gone well.

THE GOOSE EGG

"Look at that!" exclaimed Dilly with a mortified stare.

As the Twistyard crowd hustled to make the noon dropping of the triblot barrier, they all gasped and gawked in awe at the destruction that had taken place the night before. Five towering buildings, each over twenty stories tall, were nothing but skeletons of charred stones—and that's just the mess they could see from Commendus's estate. The sad structures bordered the fence line by Commendus's grand entrance.

"Do you really think noble billies did *that*?" asked Sawny. "How did they enter High Gate?"

"I don't know," said Dilly, looking stunned, "but I'm guessing Dark Hood's involved. Did you hear the gossip last night, while we were trying on clothes?"

"No," teased Boot, pushing his horse between Dilly and Sawny. Grubber was doing well, as was Boot. "What did they say about Sabbella?"

"You didn't suit up with the girls!" giggled Sammywoo, riding with Dilly. "You're a boy, Boot! Our changing room was different."

"Oh," said Boot playfully. He shivered as Sneaker's tail brushed against his neck. Boot let the ferret ride on his shoulder, like a pirate's parrot.

"So, what did you guys hear?" asked Boot, turning serious. Buck and Dod were close by, intently listening.

"The chambermaids were talking about a string of unfortunate events," said Dilly. "We've heard plenty at Twistyard about a few representatives needing to be replaced—Sirch Holden because of his boating accident, Tyran Childson because of his dreadful throat condition, Borris Goldstrum because of his bad heart, and Dudson Hullmaker because of his tragic fall—but I had no idea about the real numbers!"

"How many slots are empty?" asked Dod. His mind was muddled when it came to the exact details of the political system in Green, but he knew that there were only one hundred representatives that ultimately worked with Commendus and Bonboo to make laws and enforce the freedom. Beyond those people, thousands of lesser officials worked directly in their elected capacities to influence the representatives toward decisions that were favored by their various constituents.

"Twenty-two!" said Dilly. Her words were horribly complimented by the scene that opened up to full view as the gang exited Commendus's estate. The surrounding area looked like a bombed-out city. Ten massive buildings were completely destroyed. Three of them had collapsed, and a few more dangled precariously. At the center of the mess were the remains of the majestic Capitol Building—a structure that had occupied four square blocks and had taken decades to build.

"I can't believe it!" blurted Sawny, feeling ill. "What happened to the water? Why didn't they put the fires out?"

"Because it was well planned," said Dod, remembering the Twin Towers and how the loaded fuel tanks in the planes had burned hotter than experts had previously calculated. "They must have first damaged the water pressure in the area before lighting the fires—and I doubt a few arrows did *that*!"

"At least it was at night," said Buck. "These buildings were probably empty. If it had been during the day, thousands of people may have died."

"Why is everything black, Dilly?" asked Sammywoo.

"There was a fire," said Dilly, "a really, really, really big fire."

"Oh," said Sammywoo, satisfied with the answer. He went back to flipping Song's tail with his swot.

Everyone rode in silence until the destruction was out of view, as if to show respect for the struggling democracy. Eventually, when they passed the statue of Bonboo's parents, Dod spoke up.

"With twenty-two slots in motion and a burnt-down Capitol Building, I'd say Dark Hood has a wicked agenda. And I'd imagine he's behind the angry billies and your grandpa's poisoning, too, not to mention the flaming tent that nearly roasted your father and Bowy."

"You're probably right," sighed Dilly, almost apathetically.

"And so we've got to stop him!" said Dod, not falling into the melancholy mood that had swept over his friends.

"But there are so many of them," said Dilly. "The triblot barrier around High Gate is probably next, or maybe the whole of Twistyard, or possibly Terraboom."

"Have you ever seen a headless snake?" asked Dod.

Boot and Buck perked up. "Yes," they both responded.

"It flips and rolls for a few minutes, looking for its brains," added Boot, "and then it settles right down."

"Gross," whined Sawny.

"Well, that's what it's gonna be like for this trouble-causing machine after we get done!" said Dod. "We'll take out Dark Hood like we did The Dread, and the rest of his helpers will fall away quickly—or Pious and his men will clean them up." Dod felt proud to be Pap's grandson, and he knew Pap wouldn't have despaired over the buildings being lost.

"Right," said Boot, patting the top of Sneaker's head. "Buck and I missed our opportunity to participate in nabbing Sirlonk, so I guess Dark Hood's given us a second chance to step up. And since he's picked a fight with Bowy, he's certainly picked a fight with me!"

"I'm with you, bro," said Buck.

Dod and the brothers looked at Dilly and Sawny.

"Your metaphors could be better," said Sawny, glancing at the boys. "But I like the way you think. Anyone who's delusional enough to suppose that they're going to ruin my world and rule the ashes has got something coming to them—something ugly. We won't stand for it!"

"Right," said Dilly in a brittle voice. She then burst into tears. "I can't believe The Capitol's gone," she sobbed. "Dad and Grandpa worked on it together. It was Grandpa's last masterpiece before he died."

"It's okay," said Boot, nudging his horse close to hers. "We all remember that building, and no one can take our memories! Besides, the plans he designed are still around—I'm sure they'll get started on reconstructing it as soon as they haul off the debris."

Dilly wiped her tears with her sleeve and tried to smile. They were approaching the waiting area where hundreds of people were gathered, listening to the ringing bells. The southwest gate was much calmer than the one they had used the day before, given that only locals went in and out of it and there was no waterway to deal with. Dilly knew practically everyone in the crowd, and they were all talking about the outrageous fire.

Someone whistled a unique call and Grubber cut through the chaos, ignoring Boot, who tugged on the reins.

"I knew it was you!" said Boot loudly. Dod nudged Shooter to follow.

"Can I hitch a ride?" asked a man who stood behind Grubber, just out of Dod's view. He had a familiar voice.

"Sure," replied Boot. "But you can't take my horse. Remember, Bonboo had you train him for *me*!"

"I know," said the voice. "Grubber's yours."

It hit Dod who the voice belonged to, even before his face popped out from behind Grubber: It was Horsely's.

"Dod," said Horsely excitedly. "It's nice to see you again."

"And you, too," responded Dod. He wondered why Horsely was on foot and what had happened to the giant flutter.

"Perhaps I could double with you back to Twistyard—" said Horsely, rubbing Shooter between the ears.

"Actually," interrupted Boot, calling the shots. "I've got a ride planned for you already." He grinned ear-to-ear with delight. "Follow me this way," he said, nearly unable to contain his laughter. From every indication, Boot was proceeding with a prank and it was tingling his toes to think of it.

Dod watched Horsely limp after Boot, who strode effortlessly aboard his magnificent horse.

"Ingrid," Boot called heartily. "Have you had a chance to meet Horsely? He's one of the best maylers I've ever seen—trained by Miz himself—and it just so happens, he'd love to show you his skills."

CHAPTER FOURTEEN

"All right," said Ingrid, beaming a wondrous look of newfound pride. She was wearing yet another spiffy outfit from Commendus.

Toos leaped from his squished position next to Ingrid and hurried to his tethered horse, fearing the new arrangement might fall apart if he were still conveniently waiting for the trade with the reins in hand when Horsely approached.

"This is Ingrid," announced Boot, turning toward Horsely so he could read his lips. "She's heading back to Twistyard and needs your expertise driving this team."

"Okay," said Horsely naively. "Thanks, Boot."

"Horsely's deaf," said Boot, turning to Ingrid, "so when you talk, make sure you're facing him. He's great at reading lips—the closer, the better."

"Oh," said Ingrid. She waited to speak until Horsely had climbed aboard her wagon and squished in next to her. It was a tighter fit than it had been with Toos.

"I'M INGRID," thundered Ingrid, six inches from Horsely's face. "I REALLY APPRECIATE YOU HELPING ME WITH THE WAGON." She yelled each word slowly, as though her volume and speed would aid Horsely in reading her lips.

It didn't help.

"CAN YOU TALK?" she asked.

He didn't say anything at first. Ingrid's face was too close. Her tendency to spit when she spoke increased with her volume, which meant Horsely's face was drenched, his eyes included, and the smells that wafted from her morning breath, after a cleansing breakfast of her home-brewed garlic drippings were nearly lethal. Tears poured down Horsely's face.

"Boot!" cried Horsely, unable to see straight.

"You'll do fine," responded Boot, practically falling off his horse from laughter. He began to direct Grubber away from the buckboard when Horsely whipped the air with a shrill whistle, the likes of which Boot had never heard before. Grubber reared up, tossing Boot off his back.

"I'm sorry, Ingrid," said Horsely, unwedging himself from the seat. "As a mayler, I think I'm more needed on *that* untamed horse. Perhaps Boot will drive the wagon."

Grubber kicked around, trotting in a circle as though agitated. He snorted and pawed at the ground near where Boot sat, then threw his mane back and forth. Horsely limped to the wild stallion, put his hand in the air, and gently took the reins.

"Wow!" said Boot, still laughing but beginning to clap. "Well played, well played!" He stuck his hand up and was greeted by Horsely's lift. "I'm glad to see you've kept your sense of humor, Horsely. Go ahead and ride Grubber to Twistyard. I don't mind sharing. Besides, I think it's my turn to help this *lovely lady*." Boot turned and bowed toward Ingrid, who fiddled with her pearl necklace.

"May I sit beside you?" he asked, playing the part of a true gentleman. He had a harder time squeezing in than Toos or Horsely, but he didn't complain; instead, to make it possible, Boot wrapped one arm around Ingrid and held the reins with the other. "Can I call you Grandma?" joked Boot, nearly gleaming.

"You certainly may," agreed Ingrid, seeming to like the attention. She proceeded to explain to Boot, in great detail, why she'd never married and all about the places she'd been and the things she'd seen. It was a tear-jerking story, to say the least: Ingrid's breath was so strong that Boot often could taste it—and more than a dozen times during the drive, he silently vowed to himself that he'd never eat anything with garlic—and he constantly wished to be Sneaker, who had been given the privilege of napping in Boot's bag, since his appearance made Ingrid uncomfortable.

Meanwhile, Dod rode close enough to keep an eye on the twosome. He and his friends found it refreshing to see the adorable puppy side of Boot, the side that was wonderful with kids, animals, and old people. To watch Boot, you'd think he was having the time of his life. He frequently laughed and gave compliments, despite his watering eyes and personal discomfort. Ingrid clearly loved it. She'd have certainly traded all of her time with Toos for ten minutes with Boot.

Since the wagon couldn't take shortcuts, Dod, Buck, Horsely, Dilly, and Sawny all stayed on the long, winding road, while the rest of their friends raced for Twistyard and a possible afternoon nap. It was the first time Dod had taken the complete thoroughfare. He noticed that over a dozen small towns grew along the path, popping up in every cleared part of the forest. He also got a chance to see, firsthand, the monument everyone had called *The Goose Egg*.

A short distance from High Gate, tucked neatly behind a hill of pines, there was a massive crystal orb. It sat nestled in the lap of the Hook Mountains, with giant, snow-capped peaks behind it. Its color was smoky gray and its shape was unusually similar to a goose's egg—though the goose that could lay an egg of that size would eat towns. In all, it rose hundreds of feet from the otherwise ordinary rock and dirt, and it occupied at least fifty acres of hillside. In front of it, a wall-sized stone sign read: 'Crystalious Megaspheric Splendorium,' with small writing at the bottom, warning, 'No Climbing!'

"This is it," said Dilly. "Isn't it beautiful?"

"It does sparkle," admitted Ingrid. "I'm amazed Higga's

never shown it to me." She had Boot drive the wagon closer for a better look and then commented, "This thing would sure make a lot of necklaces."

"There are plenty of other quarries," said Dilly. "This type of crystal isn't very good—as far as crystal's concerned."

"Good enough for me," sighed Ingrid, moving to stand. "I'd be happy to bring a chunk home."

"And if you did, you wouldn't be going home, Gram," said Boot, making sure Ingrid didn't leave the wagon. "It's illegal to cut into The Goose Egg. Besides, if you want crystal, there's a decent free-dig site just a few miles from here. I've got loads of the stuff at Twistyard. Let me give you some of mine."

"Oh," said Ingrid happily. "You'd do that for me?"

"Sure thing," said Boot. "I know just the piece. It's a sparkly pink rock, about the size of your fist."

"Oooo," squealed Ingrid. "That would be fancy."

Dod marveled at the formation. It struck him as odd that the large crystal hill had naturally formed in the rounded shape of an egg, but when he suggested that it looked manmade, Sawny jumped in.

"It was the snow and rocks that carved and smoothed it." Her fingers pointed at various valleys and mountains in the backdrop, as she explained how snow and ice had once covered the area with a glacier. "So you're right in concluding that it was carefully crafted," Sawny admitted, "but wrong in assuming men had anything to do with it."

"I see," said Dod, smiling. He enjoyed the look Sawny got when she was spouting what she'd read or studied. And once she started, it didn't take much to keep her going. For over an hour of riding, Sawny explained about the types of rock and soil that were common to the Hook Mountains, and the foliage and trees that fared best in them, and the animals that relied on the plants, and so forth. It was like a detailed biology lecture.

Eventually, the discussion led into her most recent conversation with Dr. Shelderhig. She had visited him early in the morning before breakfast, and had been shown all sorts of new advancements he was pushing, including a five-colored bracelet that would give better distance readings on the location of snakes, since his current Redy-Alert-Band only had three. She also talked about his plan to introduce eight different species of fish into the lake for bug control, once the diasserpentouses were captured.

By the grueling end of the lecture, Dod was ready for Dilly's dribble about how ridiculous it was for Commendus to marry Sabbella, and how certain she was that Con would run off any day and embarrass his father the way he had before. Dod had even begun to block Sawny out in order to overhear Ingrid's description of her nightly foot-scrubbing ritual. And so it came as a surprise when Horsely asked Sawny a question.

"Did Dr. Shelderhig mention anything to you about worms?"

At first Dod thought it was a joke—Sawny had gone over so many different aspects of the ecosystem in Green that it had felt like a comprehensive list. But Horsely wasn't kidding.

"No," said Sawny. "Why do you ask?"

"Well, while at Fort Castle I read the lips of a few soldiers who were mumbling about worm experiments," said Horsely. "It made me curious—that's all."

"You went to Fort Castle?" gasped Buck.

"I meant Carsigo," said Horsely. "It's hard to keep track of the places I go when I'm not the one choosing my day."

"No kidding," said Buck, wishing the road would shrink or Boot would hurry up Ingrid's wagon.

"How did things turn out?" asked Dod.

"What?" said Horsely. He had a hard time reading Dod's lips over Sawny.

"Where did you go after Carsigo?" mouthed Dod.

"All over," said Horsely, nodding his head. "When the Zoots are having you fly them, you never know where you'll end up. But it's worth the long walk, even with a limp, just to get the chance to soar for a while." Horsely smiled and took a deep breath. "How did *you* like the ride, Dod?"

"It was great," said Dod with some reservation, feeling his question hadn't been directly answered. He wanted to know where Youk had gone, or if Youk had even been the one Horsely had flown out of Carsigo. However, before Dod could press him any more, Horsely left the road to pick pears from a wild tree, and when he came back toting the fruit, the conversation had long since shifted, with Dilly leading the new subject.

Back at Twistyard, Sawb and his friends from Raul were the first to greet them. They were waiting in the barn, bubbling over with glee.

"Finally!" said Sawb in his usual condescending manner. He ran his hand across the top of his slick black hair and grinned. "I could have walked to High Gate and back in the time it took you pathetic losers to find your way home. Did you get lost?"

Joak and Kwit grunted.

"They were busy helping Boot's mommy," taunted Eluxa, who sat on the side rail of Grubber's stall. "Or is that his girlfriend?"

Two twiggy Rauling girls laughed obnoxiously as they stared at Ingrid and Boot.

"It's nice to see you, too," said Dilly, attempting to be civil. She had just finished discussing with Boot how he could avoid trouble at Twistyard if only he'd keep his tongue, so she was trying extra hard to set an example. Before leaving for The Games, Boot had verbally clashed with Voracio and, consequently, had spent a whole week scrubbing bathrooms.

"I think I'll drop Gram off at the door," said Boot, backing the wagon up. He gritted his teeth and glanced triumphantly at Dilly, who smiled approvingly. She was proud of him for avoiding the conflict.

"Go ahead," said Sawb. "At least *she* has a place to stay tonight."

The crowd from Raul snickered.

"What's that supposed to mean?" asked Boot, stopping short of the doors.

"Why don't you ask Dod?" said Eluxa, drawing a tube of bright-red lipstick from her purse. "Isn't he psychic?" She looked in Dod's direction, puckered up, and blew him a kiss.

"Or psycho," rumbled Kwit, making eyes at Eluxa. He puffed out his chest, showing off his monstrous muscles.

Buck ignored them completely. He rode to his horse's stall, which was much deeper in the massive barn, and dismounted, but found that it had a three-foot mountain of sloppy poop in the middle—a homecoming surprise someone had left for him.

"Come on, guys," said Sawny, glancing at the crowd from Raul Hall. "We don't want any trouble."

"Then stay away," laughed Sawb. "You being here is trouble! Dark Hood and his little helper raided Green Hall, searching for something, and later came back to deliver a gift for you guys."

"A *hot* present," added Eluxa.

Doochi grinned and chuckled. "Really hot," he said, raising his eyebrows.

"Dark Hood torched your place," laughed Sawb gleefully.

"A fire?" gasped Dilly, thinking of High Gate's predicament. She turned Song around and nudged him past Boot and the wagon to get a better view of the castle. Most of it looked untouched, though Boot's huge wall of windows was bashed in and dark smoke stains colored the stones directly above it for fifty feet.

"Oh!" groaned Dilly, sad that it was true, but grateful it wasn't the whole building.

"I wanted to be the first to inform you of the tragic news—" said Sawb.

"I bet!" hissed Dilly. "You probably did it!"

"Whoa!" said Sawb, enjoying the accusation. "We weren't back yet when it burned. And everyone's talking," he added, glancing at Dod with cold eyes. "He did it. He's working with *them*."

"W-what?" stuttered Dod. He was confused and surprised at the same time, and his stomach lurched.

"We all know Dod's involved," said Sawb. "He probably set fire to his own room to make it look like he's a victim—"

"Knock it off!" boomed Boot. He'd heard enough stupid stuff and was angry that his flat had been destroyed. "We all know Dod's innocent. He was with us when it happened."

"Yeah," said Sawb. "He was with you some of the time—and riding around on a giant flutter the rest of the time. Ask any of the drat soldiers. They'll tell you the truth—"

"Before the games—" argued Dod.

"Whatever," said Sawb. "Besides, Boot, maybe you're working with them, too. It's no secret your family needs the money."

Boot looked like he wanted to explode. Had he not just barely promised Dilly he would fly clean, he might have punched Sawb.

"No shame in being poor—" said Ingrid.

Boot didn't wait for her to finish the lecture she had in

mind. He tapped at the reins and left the barn, hoping he could keep his word to Dilly for at least a few more minutes.

Eluxa slid down from the rail and stepped forward, trying to see Boot for as long as she could. "They make a cute couple, don't they?" joked Eluxa. "Look at the way he snuggles into her." She leaned on Sawb's shoulder for support as she delicately stepped over the edge of a mushy spot they had deposited for Boot in Grubber's stall.

"A SNAKE!" yelled Sammywoo, pointing his swot at a beam that ran directly above the crowd. Everyone spun to see the dangling creature. It wasn't a snake, it was part of a rope; but the possibility of being invaded from above caused Eluxa's clique to push past the boys and bolt for safety, hardly noticing the muck they stormed through. Nasty brown slime dripped from four frazzled girls who had besmudged their legs to their mid calves.

"That's the grossest thing I've ever seen—" scolded Eluxa, puckering her lips like she'd just eaten a whole grapefruit. But one of the spindly heels on her elegant boots caught a mouse hole and sunk in, right as she attempted to move, which caused her to trip and fall face first into the deepest part of the mound. Sputtering and gagging, Eluxa crawled from the pile of gooey, wet horse manure and went into spastic movements, desperately trying to wipe the concoction from her mouth and face.

"Aaaah," she screeched, complaining like she'd been gored by a bull. She was so covered in sloppy poop that no one from Raul moved to help her up, fearing they'd be unpleasantly soiled as well.

"The grossest thing, huh?" giggled Dilly, beginning to smile. She was amazed at how quickly her day had gone from rotten to refreshingly wonderful. She slid off Song and handed Eluxa a rag that Sammywoo had used as a sweat and drool cloth. "Here," she said happily, "I think you've got something in your teeth."

After the rough words and Eluxa's mishap, Dod was glad his horse's stall was much deeper in the large barn, well away from the crowd of trouble; though he couldn't help feeling sorry for Horsely, who had been left to shovel out a slide of putrid gunk that was just as deep as Buck's but surrounded by Sawb and his pals. Dod hoped Horsely wouldn't get hurt.

Surprisingly, fifteen minutes later as Dod, Buck, Sammywoo, and the sisters moved to exit, they passed Horsely and saw he appeared to be having a good laugh with Sawb and Doochi as five younger Raulings were removing the muck for him.

Inside the castle, swarms of people flocked to Dilly and Sawny, retelling what they knew of the fire. By the time the group of weary travelers had reached Green Hall, they weren't surprised to find that the place was mostly intact—only Boot's large quarters had been burned. And his solid door had been firmly shut, so the rest of the dormitory didn't even smell like smoke. It smelled like fresh paint. Workers were already vigorously applying coats of white to the scoured, empty room at the end of the hall.

"Sorry about your stuff," remarked Sawny, looking at Dod's disappointed face. "Maybe you should've stopped for cookies with Buck."

"It's okay," said Dod. "I can handle looking at it. Most of the things in there weren't mine anyway." Dod wasn't bothered by the ruined room, he was bothered that some people thought he had been involved in the attack, since they had seen him riding the giant flutter. Yet he still was grateful that he had asked Horsely to stop at his window; had he not, he wasn't sure if his medallion would have fully survived the heat, or where it would have gone. It was a narrow miss of a huge disaster. Dod felt uncomfortable as he considered how close he had come to getting stuck in Green forever.

"I've got clothes to share," said Toos, appearing from one of the other rooms. "And we've also got four spare beds in here if Pone and Voo would just move their junk."

"Thanks," said Dod, sensing doom. He wondered why Toos's cheerful face and warm offer had produced the desire to run and hide.

"See," added Dilly optimistically. "Everything's going to be great. At least we were far away when the fire happened. And that room needed a new paint job anyway." She was still basking in the shameful delight of having watched her nemesis bathe in excrement. "It just goes to show," she continued, pausing to nod at Sammywoo as well, "if you have a positive attitude, things work out for the better."

And then Dilly's luck ran out.

"This message is for you," barked one of three drat soldiers who approached Dilly from behind. They handed her a note, while eyeing Dod with suspicious glances.

Dilly,

You are hereby informed that you are under formal investigation for distrustful behavior. Your complete cooperation in this matter is required. Any attempt to do otherwise will be deemed grounds for incarceration and judgment. We have confiscated your weapons and are in the process of preparing to hear your explanation.

Voracio,

Chief Officer, Twistyard Security.

"Outrageous," groaned Dilly, not looking nearly as pleased as before.

"What is it?" asked Sawny.

"My swords!" muttered Dilly, watching the soldiers prance away. "And I was just starting to accept Voracio as a decent person." She sighed heavily and shook her head. "When did *he* get put in charge of security around here?"

"Since Zerny went missing," responded Toos. "Jibb's not at the top of his game, either—worrying about his dad and—" Toos looked side to side and approached Dilly before whispering, "The Beast!"

"What?" said Dilly.

"The Beast—The Monster!"

"Toos!" scolded Dilly, "I'm not in the mood for stories—"

"It's the truth," whispered Toos, his eyes growing big with concern. "I overheard it. More soldiers disappeared, and then Tridacello and Bowlure ran into the thing, down by Zerny's place—the same morning that Boot's room was lit on fire, while it was still dark. They said The Beast was black as coal and quick as the wind."

"You're kidding!"

"No," assured Toos. "Now Bowlure and Tridacello are both up on the fifteenth floor—"

"What?" gasped Dod. He knew what the fifteenth floor meant. The only part of the fifteenth floor that wasn't used for storage and wasn't part of the library was a special sickbay. One of Higga's esteemed colleagues, Doctor Heatherly, kept close watch on her patients there.

"I'm telling the truth—just as I heard it," said Toos. "They're both in pretty bad shape. And now that they've lived to tell—it cleans the glass, doesn't it: The rest of the missing men were killed and eaten by The Beast!"

THE BEAST

"What kind of animal did they see?" asked Dod, turning to face Toos. Mention of a monster brought back instant recollections of the bizarre dreams he had had while at home—the dreams of a black creature that was searching for him, hunting him, hungering to destroy him.

"The people I overheard didn't say much about what it was," answered Toos, nervously slicking his hair back. "They just kept referring to the thing as The Beast—like they've known about it for a while."

"Who?" asked Dilly, beginning to show signs of true interest. The intrigue over a reported monster trumped her dread over the loss of her swords and the ongoing investigation into her 'distrustful behavior.'

"I-I don't know if I should say," whispered Toos. "I'd get in a lot of trouble."

"Come on," said Sawny, hoping to prove his sources were pranking him; she didn't like the thoughts of a horrid creature near the castle.

"You can't tell a soul," whispered Toos, getting even more quiet than before. "I was doing a little favor for someone—long story—anyway, right when we got back from High Gate, I was—uh—someplace I shouldn't have been, and I may have heard—"

"Who?" pushed Dilly impatiently. She was having a hard time hearing Toos with how soft his voice had gotten.

Toos looked at Sammywoo, who was sitting a few feet away, and leaned up to Dilly's ear. "I saw Youk, Clair, and Jibb having a strange meeting—they made it sound like—well—" Toos stopped abruptly.

"We won!" blurted Sammywoo, hopping to his feet. He ran to meet Dari and Valerie as they approached.

"You survived!" said Dari, swinging Sammywoo off the ground with a hug. "I knew that swot would protect you."

"Like you promised—it's lucky!" said Sammywoo happily. "And Dilly had a magic bracelet, too. It turns red like gizzlers. And we saw the burned-down buildings, and the rocky-water thing, and the yucky dirt. And I didn't like the mean guys that picked on Boot, 'cause he was sick and everything."

"Oh," said Dari, nodding her head.

"Sounds like fun," added Valerie politely, smoothing a wrinkle out of her delicate skirt. "Tell Dilly thank you. That was nice of her to bring you home."

"I didn't mind," said Dilly, straightening her back. "He can ride with me anytime."

"Dod, is that you?" joked Dari, cleverly checking him out. "I almost didn't recognize you with a shirt on." She was referring to the ripped pajama top that had caused a stir while at Youk's house.

Sawny and Dilly both glanced at Dod with horrified looks.

"*Right-o*," said Dod uncomfortably. "I'm wearing clothes today that haven't been slashed by Dark Hood."

"Not yet," teased Dari playfully. She smelled the paint in the air and sobered. "He's got a thing for you, doesn't he, Dod? I wish someone would catch him. If any more people turn traitor on us, I'm gonna die. It's driving me crazy the way they up and slip out. You won't, right?"

"Dari!" chided Valerie.

"It's true," said Dari, flipping her short blonde hair. "Dark Hood's recruiting—and it's no secret that he wants Dod! Plenty of the soldiers think he's already joined—and Clair, of course, is certain he's a traitor."

JOIN OR DIE, echoed in Dod's mind—he could taste blood in his mouth—dust swirled around him—and in his hand he felt the weight of a heavy sword.

"Dod!" jarred Dilly. They were all staring at him as he came to himself, his fists clenched and his heart pounding.

"I was just thinking—" mumbled Dod. He really didn't want any more images or dreams or feelings of doom, and he certainly didn't take his most recent experience as a good sign.

"Come along," said Valerie stiffly, prodding at Dari and Sammywoo with her eyes. "Mom's waiting with dinner, and she won't be happy if we're late. Dad's back, and he may have guests."

The exiting threesome traded places with Boot and Buck, who strode up laughing.

"Evening ladies," said Boot.

"News *flash-o*," barked Dari. "You boys—um—*stink-o!*"

"Not me," called Buck over his shoulder, trying to explain.

"Sorry bro," laughed Boot. "You can't blame her for thinking it's both of us. Ingrid's rotten-garlic stuff is quite overpowering."

"Tell me about it," grumbled Toos, stepping back. "Try two full days, Quickie!"

"Sorry, Short Straw," chuckled Boot. "At least you didn't eat the barn floor." He then rumbled into such a fit of laughter that tears rolled down his cheeks, and Buck joined him.

"I take it you saw Eluxa," said Dilly, pulling a crooked smile.

"We did," answered Boot, almost containing himself. "I think she went a little too heavy on her makeup."

"Especially brown!" added Buck.

"Oh!" moaned Pone, striding into Green Hall with a mountain of snacks. "You'd never guess what I just saw." He bit into a cookie and then went on speaking as the raisins and oatmeal rolled around in his mouth. "Eluxa's been fouled. She's dirtier than a sick foal after a downpour."

"We know," said Dilly, beaming like she'd caused it.

"Did *you* do that?" gasped Pone, wiping crumbs from his chin.

"No—I did!" teased Sawny. "What's it to you?"

"Nothing," said Pone tentatively.

"Do you still think she's *smoking hot*?" asked Dilly, smirking with glee.

"Perhaps steaming," suggested Buck. "Warm manure does that, you know."

"Don't distress," said Boot, moving next to Pone. "She's not more than two or three months of showers away from being nearly clean again."

"Like you have any grounds to talk," choked Pone as he retreated from Boot, three cookies lighter than he had been just moments before. Fearing the rest of his food wasn't safe near

Boot's grabbing hands, Pone dashed into his room and shut the door, leaving Toos locked out.

The hall went quiet for a moment.

"Now Toos," said Dilly, "you never finished telling us about Youk, Clair, and Jibb."

"Right," sighed Toos. "I think I said plenty."

"Not enough," prodded Dilly. "You were about to tell us something when Dari and Valerie came in."

"Oh—uh—" mumbled Toos, looking like a deer caught in the headlights. He glanced at Boot and Buck, who had joined Dilly, Sawny, and Dod in listening, and scratched at his head. "Oh—right—the rumors going around—"

"Out with it, Toos!" blurted Sawny impatiently. She was ready to dive for her room and a bath, but didn't want to miss anything about The Beast.

"Well, it's just what I already told you—strange stuff is happening."

"And the meeting?" asked Dilly pointedly.

"I-I was just pulling your leg about that," claimed Toos, not sounding very convincing. "What I said is just a bunch of rumors and junk—the kind of dribble that I'm sure everyone's passing around. Who knows what's real?"

Pone cracked the bedroom door ajar and peeked out playfully. It was enough for Toos, who pushed it wide open and said, "Feel free to join us in here once you've showered, guys." He smiled at Boot and quickly added, "It's not much compared to the grandeur of your old room, Boot, but you can take my bed if you think it's any better than the others."

"I wouldn't do that, Toos," said Boot, approaching the entrance, "at least not when Pone's is perfectly undefended."

Boot bolted through the doorway and threw his body on the largest bed in the room.

"You stink!" blared Pone, trying to pry him off. "Come on guys, let's take out the trash!" he yelled, rallying reinforcements.

Boot fought off his assailants with the most unbelievable moves, holding his ground firmly while doing no lasting harm to the other boys. He was a champion wrestler. Though in time, eight pairs of arms began to prevail over Boot, at which point he cried out to Buck.

"That's my cue," said Buck, leaving the hall to join in the fray. Together the two brothers were able to successfully take Pone's bed and defend it against the clamoring rivals.

"Do you think Toos was kidding about there being a monster near Twistyard?" asked Sawny, poking at Dilly, who was busy wishing to be a boy for a few minutes.

"I don't know," answered Dilly. "If it was a shadow tale—Toos told it well."

"It was the truth," groaned Dod pathetically. His gut told him that the creature of his nightmares was in fact The Beast.

Both sisters looked at Dod eagerly—Dilly to learn more and Sawny to hear 'just kidding.'

"I've had a few dreams," said Dod sadly. "They seem to suggest that there is an animal—a creature worthy of being called *The Beast*."

"Oh!" grumbled Sawny. "First a diasserpentous—and now this! Dark Hood must be a mayler."

"Are you absolutely, positively certain that Miz is dead?" asked Dod. He felt like he was grabbing at straws, but wished to set soldiers on a good lead, hoping he'd never really need to see the likes of what he'd vaguely glimpsed during his sleepless nights at home.

"Yes," assured Dilly. "His boys gave me his trophy belt from Soosh—the one that matched Humberrone's—and if he were still alive, I'm sure he'd come back for it."

"His sons gave it to *you*?" teased Sawny, cracking a faint smile as she jabbed her sister in the ribs.

"Well," said Dilly, shaking her head and brushing Sawny aside. "Our great-grandpa hardly has a use for it. I'm sure he doesn't mind that we keep it on our wall. It's so beautiful."

Dod glanced at the Redy-Alert-Band around Dilly's wrist and imagined plenty about how she had come by the special belt.

"What ever happened to his sons?" asked Dod.

"Joop and Skap are staying with Jibb and Zerny," said Dilly. "Remember? They decided to hunker down at Twistyard."

"Hadn't heard—" said Dod.

"Because you took off for so long," chided Dilly. "Let us know next time you plan on leaving. Dari's right about people suspecting you of all sorts of things. It will be no picnic trying to bring you to Clair's dueling practices. And with the tournaments coming up, you wouldn't want to miss them."

"Clair—" groaned Dod in agony.

"You've met him, haven't you?" said Sawny. "His first week here, he kept asking for you. He said he wanted to see the face of the luckiest—"

"Don't say it," snapped Dilly. "Besides, Clair was originally taught by Sirlonk, years ago. He's stuck with the idea that Sirlonk is the best swordsmen of all time—Humberrone included—so you can see how he'd get mad hearing about a human boy defeating him, especially with all the flimsy versions of the story that have circulated. I heard one where Dod bested him with his left hand, just to be a sport and give The Dread a fighting chance."

"No wonder he hates me," mumbled Dod, feeling sorry for himself. He glanced blearily at Boot and Buck, who were still having the time of their lives defending Pone's bed.

"Get over it," said Dilly frankly. "If I worried about what other people were thinking, I'd be upset all the time. And Boot over there would be in boohoo land for life."

"So you don't mind?" asked Dod, giving her a doubtful look. From what he'd seen, Dilly most certainly did care what other people thought.

"No," responded Dilly. "If they like me, they have good taste, and if they don't—well—some people are hopelessly bent on being pathetic."

"It's good you feel that way," said Sawny admiringly. "I'd be up all night worrying about Voracio and his crazy tactics if I got a note like the one you're holding."

"Thanks for reminding me," said Dilly, her face dimming a few shades. "How bad could it be?"

"Not good," said Sawny plainly. "With Bonboo gone, Voracio's out of control. I can't believe we're related to him. You'd think he'd be extra nice to us, since he's our father's oldest brother. And aside from our immediate family, he doesn't have very many living relatives."

"Don't worry, Dilly," said Dod. "Bonboo told me he was coming back to Twistyard."

"I doubt that," said Dilly. "But I wish he were. Last I heard, he was boarding a boat at Carsigo—he was headed to Terraboom to stay with my parents and siblings up there—" She glanced down the empty hall and whispered, "Someone tried to poison him."

"Poison," muttered Dod, perking up. The mere mention of

the word reminded him of what he had spent hours thinking about while riding to Twistyard: Pap was possibly alive, having faked his death, and was cleverly hiding in the well-maintained penthouse.

"Got to go," said Dod, stepping into the busy bedroom only long enough to slide his bag under one of the beds. His heart was pounding with excitement.

"Go where?" asked Dilly, sensing Dod was up to trouble.

Dod paused. "Would you guys like to come with me to Pap's place?" he asked.

"Sure!" blurted Dilly without hesitation. "We'd love to!"

"I guess if we're quick," added Sawny, looking longingly at the entrance to the girls' portion of Green Hall.

The threesome dashed across the main passageway and loitered by the door to the seldom-used conference room, which housed the velvet curtain and the hidden access to the secret shaft. They patiently waited for a chance to slip in without being noticed by the drat soldiers who were posted on benches near Green Hall. Unfortunately, the moment Dod swung the door open, he smelled smoke and realized his plan was foiled.

"This room's closed!" snarled Jibb gruffly, rubbing at his little white beard and tipping his uppity nose at Dod. "Didn't you read the sign?" He and a crowd of guards were carefully sorting through piles of charred items—the remains of the torched room.

"Hi Jibb," said Dilly happily, pushing past Dod. "I just wanted to stop by to tell you thanks."

"For what?" asked Jibb, changing tones once he saw Dilly.

"For making sure my room didn't burn down like *his*," she said, pointing at Dod. "That must have been difficult."

"It was," he conceded, approaching Dilly. He stood in front of her, blocking her from seeing the charts and maps that were affixed to the walls. "This room's been turned into our command post," he said, "so you won't need to worry about further trouble from Dark Hood—*or his helpers!*" He glanced ominously at Dod. "If he sneezes toward Green Hall, we'll nab him."

"Good," praised Dilly. "I feel much safer." She patted his shoulder and pressed back out the way she had come, nearly knocking Dod over as she went.

"He still likes you," said Sawny as soon as the door was shut. Dilly shrugged.

"A whole lot more than he likes me," added Dod, wishing desperately to be flying up the elevator to Pap's place, his hair whizzing and Dilly and Sawny screaming.

The next two days were similarly disappointing. Pone's room was so filled with snoring and tooting at night that Dod would have preferred Youk's guest room. At least there he had had a few quiet minutes between the bursts of noise and hadn't been as bothered by Rot's pungent smell as he was by the gas that frequently drifted between bunks in Pone's room. And at dueling practice both days, Dod was the only person Clair wouldn't let touch a sword. And a few mistaken words to Voracio had landed Dod table-scrubbing duty—he'd meant to say 'It's great to see you,' but had slipped out 'It's great to *be* you,' which had been taken as a snide remark and punished accordingly.

As darkness cloaked the corridors, Dod made his way back to Green Hall after finishing his arduous duty of shining tables. He almost didn't dare hope that they'd successfully installed the new giant windows in Boot's room. He wanted to sleep there, or anywhere else that wasn't plagued with unbearable levels of noise and smell. His arms and back ached and his hands trembled.

"No more slip-ups," mumbled Dod to himself, stepping over the cracks as he went, hoping his observance of superstitions would yield a more favorable tomorrow. And then it happened. His eyes stumbled upon a small scrap of paper—the only clutter in the hall. Voracio's tight enforcement of castle rules had scared most everyone into respectful conduct. Even the likes of Raul Hall's occupants occasionally bent to scoop wayward trash.

As Dod unfolded the browning sheet, something in him whispered, *It's a clue!* He strained to read the scribbled note. Half the words were illegible and the other half were only capable of being deciphered when he held them near his glowing stone. It was a checklist, titled, *True Climbers Club*, which was abbreviated elsewhere on the list as TCC. The letters made Dod gasp. He had seen them the day before, up on the fifteenth floor, as he was being escorted out by guards. No one was allowed near the special sickbay.

Dod's insides began to tremble as much as his hands, for he knew what he needed to do, but certainly didn't want to comply. Soldiers frequented the halls, and the fifteenth floor was off limits to everyone but The Greats. Plus, there was a horrible creature that loomed close by, silently taking its victims at night.

Regardless, thoughts of Pap gave him courage. He knew Pap would seek out the truth, wherever it led. On a hunch, Dod took his glowing stone from his neck and slid it into his pocket, crept through the shadowy corridors, and entered the twenty-three story, terraced library.

This has got to connect to the rest of the fifteenth floor, thought Dod, pulling his stone out. The library was nearly pitch black. It was positioned in the middle of the castle and had only a faint glow of moonlight that crept its way in through a few ceiling windows in one corner. The ambiance reminded Dod of his nighttime visits to Pap's place.

"At least the only monsters in here are in the books," whispered Dod to himself, breaking the silence. Strangely, he felt as though he were being watched. "We're on the fourth floor," began Dod, finding the winding staircase that circled a monolith. "Eleven flights to go."

He scurried up six flights before pausing to catch his breath. The massive catacomb of books was one of the most spectacular features of the castle. It easily rivaled the college libraries Dod had visited on Earth, though the subjects of these books were much different. Scattered throughout the rooms were five-foot marble columns, topped with large, delicate glass bulbs, each containing a smokeless candle that burned brightly during the day.

Dod began to climb again when something made him freeze. He heard a noise. It was so faint that he thought it was only in his mind until he heard it again. The soft sounds were coming from the main level, where he had entered. He immediately hid his stone and peered through the decorative-iron railing, hoping to catch a glimpse of whoever was below him.

Nothing was clearly visible, and most of the distant main level was a black blur.

Fearing the sounds were from The Beast, Dod bolted up the stairs in the dark. He stumbled frequently, bruising his shins against the stone steps, but refused to take out his glowing rock, terrified of being more easily tracked. He crept as carefully as he could for the last two flights, hoping to disappear completely from notice.

Out of desperation, Dod tiptoed frantically around the

fifteenth floor of the library, searching for an exit. He huffed and puffed as quietly as he could. If he were given the chance to replay his moves, he'd have stayed his course to Green Hall. He even wished to be lying in one of the spare beds in Pone's room, enduring all sorts of disgusting noises.

When he couldn't seem to find any doors, he crouched in a corner by a stack of dusty books and quietly concentrated on leaving Green. *I've got to get out of here*, thought Dod, encouraging himself to make the medallion work. But it seemed fruitless. All of his focusing only made him realize how loud his heart was, which sent him wondering whether The Beast would be able to hear it—Dod sure could! It pounded so loudly in his ears that he almost couldn't hear anything else.

BOOM-BOOM, BOOM-BOOM, BOOM-BOOM, BOOM-BOOM!

Dod's heart continued to race. He had to do something, so he started crawling across the floor, searching for a good hiding spot—perhaps a cabinet or closet. Then he thought of Lobo, Pap's hunting dog, and the way he had tracked birds with his nose. Hiding in a small space wasn't the answer. If The Beast was following him, Dod's only chance at survival was to get out.

BOOM-BOOM, BOOM-BOOM, BOOM-BOOM, BOOM-BOOM!

Dod's heart beat louder as he boldly drew his glowing rock from his pocket and ran. With light, he easily negotiated the bends of the mazelike rows of bookshelves. As he approached the furthest wall from the stairs, he saw something truly glorious: an exit!

BOOM-BOOM, BOOM-BOOM, BOOM-BOOM, BOOM-BOOM!

A sign covered half of the door with the words, 'DON'T

ENTER!' but Dod didn't even hesitate. He seized the handle and tugged with all his might.

It was locked.

BOOM-BOOM, BOOM-BOOM, BOOM-BOOM, BOOM-BOOM!

He rattled and banged at the wooden door, hoping his efforts would break the darn thing, or better yet, alert guards. Despite knowing that his punishment would be severe, scrubbing tables and toilets sounded infinitely better than facing what he'd glimpsed in his nightmares.

Then the floor began to shake. Something was approaching. Its feet pounded against the ground like a racing horse, causing the books in the surrounding shelves to tremble until one dislodged and struck a chair, making a loud cracking sound.

Dod felt he would pass out any second and not live to see The Beast's horrible eyes, but to his rescue, a rush of adrenaline shot through him. He kicked at the door repeatedly, attempting to bash it in. *COME ON!* thought Dod in frustration, *BREAK!* Had it not been solid oak, it would have.

BOOM-BOOM, BOOM-BOOM, BOOM-BOOM, BOOM-BOOM!

Dod's heart continued to race. It nearly matched the thundering noise of the rushing feet. As they got louder, a painting fell from the wall, shattering the glass frame and ripping the canvas.

The door's useless, thought Dod. *I need a weapon—anything I can use to defend myself.* He glanced around the library, desperately wishing a sword collection would appear and catch his eyes—yet none did. The only thing that remotely resembled a weapon was part of the chair in front of him; one of its clubish legs tilted. Dod seized the seat by its armrests and threw it to the ground, freeing the broken leg, which flew through the air and landed yards away.

Without a moment to spare, Dod lunged across the ground and reached for the club. In the process, he scraped his head against the corner of a bookshelf, but was so consumed with his pending doom that he didn't even notice the blood that dripped down his face. The ground rumbled from beneath him.

Suddenly, light flooded the area as the locked door swung open. Fifteen drat soldiers stormed into the library with their torches blazing and their raised swords gleaming. Dod still clutched his chair leg, uncertain of the direction from which The Beast was approaching.

"MONSTER!" yelled Dod, staggering to his feet. He was so exhausted that his brain didn't work well enough to say much more than that.

"Where is it?" asked the lead guard, rushing to Dod's side. He eyed Dod's bloody face, the broken chair, and the dashed painting, and then he looked curiously toward the ceiling.

"I-I don't know," stuttered Dod, too frazzled to speak. He clumsily tottered to the exit and wondered where the creature had gone. The rumbling had stopped. Was the awful thing invisible? Could it imitate its surroundings so well that it matched the bookshelves?

"Stay back!" ordered the lead guard, clenching his sword tightly as he waved Dod out of the library. He shut the door to prevent The Beast from continuing to the rest of the fifteenth floor.

Dod was left alone, standing in a well-lit hall only feet from the unguarded entrance to the sickbay. He could hear the soldiers yelling to each other on the opposite side of the wall as they courageously searched for the hideous creature.

It was then that Dod gained a greater respect for the drat troops at Twistyard. Up to that point, Dod had seen them as a pesky nuisance and a threatening mob—and rightly so; they'd often been at odds with Dod, considering him a problem. But here they were risking their lives to stop the monster that was plaguing everyone.

"Thank you," whispered Dod, knowing that the men on the other side of the door couldn't hear him, yet wishing they could. His heart continued to pound as he made his way to the special hospital suite.

"My goodness," gasped a kind, older lady the moment Dod walked through the door. "What happened to you?"

"I fell," said Dod, still half in shock. In the back of his mind, he kept wondering whether The Beast could break down the door and whether the soldiers were strong enough to kill it.

"I'm Daisy," announced the woman, directing Dod deeper into the facility. She took a wet cloth and washed the blood from his face and hair, making the actual wound visible. "Heads bleed a lot—even small cuts, don't they?" Daisy gave Dod a curious look. "Nurses are gone from the station downstairs, huh?"

"I-I guess," stuttered Dod, glancing around at the fancy-looking tools. He had never been to the regular sickbay on the main level.

"Well, don't worry," she said. "We'll have you out of here in no time." She grabbed a purple jar of cream, smeared a dab of it on his head, and proceeded to rub it into his cut.

"Aaaah," hissed Dod, feeling the burn. He tried to be brave and not make a fuss. The bleeding stopped as soon as the pain started.

"I'm almost done," assured Daisy, smiling sweetly. "Count to ten and it'll be over."

Dod didn't count. His mind was distracted. The last thing he wanted was to be sent back to the dark halls. He hoped to first hear the victorious cries of the soldiers celebrating their triumph.

"That's it," said Daisy. "I told you it wouldn't take long. You can go now." She pointed toward the way they'd come.

"Can I first speak with Bowlure and Tridacello?" asked Dod, not sure whether Toos had been pulling his leg.

"Um," paused the lady, thinking carefully about the simple question. "What makes you think those people are here?" she finally offered, wearing a most peculiar look.

"I know they are," said Dod, reading her face. "Dr. Heatherly's taking care of them."

"My goodness," huffed Daisy, looking concerned. She glanced toward the main entrance, where guards usually sat. "Who are you?"

"I'm Dod," he declared, suddenly feeling confident. "I'm the one who bested The Dread at High Gate and worked with Bowlure and Tridacello on other issues as well."

"Oh," sighed Daisy, looking relieved. "You're one of The Greats—Pap's grandson. I'm sorry I didn't recognize you. Now that you mention your name, your face is familiar. The painting of you on the wall downstairs doesn't quite catch your eyes."

Hearing someone suggest he was one of The Greats made Dod squirm. He didn't consider himself anything special, let alone great; after all, he had just hurt himself while running and hiding, not fighting. But he wasn't about to dispute the issue with Daisy.

"So, may I speak with them?" asked Dod sheepishly.

"I suppose," concluded Daisy. "As you probably already know, Tridacello's not doing very well. He's still unconscious. Bowlure, on the other hand, is improving quickly. Of course, it would take a whole legion of soldiers to pry him away from Tridacello's side, so we continue to have them both in the same room."

"That's Bowlure!" agreed Dod, nodding his head.

As Daisy led the way, Dod heard singing and knew right where to go. "Bowlure," said Dod, rounding a bend, "are you practicing for your trio?"

"How'd you guess?" responded Bowlure. Both of his massive, furry arms were buried in bandages, as was one of his legs. He had a wound across his forehead and bruises on his neck, all the way to his hairline. But despite his battered condition, his smile beamed contentment.

Tridacello didn't look any worse, though a large quilt covered most of him as he lay in bed sleeping.

"Daisy!" scolded a younger-looking, tall, attractive woman—tredder-black hair, high cheekbones, and nice clothes. "We had our orders! No one was to know they were here. Voracio and Youk were very specific."

"I know," said Daisy carefully, cowering a little. "But this is Dod—one of The Greats. He was already told—I think Youk, wasn't it?" She turned toward Dod to confirm his authorization.

"Youk had a meeting two days ago and mentioned Bowlure and Tridacello," began Dod, being technically honest but omitting the part about him having not been invited to the meeting and the part about him having only learned what had been said because Toos had eavesdropped and passed it along.

"Very well," scowled the woman, scribbling ferociously on a

paper. "If Youk's telling, then it's *his* mess." She finished her notes and followed Daisy away to another room where people moaned incessantly, begging for assistance with pain. The sounds were much less inviting than Bowlure's singing.

"Doctor Heatherly's something, isn't she?" sighed Bolwure. He had worn his heart on his sleeve, and she'd stolen it.

"I guess if you like them tall," said Dod. Dr. Heartherly was well over six feet—perhaps six and a half.

"It's all relative," responded Bowlure, whose seven-foot frame towered over everyone else and whose muscle-bound bulk easily made Commendus's gigantic son, Con, look like a beanpole.

Dod hated to rush the pleasantries, but feared Dr. Heatherly would send messengers to substantiate his story, so he got to the point quickly. "What is The Beast?"

Bowlure groaned. "I don't know. It's a massive ball of trouble—its legs flailing, its razor-sharp claws slicing—" He shuddered. "I know this for sure—it's not meant to be here in Green."

"Right," said Dod. "And it must be huge. I heard it coming, and it sounded like the ground was going to open up and swallow me."

"W-What?" chuckled Bowlure, rubbing at his smooth face. "Are you sure you didn't hear something else approaching? Maybe Boot was pulling your leg. This thing, The Beast, it's as silent as an empty room, and when it moves, you'd think the wind was carrying it."

"Really?" asked Dod, recalling his recent, near-fatal close call with the creature. However, the more he thought, the more logic crept into his equation. The shaking ground hadn't begun until he had banged at the door, and the rumbling had instantly stopped the moment the guards had entered the library. In retrospect, it had sounded like a troop of men running to battle.

"I know what I'm talking about," assured Bowlure. "The Beast is silent."

"How big is it?" asked Dod, feeling like a child who was being told a spooky flashlight tale.

"Bigger than me," said Bowlure. "And I've only got two arms—this thing's got ten or more—and they're boneless, just muscle. I hope Dr. Shelderhig can discover what it is, now that he's in possession of the severed limb I acquired for him."

"What?" choked Dod.

"You didn't think I got all busted up without giving as good as I took, did you?" Bowlure grinned proudly. "If it weren't for the water close by, I'd have finished the job. The thing sensed I was winning, so it bolted for the lake and swam off."

"It's a swamp monster," mumbled Dod, wishing it weren't. He had read a book, years before, about a terrifying creature that lived in a bog and nightly ate dozens of people until the town was destroyed. But that was a make-believe story, written by some author who lived on earth and had never seen the likes of a four-armed creature like Dungo, let alone a real swamp monster.

"It moved just fine on land," said Bowlure. "It's long black hair makes you wonder which it prefers."

The room went nearly silent. Tridacello's light snoring competed with the distant moans that drifted in from other rooms.

"I hope he recovers," said Bowlure, looking tenderly at Tridacello. "He's too old for this kind of trouble. And he didn't even smell the thing—or at least he said he didn't. I could've smelled The Beast from a mile away. It must live on rotting flesh."

"Or Ingrid's special stews," added Dod, trying to raise the mood.

"Don't knock it 'til you've tried it," responded Bowlure, perking up. "That woman's got an interesting style. But I'd personally recommend sticking with Mercy's flavors for most of your meals—to spare others, anyway. It can get rough trying to practice singing with Rot after he's been eating meals with Ingrid and the soldiers. It's no wonder we're a trio short of one more."

"Don't look at me," choked Dod, reading Bowlure's expectant face. "You're as likely to get Dark Hood to join your group as you are to find me crooning."

"That won't be happening," said Bowlure, straightening his shoulders. "After the mischief he's caused, I'm dead set on him joining a different trio—one that involves Dungo and The Dread in Driaxom."

Dr. Heatherly poked her head into the room. "Why are you still here?" she glared menacingly.

"I was just leaving, thank you," replied Dod as politely as he could. He didn't want to make trouble with Bowlure's special friend.

"Stop by anytime," called Bowlure happily, and then he dove into a rendition of *Sweet Roses for My Lady*.

"Or not!" spat Dr. Heatherly as Dod passed her at the doorway. "This wing's off limits to *Coosings*—Voracio's orders!"

On the way to the stairs, Dod looked for the three letters, TCC. He knew he'd seen them out of the corner of his eye the day before, when he'd tried to visit Bowlure and Tridacello, but had been stopped before ever glimpsing the entrance to the hospital wing.

"It said TCC," mumbled Dod, peeking into the storage rooms one-by-one. He'd have had a difficult time checking around if the soldiers were spread out as they had been before.

However, with the fresh library incident, where the location in question was uncomfortably close to the sickbay, troops had been pulled in tight.

"There it is," whispered Dod. He glanced around before slipping into a vast room of strange objects. The initials TCC were embroidered in bright blue on a backpack that sat alone. *Maybe it's a coincidence*, thought Dod, creeping across the dusty floor. *TCC on a bag could be the initials to someone's name.*

But when he reached for the pack, he noticed that dust had been wiped from the shelf beside it.

Dod slid into the straps and strode out of the room, gently closing the door behind him. He wondered who had left the door ajar the day before—or if he hadn't really seen it with his eyes while being escorted out by guards—maybe he'd just seen it in his mind. Regardless, the pack fit perfectly and felt right.

I'm sure Bonboo won't mind, thought Dod. *Besides, I'll talk with him about it when he arrives.*

Without deviating in the slightest, Dod rushed through the shadowy corridors to Green Hall and sighed heavily once he'd passed under the hanging swords, oblivious to what awaited him there.

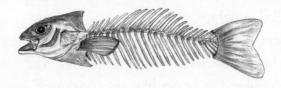

THE FACE-OFF

I t was past midnight by the time Dod reached Pone's room. Everyone had already gone to sleep, since the day's efforts in swordplay had exhausted them all. When Clair taught, he and his team of associates insisted on near perfection. Further down the hall, Boot's door was wide open and the glorious new wall of windows was sparkling softly in the moonlight.

Dod crept into Boot's quarters. It was Dod's room as well as Buck's, though to call it anything less than Boot's would be underplaying Boot's role, for on a whim he could change the order and have Pone and Voo join him in the spacious pad and have Buck and Dod go elsewhere.

The room was completely empty.

My palsarflex, thought Dod, rushing to the large closet. He hadn't been allowed to enter the area since returning from The Games and wondered how much of his stuff had survived the blaze.

Unfortunately, everything was gone. And he knew where it was—in Jibb's hands, across the hall, guarded twenty-four seven.

Dod slid to the floor and took the pack off. He put his

fingers to the laces when a tiny creak prickled his ears. *It's The Beast*, thought Dod, instantly recalling Bowlure's descriptions. His nerves were on high alert.

"Dod," whispered Dilly, startling Dod to the moon and back. "Where were you?"

"Me?" gasped Dod, nearly needing resuscitation. He huffed and struggled to catch his breath. "Why are you in here?"

"I just saw you come back," said Dilly, grinning at how white Dod's face had become. His blood had drained out in fear. "Besides, I waited up for you. I worry, Dod. Now fill me in. Where did you go after you got done polishing?"

Dod knew it was pointless to hide anything from Dilly, so he produced the list from his pocket. "I found this on the hall floor."

"The TCC," muttered Dilly. "They go way back. My grandfather, some number of greats ago, started the thing. He's the one that tripled the size of this building, making it the biggest in Green."

"I thought Bonboo began Twistyard," said Dod.

"He did—well, sort of. But he didn't build the castle, or most of the other structures. They were used by my ancients for various purposes. Bonboo was the one who invited people here to train, the way we have it today with Coosings, Lings, and Pots. Before him, things were different—"

"Oh," said Dod, trying to pull memories. He wished to understand more about the history of Twistyard, but nothing came—or at least nothing having to do with their conversation. Instead, he saw a glimpse of a gloved hand, waving mysteriously in the air like a magician's, and he felt a chill that froze the marrow in his bones.

The Beast had a master—a man with power to control it.

"So Dod," continued Dilly, jabbering on, "I'm curious, where did you go?" She took the special paper and gently tucked it into her Book of Everything, claiming it as her own.

Dod was speechless.

"You found the list, and then what?" inquired Dilly, trying to jog his memory.

"I went to the library," said Dod, hardly paying attention to his own words. He was busy feeling what to do next.

"What? At night?" chuckled Dilly. "There's no way you'd find anything written about the TCC without Ascertainy's help, and I'm certain she'd send you packing. I already tried my best when I first came to Twistyard. There's enough meat in that closet to call every wolf in the forest if the truth were made known—but it's just not out there."

Dod didn't say anything.

"Don't tell me your kin were all perfect people," continued Dilly, looking at his sober face. "If you go back far enough, everyone has trouble in their blood. It's just more noticeable in the rich and powerful families, owing to the size of their footprints. I doubt even Bonboo knows much of it, other than a few tidbits of partial truths. After his great-grandfather burned the records—well—the real story of my darker trunk is gone for good."

"And the secrets?" asked Dod, feeling an uncomfortable wave of anxiety pass through him. It was like he knew The Beast was coming. But he hated to cry wolf a second time. He'd already been wrong once that night.

"Those are about different things," assured Dilly. "Trust me."

Dod hid the markings on the pack he'd lifted. "Okay," he said. "So tell me, then, why would anyone be walking around these halls dropping lists like *that* one? It looks like it was written on old parchment."

"I don't know," coughed Dilly. "I'll need to look at it thoroughly, with brighter light perhaps. It's probably a scrap from the mock TCC. A bunch of Coosings once made a climbing club and named it after the biggie of old. Youk was in that one when he was a Coosing. I've heard a few of his tales."

Dod signaled for Dilly to come closer. He reached up and covered the rock around her neck with one hand, while stuffing his own in his pocket with the other. The closet went nearly pitch-black. The need to hide or run was instinctual. Everything in Dod was suddenly screaming, *IT'S HERE!*

He froze. *We're not home*, he thought, wishing to be elsewhere. He had been scared stiff in the library, thinking of what could be hiding in the dark, but now he beheld The Beast! Its two enormous eyes were as big as dinner plates and bulged out of its head. They glowed a murky greenish yellow except for the black centers that drifted back and forth as it climbed up the outside face of Boot's windows. It was looking in, searching the empty room, hungering for Dod just as Dod had seen in his dreams.

Dilly nearly spoke when Dod gently tilted her head. From the dark closet, they had a perfect view of the ghastly creature: its legs were similar to those of an octopus, only much larger and shaggy with long black hair; and its broad, car-sized body stretched up to fifteen feet, then condensed to twelve, working with its legs to climb; and its mouth was gigantic, spanning the width of its face, large enough to eat a man whole. It was like nothing Dod had ever seen before.

The Beast paused in the center of the glass and stared. Dod

could feel its tethered, dark brain using its senses to scan for him. It was tracking on command, communicating telepathically in a simple form. Bits of its thoughts drifted in the air. They were partially discernible to Dod's mind. *He's not home,* it seemed to say. *Shall I enter? May I feast on someone else?*

No! thought Dod. *Go away!*

But The Beast lingered, using its suction cups to stick to the glass and its claws to cling to the metal trims surrounding the individual panes. Its monstrous, frog-like face, the size of an elephant's head, pressed against the window, contorting until its mouth squished open in two places, revealing sharp, foot-long teeth.

I smell others — let me eat, it whispered.

No! thought Dod. *Go away!*

It was like Dod was having a tug-of-war with Dark Hood, and the rope was The Beast.

Dilly continued to stare, big-eyed and motionless. She couldn't believe that such a thing could exist. Its baggy, stretchy, hairy skin seemed to indicate that the monster could consume four or five men before needing to digest.

Finally, The Beast scurried down the wall and disappeared from sight. *I shall eat more soldiers,* it decided as it departed.

"We need to warn Jibb," said Dod, jumping into action. He could feel the fading presence of the monster, which gave him courage.

"It might be a trick," whispered Dilly in a quivering voice. She was past terrified.

"It's not," assured Dod, hopping to his feet. He grabbed Dilly's arm and pulled at her.

"No!" insisted Dilly, dead-stiff heavy. "Let's wait here until we know it's definitely gone! That thing is the makings of nightmares!"

"You're not kidding," sighed Dod. "But we need to hurry. It's headed for the sleeping soldiers. And Jibb wouldn't trust me; he'd throw me behind bars for causing trouble, or turning traitor, or something."

Dilly's eyes continued to watch the window anxiously.

Dod moved across the closet and pushed the door open all the way.

Dilly gasped.

"See?" said Dod. He danced his way to the center of the room and waved at his reflection in the glass. Behind his image, a smudge of mud and slime was left where the hungry creature had just been moments before.

"You've lost your freshy-mind, fool!" bawled Dilly, jumping to her feet and dashing from the room. Dod followed. Together, they bolted out of Green Hall and rallied the troops who were on watch at their entrance. Jibb wasn't there, but his cousin Dolrus saw Dilly's distress and personally nagged the other men until a number of them were sent at top speed to warn the sleeping soldiers.

In the morning, Dolrus waited for a moment when the other guards weren't watching to quietly inform Dilly that The Beast had been chased away without harming anyone, and that it had taken a few arrows as it fled to the water. "So that might be the end of it," whispered Dolrus optimistically.

"Any sign of Dark Hood?" asked Dilly groggily. She hadn't done well all night because of her fears. After seeing the nasty creature for herself, she had awakened the other girls in Green Hall and had joined them in sleeping at the feet of the guards by the entrance.

Dod couldn't blame her. He, too, had resorted to the stone

floor by the girls, finding it impossible to close his eyes until he knew someone was wide awake, protecting him.

"Sorry, Dilly. I don't know about Dark Hood," responded Dolrus, rubbing at his little white beard. "They don't tell me much."

When Boot and Buck found out about the night before, they both expressed regret that Dod hadn't roused them with the onset of the crisis, though their reasons were dichotomous: Boot because he wished to have seen The Beast, and Buck because he wished to have slept near the guards. Needless to say, neither Dilly nor Sawny felt sorry in the least for either of them—they had slept like kings, completely oblivious of the lurking danger that had plagued Twistyard.

"You didn't need to worry, Buck," reassured Boot, as they all strolled down to a late breakfast together. "Sneaker would have gnawed me lively if danger dared approach. He senses things like that."

"And yet you still have both ears," said Dilly sharply, contradicting his premise. It cheered her up to joke about the awful encounter while surrounded by friends in the light of day. "That creature was pure evil, and the look in its eyes suggested it was window shopping for dinner. If Sneaker didn't detect that as dangerous, your ferret's numb as an old hammer."

"I don't think I can stay at Twistyard," groaned Sawny, fighting to hold back tears. "Knowing The Beast is out there is too much for me. I won't sleep."

"I'll protect you," offered Dod. He felt infinitely bolder during the day.

"Me too," agreed Boot, cocking his shoulders back. "We'll all stick together. And I don't care what your uncle thinks about swords—Voracio can sit defenseless if he wants—but you can bet your front teeth I'll sneak a stash of them into our quarters before the sun sets tonight, along with a couple of bows and full quivers. The guys will trade off watching, and if anything peeps through the windows again, I'll personally drop it. I give you my word, Sawny."

"Thanks, Boot," said Sawny, feeling Boot's strong arm wrap around her shoulders. Boot caught Dilly with his other arm and insisted, "Family first, rules second—and if you talk with Voracio, you didn't hear me say it."

"I don't plan on getting anywhere near him," said Dilly. "Yesterday's lecture was harsh enough. If it hadn't been for Youk's word, I'd be on my way to harsh punishment for distrustful behavior."

"Over a couple of swords?" gulped Buck.

"They'll be *my* weapons," assured Boot. "If you happen to get caught holding one of them, you can tell them I forced you to take it."

"Distrustful," scoffed Dod. "He's the one that can't be trusted! Why didn't anyone warn us of The Beast?"

"Because Bonboo's gone," said Boot, shaking his head with disgust. "Voracio's a dim candle—no offense to your blood, Dilly and Sawny. He may mean well, but he's not very smart. And I'd say his appetite to own this place is a lot bigger than his ability to run it."

"Then he'll have to go hungry," said Dilly happily. "There's no way gramps would hand things over to Voracio."

"But he has," whined Buck, noticing how rigidly people walked in the halls, fearing Voracio's no-slouching rule would catch up with them. "He's changing the place. I mean, look!" Buck pointed at the wall in the Hall of The Greats, where workmen were taking down five of the paintings and adding two larger ones—one of Bonboo and one of Voracio.

"Please!" gagged Dilly. "I don't think I'll be able to walk this corridor anymore if I have to pass *that*!" Voracio's portrait was smiling obnoxiously like a used-car salesman. "Not only did he take my swords, he stole my belt from Miz and claims the soldiers had no part in its disappearance. What a bold-faced liar. If the guards didn't strip my wall, who did?"

"And where's the painting of Dod?" asked Sawny, glancing around to see if they had shifted it to somewhere else. "Bonboo put it right next to the proofus-print of Sirlonk and Dungo."

"Figures," said Dod. "I knew my visit would stir things."

"What?" asked Boot.

"I went to see Bowlure and Tridacello last night," confessed Dod. "They let me in because they thought I was one of The Greats."

"Cool," sighed Buck enviously.

"Yeah, it was nice until I met Doctor Heatherly. She's a woman after Voracio's own heart—the real rule-keeper type. She kicked me out!"

"So they're up there, huh?" asked Dilly.

"Yeah," said Dod. "At least Bowlure's doing well."

"And Tridacello?"

"Not so good, Dilly." Sawny looked nervous.

Dod approached the proofus-print and wished the halls were empty enough to allow him to climb on something. From his vantage, he couldn't see the black-and-white photo sufficient to satisfy his mind. He wanted to see Sirlonk's defeated face, but in the old-fashioned snapshot, the focus was more on their legs. Dungo and Sirlonk had men attaching something around their ankles. And below the photo, under glass, a browning splotch of blood and a snip of hair were placed for each of the convicts, proving they'd been processed into Driaxom with the implantation of Ankle Weeds.

"They should put it on the wall by Green Hall," said Dilly, pointing to the proofus-print. "It's our best trophy ever!"

When the group finally reached the kitchen for breakfast, they were disappointed to find that Voracio was in the room flirting with Mercy, his injured leg propped up with pillows. And since the regular eating time was over, none of them dared enter and ask for food, knowing they'd likely be punished. Instead, they kept walking.

"I know where we can get a snack," said Dilly, directing the group. "Joop and Skap asked me to stop by to taste their smoked fish."

"If you dare," said Sawny hesitantly, looking across the grassy field toward Lake Mauj.

"It comes out at night," said Dilly, enjoying the bright blue sky. "If it tried waltzing around during the day, soldiers would put it down in a hurry. Numbers are on our side."

"And I doubt Dark Hood would be taking a walk with his pet right now," added Dod, feeling his stomach rumble.

"Especially with me and mine out for a stroll," added Boot proudly. Sneaker seemed to know he was on display, for he posed on Boot's shoulder with his nose to the wind.

Sawny continued to drag her heels until Dilly persuaded a group of soldiers away from their camp, promising them a taste of the best smoked fish in Green if they came along.

Down by Lake Mauj, Zerny's house sat nestled next to the water. Tall trees and thick bushes grew so close to the dwelling that it was nearly hidden. Joop was the first to see them coming. He sat on a log in front of the cottage, carving the top of a pole into a sharp tip with barbs.

"Going fishing?" asked Dilly, approaching Joop.

"I guess ya'd say that," said Joop, his eyes flashing with confidence. He set his pole and knife down and directed the group around back, where Skap tended a large beehive-shaped rock dome, puffing smoke out the top.

"We've got visitors, huh?" said Skap, wiping sweat from his tanned brow. He and his brother were both muscular but scrappy tredders. Their clothes were dirty and worn, and when they smiled, they showed that they were both missing teeth, likely lost in fights with animals they'd trained or people they'd disliked.

"I told ya Dilly'd come down right about the time we'd be fix'n to pull the trays out," said Joop proudly. "And she's brought her clan with her—'long with a couple a swords." Joop glanced at the four drat soldiers and smiled. "Ya boys like eat'n fish too, huh?"

The soldiers smelled the air and nodded. Dilly had chosen four large and formidable-looking men.

"It's 'bout done, but while it cools, ya boys want to wrastle?" challenged Joop. His brother Skap was pulling crisscross willow sheets from the smoke, each laden with long strips of blackened pink meat.

All of the guards chuckled.

"If we win, will you still let us eat?" asked one of the big brutes, brushing a large fly from his uppity nose. Boot and Buck both grinned ear-to-ear and glanced at Dod with knowing looks.

"It's hardly a fair match," said another soldier, standing properly. He looked down on both Joop and Skap who were much smaller and skinnier, not to mention younger looking.

"Boys—it's all in fun, right?" assured Joop, beaming with

delight. "Yer commanding officers and such can't see us down here, and Jibb and Zerny are gone, so I figure there's no need to go let'n any a them know if ya lose. Fair enough?"

When none of the guards volunteered, Joop changed the terms. "If ya win, ya get twice the lump a grub we've been smok'n, and if ya lose, ya get a regular hunk, but if ya only watch—well, I'm gonna have to ask ya to watch me eat yers. I like wrastl'n."

The men proceeded to take their swords off as they prepared to wrestle. Joop drew a large circle in the dirt with a line down the center. "Who's first?" he asked eagerly.

The smallest drat stepped up and smiled. He dwarfed Joop.

"Go!" said Boot, calling the match.

Joop caught the soldier's reaching hand, twisted it as he leaned with his weight, and sent the soldier to the ground.

"One point for Joop," hollered Boot gleefully. He had obviously tried stepping in the circle with Joop.

Next, the soldier firmed up his shoulders and stayed put, waiting for an attack, but it didn't end any better. Joop lunged at his legs, knocking him over.

"Two points for Joop," called Boot, waving his fist in the air.

On the third round, the soldier placed his meaty hands on Joop's chest, attempting to push him over, but Joop ducked and lunged, planted his shoulder squarely against the man's gut, and lifted him off the ground, then twirled him around three times for show before sending him down.

"Three points—Joop wins," announced Boot, clapping enthusiastically. Dilly, Sawny, Buck, and Dod all joined in praising Joop.

One by one, the four brick-like soldiers were beaten without gaining any points. It was impressive. But just as promised, Joop gave them each a heaping pile of freshly smoked meat.

While eating, Dod prodded Boot to go three rounds with Joop, which created quite a stir.

"Only after he's had a chance to rest," said Boot.

"Maybe another day," added Dilly quickly. She knew the rivalry that Dod was blind to.

"I'm ready," insisted Joop, setting his fish down. "It'll only take a minute."

"That's true," agreed Boot, rising to his feet. "Losing's easier than winning, isn't it?"

"I don't know much 'bout losing," grumbled Joop. "Perhaps ya'd care to tell me 'bout it."

The two puffed their chests and strutted back and forth like male turkeys, until Sneaker hopped off Boot's shoulder and headed up a nearby tree. The soldiers were content to watch the match, hoping Boot would set Joop down all three times, but doubting he'd do any better than they had.

Skap rolled his eyes and stepped to the side of the circle, offering to call the rounds, though he added a string of rules that hadn't been reviewed before—like no biting, no punching, and absolutely no weapons.

Before Skap had said go, Joop stepped from the circle and laughed manically. "I can't whip ya again in front of yer friends," said Joop. "It was too pitiful last time."

"That was different," said Boot, gritting his teeth. "You'll be amazed to see what a few years can do—I'm a whole new me."

"Ya wanna bet?" asked Joop, glaring at him.

"Name it," said Boot coolly.

The frivolous fun was over. A past wound had surfaced, killing the lighthearted atmosphere.

"Yer Yonkston Ferret," said Joop, pointing at Sneaker, who was scaling up the tree.

Boot paused.

"I thought ya'd be too mousey," mocked Joop. "It's yer fluffy side that weakens ya. Ya'd never make a good mayler, Boot. Way too soft on 'em. I bet that thing wouldn't even come to ya without food."

Boot's face wore the lines of a perplexed man.

"Don't do it," said Sawny, rising to her feet. She knew how much Sneaker meant to Boot.

"We'll come back another day and settle this," added Dilly, holding out a piece of fish for Sneaker. She whistled and hoped the ferret would hurry down the tree. But he didn't.

"It's okay if ya go, Boot. My dad was right 'bout ya. Soft 'n weak!"

"Your steel-tipped harpoon!" said Boot sternly.

"What?" asked Joop.

"You heard me. If I win, I want your steel-tipped harpoon."

"It doesn't matter what ya want," spat Joop, stepping into the ring. "Yer gonna have to take it."

The two boys locked arms and pushed like bull elephants. When neither prevailed, Joop let go, dipped back, and quickly flipped his shirttail at Boot, sending dirt flying into Boot's eyes from a hidden pocket. And while Boot struggled to see, Joop pounded his legs unnecessarily hard and sent him to the ground.

"Point for Joop," said Skap, nodding to his brother.

"But he cheated!" yelled Dod.

"I didn't see noth'n," jeered Skap, turning to grab a whole

stack of smoked fish. He handed it to the guards and asked, "Did ya boys see anyth'n wrong?"

They shook their heads and dove into their seconds.

"Are ya done, Boot?" asked Joop, smiling wickedly. Dod was furious. It made him so angry to see the injustice that he began to wish he'd never told anyone about Sirlonk having stranded Joop and Skap.

"No!" huffed Boot. "But if you want to play rough, you're going to see a side of me that even I don't like to see—you're bringing it on yourself!"

"Fine by me," gloated Joop, celebrating in his point. "I like rough." He covered the top of one of his shoes with the other and grinned callously. The moment his brother said "Begin," Joop kicked his foot up in the air, sending a golf-ball-sized rock into Boot's crotch, then as Boot doubled over, he mercilessly pounced on top of him, smashing his face into the ground.

"You're a cheat!" yelled Dod. This time Buck joined him in jumping in. They both grabbed for Joop when the four soldiers pulled them back. A heaping pile of smoked fish was set in a stack for the soldiers to take to their camp when the match was over.

"They're just two boys wrestling—that's all," said one of the soldiers. "If Boot's done, we can leave. But the ferret stays—"

Dilly and Sawny started to tear up as Boot lifted his head, blood running from his nose.

"Please," said Dilly, "We're done, Joop. Let us leave with the ferret. I'll give you something else."

Joop started to laugh. "Have ya ever seen a Yonkston Ferret before his? Well neither have I, Dilly. And if ya think yer gonna take it from me, yer wrong!"

"I'll have my great-grandfather kick you from our lands!"

declared Dilly, raging with anger. She couldn't understand why they had turned so heartless. She thought she knew them, since she'd known their father, Miz.

"Go ahead and try," said Skap. "Voracio's got us work'n. I'm guess'n that'll trump yer old gramps. I doubt he'll ever live here again."

Boot rose to his feet and stepped into the circle.

"Last chance," said Joop, hiding one hand behind his back.

Boot didn't respond, but his eyes spoke volumes. Dod hadn't seen the look since the morning they'd rode for Jungo.

When Skap called the start, before Joop had whirled his trick into play, Boot seized Joop with his powerful hands and threw him high in the air like a pillow, sending him flying into a thicket of bushes twenty feet away. It was the most amazing display of strength Dod had ever seen. And as Joop landed, one of his flailing arms tried to catch his fall and made a cracking sound.

"Don't ever disrespect Bonboo or his kin!" growled Boot, and then he spun around to the soldiers that were holding Buck and Dod. They saw his fiery eyes and quickly let go.

"All right," said one soldier and "Great move," praised another. They played the part of his friends, doing their best to patch things up.

Boot stepped back into the circle and called for Joop, who remained cowering in the shrubs. "I think my arm's busted," whined Joop.

"Then you better learn to stop dishing what you can't take!" thundered Boot. He turned to Skap and added, "I'm an honorable man. Go ahead and take your brother's place. I'll finish this with *you*."

"Sounds fair," rumbled the soldiers.

Skap looked shocked. He wouldn't have been any more bug-eyed had he looked down and found he was buck-naked.

"Ya won the series by a fair stretch, Boot," he said timidly. Nothing remained of his pompous glares. "I'll help ya fetch his steel-tipped harpoon. It's rightly yours."

Boot approached the tree Sneaker had scaled and gently said, "Come on, Sneaker, it's time to go."

Amazingly, the ferret came scurrying down, and it was carrying something in its mouth—an old, dead pigeon.

"Good boy," praised Boot as the ferret climbed on his shoulder with the dried-out, shriveled bird. "You're learning to hunt, huh?"

No one said a word about his pet's choice of toys.

Skap led the group into the forest, along a narrow trail. Buried in the thickets, a large cage reached thirty feet in the air, constructed of lashed poles. It had a dozen good perching logs inside, but no birds. A rough-looking shed was tucked up next to it. Skap disappeared for a moment into the shack and reappeared with Joop's shiny, steel-tipped harpoon.

"Here ya go," said Skap, handing it over. "Do ya also want the rope that attaches to it?"

Boot took the weapon and shook his head. "What's the cage been used for?" he asked. In all the years he'd been at Twistyard, he'd never seen the structure or heard of the animals it housed.

"Zerny's pets," said Skap bluntly, pointing at the pigeon on Boot's shoulder. "He's taken to a hobby, but someth'n smudged 'em all out."

"Like The Beast?" asked Dilly. She was willing to speak with him since he had begun acting the way she had originally expected.

"Naw," responded Skap. He spit on the ground and stomped it in with his foot. "I think somebody didn't like his pastime."

The group made their way back to the house, where Joop was sitting on the back porch, massaging his shoulder.

"Are you okay?" asked Boot, approaching him. He felt bad but justified.

"Yeh," huffed Joop. "It's not broke, just sore."

"Thanks for letting me use your harpoon for a while," he whispered, out of the ear's reach of the soldiers. "Strange stuff's been happening—you know, The Beast. Dilly saw the thing last night. I'll give you your piece back once the thing's gone. Any suggestions?"

Joop's eyes were still cross, yet held a tinge of hope. Boot was being more than a sport to offer his prized weapon back at a future time, especially after Joop had been unfair with him.

"Go fer the eyes," he said in a quiet voice. "If it's what I think it is, the rest of the flipp'n thing grows back like a patch a cow grass that's been nipped. The more it eats, the more it grows."

"Have you seen it?" asked Boot readily.

"Naw—but people are talking. If it's com'n round ya, it's not good. The thing's been hit'n its marks and stroll'n off. Beasts don't do that alone. It's bad stuff. Ya might want to think 'bout leav'n for a while."

"Thanks," said Boot, letting his voice get louder, "I'll remember that move. You're a great wrestler, Joop. Miz taught you well."

After leaving Jibb's house, Dilly followed Boot's whispered advice: She thanked the soldiers and sent them on their way. By doing so, Boot hoped to keep his hands on the harpoon. In addition, he wanted a bit of privacy, since he'd found a critical clue—a real gem that the soldiers didn't need to know about.

SOMETHING'S HUNGRY

Behind the castle, Boot led Dilly and the others to a spot on the old dock that was far enough away from everything to give them plenty of warning if someone decided to approach. He insisted that they all keep quiet about what he was going to show them.

"I think we're hidden, Boot," said Dilly, beginning to speak up. "We don't need to go any farther. Nobody comes this way anymore."

"Yeah," agreed Sawny, keeping her eyes on the watery side of the wharf. She was really concerned about The Beast making an appearance, even though it was the middle of the day.

"I've got *this*," said Boot proudly, holding up the steel-tipped harpoon. "You guys definitely don't need to worry about Grumpy. If it's dumb enough to come plopping out of the water right now, I'd drop it quick. Mercy would be grilling beast burgers for dinner—and from what you've said of its size, I think the whole castle could attend that banquet."

"Right," said Dilly, fidgeting with one of her pockets. She

produced a hanky and used it to wipe dust and blood from Boot's battered face. "You don't need to impress us any more today. We all know you're strong."

"You're the tops, Boot!" praised Buck, who was still dumbfounded at how far his brother had thrown Joop. "You're only an inch or two taller, and yet, to see him fly, I'd have thought you were pitching a wrap of straw."

"It's the practice you give me," said Boot, sharing the glory with his younger brother. "You're a much better wrestler than either of them—that's why Joop felt like he needed to cheat. We've gotten better, and well, he hasn't. I kinda feel sorry for him."

"I wouldn't have climbed in the circle with Joop," said Buck, staring at Sneaker, who gnawed on the dried bird. "I saw the way he took care of business. He sent those drat soldiers packing without a point. He'd have easily messed me up. I'd be looking like your pet's treat."

"Oh—that's not true," teased Boot. "You're just too nice, so you leave all the dirty work for your mean old brother to do."

Dod stared at the rocky back wall of the castle. He would have never guessed that a building was hidden on the other side if he hadn't already seen it. The cliff looked like a serene beachfront monolith, the kind you might find while touring the Oregon coastline. The only exception was the entrance to the cavern—the very place where Dod had discovered that Sirlonk was The Dread. It gave him a rush of memories to see it.

If I had my palsarflex, thought Dod, *I'd climb the wall and see if Pap's up there.* He liked noticing that the sturdy rock surface had nooks and cracks in it which would easily make good perches for resting while repositioning the rope. It would be much simpler than his nighttime climb up Youk's wall.

"Are you going to show us?" asked Dilly, staring at Boot. She was referring to the clue he had claimed to have.

"Show us what?" asked Dod.

"Boot found a clue," said Dilly happily. She was bubbling with anticipation. "Back at Jibb's place he told me we'd all be surprised."

Boot smiled and rubbed his hand up the side of his steel-tipped harpoon. "I didn't actually find a clue," he said. The glint in his eyes indicated there was more to come.

"What—" complained Dilly.

Boot reached up and gently took the dead bird from Sneaker, who tugged back at first.

"If you've brought us all the way over here to show us the insides of that thing," said Sawny, knitting her brows, "I'm not going to be pleased."

"Hold on," said Boot, enjoying the fuss. He tilted the bird over and held up one of its legs. A small container was attached, made of a hollowed-out twig. "Sneaker found the clue!" proclaimed Boot smugly. "Take a good look at *Zerny's hobby*."

"See if it has a note in it," squealed Dilly excitedly. She didn't want to touch the dead pigeon, but was waiting with open hands to receive its cargo.

"You're in luck," said Boot, carefully picking at a tiny scroll of paper with his fingernails. He pulled it from the miniature cylinder and gave it to Dilly.

"What a find!" gasped Dilly. She read the following:

PLAN IS WORKING
5 SOLID, 10 CLOSE
NEED 15 PAPERS
TO FISHER X

7 BEFORE BIG
WILL MEET AT
HG IN CBB ON 6
REST AT SEA 2D

"It's all in code," groaned Buck. "How are we supposed to know what Zerny meant?"

"Who's to say Zerny wrote this?" said Dilly. "What do you think, Sawny? Does it look like his handwriting to you?"

Sawny peered at the letters and shook her head. "I don't think so," she said. "It's too messy. And the ink is—" Sawny bent close to the paper and smelled it, "yup, made from jumba sap. This letter was sent *to* here, not *from* here."

"Oh, I've got it!" exploded Boot. "When Zerny didn't get his special message, he had to go on a little vacation to talk to the person himself. That's why he's reported missing. He didn't want to say, 'I'm running off to consult with my evil partners in crime.' It's no wonder Jibb doesn't seem too concerned about it. I'd be freaking out if Buck went missing, especially now that Grumpy's swimming around in the lake."

"The Lake Mauj Monster," mumbled Dod.

"It might have eaten poor Zerny," said Dilly, remembering how awful the creature looked. "Besides, maybe this note isn't a bad thing. Zerny might be coordinating with Pious or one of our other allies. When he missed this, who knows what bad things may have happened."

Dod bent down to smell the jumba sap letter and shuddered. He saw massive plumes of smoke, destroying the sky for miles, he heard screams and cries from thousands, he felt the touch of death's cruel hand on his shoulder, and he saw the ghastly image of a skull, its mouth gaping and its hollow eye sockets scowling.

"It's not a happy postcard," exclaimed Dod, certain of what he knew. "This message was sent to Dark Hood."

"Then Zerny must be working with him!" said Boot. "It just makes sense. Otherwise, why did he up and build a giant bird cage in his backyard. Doesn't it seem like a strange time to start taking an interest in *this*?" asked Boot, holding up the dead bird.

"No," said Dilly. "You guys always have it out for him, like he was the prized goose before Rainfall Day."

"And the poisoning?" added Boot. "You know Zerny was visiting Bonboo. He could have easily been the one dosing him up, a little at a time to make it look natural."

"Or Jibb," added Buck.

"Why don't you like them?" asked Dilly, turning away from the breeze that was approaching from Lake Mauj. She pulled her curly hair out of her face and continued on. "We already went through this when the three of you thought Zerny was The Dread, remember?"

"And he was innocent," said Sawny, looking like she was ready to go back into the castle. The slight change in weather made little waves that turned the glassy water into a choppy mess. Now the monster could draw near without being easily detected.

"Not exactly," said Boot, shaking his head. He tossed the dead pigeon and let it fly on the breeze one last time. "When Buck and I rode to catch them, we met up at Higga's place, where they claimed they were waiting to nab The Dread—"

"Right," said Dilly. "We've been over this."

"But they weren't wearing swords," said Boot. "What kind of idiots rush out to catch a bloodthirsty villain without weapons?"

"They didn't go unarmed, did they?" choked Dilly. "Are you sure?"

"Yes," said Buck. "At first we were excited because it seemed all too easy for us—since we were toting blades and they weren't. But then Higga did her explaining and we let them go. Who knows, maybe they were up to something back then?"

Dod felt uneasy. And the moment he realized it, his heart began to pound. *The Beast is coming*, thought Dod. He didn't like that they were way out in the middle of the empty dock—nothing but rotten wood for hundreds of yards in every direction. And water sloshed under the slats below them.

Sneaker pulled at Boots hair and ripped a small mouthful out.

"Ouch," said Boot. "Come on, boy, settle down. You don't want that putrid thing anyway. I'll find you something better than a dried-out pigeon."

"Maybe that's your cue," said Dilly playfully. "He's warning you to get your stick ready.

"Yeah," said Dod, straining to chuckle. "Let's get out of here."

The breeze seemed to make strange noises, though only Dod kept turning to look.

"I'll race you guys to the thickets," said Dod, doing his best to speed things up without appearing crazy. But Sawny complained that her ankle was sore, so everyone decided they'd walk.

It was the most torturous stroll Dod had ever taken; he was certain the Lake Mauj Monster was coming. His frenzied mind struggled to hear whispers, as he had before. Unfortunately, it was hard to tell if the sounds originated from the wind or the creature. No words or phrases floated in the air.

And then suddenly, *MY FOOD!* boomed a voice as clear as Boot's. It rumbled from directly beneath his feet.

"RUN!" yelled Dod, surprised that none of the others had heard it. He stumbled from fright and bolted, knowing that The Beast's strength would easily snap the wet timbers.

"It's just Horsely and Tonnis with a few mares," laughed Boot. He glanced at Dilly and Sawny, who were both stunned with terror.

"Don't scare us like that!" cried Dilly. But Dod didn't turn toward her, he kept running as fast as he could until he reached the bushes and trees.

Horsely had approached from the opposite end of the pier at a gallop and hadn't been noticed by Dod, whose eyes had been glued to the lake.

When the others finally reached Dod, they all had a good laugh, especially Horsely. He teased Dod for not being able to identify the sound of trotting horses and insisted that even without the use of his ears, he would have known they were coming by their vibrations.

"I know what I heard!" said Dod with a determined face. He glanced at Horsely, then Tonnis. "It was The Beast. It said we were his food."

"It spoke with you?" laughed Horsely, reading Dod's lips. "You're in worse shape than I thought." He paused to get Dilly's attention and added, "Did the monster say anything to you, too?"

"No," said Dilly, only glancing briefly at Horsely and Tonnis before setting her eyes heavily on Dod's. "You nearly made my heart stop back there. Please don't tease us any more about that thing. Sawny won't sleep a wink tonight as it is."

"But I wasn't teasing," protested Dod, feeling cruelly slighted.

Horsely shook his head.

"Really Dilly—I heard something screech at us—and it sounded like—you know, that *thing* we saw the other night—"

"Or galloping feet," blurted Buck.

"Don't worry," said Boot sympathetically, looking into the air. "I once thought I heard a cow say something to me. It's pretty normal to accidentally mistake stuff like that."

"What did it say?" grilled Swany, ready to catch Boot in a tall tale.

"I don't remember," responded Boot quickly, "and that's not the point. What I'm trying to say is that Dod shouldn't feel bad. I'm sure I'd be hearing that thing's voice everywhere I went if I came face-to-face with it at night."

"Aren't you our great protector?" teased Sawny, looking skeptically at the weapon in his hand. The closer they got to the chaos of the grassy field in front of the castle and the camp of soldiers, the better she felt.

"Hey, that reminds me," said Boot, grabbing Horsely's reins. "Can you do a solid for me?"

"Sure," mouthed Horsely, "as long as you're not asking me to translate for you. I don't speak beast-talk."

"No," said Boot. He scolded him with his eyes, since he was feeling bad for Dod and wanted the teasing to end, and then asked the favor. "Can you put this at the back of Grubber's stall for me, down under the hay? I'll come for it later."

"I guess," said Horsely tentatively. "But you have to prop me if Stallio thinks I'm up to no good—fair enough?" He waved at the distant barns, where his uncle Stallio was standing by three other horses, his braid blowing in the wind.

"Have him speak with me if there's a problem," said Boot, handing over the steel-tipped harpoon. "I really appreciate your help."

Dod noticed how much Tonnis resembled his father, Sirlonk—handsome and fit—though his eyes looked soft and concerned, not proud and baneful; he didn't even join Horsely in teasing Dod.

Sawny reached up and patted the nose of a pretty palomino mare that fussed by Horsely's side. "This one's feisty, isn't she?" said Sawny, admiring the horse's delicate build. "What's her problem?"

"Everything," said Horsely. "I'd have given up on her long ago if Stallio weren't so insistent. With as many good fillies as we have out to pasture, it's pointless working with an obstinate older one like this."

"And her name?" asked Sawny, as the mare drew closer.

"She doesn't have one," responded Horsely.

"Then I shall call her Honey," said Sawny. The horse bent her head down and nudged Sawny's leg, begging to be rubbed.

No sooner had the group attempted to pass the guard's encampment than a familiar voice insisted they stop in.

"Boot!" called Ingrid. "Come and taste my stew."

Today it smelled like old gym socks rolled in garlic.

"It's good to see you out in the fresh air," said Dilly. She stepped forward and sampled the old woman's concoction. "This is wonderful," she lied, trying hard not to vomit. "I think the soldiers are lucky to have you cooking in their camp today."

"I'm down to only five times a week," said Ingrid sadly, rubbing one of her legs. "But I do what I can to help with the cause. Besides," she added, glancing at a matrix of loaded tables, "we owe these men our thanks, wretched as they are."

Dod smelled the air and thought that the soldiers probably wished Ingrid's graciousness had been spent in knitting sweaters or learning to speak kindly, for Dod knew he couldn't stomach what she'd made. It reeked. Yet surprisingly, the troops dug into it readily, despite their sour faces.

"Why do you do it?" asked Buck of Dolrus, when he was out of Ingrid's earshot. "There's plenty of better food for the taking." He pointed at a table that was laden with ham, bread, fruit, and other delicious-looking items that had been provided for their lunch.

Dolrus groaned and blushed. "They say it keeps you-know-what away," he finally admitted. He couldn't openly say 'The Beast' or he'd be hauled off and punished by his superiors. Talk of the creature was not allowed around civilians—Voracio's orders.

Later that night as the sun set, Green Hall buzzed with views on what to do. They were all terrified and convinced that the guards who waited at the entrance wouldn't be able to respond fast enough to save them from The Beast, and they were disappointed that the guards' orders hadn't been changed to accommodate the possibility of danger at the windows. Fortunately, Boot had a plan.

"Don't worry," explained Boot, popping his head out of the largest hall closet. "We'll sleep a little tighter than usual and protect each other. We've got plenty of talent right here—more I dare say than out there—" Boot pointed toward the handful of guards that were stationed on the other side of the double doors, at the dorm's entry.

"With what?" asked one of the younger Greenlings.

"With swords," responded Boot. "But not a word of it leaves Green Hall. I'm putting my head in your hands to keep this a secret. You know the wrath I'd reap from Voracio and the soldiers if it leaked out that I smuggled weapons into this place—"

The mob of Coosings and Greenlings watched as Boot disappeared into the closet and came back hefting a black metal chest. He popped the lid open, revealing it held twenty swords.

"Wow," gasped Pone, being the first to speak. "How in the world did you come by them?"

Boot smiled and dipped back into the closet. He returned with a second chest, and then a third, and then a forth. Eighty swords in all.

"One a piece," he said happily, beaming with pride, "and a few extras for good measure. We'll all sleep better knowing that we've got them, and I intend on having you each keep them beside you at night—we'll hide them during the day."

"You weren't kidding," said Dilly, who was completely shocked.

"Nope," said Boot, pulling three bows from the closet. "I told you I'd protect Green Hall." He reached back, fidgeted momentarily, and produced his steel-tipped harpoon. "If that thing comes near us, I'll drop it or die trying!"

Without a word, Buck raised his fist in the air and the whole crowd followed. "We're with you, Boot," said Buck, reaching to choose a blade.

"I figured it's about time we tote these things," said Boot proudly, doling out the weapons. "After all, we endured plenty of training at the hands of Sirlonk, and recently we've had a fair dose from Clair as well, so it only makes sense that we sword-up against The Beast."

When Dilly reached for a blade and scabbard, Boot caught her by the wrist. "These aren't for you," he said.

"But Boot—" she protested.

"I've got something else in mind," he chuckled, reaching behind him into a large gunnysack. He produced a magnificent rapier with a ruby encrusted handle. '*Tillius, Freedom for All,*' was etched up the side in fancy writing.

"What?" gasped Dilly and Sawny both.

"Where did you get *that* from?" asked Dilly. "It was stolen years ago, when I was young."

"I know," said Boot, nearly bursting the three top buttons on his shirt. "But when a friend of a friend told me he'd seen it floating, I let him know you'd like it back."

"Wow, thanks," said Dilly reverently, carefully inspecting the craftsmanship. Bonboo's father had received the sword from his father and had wielded it in the fight against Doss. "I thought we'd never see this again. Once it disappeared from the glass case in the Great Hall, we feared it was gone forever. My great-grandpa will be so pleased."

"Always trying to help," said Boot happily. "Just—well—when you give it to him, perhaps you could think of some other way you came by it. I'd rather not get the glory on this one, especially with your uncle Voracio looming around like a black rain-laden cloud. You know him—no good deed goes unpunished."

One by one, every member of Green Hall took a sword and sheath. They were all fair to good with the weapons, and together, they were a formidable bunch. It changed the mood in the dorm substantially.

Boot designated sleeping arrangements: the boys occupied two rooms with windows, and the girls shared a spacious, windowless recreation room that was squished between them. He also assigned hourly watches to guard the doorways and windows throughout the night. If anything attempted to enter, the people on duty would ring their bells and everyone in Green Hall would rise up with their swords to defeat the creature. It was a fantastic plan.

"How did you get the weapons past the drat soldiers?" asked

Dilly, pushing Boot mercilessly once the group was settled for the night.

"Come here," he whispered. He led Dilly and Dod to the hall closet where he'd hidden the arsenal. "Do you notice anything odd?"

Dilly and Dod searched the room. Nothing seemed unusual. It was ten feet wide by twenty feet deep, windowless, and lined with shelves from floor to ceiling. Most of the supplies that littered the closet were uninteresting: blankets, pillows, ropes, cleaning rags, brooms, tools, and the like.

"Can you keep a secret?" asked Boot. He was dying to tell someone what he knew.

"Of course," said Dod. Dilly's eyes answered for her.

"What would you never touch?" he asked, peering around the closet. He enjoyed turning the conversation into a game.

"I don't know," said Dilly quickly.

"Think about it—realistically—what would no one ever touch?"

Dilly glanced across two sets of encyclopedias while Dod focused on a shelf of sewing equipment.

"Think *never*," hinted Boot, smirking.

Eventually, Dod and Dilly both looked at the same spot. High up in one corner, on the top shelf, a container held the grossest-looking toilet cleaning brushes they'd ever seen. Brown goo, which appeared to be poop, clung to the crude instruments—and the brushes faced outward, making it impossible to draw them down without grabbing the ends that had been plunged into toilets.

"Up there!" said Dilly, repulsed by the thought that they hadn't been thrown out. "We have newer ones that work much better! Why do we still have those old things?"

Boot chuckled. "See?" he said. "I knew you'd figure it out. Go ahead and get them down."

"Eew!" shrieked Dilly. "No way!"

Boot closed the closet door, pushed a three-step stool over to the corner, and one by one removed the filthy looking items. "It's not what you think," he said, raising one of the nasty brushes to his face. "See?"

Dilly shut her eyes in horror and shuddered. She couldn't believe Boot was licking the brown goo.

"It's chouyummy," said Boot gleefully. "I put it there myself. And these scrubbers were new when I soiled them."

"What?" choked Dilly, peeking through slits.

"You can look," he said, swinging one of the brushes toward her.

Dilly stepped back. "I'll trust your word."

Boot finished clearing the shelf, then worked with a screwdriver to unwedge the container that had held the cleaning supplies. As he pulled back the massive box, an opening appeared. "Voila!" said Boot proudly. "It's my secret passage!"

"You have got to be kidding!" said Dilly in shock. "How did you know about *that*?"

"I may have had a tiny hand in its birth," responded Boot. "But remember—you can't tell anyone. You both promised!"

"We know," said Dod, wondering how and why Boot had created the escape route. The first thought that came to Dod's mind was Dark Hood's magical disappearance—the night he and his little helper had been surrounded by guards, inside and out.

"Where does it lead to?" asked Dilly, rushing to poke her head in. She pushed past Boot and jammed a smokeless candle up the darkened crawlspace.

"The boys' changing room upstairs," said Boot.

Dilly retreated.

"Do you remember the year the pool broke and flooded part of the fifth floor?"

"Yes," said Dilly. "It was scorching hot and we couldn't swim for weeks."

"Well—" proclaimed Boot, pointing at the hole. He paused.

"Well what?" asked Dilly.

"That's when they redid the flooded-out parts of the fifth floor—and uh—I may have helped the workers a tad more than they knew."

"Bonboo would be ashamed of you!" said Dilly with disgust. "You can't go changing the castle without asking for permission."

"Do you think Bonboo would like his favorite great-granddaughters to be left helpless with a hungry, vicious beast on the loose?"

"No," said Dilly slowly.

"It's not like I did it to be bad," argued Boot. "It's just—well—you know me. I thought I'd help the workers—and then I was curious whether it connected to Green Hall—because I suspected it did—and then once I knew, I didn't want to close it off for good—"

Boot rambled until Dilly broke in. "It's okay," said Dilly. "We'll keep this a secret, right Dod? I won't even tell Sawny."

Dod nodded uncomfortably. He was happy that Boot had found a way to sneak the swords into their quarters, because he definitely didn't want to see the Lake Mauj Monster again without being armed. But it was disconcerting to be sworn to secrecy about the very route that Dark Hood had likely used to escape—and it made Dod wonder how the villains had discovered Boot's handiwork.

"I hauled the boxes in this—one at a time," said Boot, lifting a sizeable burlap sack from the floor. It had 'POOL TOWELS' embroidered on the side in big block letters. "Once I got them to my *special* changing stall, well, the towels became swords."

"And didn't Buck help you?" asked Dilly, imagining how many trips it had taken.

"Buck doesn't know about my creep hole," said Boot defensively. "Like I said, I made it myself and I've kept it a secret—all these years—just in case. Up to now, I've only used it one or two other times."

"For what?" begged Dilly curiously.

"For I can't remember!" returned Boot. He grabbed the mess on the floor and worked to reassemble his gross-looking façade. "Please keep it a secret," he groaned as he worked. The concern in his face seemed to relay a heavy dose of regret in having finally shared his nifty creation.

"Don't worry about me—I trust you completely," said Dilly. "I'm just glad you've got your spear-thing."

All night, Dod tossed and turned. He only spent one hour on duty, but worrying about the creature kept him awake. In his mind he could see its menacing eyes; they glared, glossy and cold, searching, hungering. And behind their stare, Dod could feel the tug of Dark Hood's controlling power. It haunted Dod's dreams as it had before, while at home.

Nothing happened.

In the morning, everyone hid their swords in their bedding and acted as though things were normal. Night after night, they continued the same ritual. Slowly, the tension they had felt over The Beast began to dissipate. They would have hoped that the soldiers' arrows had hit their marks and ended the creature's life if it weren't for two horses that had gone missing the first night; a few remains had been discovered on the shore of Lake Mauj, suggesting the monster had eaten them—and to Sawny's great lament, Honey was one of the two.

After a week, the hardest part about the evening ritual was keeping the more rambunctious individuals from sparring. Boot hated bossing people around with an iron hand—it wasn't his style. However, after a few minor injuries, he nearly stripped the masses of their swords. They couldn't help wanting to practice. Clair's classes consumed the bulk of their days in preparation for the upcoming tournaments, and they all hoped to do better than they had done in the past, especially against Raul Hall.

Sawb and his lot strutted around Twistyard like kings all week, gloating in advance of their upcoming victories. They knew that they were the best at swordplay. Even Tonnis put on more airs than usual and appeared to be a true member of the gang. Of course, Clair had spent extra time helping him with his sword skills, out of respect for his father, Sirlonk. Clair treated Tonnis the exact opposite of the way he treated Dod. He praised Tonnis so much that Sawb and his pals seemed to buy it. And every chance Clair got, he reminded everyone that despite Sirlonk's evil deeds, he had been and ever would be the best, most amazing swordsman of all time.

But even Raul Hall's pretentiousness dimmed each night as the sun set. It was clear that they, too, had heard of or seen The Beast. Sawb had resorted to drawing upon his family's resources in Green to pay for thirty private tredder guards, who kept vigilant watch at the windows and doorways of Raul Hall at night.

And for good reason!

CHAPTER EIGHTEEN

THE "PICNIC"

One early morning, before the corridors were bustling with traffic, Dod made his way to the Hall of The Greats, hoping to catch a better glimpse of Sirlonk and Dungo in the proofus-print. But as he approached, his stomach for reveling in his victory over The Dread weakened until it only rumbled from hunger. Tonnis was standing by the wall, gazing up at the portraits.

"Hey, Dod," he said, without taking his eyes off the wall.

"How'd you know it was me?" asked Dod.

"You did that three-step shuffle thing with your feet," he responded.

Dod suddenly felt very self-conscious about the way he walked. He'd never noticed that he had a particular pattern of stepping, yet he knew exactly what Tonnis meant the moment it was brought to his attention.

"You're very observant," said Dod, attempting to change his routine as he approached.

Tonnis sighed heavily. "You ready to get beat?" he asked, finally swinging his head to look at Dod.

"I guess," responded Dod, knowing he'd go down quickly against the Raul Coosings. He had practiced really hard at home with The Guys—hard enough to feel decent. Still, he'd also watched the way Sawb dueled. Even Eluxa, who usually played the part of a head cheerleader, had moves that were remarkable. Swordplay was in their blood.

"Come on," jabbed Tonnis, flipping his bangs from his forehead. "At least pretend to be good."

"I'm not," said Dod flatly.

Tonnis looked Dod up and down.

"I'm serious," said Dod, feeling sorry for Tonnis. Pap's picture was on the wall for the great good he had done and Sirlonk's for his wickedness.

"Huh," grunted Tonnis, turning back to the wall. He hid his thoughts well. Dod wondered how Tonnis felt about his dad, whether he secretly sided with him, or whether he felt ashamed. Neither emotion showed on his face—only indecision.

"So what brings you here?" asked Tonnis.

"I-I was just passing through," stuttered Dod. He lied, and he knew Tonnis could tell.

"The other way's shorter," said Tonnis, turning back to Dod. His conflicted eyes beat down on him. He could be a hero or a villain—or neither.

"I know," mumbled Dod, eager to move on. He turned to walk away, wishing to disappear because that would be faster, when he heard something amazing.

"Sorry about Pap," said Tonnis quietly. "I liked him."

Dod was dumbfounded. He knew that Tonnis wasn't typical of the Raul Hall crowd, but to hear a Chantolli apologize was beyond shocking.

"Thanks," said Dod. He searched his brain for anything else he could say—anything that would return the pleasantry. "I'm sorry about your dad," stumbled Dod. Once the words had escaped his lips, he wished to take them back. They were too daring.

"Yeah," said Tonnis, "me too!"

"And—a—how's your mom doing?" added Dod, red in the cheeks with embarrassment over bringing up the subject of The Dread. It was particularly awkward since Dod had been the one who had stopped him, effectively condemning him to a living-death sentence at Driaxom.

"She's doing okay, I guess."

"I heard she's got a visitor," continued Dod, trying to chuckle. "We rode home from Fort Castle with Ingrid in our group. That woman is one-of-a-kind, isn't she?"

Tonnis didn't respond.

"I mean—she's got a smell that's all her own," added Dod, giving him a knowing look. It was out of character for Dod, who wouldn't normally say rude things about others, yet being caught in a weird and uncomfortable conversation with Tonnis drove him to try to fit in with the Raul Hall type.

Tonnis still maintained his silence, though he cracked a rare smirk.

"Are you spouting on about me?" blared a voice from a distance away. Dod recognized the thumping and immediately died inside.

"Ingrid, it's nice to see you," said Dod, feeling more two-faced than ever before. He couldn't believe the irony. In trying to bond with the son of a mass murderer, he'd turned into the horrible person, while the criminal's son had stayed decent.

"But not smell me, huh?" chided Ingrid. Dod feared if she came too close, he'd get a cane to the crotch.

"I-I just meant that you're always cooking your stews," said Dod, stumbling over his words. "I-I can tell that you do a lot of cooking—you smell like you cook stuff—"

"And he likes your stew," interrupted Tonnis. "He was trying to tell me that he hoped you'd invite him for a big bowl today. The smell makes him hungry." Tonnis glanced at Dod and added, "Doesn't it, Dod?"

Dod nodded hesitantly. It did make him hungry—hungry to run and hide and hungry to never eat anything with garlic.

"Then I'll count on you for lunch," said Ingrid, softening before she reached them. "Will you be joining him, Tonnis, or are you as defiant and stubborn as your mother?"

Tonnis bristled. "I'm my *mother's son!*" he said, staying cool.

Dod left the conversation before he tripped into deeper water by affiliation. He knew what Ingrid had said about Juny, and he assumed she felt the same way about Tonnis—that they were traitors, secretly carrying on with Sirlonk's evil designs. Tonnis's posture shifted, showing he had some of his dad in him, too; he wasn't going to back down from Ingrid.

Before hitting the Great Hall, Dod bumped into someone else. It was Bowlure.

"Have you seen Tridacello?" asked Bowlure, knitting his brows.

"I haven't," said Dod, "but you look great. I can't believe you're all better."

"Well—Doctor Heatherly," said Bowlure affectionately, "is nothing short of a miracle worker."

"I can see," said Dod. "And how is Tridacello doing?"

"That's what I'm wondering," responded Bowlure, scratching at his sweaty head. He huffed slightly between speaking, as though he had been hurrying. "I can't seem to find him. When I woke up this morning a little earlier than usual, I discovered his bed was empty—and no one knows where he's gone off to—or if—" Bowlure paused and looked down at the ground sadly, "perhaps someone's taken him."

"Did he ever perk up?" asked Dod.

"No," groaned Bowlure. "He's been as silent as a log for over a week—just sleeping. That's why I'm so worried. Who could have stolen him while I snoozed? They'd have needed to walk past the guards with him in their arms, and that's about as likely as it is that they snuck him out the window."

"He'll turn up," said Dod, wondering what had happened. It was mysterious to say the least. "Do you want to catch breakfast with me? Maybe Tridacello's beat us there. Sleeping for long periods like that makes you hungry."

"I suppose you'd know," agreed Bowlure. He joined Dod in sauntering down to breakfast, taking one stride for every two of Dod's.

When Mercy heard Bowlure was seated in the Great Hall, she came out to greet him. "I wanted to see with my own two eyes the strongest man at Twistyard," teased Mercy, approaching their table with a special, heaping platter of various foods: piles of ham, hash browns, pancakes, eggs, fruit, and spice cakes. She set the load beside Bowlure and chirped, "It's remarkable how you claimed an arm off The Beast." Then she caught herself and looked both ways nervously.

"I mean—well—you know what I mean," whispered Mercy. "I'm not very good at secrets. Please don't let Voracio or Youk know. They think my lips are as tight as my freshwater clams, and the way Voracio's been stopping in, I'm guessing he fancies me." Mercy pressed at her new apron and fiddled with the strings to its closeable pocket in the front, making sure they looked their best.

"You're fine, Mercy," said Bowlure, glancing around the empty room as though one of the few people who were seated would suddenly turn into Tridacello. "I don't know why Voracio's trying to keep the thing hidden from everyone. He ought to be spreading the word, don't you think?"

"Goodness, yes," agreed Mercy. "I'm scared sauceless and frumpy—and that's with two guards at my door—but I'm still glad I know. You wouldn't want to learn the hard way about—*the thing.*"

"Nope," said Bowlure. "It's a horrible pet, isn't it? Have you heard any more on where they're headed with catching Dark Hood? Since Tridacello's been out cold, I've been left in the dark. He was always the one to be told news."

"Ummm," hummed Mercy, fidgeting with her graying curls. "I can't exactly say. Like—um—I can't say that they nearly had him this morning, really early, dashing from the Sonto Museum. What would he want from there, anyway?"

"You don't say."

"No, I don't," whispered Mercy. "And I certainly can't say that Voracio himself was almost killed by Dark Hood and his helper. He happened to be out for a morning stretch and saw them escaping from guards. And I can't tell you—though of course I would if I could—that Voracio's getting another zipper, right now as we speak, this time on his arm."

"Did he fight with Dark Hood again?" asked Dod, unable to keep quiet.

"No," said Mercy. "He wasn't wearing a sword, so he tried to hide from them, but ended up cutting his arm on something sharp. You have to watch where you dive."

"And The Beast?" asked Bowlure. He didn't try to play games or dodge the name.

"If I were to tell you," said Mercy, "which of course I can't, I'd say that they didn't see it this time."

"At least that's good news," sighed Bowlure. His voice was hard to hear over the rumbling of his enormous stomach. He dug into the piles of food that she'd placed beside him and focused on eating.

Shortly thereafter, someone stormed from the kitchen, looking distressed, and requested Mercy's help to save the rest of breakfast before all was lost. Apparently, a number of Sooshlings were assisting with the cooking and had inadvertently caused trouble.

As Dod ate breakfast, he prodded Bowlure for more information about his encounter with The Beast.

"While fighting, did you hear the creature say anything to you?" asked Dod, looking expectantly at Bowlure.

Bowlure squinted his eyes, wiped egg yolk from his lips with a towel Mercy had left, and tried to read if Dod were joking. "I speak the same language you do, Dod."

"I know that," whispered Dod, attempting to keep things quiet. More people were beginning to fill the eating chamber as the morning sun rose in the east. "It's just—well—when I saw the thing, it said stuff—not to me—but with its mind—kind of like I could hear its thoughts."

"Oh," said Bowlure, clearing his throat. "Is that before or after you heard it shaking the ground." He smiled and plopped two whole pancakes into his mouth.

"No," explained Dod. "I saw it for real—later that same night. It climbed the wall and peered into Green Hall through the window. Dilly saw it, too."

"I bet she's not sleeping," grunted Bowlure.

"That's true," added Dod. He studied Bowlure's face. "So, you're sure you didn't hear anything?"

"Yup," responded Bowlure with a clear throat. He could chew and swallow fast, which made his speech less Pone-like, despite the mountains of breakfast he was consuming. "But I'm not being aided by a swapper, and I'm not psychic."

"Me neither," insisted Dod quietly. "I can't figure out why I heard stuff."

"What did he say?"

"That he wanted to eat us."

"Oh, I see," chuckled Bowlure. The food was cheering him up. "I heard stuff too, then. He was telling me, 'I think I'm gonna rip your arms off and stuff you in my mouth,' and I was saying, 'I sure as heck don't think so, you big, hairy, bug-eyed thing,' and then I let him have it and he ran off."

"I'm serious," whispered Dod. "Am I crazy? Is it just me? Why did I hear him in my mind?"

"Maybe you saw his ugly face and your creative side did the rest," answered Bowlure, giving a serious look. "Either way, you're still here, and I'm still here, and I hope Tridacello's still here somewhere—so that's what matters. Don't beat yourself up over your mind playing tricks on you. Besides, maybe you did hear the thing's thoughts. You're special, Dod, and I'm sure you don't need me to tell you that."

"Thanks," said Dod. He actually did need to hear it. Just feeling Bowlure's friendship bolstered Dod's confidence in himself. He'd done unusual, good things before, but still had a hard time believing he could do anything worthwhile in the future.

"Oh, one more thing," begged Dod, as Bowlure prepared to head back to the fifteenth floor. "What was Dark Hood doing while you were fighting the monster? Did you see his hands?"

"Dark Hood?" said Bowlure, looking confused. "No. I didn't see him or his helper. He'd run off earlier. Tridacello came and got me after Dark Hood had already slipped the soldiers. We only ever saw The Beast—while trying to find where Dark Hood had gone."

As Dod cleared his tray and Bowlure's serving platter, he watched Bowlure happily jog away, ignoring the strange looks that people gave him. *What a man!* thought Dod, grateful to be friends with Bowlure.

At the side annex to the kitchen, where dishes were scraped—all leftovers for the pigs and chickens—Dod met up with a cluster of Sooshlings who had been kicked out of their breakfast cooking duty and reassigned to dish scrubbing duty. Their faces looked dejected.

"Don't worry," reassured Tinja, tying a thick, waterproof apron around his waist. "We didn't want to be in there with the ladies anyway."

Dod found it odd that Twistyard's Hatu expert was joining the Sooshlings in their obligation. The Greats never took part.

"Remember," said Tinja firmly, "we're watching, not just scrubbing."

"Right!" said a younger Sooshling, his messy hair jutting in every direction. "If we see the signs, we'll give the signal."

"And do what?" asked Dod eagerly, becoming part of the conversation by proximity. He was the only one close enough to hear what the Soosh Hall crowd was saying.

"Is it okay if Dod knows?" asked a boy who wore a distractingly large splotch of food on his shirt. He looked up to Tinja for approval.

"Dod's in," said Tinja, scratching at his stubbly head. "He knows a lot about billies and the trouble they cause—right Dod?"

"They're pretty mean," chirped Dod, glad he wasn't being rejected. The mere mention of noble billies triggered a wave of images to flood his mind. It was a sudden repeat of the experience he had endured after smelling the jumba sap letter. This time, the smoky air seemed to fill his lungs as much as his mind, causing him to double over, coughing. It felt real. And the cries of the dying were pitiful.

"You've got the right idea," said Tinja, thinking Dod was faking to make a point. As Dod began to recover, Tinja nodded and spoke with a tongue that was drenched with disgust: "They like to burn things, don't they? They burn ships, they burn houses, they burn people—it's their handprint. And with the blazes we've seen over the past month, I'd say anyone dumb enough to think billies haven't joined with Dark Hood and Dreaderious are dumber than a swarm of moths by a flame."

Dod kept seeing glimpses of the gruesome skull he'd seen before, its mouth open and its hollow eye sockets scowling.

Tinja lifted his pant legs and the boys around him ooed. Dod moved so he could see what stirred the bunch. Tinja's lower legs were scarred white and hairless.

"I walked through coals and hot ash to escape their wrath," he muttered bitterly, revisiting the moment in his mind. "And my brother's shoes saved me—their soles were thick—kept me going 'til I got out. He was already dead by their swords so he couldn't have used them anyway."

"I'm sorry," said Dod, crinkling his face at the sight of Tinja's legs.

"And when I lay there dying on the beach, what did they do? They gave me *this*!" Tinja pulled back the collar of his shirt so the boys could see a branded mark on his shoulder. It was the face of the skull.

"When everyone said The Dread did it, claiming a few tredders burnt the place down, it made me angry. I survived. I saw them with my eyes. I smelled their putrid sweat and fishy brine. I know whose hands to thank—the noble billies! But did anyone listen to a boy? No! And they still claim I'm a fool for remembering."

No one said a word. They just listened.

"So keep your eyes open," he added, gaining composure as he reached for a large scrubbing brush. "They're working with Dark Hood. I can feel it. They're the ones that caused the fire at High Gate—and here, too."

All the way back to Green Hall, Dod kept thinking about Doctor Shelderhig's lady friend, the expert in things related to billies. Surely Commendus had been worried that the pirate-like people were possibly causing trouble or he wouldn't have housed Newmi. And after the massive fire at High Gate, Dod wondered what would become of the final Bollirse game, scheduled to be played in Champion Stadium. Would Commendus even allow the Raging Billies to try for The Golden Swot? And if so, would the fans be permitted to watch?

Dod had agreed with Bonboo when Bonboo had spoken to Tinja about not judging all billies because of the actions of a few, but now that High Gate had already suffered such a devastating fire, things seemed less clear. Not to mention, the thousands of people who kept crying in Dod's mind concerned him. He hoped that it wouldn't happen at all, and that if it did, it wouldn't be the burning of High Gate.

"You got up early," said Boot, being the first to greet Dod

the moment he walked into Green Hall. "...almost earlier than me." Boot was coming out of his special closet, sweating and huffing like he'd just finished a race.

"I couldn't sleep," said Dod, wondering what Boot had been up to.

"Come here," mouthed Boot. He opened the closet and rolled back the rug on the floor. One of the planks came up easily and then a block of slats rose together. It was a secret cache. Boot had filled much of it with the boxes that had held the swords, but he had also hidden a sizeable amount of other stuff around them, including what looked like a mannequin—which is the object he reached for.

"Don't tell Dilly about this or she'll be rooting through my stuff," said Boot. He set up the dummy, re-situated the flooring, and shut the door, then proceeded to show Dod a string of sword moves that were remarkable. Some of them involved Boot rolling and twisting his body like a gymnast, which was amazing to see, particularly because of the precision that was needed in order to perform them in such a small space.

"You've been practicing!" exclaimed Dod with a roguish grin, thinking of the Raul Coosings that would be surprised.

"I've been beat one too many times," responded Boot. "Over the past five years I've been improving, but I haven't shown anyone my new moves—I haven't even used them at the tournaments. I've been waiting, perfecting my skills, and now I'm ready. This year they won't know what hit them."

"That's awesome," said Dod. "You're full of surprises lately, aren't you?"

"Yes," admitted Boot hesitantly while cleaning up. "I'm not a kid anymore, Dod." He turned and gave a sobering look.

"Things need to change—they can't stay the same—and I intend on doing stuff! This place, and everything that Bonboo's worked so hard for, is falling apart."

Dod sighed. He was glad when Boot mentioned Bonboo. For a tenth of a second, he had worried that Boot was a turncoat, bent on recruiting Dod to Dark Hood's side.

"We've got to rise up and put things back together, Dod. You, and me, and Buck, and Dilly, and Sawny, and the rest of us. If we sit around waiting for Voracio, or Youk, or the drat soldiers, we'll be waiting a long time.

Dod nodded.

"That's why we need to attend the picnic today," said Boot, cracking a smile. "The two of us can rub shoulders with the right people and keep them better leashed, so to speak."

"Huh?" chuckled Dod. He didn't get it.

Boot swung the door open and reached for a pair of pants that was sitting on the top of a pile of clothes on the floor in the hall. He dug into the back pockets and pulled out a delicate note.

"See—we have a picnic to attend," said Boot. He handed the note to Dod, who read it out loud.

Dod,

It would be our pleasure to have you attend our patio picnic tomorrow, scheduled for noon sharp. The food will be the best you'll eat all month, so come hungry.

Pooraah,

Saluci

"What?" gasped Dod. "When did you get this?" He turned the note over and admired the intricate, gold trim. It was a first-rate invitation.

"Dari handed it to me yesterday while you were busy going rounds with Clair. She wants you to dress up a little, too, since Neadrou and a few other influentials will be present."

"I wasn't going rounds with Clair," muttered Dod, "I was getting yelled at."

"But you took it well," said Boot. "That's nearly as good as responding. Besides, while he beat you down, Toos dumped ants in his sack lunch—the really big ones with black-and-red heads. That's a point for you, right?"

Dod smiled. "I guess you can come with me, Boot. I'm sure you're plenty mature enough to rub shoulders with Youk and his friends."

"Thanks Dod," he responded, smelling his sweaty shoulder. "Do you think I need to shower first?"

"Okay, maybe you're not mature enough," teased Dod.

Boot pushed him playfully.

A sudden idea burst into Dod's mind. It was almost too bold to consider, yet he couldn't help embracing it. "Boot," he said, "I'm going to need your help this afternoon."

"When?" asked Boot.

"During lunch—if it's even possible."

Boot's eyes sparkled with glee. "You're up to something, aren't you," he said, rapping Dod on the shoulder. "What are you planning?"

"Have you ever heard of the TCC?" asked Dod.

"Yup," said Boot. "I think Youk was a member of it when he was a Coosing, years ago. They scaled all sorts of things for the fun of it and regularly practiced on the back wall of this castle, up the cliffs—True Climbers Club, right?"

"Sure," said Dod. He and Boot walked down the hall to Pone's room, and Dod buried his head under the bed where he'd stuffed his bag and the TCC pack. His bag was still there, his sword from Pap included, but the backpack was gone.

"Have you seen a pack with the letters TCC on it?" asked Dod, scanning under the other beds in the room.

"Nope," said Boot, "but you're welcome to write TCC on one of my bags, assuming we can find one that didn't burn in the fire or get confiscated by the soldiers."

Dod scurried around the room, wishing it would turn up. He hoped it was an accident. He hadn't gotten a moment to himself, so he still hadn't even looked inside the pack, though he assumed it held rappelling gear—probably from the mock TCC of Youk's day.

"Can I help you?" asked Boot, noticing how Dod's face had dimmed with distress.

"I thought I had some climbing supplies," groaned Dod. "I was hoping—well—if we were already on Youk's balcony, and if the moment were right, I'd pop up the wall and visit Pap's place."

"Oh—right," said Boot, nodding his head. "Why don't you use your palsarflex? That thing has got to be better than anything else."

"We lost it in the fire," moaned Dod pathetically. "And if it didn't burn, it's sitting near the entrance to Pap's place, guarded around the clock by drat soldiers."

"No it's not," said Boot.

Dod looked hopeful.

"Come on, you don't think we'd leave something like *that* out in the open, do you?" Boot led Dod back to the magical closet, closed the door, and once more opened his cache of supplies.

"You just needed to ask," said Boot, loading a backpack with the palsarflex, two buster candles, eight foot-long daggers, and a few other miscellaneous things. "I'll even carry the pack for you if you let me come along," added Boot eagerly, looking as excited to see Pap's place as he had been the first time they'd tried.

"Sure," said Dod, starting to laugh. "Now all we need to do is think of a way to keep Youk's guest's from noticing us while we scale his garden wall." It was beyond crazy to hope that the party would be contained behind Youk's foliage, or otherwise occupied to the extent that Boot and Dod could climb the barrier unnoticed; nevertheless, a few hours later, Boot and Dod dressed up and went to the party—carrying the bag!

"If we pull this off," said Boot excitedly, taking two stairs at a time, "it'll be the best ever! We'll get fed, rub shoulders with a few influential people, and end our day searching through Pap's gear. What more could we ask for?"

"An empty patio," mumbled Dod nervously. The closer he got to Youk's house, the more he realized his plan was ridiculous; and he hoped Boot wouldn't try to push it through anyway, despite the impossibilities, and land both of them in Voracio's meaty hands as troublemakers.

Valerie greeted Dod and Boot at the door with pleasant words of salutation, while Dari, on the other hand, spewed a string of things that were less welcoming.

"Who told you to invite *him*?" asked Dari, glaring at Dod and pointing at Boot.

"I thought you wouldn't mind," said Dod, caught off guard by her attack.

"Well, my little *friend-o*, the note says Dod—doesn't it?"

"Dari!" scolded Valerie. "They're our guests."

"Only one of them," barked Dari defiantly. "The other isn't technically a guest—he's more of an intruder."

"Whoa," said Boot, putting his hands over his heart. "That hurts."

Dari glanced at Dod, then Boot. "Got ya!" she blared obnoxiously. "Come on in. Everyone else is already out back."

"You can't tease like that," said Valerie, disgusted by her sister's unruly behavior. "Remember what mom said about having manners today."

"That's just in front of the stiff-hats, not Dod and Boot," responded Dari, grinning ear-to-ear. "Come and see my new plant before you join the others. Neadrou bought it for me—it eats bugs like a gecko."

"Sick!" said Boot. "Show us the way."

Valerie primped at her fluffy dress and floated delicately out the back door, while Dari charged down the bedroom hall in her best jumpsuit.

"I put the little striker in my dad's biggest planter box, just outside of his bedroom. If it ate worms, I'd be set. The box is full of them. It's probably because my dad is always rotating plants around—inside for a while, outside for a while. But it works. Take a look."

As Boot and Dod rounded the corner at the end of the long hall, a five-foot by ten-foot box held a wide array of gorgeous-looking plants, many of them flowering. It occupied the bulk of a small sitting room.

"It's a jungle!" admired Boot playfully. "Sneaker would love something like this."

"Yup," chattered Dari, "it's my dad's pride and joy. He spends more time sitting here, talking to his precious plants, than he spends sleeping in there." She pointed at his bedroom door. "But my mom says it scares Sammywoo."

Dod thought of the two nights he'd spent down the hall and nodded in agreement that something surely frightened the boy; his screams had been blood curdling.

Dari knelt down, produced an ant from her front jumpsuit pocket, and held it out on her flat hand. The plant nearest to her looked similar to a standard houseplant—Aunt Hilda had kept an identical one, or so Dod thought—however, within the blink of an eye, a lightning-fast tongue shot out of a rolled leaf near the bushy center and whisked the bug off.

"Wow!" gasped Boot. He bent down and tried to look into the rolled leaf.

"Don't get your face too close or it'll suck your eyeballs out," claimed Dari. "Neadrou warned me."

"No," said Boot, not buying it. He gawked with fascination and begged for an encore.

This time, Boot got to hold the ant. The plant took longer to respond than it had before, but eventually its sticky tongue flipped out and whipped back, consuming the fleeing victim.

"That's cool," sighed Dod. He wasn't as excited as Boot, who wished to own one. Dod's zeal was sucked dry by the agony he was feeling over the task of finding a way up the patio wall.

Out back, three elegant tables held fancy dishes and silverware, and a forth held platters of the most bizarre foods. Dod didn't recognize a single item on the menu; perhaps the meat was a roasted bird of sorts, though its feet seemed to be hoofed; and the salad had leaves that resembled weeds Dod was certain he'd sat on while watching some of his fellow Coosings duel during Clair's practice hours; and the fruit was carved into little animals and glazed with various sauces, making it nearly impossible to determine the type; and the drink was a dark-green, mushy goo that brought back childhood memories of stirring rotten grass in a bucket with a stick, claiming to be making witches' brew.

"I hope you've brought your appetites, boys," said Youk, breaking from a circle of men to greet Dod and Boot. "My wife is the best cook in Green, and she's really outdone herself this year!"

"I'd say," agreed Boot, glancing hungrily around at the heaping piles of food on the table. "She's made the traditionals—not very many people take the time anymore, do they?"

"And we helped a lot!" blared Dari enthusiastically. "Especially me. I chopped the tinshoops into perfect squares and ground all the hillterberries by myself, not to mention doing tubs of dishes. The kitchen's a complete disaster. It's good we're eating out here."

From a distance away, Valerie looked up from her conversation with six high-society women and cringed.

"You're right," agreed Youk, smiling at Dari. He was more amused than embarrassed by her outbursts.

Dod scanned the open placement of the tables and then hesitantly glanced at the towering patio wall. To his surprise, he saw a rope ladder that was stretched the full forty feet. It was wonderful and horrible at the same time.

"Who's been visiting the rooftop gardens?" choked Dod, shocked that the forbidden nesting grounds had been invaded.

"That's for Rot," said Youk. "He's still trying to determine why our rare singing doves have been disappearing. You've got to see what he's done." Youk directed Dod and Boot to follow him. A distance into the thickets of Youk's patio garden, there was a beautifully-crafted cage containing a dozen pairs of doves.

"Rot's trying to raise their numbers here at Twistyard."

"Is he friends with Zerny?" asked Boot, giving Dod a chuckle-eye.

"I'm not exactly sure," answered Youk. "Why do you ask?"

"They both like raising birds," responded Boot. "Zerny's got a cage that's ten times as big as this one."

"Ten times as big," repeated Dari, wearing a gleeful look on her face. "Rot could stay with Zerny and Jibb, and just like that our house wouldn't stink anymore. It would be perfect, Dad. Don't you think?"

"Honey," responded Youk, grasping at his daughter's shoulder, "Rot's doing a lot of good here. And we've got the ideal spot for his studies—not Zerny and Jibb. Besides, Bonboo's been gracious to let us use this large apartment and gigantic patio. It's unmatched. The least we can do is temporarily share it with Rot."

"Please come now," called Saluci, beckoning for everyone to assemble. She was approaching the food table with a steaming platter of what looked like fried grasshoppers and beetles.

"Simply marvelous!" exclaimed a man as he parted from the biggest crowd. It was Neadrou, head-to-foot in bright red. He'd have been invisible in a tub of ripe apples.

"Follow the tags," advised Saluci, sweeping her way to the head of the largest table wearing a gorgeous, sparkling dress. It had thousands of tiny shells sewn into the fabric, making it look like a wave of pearls. The afternoon sun momentarily caught her and blinded the crowd.

Dod and Boot followed Dari, who led them to where Dod's name was written; Boot didn't have a tag, but two up from Dod the seat was empty, so he took it. Dari and Valerie sat across from one another, with Dod on the table's end, between them.

"Con won't mind," said Boot confidently, looking beside

him at Valerie. He slipped Con's tag into his back pocket and added, "If he's not here yet, we'd better eat while we still have a chance—that boy's as big as a barge. I'd pull a frog out my nose if he eats anything less than half-a-cow per day. Who invited him?"

Dari laughed and Valerie shook her head reproachfully.

The comment was less funny once Boot realized Commendus was close by, hearing every word.

"It's nice to see you again," said Dod, tipping his head toward Commendus and Sabbella as they walked past.

"Occasionally the world must wait," responded Commendus. "Events like this are important. Saluci and Sabbella have always been close. It's a pleasure to be able to celebrate with them."

Celebrate what? thought Dod, unaware of the special nature of the gathering. He looked toward Neadrou and noticed that he continued to stand while everyone else sat.

"As you all know," began Neadrou, "the Zoots have devoutly remembered this day for over three thousand years. We can never forget the nobility that has been so graciously bestowed upon us. In the days of Dossontrous—"

"Here it comes," whispered Dari to Dod. "He's soon going to reach the part where he shakes his fists in the air and chants, 'We will rise! We will rise! We will rise!' I can almost quote the man by heart."

Valerie kicked Dari under the table, reminding her to be quiet, and Dari returned the favor with a bigger nudge that left Valerie's eyes watering.

Dod looked the crowd over and wondered where Sammywoo was.

"He's with Rot," said Dari softly, reading Dod's glances. "Sammywoo wasn't allowed—no one under twenty-five."

"Oh," responded Dod with a quiet nod. He suddenly felt

out of place. And it wasn't just his age. With new eyes, Dod could see that nearly everyone in the room was related. It was a gathering of Zoots—the stuffiest, uppitiest, we-have-the-best-blood-in-all-of-Greeniest people in the world. The only family that matched them was the Chantollis in Raul. Terro, and his son Sawb, and most certainly his brother Sirlonk, knew that they had the absolute best tredder blood.

The clan of nobles listened intently to Neadrou until, as Dari had forecast, he shook his fists in the air and yelled, "WE WILL RISE! WE WILL RISE! WE WILL RISE!" His voice echoed ominously off the stone walls.

Dod's sense of discomfort was magnified by his memories of Neadrou's backstabbing moment at Carsigo, where he had 'forgotten' Dod's identity in front of General Faller. The whole nature of the gathering was turning creepy, like a secret, extremist cult's rally. And then Neadrou laughed and everyone clapped. It was a performance of sorts, a reenactment of things their forefathers had said, not an actual call to arms for the Zoots to take control of Green again.

Dod sighed.

"We can eat now," said Dari, nudging Dod. "And the youngest go first, so that's us."

Boot beat Dod to the food and stole the front of the line. He piled a double-sized plate with a healthy clump of everything offered, then stopped in front of Saluci while on his way back to his seat, bowed courteously, and thanked her for the fabulous lunch, noting that she looked every bit as royal and beautiful as the paintings of Queen Shurry from Dossontrous's day.

Dod's plate was the opposite of Boot's. He feared that the flavors would make him ill, though to his relief, they were delicious. Even the serving of fried water creepers tasted marvelous, like shrimp.

Dari dominated the conversation with comments about everything, but especially about her deceased relatives and their unconquerable spirits. The occasion drew it out of her. As she spoke, memories filled the gaps in Dod's mind. Dozens of her ancestors had ruled large parts of Green, before Bonboo's had taken a more prominent position in the world.

"So in a way," explained Dari, "if it hadn't been for them, we'd probably own a castle like this right now."

"Dari!" scolded Valerie for the hundredth time. "That's not polite to say. Don't disparage the Tillius's. They've been good to *us*."

Boot and Dod were both thinking the same thing—they were glad Dilly wasn't part of the conversation. Hearing Dari slam on her distant ancestry would have crinkled her collar—and needlessly so; the truth of what had really happened was long gone, making it pointless to take offense.

Dod kept glancing at the rope ladder, wishing he could snap his fingers and make everyone else disappear for about one minute. That's all it would take.

Someone tapped at Dod's shoulder. It was Tridacello, standing with the use of a cane.

"Tridacello," gasped Dod, surprised to see him. "It's wonderful that you're out."

"At last!" responded the old man, reaching to flatten his straying wisps of white hair. "I'm glad to be up and moving. All that resting was driving me crazy—"

"Oh," said Dod, "Bowlure hadn't mentioned you were awake. I thought you slept right through your recovery—just like me."

"No—well yes," mumbled Tridacello feebly. "It's hard to explain."

"Recovery from what?" chirped Dari.

"Getting old," fibbed Tridacello, looking two tables away at Neadrou. It was largely true. His current state didn't appear wonderful, just better than being unconscious in bed. The Beast had left him acting his age of two hundred and thirty-eight.

"I guess you're crawling close to the drop-off now, aren't you?" said Dari, mortifying Valerie. "You're the oldest here, and your wife's been gone decades and your sons are slowing, too."

Tridacello didn't respond to her. He furrowed his brow in thought.

From the grassy courtyard twenty-five stories below, a loud horn trumpeted, and it didn't stop.

One middle-aged gentleman rushed to the balcony's edge and peered down to discover what the fuss was about. "You've all got to come and see this!" he called to the diners. "It looks like Con is here, and he has a special presentation for us."

Commendus and Sabbella hopped up with excitement and prodded the crowd to their feet. They knew what Con had planned, and they were giddy with anticipation. Everyone made their way across the half-acre balcony of gardens to the ornate railing, where they lined it for the show. Even Tridacello stepped a fair pace without his cane to get a good view.

But Dod caught Boot by the arm and slipped behind a large bush on the way, letting the procession pass without them.

"This is our chance," whispered Dod impatiently. His heart was pounding in his chest.

"Can't we first take a peek?" responded Boot, looking longingly toward the others.

"No!" snarled Dod. "This is it! Quick!"

Together, Boot and Dod scurried silently across the patio, around the tables, and up the rope ladder. Once in the rooftop thickets, they dashed through the foliage to the edge where they could better see the spectacle that Con had orchestrated, while staying concealed from view.

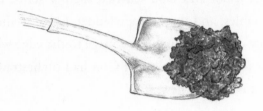

PAP'S HOME

"Wow!" gasped Dod, amazed by the crowd of performers. Hundreds of men and women danced and waved rags in rigid order as a five-wagon orchestra parked nearby, playing beautiful music.

"He couldn't just be on time," mocked Boot. "Con does stuff like this. He spends through his dad's money as though he were bailing water from a sinking ship. We'd all rather he keep his gold and be a little more free with his friendship and decency."

"Wasn't he a Green Coosing?" asked Dod.

"Coosing—Yes. Green—No! Sawb had him as a Raul Coosing for about eight months. It was sheer torture on all of us here at Twistyard. Just ask Doochi—he bunked beside him. I bet he'd take being trapped again in the dark, cold storage chambers over having to return to the days when he shared a room with Con. The big lug is trouble. He's constantly doing stuff he shouldn't, and disrupting things for everyone, and his pranks, Dod—they're not even remotely funny."

Dod smiled. "And you're sure he's not your twin brother?" Dod noticed how many things Boot listed that were perfect descriptions of himself.

"I see what you mean," admitted Boot honestly, "but Con—he's mean to the core, Dod, not just carefree like me. I've seen deep into Con's dark soul, and I can't say I noticed more than one or two specs of gold. It's dismal down there—a real wasteland. That's why even his own father cast him out. After Con got drunk and hurt a bunch of people at High Gate, he served time but couldn't go home when he was done. He's been off in the military."

"A secret weapon against Dreaderious!" jabbed Dod.

"That's the spec of gold," said Boot. "He's so awful, if you have a common enemy, he's useful. Of course, truthfully, even with your foe, mercy should always be part of the equation."

"And this hasn't got anything to do with Con chasing after Dilly?"

Boot rolled his eyes and quieted down. They both watched the magnificent presentation for ten minutes before sinking deep into the forested rooftop.

"Why do you suppose Saluci invited Tridacello?" asked Dod, pushing branches out of his face.

"You don't know?" chuckled Boot. "I thought you and Tridacello were really close."

"Not so much," responded Dod. "Though I think he does a lot of good—and Bowlure loves him."

"Then I'll tell you frankly," said Boot, dipping to his knees to squeeze through a tight spot. "Tridacello was married to Neadrou's oldest cousin, Jazzui, and from what I've seen over the years, he's become as much a Zoot as she ever was."

"One of them," muttered Dod with surprise. "I never would have guessed."

"Don't get me wrong," added Boot quickly. "The Zoots do a lot of good—usually for everyone to see—and they love being in charge of stuff. I suppose that's why Sabbella's drawn to Commendus—he acts like a Zoot."

"Am I the only one who's not connected?" complained Dod, thinking of his family's duplex back in Cedar City. "Dari and Valerie have their Zoot blood, Dilly and Sawny are Bonboo's great-granddaughters, and Sawb's father presides over all of Raul, nearly like a king."

"You're hardly one to talk!" snapped Boot. "He pulled back a bushy clump of branches and gazed at the tip of Pap's penthouse, up another stone wall and hidden behind trees. "If I had a gramp like Pap—that would be something—not that I'm not proud of my own dad—but I'd take Pap over any of the Zoots—or all of 'em put together. I wish my grandpa had been like Pap."

As Dod and Boot approached the last climb, Dod felt as though eyes were watching him, just as he'd felt in the dark library. It rattled his nerves enough that he let Boot go first up the palsarflex.

On top, the well-manicured yard looked just as amazing as it had looked before. Ripe vegetables and fruit were everywhere, and surrounding them were rows of weed-free, freshly-turned dirt. The sight reminded Dod of Pap's gardens in Cedar City. He had been known for his giant tomatoes and peppers.

"I think Pap's still alive," whispered Dod.

"What?" said Boot. "That can't be."

"How do you know?" asked Dod, bending to walk under an apple-laden branch. "He's good at being sneaky. I think he faked his death at High Gate. When the others died, he somehow didn't—kind of like what Bonboo did, remember?" Dod knew it didn't make sense, but neither did the circumstance.

"He's dead," assured Boot sadly. "Trust me. I know."

"But Bonboo told me that I'm the only one with a key—and that I'm to maintain this place. And look at it, Boot, someone's been working hard up here to make it beautiful. I'm betting Pap's hiding out."

Boot surveyed the scene and picked up a dirty shovel. "I wish you were right—but you're not! We'd better be ready. You've got a squatter!"

Boot's determined eyes and fighting stance quickly changed Dod's happy feeling about the place. He grabbed a thick stick and joined Boot in hunting for the intruder. Together, they combed through the small orchard and vegetable gardens first, then the flowering bushes and thicker foliage by the edges.

Eventually, they made their way along a path that turned into a staircase, leading down to a gigantic cage. Bars crisscrossed the open roof, and bushes, trees, and grass filled the inside like an overgrown yard. Since the enclosure was thirty feet below the level of the gardens surrounding the house, the walls were made of the castle's stone.

An iron gate met them at the base of the stairs. It was closed, but not locked.

"Do we dare enter?" whispered Dod, nudging the squeaking mesh of metal.

"Yeah," said Boot excitedly. His face looked more fascinated than concerned. "The stories are true—at least partially, anyway." He pushed his way into the massive cage and gazed around, as though imagining.

"What stories?" begged Dod apprehensively.

"About '*The Zoo*' here at Twistyard," responded Boot with kidlike, glossy eyes.

The enclosed field was two acres, and lining the stone walls intermittently were majestic archways, opening up to sheltered corridors or halls.

"The Zoo?" gasped Dod. Convoluted images flashed through his mind of strange creatures, each with horrifying capabilities. It was like a three-second nightmare. "Who kept them here?"

"Dunno," mumbled Boot, making his way to the first sheltered alcove. He was mesmerized by the scene. Individual pens of various shapes and sizes lined the inner walls, the smallest of which could easily house bears or lions, and some had recessed floors occupying much of their space, with water stains marking the sides of the empty pools.

"This place is huge!" said Dod with amazement. Nearly the entire space under Pap's house and yard was occupied by the enclosures and the central, open courtyard. "Why would they keep animals up here?"

"Because they didn't want people seeing them," responded Boot. His shovel accidentally bumped one of the bars and it rang like a bell, chilling Dod's blood.

"The Beast!" snapped Dod. He froze in his tracks. "What if Dark Hood is living up here, and he's keeping his pet caged in this enclosure?"

"Then we're dead," chuckled Boot. "But I doubt it. Look around. No one's used this stuff for decades."

"You think?" asked Dod nervously.

Boot pointed at the stone flooring that had weeds, moss, and grass growing on it. "Yup," he said confidently. "Someone's been taking care of the upper level, but not this place. They've left it alone."

Dod's tense nerves relaxed a few notches. "What do you know of The Zoo?"

"Only the kind of stuff people joke about around campfires—how some crazy guy occupied this castle hundreds of years ago, well before Bonboo's parents—and he wanted to rule over everyone, so he made an alliance with two other families, hoping that together they'd take Green, Raul, and Soosh by crafty force. The Zoo ended up being one of the group's mad, ill-fated ideas—actually, its last. Supposedly, they brought deadly beasts from other worlds to this one as babies, smuggled through a Mauj portal at The Lost City, and then raised them here at Twistyard, preparing them to attack and destroy."

"The Lost City?" mumbled Dod.

"I know," assured Boot. "It's mostly made up. People have been searching for The Lost City for hundreds of years, and yet no one has been able to prove that it ever existed. If there were a secret cluster of buildings anywhere near High Gate, we'd have found them, especially since they reportedly contained piles of riches—stuff the Mauj visitors from Soosh had to leave here in Green when they fled their beautiful homes. They say this castle's owner unleashed his zoo of monsters on them."

"Okay, that's freaky," said Dod hesitantly, looking around at the cages as they walked the shadowy corridors. Large, empty hands of stone reached from the walls every fifty feet, where monstrous torches would have burned, lighting the chambers.

"I know it's all fabricated from the blurred recollections of a few delusional people," admitted Boot. "It has to be. But it makes for a great bedtime story, don't you think? The lunatic that supposedly trained the creatures had to destroy the Mauj visitors living in The Lost City before his alliance would help him gain control of Green, so he drove the Mauj out with his demons. They say he found that his tricks for training his pets didn't work well enough: They turned on him and each other, and none of them were ever heard of again."

"Now that's got to be hokey," scoffed Dod. "If it really happened, wouldn't the history books talk about these awful animals? After eating the crazy guy, they would have roamed around killing other people, too. And if the city had possessed great riches, once the Mauj were gone and the beasts were gone, people would have rushed the place and taken its treasures. How can you lose a whole city? That's nuts. Nobody would believe that."

"Except Toos—and about a million others who have devoted countless hours to scouring the mountains above High Gate." Boot smiled and ran his shovel across a row of bars. "It's a fact that someone kept pets right here."

"But you're not saying—" began Dod.

"No," snipped Boot. "This place was probably a barn of sorts for flutters." He pointed his shovel at the roof of crisscrossing bars of iron as they stepped back out into the open courtyard. "See—flutters."

"Oh," sighed Dod.

"Besides," added Boot, "Bonboo's relatives reportedly built this castle, and judging from all the good Bonboo's done for Green, I can't imagine any of his forefathers being bloodthirsty lunatics."

"What about the TCC?" blurted Dod.

"Youk's thing?"

"No, the real one—the group started by Dilly's distant ancestor."

"Oh," said Boot, melting a suspicious grin. "That TCC. I

can't say I know much about them. You'd have to ask Dilly, I guess—if you dare. She's touchy about the fringes of her blood."

"But these cages—" insisted Dod, following Boot out of the enclosure and up the stairs.

"Flutters—"

"And The Beast?" begged Dod. "Maybe some parts of the outrageous tale are true. Dark Hood could be a great-great-something of the evil guy who built The Zoo—"

"You mean Dilly's distant grandpa?" choked Boot, turning to grin at Dod. "So you think one of her uncles or cousins is Dark Hood?"

"Well—"

"You've nearly met them all," continued Boot.

"No I haven't—"

"Yup—Voracio,"

"He's the only one I've met," barked Dod, approaching the last step. They had given up on sneaking and being quiet. "I've met him—and Dilly's father, of course."

"Yup," said Boot, shaking his head in the sunlight. "It's sad to say, but Bonboo's been unlucky with his family members—they've all had unfortunate accidents over the years 'til Chikada and his bunch are just about the only ones left alive. Bonboo hasn't a single living cousin or descendant of one, and he himself was an only child. It's a good thing Dilly's got six siblings or the Tillius's legacy would end flat."

"That's too bad," said Dod, still trying to piece things together. "But The Beast—there must be a connection to these cages." He looked over his shoulder toward the pit of forgotten enclosures and then around at the contrasting, well-tended gardens encircling Pap's house.

"No," assured Boot. "Whatever animal you saw with Dilly came from Soosh. They've got lots of strange ones. I'd imagine Dark Hood's a mayler—"

"Then it's Miz," huffed Dod. "He's not dead, and now that he's got his two sons staying here, they're all working together."

"Nope," said Boot sadly. "Miz is dead. And he wasn't the type, anyway—his boys are more so than he ever was. It's unfortunate that nice people often have mean kids."

"Spare the rod, spoil the child," said Dod, quoting his Aunt Hilda.

Boot gave him a raised-eyebrow glance.

Dod suddenly felt someone's presence and knew where to look. "He's in the statue!" blurted Dod, spinning to face a glorious sculpture. It was the crowning centerpiece of Pap's elegant rooftop estate. "He's right there," insisted Dod, approaching the marble figure and pointing his stick menacingly.

"What?" said Boot, playing with his shovel rather than following. "Do you really think someone's inside *that*?"

The work of art looked like a rough, solid block of stone with hands, feet, legs, and faces poking out, as though the sculptor had stopped in the middle of the process.

"Come out!" demanded Dod, standing in a fighting position.

Boot jogged over and joined what he thought was a game. "I'll pop your hands off if you don't obey!" he rumbled, waving his shovel in the air. He struck the base of a giant sunflower and sliced the stalk in half. "I'm warning you! We can either do this the easy way or the hard way."

To Boot's surprise, the sculpture made a noise. "All right," it said timidly. "There's no need to hurt me. I'm your friend."

Boot nearly fell over with astonishment as he stumbled

backward, fearing the faces were coming to life. Dod held his ground.

A scrawny, wrinkly, gray-skinned man came crawling out of the base through a small hole that opened up. His eyes blinked in the sunlight as he drew himself up to a stooped position, showing subjection.

"I'm Pap's friend—Abbot," he said carefully, shivering with fright. The man reminded Dod of a stray dog he'd taken in for a while.

"Why are you here?" demanded Dod.

"It's my home, sir," said the man with a quavering voice. "Pap saved my life and brought me back—to keep me safe. Others didn't understand—they just don't understand."

The old man hobbled to a bench and sat down, all the while mumbling to himself. He seemed to fade in and out of reality, which helped to explain his disheveled appearance. His dirty, long-sleeved shirt hung on him pitifully, his pants were shredded at the ankles, and his feet were bare.

"Where's Pap?" asked Dod, lowering his stick.

"Pap knew the truth. I didn't do it," continued the man, rambling to himself. He stared at the ground with his deep-set brown eyes.

"But what of Pap?" begged Dod, moving closer to the man. "Can you tell me where Pap is?"

"Pap?" gasped the man, emerging from his trance-like stupor. "You're his grandson—don't you know what happened?"

"The poisoning?" sighed Dod, wondering how the man knew he was related to Pap.

"Well, yes," said Abbot, shifting back and forth. He eyed Boot's intimidating posture and bowed his head again. "I'm sick with sorrow. Pap was my best friend—and nearly my only friend. Now that he's gone, it's unbearably lonely up here. Even the gardens lag at cheering me up, and the dirt has lost its pleasant smell."

"Then move out," grumbled Boot, eyeing the stranger suspiciously.

"Oooh!" moaned Abbot, shaking his head and flopping it into his hands. "I'm as good as dead. They'll find me—they'll kill me—they'll see that I suffer. Sir Boot will tell them where I am. He hates me. He thinks I'm foe."

"What?" gasped Boot, moving in on the man. "How do you know my name?"

"Don't hit me, sir," cried Abbot, cowering down. "Please, sir, don't hit me."

Boot lowered his shovel and tossed it aside. "We just want the truth," said Boot, feeling sorry for the man. "How do you know us?"

The old man rose to his feet and hobbled back to the statue. He dipped inside and returned with a pair of noculars. "I watch," he said carefully.

"You've been watching us?" snapped Dod, feeling uncomfortable.

"I'm lonely," whined Abbot, furrowing his brow. "I watch everyone. It's the glue that keeps me together—especially since Pap's gone. He's the only one who knows—I didn't do it—they just don't understand."

Abbot whirled into a bout of mumblings again, insisting he was innocent, while Boot looked to Dod for direction.

"Perhaps we can talk with Bonboo for you," suggested Dod, not sure when he'd do it since Bonboo hadn't returned.

"No!" insisted Abbot, pulling at his gray hair. "They don't

understand, sir. Please don't tell. Leave me as a ghost—I beg of you!"

Abbot fell to his knees and caught hold of Dod's shoes, burying his face into the ground. "Please Dod, sir," he begged, "let me stay. I'll care for the gardens and dust your house, sir, and keep things just as Pap wanted. Please."

"All right," agreed Dod, noticing scars on the man's feet and ankles. He could imagine they climbed his legs as well and were hidden beneath his long-sleeved shirt. "You can stay for now, but you've got to explain yourself. How did you know our names—and that Bonboo gave me Pap's place?"

The old man tilted his head and peered up. "Everyone knows of Dod, sir—you're the one who defeated The Dread—and you walk like your grandfather." He glanced cautiously sideways and added, "Sir Boot—well—you're something to watch—always on the move with the crowds. Pap spoke highly of you."

Boot smiled and the tight muscles in his neck relaxed. "Just don't tattle," he said jokingly. "We'll keep your secrets and you keep ours—fair enough?"

Abbot nodded carefully. "They don't understand," he muttered.

Dod and Boot helped the man to his feet and they walked to the house together, with Abbot whispering things to himself.

"I can't believe Bonboo gave you all of this," said Boot to Dod, being the first to reach the patio door. "It's too bad he wants you to keep it a secret or we could host parties up here."

"It's like a dream," confessed Dod. "You wouldn't imagine how much bigger this place is than the one I go home to."

"Join the club," laughed Boot. "My mom lives in a three-room cottage out in the hills—no running water. But one day soon, when I get a little money, I'll rent a place for her in the heart of Ridgeland with better facilities. She'll be dazed when she sees how much easier life is when she doesn't have to pull water from the well or go to the slat-shack for relief. I think bathrooms are the coolest inventions the Mauj ever came up with."

"Why don't you ask Dilly or Bonboo for the money? They both love you," assured Dod.

"They don't have much to spare anymore," said Boot. "A lot of their riches were stolen a few years ago—that's when Bonboo started getting other people to help finance Twistyard, and that's also when The Greats stopped getting paid to teach. Recently, I overheard Voracio discussing money problems with a group from High Gate—Commendus's colleagues—and they were calculating the worth of the Tillius Woodlands and Lake Mauj. Dilly would die if she knew they were considering selling them off."

"Really?" gasped Dod, entering Pap's place. It was news to him. He had felt bad when he had heard that Dark Hood had stolen the Farmer's Sackload, but he hadn't realized the dilemma it had created. Bonboo's collection of pure-sight diamonds had been used to sure up loans during tight years. Without them, creditors were becoming difficult.

"You had a break-in, sir," interrupted Abbot, keeping his eyes to the floor. "I fixed the door and cleaned the house, but they stole your books, sir. I shouldn't have left."

"It was The Dread," said Dod, patting Abbot on the shoulder. "You couldn't have stopped him if you had been here. And I don't think he was alone." Memories of the dark night flooded Dod's mind. As he stood in the cluttered hallway, he felt uneasy. "The Beast was with him," added Dod.

"The Beast?" choked Boot. "How do you figure? It seems Dark Hood's pet didn't turn up 'til recently."

"He was here," insisted Dod. "I found long black hair on a hook and wondered what it could have come from, but after seeing The Beast for myself, I'm pretty confident he left it."

"Tooshi-wanna, Tooshi-wanna," blared Abbot, his eyes filling with fear. Once again he drifted into a daze.

"What's he saying?" asked Boot.

"Tooshi-wanna, Tooshi-wanna," repeated Abbot. He raised his hands in the air, bent his fingers like claws, and danced in a circle while chanting.

"He's gone mad," said Dod, trying to settle him down. But Dod's efforts were useless; the old man's mind was a blur of nonsense. Nothing seemed to bring him back, though he stayed near Dod and Boot no matter where they went, so the howling and dancing continued as Dod attempted to give Boot a tour of the spacious penthouse, raising his voice to be heard over the noise.

From room to room, Dod and Boot went searching for cool things to bring back to Green Hall. Dod's angle was different than it had been before: He was looking for anything valuable to sell, hoping he'd find a stash of treasure somewhere amidst Pap's relics that would solve Twistyard's financial problems. But nothing significant turned up. The most cashable items appeared to be Pap's swords, yet they wouldn't fetch enough to make a dent in the debts.

Boot was good at blocking out the chanting old man who followed them. He loved Pap's interesting artifacts and managed to find and hoard a whole pile of gadgets that tipped him giddy as a boy on Christmas morning. He beamed gleefully as he filled one of Pap's packs with the gear.

The best of Dod's finds was a second palsarflex and two

peculiar-looking harnesses with ingenious clamps. Climbers could scale up or down, then rest in a seated position while situating their alternate line. *No more perching on knives*, thought Dod happily. And it wasn't long before Dod and Boot tested the equipment on the back wall of the castle, lakeside, since reentry to Youk's party wasn't likely to bring cheers of joy and the quick-rappel shaft only led to a room full of drat soldiers.

"Do you think it's safe to leave Abbot up there?" asked Dod, feeling guilty as he followed Boot down the palsarflex line. He could still hear the old man raging on in the distance.

"It's his home," mumbled Boot, parked at the bottom of the first rope as he waited for Dod to hand him the second. Boot wore the heavy pack full of new items, while Dod wore the lighter one they'd brought from Green Hall. "Besides," continued Boot, "I don't think he's likely to break anything. He'll probably dance himself to sleep under the apple trees and wake up cheery as a morning sparrow."

"I guess," conceded Dod, sighing heavily. He felt bad for Abbot and wished he didn't have to stay alone. "What do you think is wrong with him—the way he zones out and splits from reality?"

"I don't know," said Boot. He latched his harness to the second line and zipped down fearlessly, never doubting the strength of the five red balls that fastened the rope to the rock wall. In the distance thirty stories below them, small waves teased the edges of the rotten, empty dock. Only seabirds and swallows noticed the boys' descent.

Dod carefully tugged at Boot's line, testing its capacity before hitching his straps to the rope, then he wiggled the other line gently until the balls let go.

"Are you trying to hit me?" teased Boot, ducking as the

flailing rope and five balls followed gravity and narrowly missed conking Boot across the head. "If I were out cold, you'd find this wall a bit more precarious."

"Sorry," said Dod, coiling the line. He inched his way to Boot and handed him the spare palsarflex. As much as he could, Dod tried to avoid looking down. He wished there were one secure rope to the bottom, so he could quickly descend and not need to worry about his equipment malfunctioning. Not to mention, Boot's extra weight on the lines didn't instill confidence.

Gradually, the twosome worked the wall and obtained the ground. It was no small feat. Boot bent down and scratched TCC in the dilapidated plank where their feet had first touched. "I think we've just started our own True Climbers Club," he gloated, handing Dod a pocket knife. "Sign your initials."

"Cool," sighed Dod, just glad to have made it.

Over the course of the following week, Dod slipped out every chance he got and scaled the wall to Pap's place. Each visit, he was greeted warmly by Abbot, who insisted that Dod was a lot like Pap. The old man was intelligent and clear-minded some of the time and loonier than a drunk baboon the rest. His volatility shortened their chats and greatly restricted the things Dod dared speak about with Abbot, since the old man's tendency to lose reality correlated perfectly with difficult questions.

However, Abbot was a great resource. He'd watched everyone so intently with his noculars that his observations were unique. Dod gleaned useful tidbits from the old man and wrote them down: Rot was often in the rooftop gardens, pointing his noculars away from the castle as much as he was tracking the flow of birds in the thickets; and Youk and Saluci were unusually interested in the rare doves that Rot raised on their balcony, so much that the birds appeared to be their pets, not Rot's; and Abbot claimed he'd spotted Zerny coming and going from his lakeside house, though the rest of Twistyard feared he had become a casualty of Dark Hood's activities; and Clair was holding a special dueling class early in the morning, a distance away, for a select few people who Abbot couldn't identify.

Dod avoided most of Clair's regular instruction sessions throughout the week and instead used the time for his own climbing practice. He'd already learned that Clair wouldn't let him touch a blade of any kind, regardless of Dilly's best words on his behalf. It seemed hopeless that Clair would ever warm up to Dod. Though Dod did secretly look forward to the upcoming tournaments. He couldn't wait to see how people would react when Boot stomped on the others with his hidden talent of sword fighting, and Dod hoped Boot would face-off with Clair and set him straight, too.

Nightly, Green Hall continued their regimen of posting watches and squishing together into three rooms, despite the fact that The Beast hadn't been seen by anyone for over a week. Boot was cautious. Even though his remodeled room had received its new furniture and had been given a wonderful planter box like Youk's, he still slept in Pone's room. And he forced Sneaker to do likewise, which was a bit of a tug since the ferret loved spending its spare time sprawling out in the top branches of a little tree that consumed the center of the planter box.

Dod's nightmares tormented the surrounding sleepers and especially frightened whoever was on watch for The Beast. After meeting Abbot, Dod couldn't stop having a recurring dream that left him sweating and panting when he awoke, though the details were convoluted enough to render him aimless as to the direction they were pointing. He kept seeing a quarry of white stone, the hot, suffocating air filled with dust and the pounding sounds of metal tools crushing giant rocks into little pebbles. Pain and suffering drenched every nook and cranny. It was a miserable place, or that's how it felt in his dreams, which caused him to cry out into the stillness of the night with garbled pleadings for deliverance.

Dilly eventually took notice and insisted Dod inform her of every aspect of the dismal images, hoping they were somehow pointing toward the truth about Dark Hood. However, after recording the information in her Book of Everything, she hardly sought conclusions. In truth, she couldn't: Her mind was highly preoccupied with visions of victory as the sword tournaments were about to begin.

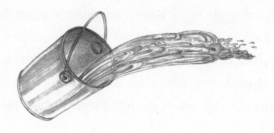

CHEAP SHOT

D illy was up early in the morning on the first day of the Twistyard sword tournaments. She couldn't contain her excitement any better than a rattled can of pop could hold back its fizz.

"Get up, get up!" she insisted, rousing all of Green Hall out of bed at five a.m. Sawny was less enthusiastic, but rigidly attached to Dilly's side for emotional support—she understood well how significant the dueling matches were to Dilly.

"This is our year, I can feel it," chirped Dilly gleefully, her eyes a misty gloss of hopes. "Hurry now. I've pulled lines and arranged to have Mercy serve us first—one of the special meals Humberrone routinely ate before going into battle."

Steak, thought Dod sleepily, remembering Saluci's cooking—the good-luck breakfast she'd fixed for him the morning he'd ridden the giant flutter with Sammywoo.

"As long as it's not beetles and crickets again," moaned a tired Toos, emerging from his covers with a blade print on his cheek. Sleeping with swords was a bit of a challenge at times, but infinitely better than waiting unarmed for The Beast.

"Bugs?" whined Donshi, walking through Pone's room toward the hall. "Are we really going to eat bugs, Dilly?" Her crumpled blonde curls and sleepy blue eyes attested to the fact that she hadn't seen a mirror yet. Circumstances were inconvenient for everyone, especially for the Green Hall girls who slept in the windowless recreation room between the two overloaded boys' rooms. But they all slept safely. And had the arrangements been any less squished, they wouldn't have slept at all—they'd have spent their dark hours wide awake, wondering if the nasty creature, with its foot-long teeth and monstrous head, was coming to dine on them.

"Not bugs," responded Sawny factually, "they're mollusks. Mercy makes a wonderful seafood dish. If you close your eyes, it's less startling, and once you've tried it, you'll finish your plate clean."

"Yikes," rumbled Sham, working his fingers through his morning hair. "Can't I have a steaming plate of pancakes, bacon, and biscuits?"

"Or hash browns and eggs?" added Voo from under his covers, peeking out.

"I'd like them all," insisted Pone, rising to his feet and stretching like a bear that had just emerged from hibernation. "I'm starving. It makes me twice as hungry to be up at night watching for that pond creeper. Maybe we could set out refreshments tonight. It would make the time fly by—"

"And the ants crawl in," ribbed Dilly playfully. "That's why *we* don't eat in *our* dorm."

"Speak for yourself," mumbled Buck from under a heap of covers. He knew Pone was notorious for bringing all sorts of food into Green Hall.

"Sneaker would clean up the crumbs—let's do it," added Boot, rising from a blanket on the floor with his pet ferret in his arms. Boot had taken his turn roughing it, not allowing his status at the top to change his position in the rotation of mattressless slumber.

"I doubt your ferret would be able to find all the piles that would wind up in here if we bumped the rules," said Dilly. "But—well—perhaps if you win your matches today, we could become a bit forgetful."

"Then I'm gonna be feasting on cookies and fried chicken tonight, boys!" blared Pone eagerly, hopping around the room with his arms in the air. "Mr. Clair's a great sword instructor. I'm twice what I was before. It's like he discovered a well of skills within me and drew them to the surface."

Huh, thought Dod sadly, rubbing debris from his eyes. Clair hadn't drawn anything out of Dod but frustration and anger, so the matches weren't looking favorable for him. Add to that the fact that he hadn't slept well, because he had suffered through three nightmares during the brief catnap he had slipped into after taking the twelve to one shift in the hall. But at least he knew he wouldn't make a complete fool of himself when he dueled, thanks to the superb instruction he had received from The Guys back in Cedar City.

Half the hall began to bustle while the other half tried to ignore the commotion.

"Last one ready for breakfast gets a double turn watching for Ugly tonight," yelled Boot, putting a spur in their flanks. "We need all of us to move as one today—complete unity. Win or lose, each match will be supported by the group. WE'RE TAKING RAUL DOWN!"

Boot's words and thunderous voice rallied the troops to hop up and get hustling. Excitement floated in the air as conversations drifted into the history of competitions with Raul Hall.

Dod left Pone's room and ventured to Boot's newly furnished flat. Dod's clothes from Pap were in the closet where he and Dilly had been seated when The Beast had made its awful appearance. The dark morning, barely hinting that the sun was coming, brought back ominous feelings. The room was shadowy like the middle of the night, and the moon was still lingering, three-quarters full.

Dod slipped out of his pajamas and began to look for his pants.

Suddenly, like a soft whisper, Dod heard a familiar voice in his mind. *Perhaps up there*, it said. *I'm still hungry — and he's home now.*

Dod knew it was The Beast! He felt its searching, tethered brain considering a climb to his window.

Without hesitation, Dod dug into his limp bag on the floor and drew Pap's beautiful golden sword. His heart was thumping at a gallop in his bare chest and his breath was stolen. He wished he knew how close the monster was, for he wanted to bolt to the safety of his friends, but he didn't relish the thoughts of exposing himself to the wall of windows if The Beast were nearby, and he hoped to first find his pants before entering the bustling hall of girls.

"Dod, are you in here?" called Boot, carefully sneaking into the bedroom and closing the door behind him. He locked it. "I've got a little surprise for you, Dod, come on out. You've got to hurry."

Dod felt sick to his stomach. He couldn't hear The Beast

very well, but it mumbled in the morning air, suggesting it was still hanging around.

"I-I'm in the closet changing," gasped Dod, struggling to speak. He was frantically groping for his pants, while securely holding his sword. "And The Beast is really close! Watch out, Boot! I think it's coming!"

"I know," said Boot casually. "Come on out and I'll show you."

I smell them! boomed The Beast eagerly. *Let me feast!*

No! Go away! thought Dod, shuddering. He grabbed the first piece of clothing his hands touched in the darkness and pressed for the closet door.

The creature was nearing the window, scaling the wall. Dod could instantly sense its approaching presence. Any second he knew its bulging eyes would be popping into view.

"RUN!" shouted Dod, bare-chested. He flew around the corner with only one leg in his trousers.

To Dod's amazement, Boot stepped in front of him, calm as a summer's afternoon, and wiggled his hands in the air, showing off a handsome pair of sparkling-white gloves.

"Don't dash away," said Boot. "I'm not done."

"The Beast," muttered Dod in a frazzled, desperate voice, fighting to leave the bedroom. But Boot grabbed Dod's arm with his powerful grasp and held him back.

"Where?" asked Boot, smirking. He didn't look the least bit nervous.

"It's climbing the wall!" exclaimed Dod. He was terrified of the approaching creature and beyond dumbfounded by Boot's lack of concern, as though Boot's fancy slips were going to save him. Dod clutched his sword tighter, until the blood drained from his knuckles.

"Open up," hollered Buck, rapping at the entrance. "Don't leave me out here with *them*—"

"Just handle it," responded Boot, still clasping Dod's arm. He slowly let go and then shrugged his shoulders. "I guess Buck can be in on it."

Dod flung the door open and was nearly trampled by Buck and Pone, who both stormed in and locked the door behind them.

"Please!" yelled Toos from the other side. "They'll take it out on me—"

"And they should," said Buck, leaning his back against the door, making it nearly impossible for Dod to escape. "You did it, not us."

"It was Pone's idea!" pled Toos. "Let me in, let me in."

"Let *me* out!" cried Dod, not caring for their games. He couldn't feel The Beast anymore, but he figured the commotion around him had masked its approaching presence.

Pone and Buck stared, flabbergasted. Neither of them moved from the door.

"I think you might want to put those on before venturing out," said Buck, pointing to Dod's pants that were trailing awkwardly from one leg.

"It was Pone's idea," screeched Toos as a wave of girls' voices overtook the hallway. Water noises followed.

"If you didn't want to get wet, you shouldn't have started it!" huffed Dilly, clearly lecturing a drenched Toos. Boot and Pone laughed hysterically, safe inside the locked room.

Dod looked intently at the wall of windows, knowing his sword was all that stood between him and a huge tragedy.

Nothing happened.

The pristine view of the setting moon felt like an empty,

well-spun web. Any second, The Beast could smash through the glass and gobble them up. Dod didn't dare blink.

"We don't use real swords at the tournaments," chortled Pone, grinning gleefully as he gazed upon Pap's rapier.

"I know," snapped Dod. "The Beast is just outside our window."

"What?" gasped Buck. He stood up straight and pulled at the door frantically, though without luck since Pone's big body was plopped on the floor in front of it.

Boot and Pone laughed until Buck's face turned cross. "You too, Dod?" he frowned, shaking his head. "I should have known! Boot's well aware of how terrified I am of The Beast."

"I'm being serious," insisted Dod. His sober face, amidst the frivolity, was his most convincing piece of evidence.

Buck turned and yanked at the handle, while attempting to dislodge Pone with a kick.

"Calm down," sighed Boot, jumping to his brother's side and aiding Pone in reemploying the lock. "It's nothing. I'll prove it."

Boot jogged across the spacious room, popped one of the sliding panes open, and stuck his head out. He looked down, he looked up, and then he pulled his head back in. "See?" he said happily. "There's absolutely, positively, and most certainly nothing to be afraid of."

Dod was horrified at first. It was like he had just watched his best friend put his head in the mouth of a ravenous lion. Slowly, Dod felt his muscles tingle and relax. The Beast was gone.

"It's the first day of the tournaments," said Pone to Buck. "What did you expect? We always pull a few pranks before the matches commence. It clicks our heels and sets our jaws, so by the time the swords start clanking, we're already full speed."

Dod dipped his weapon to the ground and put his pants on. He wasn't sure what had just happened. The voices in his head had undeniably sounded like The Beast. It couldn't have been a joke. But where had the horrendous creature gone? And why hadn't it swallowed Boot's head?

"I can duel without being ruffled all morning," whined Buck, plodding his way to the closet Dod had exited.

"But I do better after ruffling," responded Pone lightheartedly, "so thanks for your contribution to my preparation. A couple more pulls and I'll be three-kites high. No one will touch my sword skills today."

Dod followed Buck and searched for a good, lucky shirt. He needed all the luck he could get. His adrenaline rush had left him exhausted.

"Sorry I didn't play along very well," said Boot to Dod as he stood at the entrance to the walk-in closet. His voice was wet with guilt as he misread Dod's concerned face. "At least you scared Buck."

"Yeah, you had me hooked," said Buck encouragingly. "You're a natural actor."

Dod wasn't sure how to respond. He did feel a little loony every time he heard voices in his mind, or saw glimpses of images, or had nightmares. And he didn't want everyone to think of him as a cracked nut, like Boot did of Abbot, so he finally decided to keep quiet and pretend as though it had been a prank.

"I'm still getting used to your customs around here," confessed Dod uneasily. "So—uh—sorry, Buck, if I got you riled."

"We're level if you let me wear this shirt," responded Buck, dangling a sky-blue button-down from his fingertips. It matched his eyes perfectly.

"Sure, take your pick—and you too, Boot. That's why I got them. What's mine is yours." It made Dod feel better to have something to offer his friends.

Since the fire had destroyed the clothes in their closet, or at least had caused them to be confiscated, Boot and Buck had been left with only a few items they had obtained from begging. Dod, on the other hand, had brought back a wide variety of things to wear from Pap's stashes, a heaping backpack load each time he had met with Abbot, making him rich in apparel by comparison.

Fortunately for his roommates, Dod had purposefully stocked up on larger sizes, knowing that Boot and Buck needed new clothes, too; Dod had brought back pants and shirts that didn't fit him, stuff that wouldn't have fit Pap, either. But the items had been in with Pap's possessions, so they were technically Dod's, regardless of their original owner.

"Thanks, Dod," said Boot, seizing a regal-red blazer. He pulled the jacket over his white shirt and strutted up and down the closet with a stiff back. "This is perfect. Now I'll have a jacket to take off when I enter the ring. It's a good tactic for intimidating."

"Oh, nice," said Dod, biting his tongue. He couldn't help thinking Boot looked like a carriage boy, waiting to open the door for someone important. The gloves completed the image.

Buck slid into the blue shirt and disappeared in search of a mirror. No sooner was he gone than Boot changed gears.

"Here," said Boot quietly, kneeling down beside Dod, who was lacing his shoes tightly. Boot took the gloves off and gave them to Dod. "I want you to have these, but you can't tell the others who they're from. It's our little secret."

Dod crinkled his brow.

"Do you recognize the golden trim?" Boot tipped the gloves over, palm up, and revealed insignias in each—Chantolli insignias!

"These were Sirlonk's," said Boot proudly. "When you cross blades today, you can be wearing them. Only Pap bested The Dread with a sword—only Pap—and you're his grandson—and you sent Sirlonk off to Driaxom, where he belongs." Boot got a smug look and added gleefully, "And I doubt anyone else will recognize them—except Clair—he's a detail freak. It'll smoke his socks to see you routing the others while shamelessly flaunting your slips from an *old friend*."

"Thanks," said Dod sincerely. He felt bad that he had been frustrated with Boot. In retrospect, Boot's actions were motivated by his desire to do something nice.

"Oh, and one more thing," said Boot, rising to his feet. "If I were you, Dod, I'd skip the green gooey stuff with the little pink balls. Mercy claims it's part of the meal, but I know she's stretching it. That dish comes straight from her childhood, not Humberrone's. I knew him, and trust me, he hated the pink balls. He said they made him nauseous."

"You knew Humberrone?"

"Sure," said Boot. "He didn't stay here all of the time, like Pap, but when he was here—wow! I tried to attend his lectures and trainings as much as I could. The man was really something. Did you ever meet him?"

"No," mumbled Dod.

"Too bad," said Boot. "I'm sure the two of you would have hit it off. He was quick with ideas, like you and Pap."

On the way to breakfast, Dilly and Boot scurried back and forth, attempting to enforce the truce that had been negotiated before leaving Green Hall. Too many pranks had gone wrong. It was like April Fool's Day—times two or three.

Toos had a bluish tint to his face and smelled like a hedge of roses. Not only had the girls drenched him with water, they had sprayed him with perfume that had been adulterated with blue dye. But he wasn't alone; four other Greenling boys smelled and looked the same. It was their punishment for dousing the girls with buckets of water.

Sawny explained to Dod that the pranks were lighter than usual, considering no one was in need of stitches and to the best of her knowledge, nothing important had been irreparably destroyed.

"Then what happened on the bad years?" chuckled Dod, noticing Sham was missing an eyebrow. Someone had shaved it off during the night.

"You don't even want to know," said Sawny, delicately pushing her hair out of her face. "One year we forgot to lock the door to the girls' hall, so during the night, the boys dumped a gunnysack of water snakes into our entryway and shut the door tight. By morning, everything was crawling. I personally found three snakes in my shoes, one in my jacket pocket, two in my drawers—which I haven't the slightest how they wriggled their way in—five in the shower, one in my stack of books from the library, and the worst of all—you won't even believe it, Dod—" Sawny shivered just thinking about it before explaining. "By far the most dreadful was the first one I discovered—it was squished flat in my pillowcase. I slept on a snake, Dod! It was horrible!"

"That sounds pretty crazy," admitted Dod. "The most troublesome prank we ever did back home was sending love notes to a dozen girls at school from this creepy guy in town. But Pap pulled a tight one when he was younger. He was hanging out with his buddies at night, causing trouble, when one of them got the wild idea of tipping an outhouse."

"An outhouse?"

"You know, an outdoor bathroom."

"Right—a slat-shack," said Sawny.

"Well—the slat-shack was my grandpa's—"

"Why would he tip his own bathroom?" interrupted Sawny.

"I don't exactly know," said Dod, straining to remember the details. He knew there was more to the story than he'd ever been told. "Maybe peer pressure," he finally said. "Anyway, that's not the worst part. When he and his buddies gave it a good nudge, it wasn't empty! They tipped the outhouse over with my grandpa's old man inside—and he was a grump to start with."

"There's your reason," said Sawny. "Bonboo had a mean uncle when he was younger—and if I tell you about him, you can't tell Bonboo, because he'd die if he knew my dad told me the story." Sawny cleared her throat and proceeded. "One day Bonboo decided to get back at the man for all the wretched things he'd done to everyone, so he nudged a creek off course and flooded the man's garden—"

"That's not so bad—"

"And the garden happened to be the man's pride and joy. Naturally, the man rushed out into the mud to save it—"

Dod stared. He knew there was a big punch line coming. Sawny's eyes were getting bigger than he'd ever seen them before.

"And as he waded into the mud, he stepped on a Hissolop weed. The poisonous thorn struck the mean man and he died right there in the middle of his swampy garden."

"That's awful!" gasped Dod.

"Yup," said Sawny. "Poor Bonboo hated himself for causing

the death of his uncle. He couldn't get rid of the guilt he felt. Every night, he'd look into the starry sky and wish he could go back and undo the harm. But it didn't force good to come. All of the wishing in the world wouldn't bring the man back. So when Bonboo got a little older, he sought help from an old woman who told him a secret that changed everything—"

"Really?" asked Dod, entering the Great Hall beside Sawny.

"Yup," she said, stopping to look both ways. She bit her lip and then signaled for Dod to get closer. "Here's the secret," she whispered, barely audible.

Dod waited, tingling with anticipation.

"BOO!" she screamed, flipping her fingers for emphasis.

Dod tripped backward and fell over.

"Sawny!" blared Dilly, "We all came to a truce!"

"Not me," said Sawny in a refined, defiant manner. "I've been waiting months to dish him back for the night ride we shared by Commendus's pond." She then smiled ear to ear and helped Dod to his feet.

"I deserved that," chuckled Dod, impressed by Sawny's abilities.

"Did she tell you about our mean uncle?" asked Dilly, trying not to smile.

Dod nodded while Boot, Buck, and Pone all laughed.

"I love that one," said Boot. "Nobody spins it better than Sawny."

"It's because she's so factual the rest of the time," insisted Buck. "People who don't usually tease are the best when they do—kind of like Dod. He really had me going this morning. I was certain The Beast was about to crash through our bedroom window."

"Turnabout's fair play," chirped Sawny, nudging Dod jokingly on his shoulder. "One prank a year is about perfect for me."

"Who's teasing whom?" asked Mercy, emerging with a line of helpers. They followed her with trays of seafood. Dod took one look and knew why Toos had fussed about bugs.

"I've done all I can to give you the edge," said Mercy, displaying the wide array of interesting dishes. They were less glamorous looking than the specialty items Saluci had fixed for the patio picnic, but they smelled similar. Dod hoped they tasted as good.

"Now remember," said Mercy, "this is the exact meal Humberrone would eat before heading out on his most important missions. I fixed it for him many times."

"Looks wonderful!" praised Boot, stepping over to give Mercy a squeeze from the side. "I can't believe you made all of this for us—and so early in the morning—"

"I prepped most of it last night," confessed Mercy, basking in the adoration. "Besides, I'd happily stay up three nights straight if I thought it would help Green Hall tip Raul Hall on their sides. And I'm not embarrassed to say it. They've become so pompous and booshy that I can barely stand to serve them some days. And do you think the Raulings take their turns in the kitchen now that Bonboo's gone?"

"But what about Voracio?" asked Dilly. "Doesn't he make them?"

"I've mentioned it to him—but there are some feats even he can't seem to do—despite all of the wonderful things he does right." Mercy beamed a fresh glow when Voracio's name was brought up.

"We're glad you're rooting for us," said Sawny. "It means a lot."

"Well," huffed Mercy, picking at her short, graying curls, "after Sawb played cowardly with his sword across Dilly's fingers, I've been counting down the minutes to this day. Please set him straight."

"Oh, I will!" insisted Dilly.

Or Boot certainly will, thought Dod gleefully.

The food was unusual to say the least. Much of it resembled smoked oysters, though the fleshy chunks seemed to have leg-like strings that shot outward, giving them the appearance of bugs. But Sawny was right—with closed eyes the meal didn't taste bad, just a little muddy.

Once Mercy was gone, Dod couldn't help asking: "Why in the world did Humberrone eat stuff like this?"

Buck nodded in agreement, since his finicky stomach forbid him from tasting half of the lucky breakfast.

"It probably reminded him of his mother's cooking," said Dilly, fiddling with the food on her plate. "People from Soosh eat the strangest things. Ask Jim sometime what his mom likes to make. I remember hearing that one of their holidays is a lot like Rainfall Day, but rather than roasting a goose, they eat piles of giant frog legs."

"Gross," gagged Sawny. "Who would ever think of eating a frog's legs? I'd have to be starving to death before that would cross my mind."

"My dad used to eat 'em," confessed Dod proudly. "When he was a kid, he'd hunt the really big bullfrogs with his friends and cook their legs over a campfire."

"And you're not from Soosh?" joked Sawny, eyeing Dod with a curious grin.

"Definitely not," responded Dod.

"So where are you from?" asked Donshi, closing her eyes as she gingerly took a bite of her food. Dod didn't know what to say. It was the kind of question he tried to avoid.

"I dare you to eat the fish eyeballs," blared Dod, poking

Pone who was seated beside him. He acted as though he hadn't heard Donshi.

"Eew, don't do it!" snapped Sawny from across the table. She looked away from Dod and Pone.

"Do it! Do it! Do it!" chanted Boot, Voo, and Sham.

Pone smiled and slid the fish serving platter over. He took his spoon and scooped the eyeballs out of their sockets, one by one, until he had a pile of nine on his plate. The tenth eye was nowhere to be found.

"Don't be foolish," chided Sawny, cringing as she peeked through her fingers.

"I'm not," assured Pone. "I'm hungry. Besides, who knows how much luck they'll bring me. I bet Humberrone ate eyeballs for snacks."

"Would you jump off a building if Dod dared you to do it?" asked Sawny. Dod thought she was sounding a lot like his mother.

Pone cleared his throat and stuffed the marble-sized eyeballs into his mouth until his cheeks resembled those of a greedy squirrel. "Now what were you saying?" teased Pone, turning toward Sawny as he sloshed the eyes around with his tongue.

"That's disgusting," said Buck, not amused. "At least swallow your food. We don't all enjoy your choices."

Once Pone had chewed them down, he slid a bowl of slime in front of Dod and said, "Your turn." It was the green gooey stuff Boot had warned him about.

Don't eat it! thought Dod, noticing how many little pink dots it had. He glanced at Boot and was surprised to find that he was nearly done with his third bowl of the 'unwanted' dish. It reminded Dod of the time he'd tried hard to convince Josh and Alex that they wouldn't like homemade peach ice cream.

"Come on," taunted Pone. "I see you've tried everything else, why not finish with sloosha? We'll be invincible today, like Humberrone." He reached into the bones of the fish platter, drew out the missing eyeball, and plopped it on top of the green goo."

"Of course," sputtered Dod, scooping the eyeball up with his first bite. He couldn't resist the pressure he felt—not only from Pone, but from the crowd of Coosings and Greenlings that were now watching to see if he would follow through, which only seemed fair after Pone had eaten nine giant fish eyeballs because of Dod's dare.

Surprisingly, it went down smoothly and didn't taste bad. *Chopped pickles and tuna*, thought Dod, feeling a wave of relief. He dug into the bowl with vigor.

Boot watched him and smirked. "Do you like it?" he asked.

Dod nodded. "At home I eat this stuff for lunch all the time," he said.

Before breakfast was over, a wave of people entered the Great Hall from the front courtyard. It was Sawb and his associates from Raul. They approached the special feast like a pack of hyenas.

"Seafood?" scoffed Sawb, wearing an expensive three-piece dueling suit. He reminded Dod of Sirlonk in the fancy outfit. Dod instantly knew who Boot was wishing to emulate when he had chosen the blazer.

"Too bad there's none left for you," said Dilly smugly. "I suppose if you wait, Mercy can bring you some pancakes and eggs while we go out front to warm up a bit."

"We've already eaten," snorted Sawb. "You've got your stinky rituals and we've got our—well—more refined ones. Roasted pork and beef will keep us fighting long after your pond slugs have dwindled and gone. Besides, Humberrone was nothing special." Sawb rudely prodded at Sham's full plate with his finger and laughed.

"Roasted pork," whined Sham enviously.

"We'll see who fares better," said Dilly, trying to be mature. The fire in her eyes suggested she didn't need any warming up, she needed a little cooling down.

"What is this stuff?" asked Eluxa, squeezing between Buck and Boot to grab a messy platter of scraps. Her perfume was strong enough to drift across the table to Dod and Pone.

"It's — uh — well," said Pone, trying to answer Eluxa, but appearing horribly distracted by her black leather dueling outfit.

"It's a traditional good-luck breakfast," responded Sawny flatly.

"Oh — then you should break from tradition," giggled Eluxa, poking at the slimy, brown-and-black slug-like scraps. When a big one stuck to her pointer finger, she dramatically screeched as though being bitten, dropped the tray, and flipped her hand in Sawny's direction. The greasy gob of mollusk flew past Boot and landed squarely in the center of Sawny's pink-and-white shirt; it dripped down, leaving a large brown smudge.

"Oops," said Eluxa coyly, lifting her clean hand to her mouth. She enjoyed the bout of laughs that rumbled from her surrounding crowd of Raulings and Coosings.

"Yup—I'm sure that's lucky," mocked Sawb, strolling closer to get a better look.

Sawny's eyes were moistening.

Boot stood up and cleared his throat purposefully loud. "That shirt was her mother's keepsake from her days as a champion—I think you owe Sawny a big apology." Boot glared at Eluxa.

Sawb put his dirty hand on Sawny's shoulder and wiped his

fingers off. "Oops," he said, copying Eluxa. "I think I had an accident, too, Boot. What are *you* going to do about it?"

Lickety-split, Dilly flew to her feet and planted her half-full plate of stinky seafood in Sawb's face.

"FOOD FIGHT!" yelled Toos, eager to unload his unwanted piles of mollusks and fish. He hurled the gooey mixture into the air toward Eluxa and grinned gleefully when it splattered on her and two other Raul Coosings.

Sawb wasted no time in pasting his fist across Boot's face as payback for Dilly's outrage, which caught Boot off guard and sent him flailing backward onto the table.

Before Boot could return a blow, Voracio's voice broke through the noise like a clap of thunder.

"STOP!" he yelled, his nostrils flaring angrily as he hobbled from the kitchen. "I want this mess cleaned up right now! And if I hear so much as a peep—even a tiny peep—I'll personally take a stick to your backs."

Sawb waved his hand and the others from Raul obediently began to retreat the way they had come.

"I said CLEAN IT UP!" raged Voracio. "Where do you think you're going?"

Sawb spun around, food still dripping off his face, and looked Voracio up and down. They stared each other in the eyes for an awkward moment of silence, and then Sawb turned and led Raul Hall out the door, uncontested.

"Well—CLEAN IT UP!" yelled Voracio angrily at Boot, who was rubbing his sore jaw. Voracio's voice was even louder than before. "There will be repercussions from this—mark my words! I'll have my people inform you of your punishments. All of Green Hall will pay for this disorderly conduct."

"And Raul?" asked Boot indignantly, feeling maligned.

Fire nearly shot from Voracio's eyes. "That's it, young man!" he boomed, rushing to grab Boot by the collar. "You won't be dueling today—or anytime this week. I've seen enough bad behavior from you to last a lifetime. If your labors in the stalls don't improve your attitude, you're out of Twistyard—and I don't care what Bonboo says!"

Boot's posture was stiff and insolent.

"My grandfather doesn't know you as I do," added Voracio frigidly, momentarily cracking a wicked grin. "Perhaps I shall inform him in a letter—"

"I'll muck the stalls for you," snapped Boot, "but the rest of Green Hall stays out of this. No more punishments. I provoked the trouble, not them."

Voracio glanced angrily at Dilly and Sawny, then around at the others before his glare settled back on Boot. "Don't worry—you'll get it the worst!" he growled heatedly.

Boot calmly put his hand on Voracio's shoulder, forced him back a few paces, and whispered something in his ear.

Voracio's nostrils flared again, yet this time it wasn't accompanied by his violent tongue. He stood still, speechless, looking at the Greenlings and Coosings for nearly a minute, thinking through his options. "You're all free to go warm up," he finally grumbled, "but I won't tolerate any more insubordinate conduct. I'm serious. If you cross me again—" he shook his head and struggled to find his words, "well—you'll really be in trouble."

"You heard him," echoed Boot quickly, forcing a smile. "Let's fix this mess and get going—we've got matches to win!"

Boot was an invincible hero of sorts, or so he seemed. But when everyone else made their way toward the matches, Boot took

Dilly aside and put her in charge. "I've got a few responsibilities to take care of," he said, pointing at the barns. "You'll have to tell me how things go, okay? Knock them over, Dilly! You're the best. And if Sawb tries to give you any more trouble, let him know I'll personally escort him by his ear to the portal at High Gate and see to it that the last parting gift he receives from Green is my footprint on his royal backside."

Dod wanted to cry for Boot, who acted like it didn't matter that he would be spending his time arduously shoveling horse manure all week instead of dueling. It wasn't fair.

"But I thought things were settled," gasped Dilly, suddenly noticing the bruise that was growing on Boot's cheek.

"Everything's fine," assured Boot. "I'm not that great with a sword anyway—and after this tussle with Sawb—he'd be out to clean my attic."

Horsely and Ingrid emerged from the largest barn and approached Boot, Dilly, and Dod. Horsely limped, but still steadied Ingrid in a gentlemanly way.

"Did you fight with it?" asked Ingrid, looking at Boot's injured face.

"What?" choked Dilly.

"The Beast," said Ingrid ominously. "Leave it for the drat soldiers. I don't want *you* getting hurt, Boot." She waddled closer and inspected his bruise.

"I'm fine, Gram," said Boot in his carefree, jovial voice. "The Beast didn't do this, I—uh—fell on the table at breakfast."

"That's awful!" exclaimed Ingrid. "I hope it doesn't affect your skills today. I got up bright and early so I wouldn't miss a thing—and I did you a favor, too." Ingrid looked pleased.

"Oh," mumbled Boot. "What did you do?"

"The ritual thing—with your foes."

"Huh?"

"She went with Sawb and the others to the terrace for their annual pre-game roast," said Horsely, jumping in to explain. "I drove her in the private carriage—"

"With Juny," added Ingrid. "I kept my eye on her the whole time, but I kept my ears on Slob. He's got plans for you. He told everyone he was going to get you thrown out of the matches today. Keep your wits about you and stay away from Slob. Clair seems to favor Raul over Green, thanks to his boyhood delusions about Sirlonk being remarkable with a sword, so it wouldn't take much to send you packing."

"Too late," slipped Dilly.

Boot gave her a pleading look.

"Too late for what?" asked Ingrid, clutching her cane for support.

"It'll be too late to get a seat if you don't hurry," rushed Dilly. "Mr. Clair told us that he likes to start things early."

"No worries, honey," said Ingrid, pushing past Boot and Dod to Dilly. "I can keep up with you if you help me." She poured her large arm around Dilly's neck and leaned. "Let's hurry," she said, "I'm excited to see what the tournaments are like. I've heard so much talk—and Boot's the best, isn't he?" She tilted her head to smile fondly in Boot's direction.

"He sure is!" responded Dilly, more to Boot than to Ingrid. "No matter what people say, Boot's a gem!"

Dod lingered back with Boot and Horsely, while Dilly began the chore of helping Ingrid to the rings. And before Boot had finished whining to Horsely about his unfortunate circumstance, a battalion of drat soldiers rode up on horseback to speak with Horsely. Jibb was in command, wearing a sword at his waist and carrying a bow; he also had a quiver of arrows slung across his back.

"We've been looking all over for you," huffed Jibb loudly over the snorting horses. "We had another incident—" Jibb glanced at Dod and Boot with annoyance as though their presence was hindering his discussion.

"It was The Beast again, wasn't it?" said Dod eagerly.

"How do you know anything of *that*?" demanded Jibb, turning his full attention on Dod. The waiting soldiers all watched. "Who's been telling you there's a beast?"

"I saw it, remember?" responded Dod. "I'm sure Dolrus told you. The Beast nearly ate me and Dilly."

"Oh—I suppose you know, then," admitted Jibb. "I hope you'll use great discretion with that knowledge. Voracio and Youk are both stone-stiff serious about others not hearing of The Beast."

"So, it came back?" asked Boot.

"Yes," sighed Jibb. "Fortunately, my men on watch heard a commotion and gave pursuit, chasing it from the holding yards, and no one we know of is missing—just three hogs that were scheduled for this evening's dinner."

Boot began a sentence when Horsely interrupted, thinking it was his turn to speak since he was reading Jibb's lips, not Boot's. "I still haven't found it yet," he said, "but I'm sure it's got a slide somewhere close by. I'll search more of the shoreline today."

"Then let me send a few of my men with you," insisted Jibb. "We don't want you to disappear."

"I won't," laughed Horsely arrogantly. "They rarely come out during the day—or at least that's what Dr. Shelderhig said, and I'd say he's always right. But if you think I need backup, send Boot with me."

"Boot?" chuckled Jibb, glancing in Boot's direction. "He has other engagements—the tournaments—and I highly doubt he'd set them aside for our benefit."

"I'll tell you what," bargained Horsely, working hard to hold back a smile, "If you'll have a dozen of your best workers clean out all of the stalls in the big barn, I'll convince Boot to skip the silly tournaments and he'll accompany me to search for The Beast's lair. Do we have a deal?"

Jibb laughed. Boot and Dod played their best stubborn eyes behind Horsely's back.

"I'm serious," insisted Horsely. "Voracio doesn't understand how hard it's been on my uncle Stallio to fill spots in the barns these days, especially with your dad gone. If Voracio's not going to rotate the resident Pots or Lings or Coosings, he should have the soldiers help out. The barns need to get cleaned somehow, and I'm not the one to do it, and neither is Stallio."

Jibb squirmed in his saddle. "And if Boot won't go?" he asked.

"There's no way I'll miss the tournaments!" spat Boot, but out of Horsely's range of vision.

"Then I'll spend my days searching for the lair with your men," agreed Horsely, "and my nights shoveling 'til it's clean—fair enough?"

"You've got a deal," gloated Jibb happily. "Let's see you strike this one."

Horsely and Boot had a mock argument, back and forth, with Horsely insisting Boot owed him and Boot insisting that as the head Green Coosing he couldn't miss the matches. It was humorous for Dod to watch. He knew the game.

In the end, Horsely made some obscure reference about having saved Boot's life and Boot pretended to sulk, then agreed to ride with Horsely in search of the monster's lair. Jibb nearly fell off his horse with astonishment.

"I'll be watching for your workers," added Horsely, beaming at Jibb. "Please get your men going on the big barn—and use as many as it takes. It's a real mess!"

When the soldiers were gone, Dod and Boot both clapped. Thanks to Horsely's quick thinking, Boot's obligation of mucking out the entire large barn was taken care of, which would have been a two-week job if Boot had done it alone.

THE TOURNAMENTS

D od jogged and caught up with Dilly and Ingrid before they had made it to the rings. He was still disappointed that Boot wouldn't get a chance to reveal his secret talent, but he felt much better knowing that Boot would be riding the shoreline of Lake Mauj with Horsely instead of shoveling manure.

"Dod," said Dilly, "Ingrid thinks we ought to go and live with Commendus for a while—because of The Beast. What do you think?" She had clearly given Ingrid her opinion and was merely waiting for Dod to second the motion.

"Not a chance!" wheezed Dod, trying to catch his breath.

"But didn't the two of you see the gruesome thing try to enter Green Hall?" asked Ingrid, searching Dod with her eyes. "It's ludicrous for you to stay here! I'd leave if I weren't pressed by my duty to keep a watch on Juny. Even Bonmoob's decided this place is too dangerous."

"That's why we're staying!" insisted Dod. "We're going to rid Twistyard of its pest problem."

"Huh," huffed Ingrid. "Stay safe. And if that monster tries to enter Green Hall again, get out! If I lived in Green Hall, I'd leave. I'd make Juny accompany me to Commendus's palace—that is, if I had your connections, Dilly."

"Oh—I'm sorry," said Dilly, suddenly realizing what Ingrid was getting at. "Would you like me to ask Commendus if you could stay with him for a while?"

"Would you do that for me?" choked Ingrid excitedly. She calmed her face and added, "I hadn't even thought of it, but now that you mention the possibility, it sure would be nice—assuming I could bring Juny with me."

Dod and Dilly smiled at each other. They both knew that Ingrid had placed her words from the start with that goal in mind.

"I'll send him a letter if he doesn't come to the tournaments," responded Dilly, "though he usually shows up to watch the better matches."

The threesome approached a string of temporary bleachers that were nearly filled to capacity. Dilly hadn't been entirely off when she had suggested that Ingrid would need to hurry if she wanted a seat, especially near the level-five ring.

The tournament matches were divided into classes based on past performance and training. All of the Coosings from Raul and Green, and most of the Coosings from Soosh, were ranked high in their dueling abilities and were, therefore, put in the level-five bracket. Many of the Greenlings, Raulings, and Sooshlings were level four or three, and Pots were usually in level two or one. Still, noteworthy exceptions abounded, including a number of talented Pots from Raul who were level five, hoping to make a big enough impression on Sawb to catch his eye.

Hundreds of people sat on wooden bleachers, surrounding five circles in the grass. During each match, both contenders had to stay within the circle while showing off their skills against their opponent using spar swords. Two judges sat on opposite sides of the ring, quietly evaluating the duel. Each pair of competitors was given five minutes to prove their position. If the actions displayed were considered too hazardous, a whistle would blow, ending the match prematurely, and the judges would call a winner—though it was typically in the best interest of both contestants to show respect while dueling, because in most circumstances where a match had ended short, a tie had been called, resulting in half-a-point for each person.

For the first three days of the tournaments, everyone participating would be given an equal number of matches; after that, on the fourth and fifth days, only the people with enough points would be allowed to progress and compete for championship titles, including best three individuals and best pairs in each level, and based on the sheer number of competitors in the final matches, best Hall. Raul usually swept them all.

"You're in luck," said Dilly, leading Ingrid toward a front-row spot where Juny had saved her a place.

"I'll be watching," huffed Ingrid, taking her seat. Juny looked up and thanked Dilly, as though she had just taken care of Juny's aging grandmother. It seemed to indicate that despite the rough statements Ingrid made about Juny, the two women had a decent friendship.

"You better hurry, Dod," called Pone from outside of the bleachers. "You've got to sign in or Mr. Clair won't let you duel—and you're up first in the level-five ring."

Dod suddenly felt panicked.

"Quick," said Dilly, grabbing Dod by the hand. She pulled him through the congested grounds to the registration table before he had a chance to think twice. "Just do your best," she whispered. "Win, lose, or tie, it'll still be fun. At least today Mr. Clair will let you touch a sword."

Dod took a string of long, heavy breaths. He was feeling unsettled.

"You're dueling against Harrick," said Sawny, "so watch your legs—and he jabs more at your left than your right."

"Th-thanks," stuttered Dod nervously.

A hand slapped heartily on Dod's back and startled him. "You cunning *devil-o*, you!" blared Dari. "How'd you get picked to fight in four of the first six matches? *That-o* doesn't sound like a blind draw to *me-o*?"

"What?" gasped Dod.

"I'm sure it was fair, Dari," said Valerie in a proper voice, standing a few paces away with Sammywoo.

"You're gonna win, aren't you Dod?" plugged Sammywoo, noticing how white Dod's face was turning. "Just pretend you're fighting with The Dread again."

The boy's words pricked at Dod, causing him to reach into his pocket. He drew out Sirlonk's gloves and slipped them on, thinking of Boot's friendship. "I'll give it my best," responded Dod, "but you need to know, I'm not feeling well."

"I've heard that excuse all morning," screeched Dari. "My dad says it's a proud man's way of hedging his bets against failure."

Dod glanced back toward the level-five ring and saw Youk taking a seat at one of the two judges' tables, wearing his fanciest white hat.

"I thought you'd coward out!" grumbled Clair from behind a string of registration sheets. The line had thinned, making Dod next.

"Nope," said Dod flatly. "I'm here to have fun." It was a lie, but he hoped Clair would believe it.

"Then try smiling," said one of Clair's assistants, handing Dod a list that had his name on it. "Sign here and go choose your weapon. We're about to start, and you almost missed your first match. It would have been a tragedy to bump you without seeing your moves. We're all dying to know what you've been hiding. Look around, it's standing room only today."

Clair grimaced when his assistant indicated the crowds were larger because of Dod.

"It's the good weather," grumbled Clair, rising to his feet. His chest was as wide as two regular people. Clair's eyebrows raised with agitation when he noticed Dod's gloves. Boot was right—Clair quickly perceived they were Sirlonk's.

"I'll help you choose your sword," said Dilly, rushing Dod over to a gated area where swords were dispersed. Dod hefted three before settling on a lighter, skinnier spar sword.

The ring felt small once Dod stepped into it and prepared to duel, though part of the shrinking feeling came from having Youk's critical eyes beating him mercilessly from one side and Clair's angry eyes thrashing him from the other; not to mention, Harrick had a standard, Raul Coosing set of arms that hung from his towering frame, indicating he'd have no difficulty in reaching Dod, no matter where Dod fled to in the circle.

"Bow first, and then on three," said Youk.

Dod tipped his neck and counted with the judges. The instant they said three, Dod felt Harrick's retractable blade pushing against the left side of his chest and heard the crowd gasp. Harrick was lightning fast, or had cheated. Either way, Youk and Clair were observers, not referees, so Dod couldn't tell whether they liked what they had seen or not. Regardless, it hurt! Even though the blade collapsed inward, as designed, the pressure it took to force the metal parts to slide was enough to make Dod yelp.

But Dod's cries were followed closely by Harrick's, for Dod's arm had shot up like a spring-loaded Jack-in-the-box, the moment he felt the attack, and on the way to dismissing Harrick's pounding blade, Dod's sword had caught Harrick between the legs, causing him to howl and stagger backward.

"That's what I'd have done!" shouted Ingrid from the sidelines. "Get the cheater again while he's doubling over!"

Dod ignored Ingrid's suggestions; instead, he pointed his sword outward and waited for Harrick to rise.

"You'll blibbin pay for trousing my tenders," blared Harrick the moment he gained enough breath to speak. And he didn't rise before swiping his lengthy arm at Dod's legs, hoping his sword would cause pain.

"Get up!" yelled Sawb from beside Clair, his face exploding with frustration. "You're dueling! You can rest your lowers later! Make a move or I'll move you to the Pots!"

Dod's confidence grew as he looked around and noticed how pleased his friends were and how cross the members of Raul Hall appeared.

"Take this!" blared Harrick, jabbing toward Dod's stomach. Dod deflected the move, hopped to the side, and poked at Harrick's posterior. Harrick stumbled clownishly. Sammywoo giggled so loudly that Dod easily spotted him in the crowd and bowed a quick nod before repositioning to defend himself.

Bit by bit, Harrick regained his composure and agility. His lunges and jabs improved until, by the end of the five minutes, Dod was straining to deflect them. Amazingly, the training Dod had received from The Guys in Cedar City was just enough to carry the match.

"Point for Dod," said Youk happily after consulting with Clair, who looked so irritated that he couldn't have brought himself to declare Dod the winner even if he had been offered mounds of gold to do so.

Dilly and Sawny were the first to rush Dod, followed quickly by a wave of other Green Coosings and Youk's children. It was more than a win, it was payback for Boot and Sawny, and it was a forward push for all of Green Hall as they prepared to face their own duels. Winning the first match was critical.

In the second lineup, Dod was set against a Pot from Raul who had everything to win and nothing to lose. The boy towered over Dod menacingly and fought well from the start. His movements with his sword were sleek and refined, suggesting he had been trained by an expert before coming to Twistyard, and his clothes made it clear he was from an important, wealthy family in Raul. It was only a matter of time before the boy would become a Raul Coosing—and if the boy beat Dod in the match with a healthy womping, enough to humiliate Green Hall, it would certainly help expedite the process.

"Take him down, Klide!" yelled Sawb. "Don't let a human beat a tredder. Show him what Raul's made of!"

Dod bolted through a string of routines that Jack Parry had taught him, the kind of moves that people in Green, Raul, and Soosh had never seen before, so it threw Klide off his game and made the first three minutes pass with Dod shining like a gold penny, despite a growing feeling of unrest in his gut.

Unfortunately, about the time Klide began to press harder, Dod's stomach rumbled uncomfortably, and he threw up.

"Gaaaah!" blared Klide, stumbling backward to get away from the mess. One of his legs was splotched.

Dod hadn't been joking when he'd told Sammywoo that he was feeling sick, and that feeling had only gotten worse, even after his invigorating win against Harrick. It was nausea — a full-out onset of what felt like food poisoning — and it approached so suddenly that Dod knew what it was from: the dreaded green gooey stuff with the little pink balls. Boot had been telling the truth when he had warned Dod of Humber-rone's preferences.

"Sorry," mumbled Dod, tipping his soiled sword in Klide's direction. No matter what, Dod was bent on giving the match his best efforts.

"Gross!" screamed Eluxa from the bleachers. "Call it already, Clair! Give a point and clean the place up before we all start smelling it."

Klide tried to ignore the way his pants stuck to one leg, but it clearly hurt his game. And when Dod pressed at him—white-faced and ailing—Klide retreated too far and misstepped out of the ring, triggering a whistle.

"Point for Dod," said Youk. It was indisputable. The rules were clear on the need to stay within the circle for the full duration of the five minutes.

No one rushed to Dod as they had before, but there were still plenty of cheers from the crowd that loved Green Hall. Ingrid waved her cane in the air while Juny sat still, clearly rooting for Raul Hall. The two women looked completely opposite. Juny was the epitome of a princess: well-combed, long black hair, outrageously beautiful dress, perfect figure and posture, and fittingly appropriate facial expressions. Ingrid, on the other hand, roared and fussed like a soccer mom, hung out on all sides, wore plain, cheap clothing, and didn't worry two hoots about her posture, so she slouched as comfortably as she could.

"Are you all right?" called Dilly from the sidelines, waiting for Dod to exit the ring. He took a staggering bow for his fans and hobbled toward her.

"I'm ill from breakfast," said Dod. "It was the pink things—"

"Sloosha?" interrupted Dilly. "I thought you ate the stuff for lunch all the time back home."

"Well—" sighed Dod, heavily tottering, "I misspoke. The stuff tasted like something my mom fixed for us, but it was different." In Dod's head he couldn't help thinking he'd never eat another tuna-and-pickle sandwich as long as he lived, let alone consider downing a whole bowl of green gooey stuff. "I should have listened to Boot."

"Boot? He loves sloosha," said Sawny, peeking out from behind Dilly. She was clearly germophobic and wasn't going to take any chances on catching whatever Dod had.

"I know," groaned Dod. "He likes it, but he said Humberrone hated the dish. Maybe it's a human thing."

"Could be," said Dilly, stepping back. She wasn't going to take any chances either, considering she'd waited all year for the tournaments and knew a health issue would ruin her odds of victory.

Dod felt exhausted. He sat down on the grass in front of the bleachers and rested, still holding his messy sword.

"That was awesome!" thundered Pone as he came bounding from the bleachers. He held out a beautiful pocket knife. "I knew you'd pull it off, Dod. That's why I bet on you."

"With whom?" charged Sawny. Betting was the sort of behavior Bonboo had constantly chided the Coosings to rise above, for he considered it a vice.

"Well—it was more of a prize to the winner," corrected Pone sheepishly, catching Sawny's eyes.

"And the giver of the prize?"

"It was Joak," said Pone proudly.

"Then you're fine," gloated Dilly, glancing up at Joak who was scowling at her. Joak sat snugly between Kwit and two girls from Raul. They were patiently awaiting their matches.

"If you never do it again," insisted Sawny, still hiding behind Dilly. She didn't care if Joak was the loser—Bonboo's rules were meant to be kept.

Sawb strode up and bumped Dilly and Sawny aside. "You've had two lucky spins, Dod. The next run will show how truly pathetic you are."

"Do you want to bet?" snorted Pone, stepping in front of Dod. He held Joak's knife in his hand and flaunted it in Sawb's face. "I haven't taken anything from you yet."

Sawb glowered at Pone and marched away.

"I didn't think so!" called Pone triumphantly after him. "When you man up, let me know!"

Sawb looked over his shoulder coolly, as though he were thinking about punching Pone, and then he sauntered away to see how the level-four matches were coming.

Dod was shocked that his two measly wins had busied the air with hope for Green and despair for Raul. It was silly. But he dreaded telling his fellow Coosings what he knew—that he was too weak and ill to fight again.

The next round was between Tonnis and Jim. To hear the Coosings from Soosh cheer Jim on, you'd think he was facing The Dread. And in the midst of them, Tinja and Strat stood like parents of the motley bunch of boys. Strat whispered something in Jim's ear, tapped the hilt of the spar sword three times, and handed it to Jim.

Juny sat a little taller on the bench when her handsome son entered the ring, shoulders steady and chest out. He was clearly her pride and joy, and he knew it.

"Give it to him, Jim!" shouted Ingrid from right beside Juny. "The boy's a soft patsy—and maybe a traitor, too!"

Tonnis looked hurt, yet he didn't respond. His solid frame and fighting stance were more than ready to deal with Jim.

On three, Jim leapt at Tonnis and swung his sword viciously. Nevertheless, Tonnis had plenty of his father in him; he easily deflected the blows and waited for more.

"Take this," yelled Jim angrily, diving at Tonnis's legs in a clever roll. He fought for all of Soosh, as though Jungo sat upon his burgeoning shoulders.

Tonnis tipped Jim's blade away with little effort and repositioned for more action.

Again and again, Jim did his best to level the demoted Rauling, but without any luck. Tonnis deflected every assault. Finally, with only thirty seconds to go, Juny broke from her silence and shouted to her son. "Show them you're a Chantolli, my boy! Show them!"

Tonnis lit on fire, as if the flawless defensive routine he'd just performed was only a warm-up. He surged upon Jim with such vigor that he forced him from the ring, assuring himself the victory point, though it was Tonnis who was first to greet Jim after the match.

"You're getting better," he said genuinely. "All of Soosh can be proud of the way you handled yourself—"

"And all of Raul should be proud of the way you fight," said Clair, racing over to pat Tonnis on his shoulder. "You're the best

I've ever trained. Your father would be proud." Clair panned his eyes across the sea of people and paused at Juny and Ingrid.

Sadly, the other Raulings and Raul Coosings hardly nodded at Tonnis after he'd won. And to see the mob of support that encompassed Jim, you'd think he'd taken first place in the tournaments. Dod felt bad for Tonnis, though he was glad that at least Tonnis had a mother that believed in him. It reminded Dod of his own mother's undying devotion to her kids.

Pone bent down beside Dod and took the sword from his hands. "I'll tidy this up for you," he said, wiping the blade clean on the grass. "Now it'll shine in the sun as you topple Ulrich."

A bulky, tanned Raul Coosing stepped into the ring and urged Dod to join him. He couldn't wait for the chance to duel against the famed Dod.

"I can't do it," choked Dod to Pone. "You'll have to give the sword back for me. I'm not well — really."

Pone tried to convince Dod otherwise, and was soon joined by Buck, Sham, Voo, Toos, and many others who were eager to have Green Hall rise, but their efforts were in vain. Dod's issues left him a helpless spectator for the rest of the day, giving a handful of people easy points by forfeiture.

Things went well for Dilly, who had a perfect string of sets — she won all six. And Sawny took four out of six, which wasn't bad either, tying with Buck, Pone, and Toos.

Raul Hall gave more ground than they had in years, though nothing serious; Sawb, Joak, Kwit, and Tonnis went undefeated, and even Eluxa won five out of six. They were still securely on track to dominate the finals as usual.

By the end of the day's rounds, Dod was starting to feel

better. His head had cleared enough to walk again, so when Tonnis won his last match, Dod approached him to offer praise.

"Nice moves," he said, feeling awkward that nobody else was interested in speaking with Tonnis. The match Tonnis had just won against a fellow Raul Coosing was the best of the day, at least from Dod's angle. And not surprisingly, everyone from Raul had favored the other guy.

"Thanks," responded Tonnis, hiding well whatever he was feeling. "You did all right, too." He flipped hair from his forehead and smiled.

"Whatever," said Dod. He dug his hands into his pockets and felt the white gloves he'd deposited after the morning's excitement. "Here," he said quickly. He held the gloves out. "You're one heck of a Chantolli."

Tonnis took the presents, tipped them over, and eyed Dod suspiciously once he'd seen his family's insignia.

"Don't ask," said Dod before Tonnis had said a word. "It's kind of a long story. Anyway, I think you're the best I saw today—for whatever that's worth."

Tonnis silently nodded. He slipped the gloves on for a minute. They fit perfectly and didn't bunch like they had for Dod. Deep thoughts filled Tonnis with emotions that hid behind his eyes, except for a wave of subtle expressions that crept across his face.

"You can keep them," he finally said in a calm, composed voice, stripping the slips off. "I don't like to hide my hands when I duel."

The moment was uncomfortable.

"Did you win?" hollered someone from a distance, approaching quickly. It was Boot riding up on Grubber, with Horsely riding a beautiful tan stallion at Boot's side.

"Sort of," choked Dod, shoving Sirlonk's gloves back into his pocket. "I won two before the pink balls got me good."

"Oh, nasty!" roared Boot with delight. He turned to Horsely and explained, "I warned him about sloosha. Not everyone can eat it and still see straight."

"So that's what happened," chuckled Tonnis, glancing at Dod pleasantly. Whatever tension had been in the air before was now gone with Boot's arrival. "You should have seen it, Boot. This guy was in the ring with Klide when it surfaced. The place went nuts—especially Eluxa."

"What a day to miss!" groaned Boot enviously.

"Sorry about this morning," added Tonnis. "Classic Sawb. You don't have any spots open in Green Hall, do you?" Tonnis laughed as though it were a joke. "I'm ready to trade up. Perhaps Toos would fare all right as a Rauling—you think?"

"I feel for you," said Boot sarcastically. "It must be miserable walking around with the guys that win everything and are always getting out of trouble thanks to Sawb's hot glare." Boot rubbed his bruised jaw for emphasis. "If it weren't for Horsely, here, I'd be shoveling the stalls for the next two weeks—compliments of Voracio. You'd think he'd cut us some slack since Dilly and Sawny are family—"

"Often it's twice as bad if you're related," spat Tonnis, momentarily serious. "But not if you've got brothers like yours: Buck and Bowy are solid, aren't they?"

"They're solid," repeated Boot, nodding his head. "And Dod, over here, is practically a brother, too. He's amazing. If you square off with him, be kind, okay?"

Tonnis nodded.

Dod felt an unusual brotherhood—a bond that was thick

between Tonnis, Horsely, and Boot. It stretched beyond the bounds of the petty day-to-day feuds that certainly existed between Green and Raul Halls and was broad enough to encompass an old, injured Green Coosing.

"Here," said Boot, dropping his hand down to Dod, "let me give you a lift to the castle doors. Your face is still a little pale."

Dod gladly accepted. He and Boot rode to the grass in front of the Great Hall, while Horsely hung back with Tonnis.

"How was your hunt?" asked Dod, eager to hear about The Beast.

"We didn't find its lair, but we made progress. According to Dr. Shelderhig, the creature we've been hearing about is called a duresser. They're only found near one lake in Soosh, because they need water to survive and the lake they're indigenous to is so far from any other pond or stream that they haven't migrated. Did you know that they can get up to fifteen feet long?"

"That's about the size of the one I saw," said Dod, remembering the monster's horrible face.

"Dr. Shelderhig said that the arm he got from Bowlure indicated that the creature's about full grown, so you're right, it's got to be huge. In Soosh, they mostly live on wild horses that come to drink—crazy, huh?"

"I can imagine them eating a horse. The one Dilly and I saw had such long, sharp teeth that it looked strange, since its mouth was plenty big enough to swallow us whole—but a stallion might take a few bites."

"Yup," agreed Boot. "After spending the day listening to Horsely, I'm glad we've got hundreds of drat soldiers around here to help solve the problem. Searching for The Beast's lair on horseback during the day is one thing—fighting with it hand-to-hand during the night would be something else. But I'm not ready to head to High Gate, no matter what Horsely says."

"I know," said Dod, "though hanging around here makes you want to dive into Ingrid's stew, doesn't it?"

"Really?" poked Boot, stopping Grubber close to the castle doors.

"No!" gagged Dod, thinking about the noxious odors it created. His stomach was only good for something light, if anything, and just the wafting smell of barbequed pork that flowed from the Great Hall entrance was enough to help Dod decide he'd wait until breakfast to eat.

"Thanks Boot," he said, sliding off. "I'll see you back at Green Hall."

"Right," nodded Boot. "And I'll take your shift for you tonight—you need lots of sleep if you're going to win the rest of your matches. You're down four points—I think you can only give one or two more if you hope to play the last two days."

Dod felt lucky to have Boot as a best friend.

The next morning, Dod awoke early with another horrible nightmare. He knew it was important, because the same images had plagued him in his dreams for two weeks. Yet it wasn't just the white-rock quarry that bothered him, with its suffocating air and sweltering heat, it was the dismal, lonely, forsaken feeling that accompanied it. It stirred emotions in Dod that went even deeper than those he felt over the glimpses of smoke, fire, and destruction. They were all connected somehow.

"You should get a few more winks," said Boot, hovering over Dod as he came to himself. "Don't worry about The Beast.

I won't let it get you." Boot assumed Dod's ghastly nightmares were triggered by his fear of the Lake Mauj Monster.

"It's not that," confessed Dod, wiping sweat from his brow. His hair was a mess from tossing and turning. Boot took a seat on his bed and listened.

"I've been seeing an excavation site—sad people everywhere—and the dust is awful, so thick you can't breathe."

"You hate work, and you feel pressure from Voracio—" started Boot, trying to draw meaning.

"No—that's not it," said Dod, scratching at his head. He pushed his covers off and looked at his pink feet, then his ankles.

"You don't sleep well without your shoes on—" tried Boot, making a second attempt.

"No—that's not it, either."

"Then maybe it's because you're homesick. I get homesick sometimes—not for my mom's place right now, but for how things were before my dad's death, back when everything was simple and happy—though Bonboo's been like a father to me for over thirty years—I can't complain—he's more than made up for Voracio's accident—"

"Right," sighed Dod, feeling guilty that he wasn't sharing what he suspected about the fateful incident.

"I just don't know," continued Boot, rambling on, spilling his feelings more than usual because the darkness hid his embarrassment. "I guess I'm discontent—I keep wishing for what I had. Maybe that's what's making you lose sleep—Pap's gone." Boot teared up and quickly rubbed at his eyes like he was tired. "I miss Pap, too, you know. If I could go back, I'd make sure that poisoning didn't happen—I'd trade cups and die instead of him—or whatever it would have taken. It's just unbearable. And the boys from Soosh—"

"You couldn't have done anything had you been there," insisted Dod, wanting to cry. He had a deep well of tears that he had saved—plenty from when his father went missing, and a bunch more from Pap's death. "You'd have died along with them, and we'd have never met," choked Dod. "Thanks for being a true friend."

Boot gave Dod a heavy hug, the kind you give to a person who's standing beside a casket, and then rose to his feet before it got awkward. "I guess we can't change what's already happened, we just have to focus on what to do next—and I'm thinking you need to show everyone that Pap's grandson is the best swordsman at Twistyard."

"But I'm not," said Dod, his voice quivering from thoughts of the deaths that had altered his life.

"I think you might be—well, second to me anyway," said Boot with forced confidence. He puffed his shoulders and chest for emphasis and trotted quietly around in a circle, pretending to be a commanding general, until he tripped on a rug and toppled to the floor.

"You're the best, Boot," said Dod, feeling a little better. True friendship was the most soothing balm for sorrow.

"Best?" chuckled Boot from the floor, rubbing his ankle.

"Yes," assured Dod. "I wish you were in the tournaments right now. Someone needs to set Sawb in his place."

"If you don't, Dilly probably will," said Boot, shifting to reality. He already knew Dod was a mediocre swordsman, for he had practiced with him before. "Besides," he continued, lowering his voice when he noticed Pone stirring, "I've got to find The Beast's lair. Horsely's certain we'll be able to see a slide into the water near the entrance."

"And then what?" begged Dod, imagining the horrible creature rising from the lake to consume Boot and Horsely.

"I don't know," admitted Boot casually. "We'll probably poke around to see if it's home."

"I'm coming with you!" insisted Dod. He knew that he could hear the monster's thoughts, so he figured his presence would better ensure Boot's safe return.

"But the matches—" said Boot.

"We both know that I'd lose more than two rounds between today and tomorrow," answered Dod.

"Me too," whispered Buck from under his blanket near Dod's bed. He stuck his head out and looked at Boot. "You know I wouldn't have left your side yesterday if you'd have told me you weren't going to stand in the tournaments. If Voracio's pulled your matches, he's tanked mine as well. We stick together."

"Shhh," said Boot, suddenly realizing everyone was waking up. He pointed at the door and slipped out of the room. Dod followed with Buck sleepily on his heels.

In the hall, Boot's face seemed ready to burst. "I've got to tell you something," he rushed. "Last night I overhead news that's going to shake things up today—and I mean really shake things up."

"What?" gasped Dod.

"You know how Sawb's been making excuses for why his dad didn't show up to Carsigo, and he's begun a new string of lines about how he doubts his dad will be coming to the tournaments because he's so busy—"

"Yes," said Buck, nodding Boot to continue.

"Well—he's missing!"

"What?" said Dod and Buck in unison.

"Terro's missing. He came to Green months ago on important business—checking their holdings all over the world here, or at least that's what he supposedly said he was doing—"

"But Sawb's gotten letters from him—even recently," insisted Buck, giving Boot a skeptical look. "Who've you been listening to? Sawny?"

"What I heard wasn't a prank. Youk was instructing men to leave yesterday for distant lands. He wants the word out so that all of Green can begin searching. Terro's family and council back home in Raul are insisting we find him or they'll cause severe hardships for us."

"Like what—no more chouyummy?" scoffed Dod, wondering what they could do through the one and only portal.

"No," said Boot. "People in Raul own a lot of stuff here in Green, and they have allies. They've given us two weeks to find and deliver Terro or be punished."

"But that's not right," said Dod. "What if Terro's busy being Dark Hood?"

"Oh!" groaned Buck. "That would be awful. Our governments would fight things out—and it's not an equal battle: They own way more of Green than we own of Raul. The best we could do is shut down our guest services and diplomatic offices in Raul, while they full-out assault our cities with hired soldiers."

"It could happen," said Boot. "It might be Terro's way of seeking Jungo. Sirlonk was Terro's only brother."

"You guys!" huffed Dilly, startling them half to death. She and Sawny were dressed for the day and had come up behind them sneakily. "Boot's always stretching things. While *we* were having a celebratory evening sip of juice on Youk's patio last night, he and Mr. Clair explained it all. Terro's done this before.

He comes here on business and enjoys the open sea so much that he hates the thoughts of rushing back to bureaucratic stagnation. But as we all know, he loves his power enough that he wouldn't hand it over to anyone else, so his council puts teeth into Green's arm to deliver him back to them. They want him to fulfill his responsibilities."

"It's his wife's way of saying it's time for him to come home," added Sawny, smiling sweetly.

"So you don't think he's Dark Hood?" asked Dod, mulling it over in his mind.

"No," laughed Dilly. "He's got all the power he wants back in Raul and plenty here in Green—why would he sneak around fighting with people, stealing stuff, and playing with an ugly pet duresser? That seems like a lot of work for someone who's got it made."

"How'd you find out it was a duresser?" begged Boot, dimming with disappointment. He had thought he was one up on Dilly with that news.

"I've got friends," gloated Dilly, flipping her bouncing curls. Sawny elbowed her sister in the ribs. "Sawny and I have friends," she corrected.

"Shelderhig," snapped Buck.

Sawny nodded proudly. "He returned my letter and confirmed what I already knew. There are plenty of books that talk about duressers."

Everyone gave Sawny a blank stare.

"Am I the only one that reads around here?" asked Sawny as she shook her head with playful disgust. "The library has a lot of answers if you only look."

"Anyway," said Dilly, "back to Terro. Sawb's not worried.

He got a letter three days ago from his father, stating he'd try to make it to the final matches. I bet he'll show. He hasn't missed the awards ceremony for years. He's really proud of how well Sawb can duel."

"Then why did I hear Youk sending men to look for him?" asked Boot. He smiled as he waited for the answer, assuming she'd struggle.

"Because Youk knows where he is," replied Dilly flatly. "Youk sent men to inform him that his vacation is over, just in case Terro has gone off the deep end."

"Oh," said Boot.

The explanations seemed logical, but felt wrong to Dod—something was amiss—and by the time he had discovered what it was, he wished he'd never entered Green in the first place!

CHAPTER TWENTY-TWO

A BIG FAVOR

Boot, Buck, and Dod spent the day with Horsely searching for any signs of The Beast's lair. Since the closest parts of Lake Mauj had already been checked, they rode their horses through the surrounding forests and fields, probing every body of water they could find. Nothing turned up, but they had plenty of fun. Buck even slipped in an hour of fishing on the shores of the Blue Tip Pond, while Boot taught Dod and Horsely about fighting with sticks on a wet log.

At dinner, Dilly dominated the conversation with news about the matches. She had fought a second perfect day, which nearly guaranteed she'd make it into the finals.

"So, when do you fight Sawb?" asked Boot, piling his plate high with Mercy's blizzard casserole. It tasted like lasagna.

"He's not one of my regular matches," responded Dilly sadly. "I think Mr. Clair or one of his helpers must have fudged things. Sawb's had easy targets both days, and his schedule for tomorrow looks pretty much the same—"

"Clair likes fudging—" popped Dod, thinking of his experiences with the cantankerous man.

"It's not favoritism," interrupted Toos. "It's Sawb's lucky dueling ring—with the sapphire snake eyes. Have you seen how he's been wearing it for the past week? The ring channels good things in his direction."

"Right," laughed Boot.

"Don't knock it," said Toos, looking pretty serious. "Lots of people use stuff to attract fortune; like Joak has his cooplick-hair shoelaces that he only wears on special days, and Tinja has his funny-looking hat that he struts around in before taking his ten best pupils to the Hatu competitions."

"Have you got something?" asked Sawny, glancing up from the book she was reading—*Tipping the Scales in the Ring.*

Toos ran his hand across his slick hair and blushed. "I'm still experimenting," he admitted. "Nothing's worked quite right yet."

"I wonder why," teased Boot. He didn't believe in luck as much as he believed in making his own luck.

"I know what I'd use if I could," beamed Dilly. "I wish I could wear my trophy belt from Miz. It's the spitting image of the one Humberrone occasionally wore. If only Voracio would give it back."

"Ask Jibb," teased Boot in a taunting voice. He knew Jibb had a crush on Dilly.

"I already did," lamented Dilly. "He's certain it's not among the confiscated items."

"Dark Hood stole it," said Dod. The thought flowed into his mind like a fact more than an opinion and rolled off his tongue before he had considered what he was saying. It was really just a hunch.

"Yup," mumbled Pone with a mouth full of grapes, "I'm sure that's what Dark Hood was after. He wanted to have a lucky belt—preferably one that matched his cloak—so he broke into Green Hall with his helper, faced hundreds of guards, and mysteriously slipped out, all because he knew he wouldn't sleep until he'd taken Dilly's from her."

"What did it look like?" asked Dod. Even if everyone else thought he was teasing, he knew what he felt: Dark Hood had it.

"It had an auburn base with strands of red and orange woven into it," said Dilly, fondly remembering her wall piece. "And every few inches it had white bones or teeth sewn into the center that made the strands bulge artistically." Dilly sighed. "I loved that belt!"

"What about your Redy-Alert-Band?" asked Buck, thinking she was sounding like a whiner. While searching through the swampiest regions near Twistyard, Buck had mentioned how convenient it would have been to be wearing a Redy-Alert-Band, since snakes were everywhere.

"It's good," said Dilly quickly, holding it up for inspection. "But Miz's trophy belt would guarantee I'd beat everyone this year."

"See what you've done?" ribbed Boot as he pushed at Toos's shoulder. "She was perfectly happy with winning the old-fashioned way until you went and suggested a shortcut."

"Well, if it helps—" began Toos.

"It wouldn't," said Sawny, flipping to the back of her book. "They say right here that people commonly put their trust in trinkets to make them duel better, when in actuality it's all in their minds."

"But if it works," persisted Toos, "who cares if it's in your mind?"

Sawny thought for a minute and then nodded. "I guess

if you can trick yourself into thinking you're better able to do your best, you might be more likely to do it. You may be onto something, Toos."

Having Sawny partially validate Toos lifted his chin sky-high. He shoved Boot back and grinned contagiously.

"Then get looking," teased Boot, nodding at Toos.

Before dinner was over, Dod excused himself and ran for his climbing gear. He thought he recalled seeing a drawer of belts in Pap's place and hoped maybe one of them would cheer Dilly on to victory. It was at least worth a try—plus he wanted to ask Abbot if he knew about the Soosh Mayler Belts and why Dark Hood would want one. Perhaps it was a symbol of status that would help the villain cause trouble in Soosh or fit in with certain crowds.

At the base of the cliffs behind the castle, Dod paused to consider where to climb. He'd been up a string of easy routes, but was reluctant to try 'The Tipper,' as he'd named it—a part of the back wall that had a difficult section where it jut out precariously before correcting inward, making it a real challenge even with two palsarflexes. Below it, a few initials were carved into the rock, likely from daring members of the TCC.

"Not tonight," said Dod to himself, glancing up at the golden sky. The sun was preparing to set on the other side of the castle, and Dod hoped to return while it was still light, not wanting to fumble his way down a shadowy wall only to find the duresser waiting on the dock to gobble him up.

Quick as lightning, Dod shot up the easiest route and bolted for Pap's house. Abbot greeted him pleasantly with a plate of freshly-baked cookies and slipped into a string of things he'd seen from the roof, including a duel between Sawb and Pone, where it was Abbot's opinion that Sawb had cheated.

Dod couldn't help feeling a bit sorry for Pone, who had been seated near Dilly when she'd insisted that Sawb had fought nothing but light-weights.

"Why weren't you in the matches today?" asked Abbot, his graying eyes pensively pressing.

"I got sick yesterday and missed a bunch of rounds, so I figured it'd be a waste to continue." Dod didn't mention his search for The Beast's lair, since any mention of the creature sent Abbot into chanting.

"I saw the two matches you fought—and even with an upset stomach, you pushed mightily, sir." Abbot hunched as usual and looked at the floor more than anywhere else. "It was disappointing that you didn't persist."

"Right," sighed Dod, glancing at Abbot's bare feet. His gray, wrinkly skin reminded Dod of a leathery corpse he had once seen while visiting a mortuary. "Thanks for the cookies," he choked, feeling Ponish as he spoke with his mouth full of plum-and-sugar delights.

"My grandma's recipe," mumbled Abbot, beginning to compulsively nod his head. It was a bad sign. Abbot's body would often spasm during his episodes.

"Did Pap ever have a Soosh Mayler Belt?" rushed Dod, wiping crumbs from his lips. He hoped to get an answer before it was too late.

"A belt, a belt, a belt," repeated Abbot. His fragile mind was slipping in and out, like a dysfunctional robot. "Was it brown and orange?"

"Yes!" said Dod excitedly, feeling like he'd hit the jackpot. "Where is it?"

"A belt, a belt, a belt," mumbled Abbot, his head shaking more violently. "Stolen—with the books."

"What?" gasped Dod. It made partial sense, yet none at all. The Dread had stolen Pap's belt, and Dark Hood had stolen Dilly's—but why? Dod reached out and put his hand on Abbot's slouching shoulder and the shaking slowed down.

"Show me your garden," said Dod, helping Abbot move. As the old man began to walk toward the patio door, his full senses returned.

"I don't know what Pap used the belt for, sir," said Abbot calmly. "He always kept it on the wall above his swords. I think it was a present from someone special."

Crossing back and forth around the statuary and fancy objects in Pap's hall flooded Dod's mind with images of his nighttime escape from The Dread and The Beast. It also made him think of Sirlonk, sitting in chains in Commendus's dungeon, stubbornly refusing to say a word.

Sirlonk knows so much, thought Dod in aggravation. *He stole the books and belt, originally used the duresser, and obviously is acquainted with Dark Hood, not to mention he knows who poisoned Pap!*

"I've planted some new flowers," said Abbot, stumbling over his own feet near the door. "You'll find them beautiful when they bloom. They're called White Rock Peepers."

Dod's mind raced through his nightmares, triggered by Abbot's mention of white rocks. "Do you know where they quarry white rocks?" asked Dod.

Abbot stopped moving. He stood speechless, studying the ground. For a moment, Dod wondered whether he had died, but since he was still standing with his hand on the back door and hadn't collapsed, Dod assumed he hadn't passed away. Silently, Dod waited. He knew if he rushed Abbot, the old man's mind would topple over like a ten-story building made of cards.

After a long time—minutes of nothing but the sound of a pesky fly—Abbot spoke. "The pit is in Driaxom, sir. They quarry white rocks, crush them to dust, and put them in bags."

Abbot pushed the door open, but Dod was now the one with paralyzed legs. His gut was saying things his mind and body didn't want to hear: He needed to go to Driaxom to speak with Sirlonk!

"Are you coming, sir?" asked Abbot.

Dod slowly followed. *That's ridiculous*, thought Dod, taking heavy, plodding steps. *If someone needs to go to Driaxom, it should be Commendus or Bonboo. They might get Sirlonk talking. What would he say to me? Probably nothing!*

Abbot made his way to where a resplendently stunning array of flowers was blooming, each at the height of its beauty. And in the center of them all, one gorgeous, five-inch-wide, pink-and-maroon trophy shot above the others, it's petals nearly on fire with color, as though to prove that it was the best.

"This is my favorite one," said Abbot carefully, pointing his frail finger at the gigantic flower. "I call it Pap because it outshines the rest. You won't believe me, but all of those little ones over there are the same kind. It's strange to see how seemingly identical seeds can produce such a wide variety of results."

Dod stared at the patch of smaller replicas of 'Pap' and felt uncomfortable. They were tiny, like clover puffs, and didn't even resemble the magnificent specimen.

"It's their choices, I guess, that make them small," said Abbot. He was having a clear-minded moment, completely unaffected by the bouts of mental illness that stormed in and out like summer squalls.

"Their choices," mumbled Dod, feeling his heart leaping out of his chest. Which kind of flower was he, a little gumdrop-sized splash of color amidst the fields of identical blooms, or the towering masterpiece of nature?

"How do you visit someone in Driaxom?" choked Dod nervously. He didn't even want to think about it, and he knew that the subject would likely send poor Abbot away chanting, but the marks on one of Abbot's ankles were too familiar—Dod vaguely remembered similar images from his nightmares of the quarry.

Abbot's head began to nod. "I didn't do it," mumbled Abbot to himself.

"I know," said Dod, jumping to Abbot's side. He put one hand on Abbot's shoulder and pointed at the prettiest flower. "Pap knew you didn't do it, and Pap's my grandpa, so I know you didn't do it! Please Abbot, stay with me, here. I need to know about Driaxom. I need to visit someone there."

Abbot huffed loudly, gasping for air, and looked up at Dod with glossy, foreboding eyes. "No one visits Driaxom!"

"But I must!" demanded Dod, persisting against his own will as much as Abbot's. "Really bad things are about to happen, and I'm that flower, I'm like Pap, I'm the one that has to do certain things—discover certain things—or we lose!"

Dod was filled with emotion as he petitioned Abbot. In his mind, new glimpses swirled around of a city—flames licked the smoky air as they devoured miles of buildings, and from the ashes an army of beasts rose up. It was the utter destruction of High Gate!

"Please," begged Dod, "tell me."

Abbot shuddered and continued to breathe heavily, but he

started talking. "I know someone—a friend—he might be able to figure a way—but you shouldn't go, Dod! Don't go to Driaxom!"

"Who?" asked Dod.

"Don't go, don't go, don't go," muttered Abbot, beginning to slip from reality.

"WHO?" shouted Dod, overcome with frustration.

"Don't beat me, sir," yelped Abbot, falling to his knees with his face to the ground. "Please don't hit me, sir." Abbot's long-sleeved shirt drifted up a little, revealing atrocious scars on his lower back.

Dod knelt down on the ground beside Abbot. "It's me—Dod—Pap's grandson. I'm right here, Abbot."

"Please, please, please," muttered Abbot quietly, slowing trailing off. After a minute, his quivering ended and he gently looked up. "I could try," he said, once more coherent. "Meet me tomorrow by the far end of the old dock, about noon."

Dod was shocked. He didn't know Abbot ever left the rooftop.

"I'll try," grumbled Abbot, his head beginning to nod. "I'll try, I'll try, I'll try."

"Thanks," responded Dod, patting Abbot lightly on the back. "I'll wait for you."

All the way down the wall and back to Green Hall, Dod puzzled. He wasn't sure who Abbot knew, or how Abbot would climb down the wall, or what Abbot's friend could do—assuming he had a living friend that wasn't just in his delusional mind. And the more Dod thought about it, the more crazy it seemed; however, since the likelihood was very low that anything would come of his discussion with Abbot, Dod pushed the conversation from his mind and pretended to not worry.

"How was your climb?" asked Dilly, snagging Dod the moment he entered Green Hall.

"Fine," said Dod, plodding tiredly.

"And Abbot?"

"Same as always," sighed Dod. Dilly had never met Abbot, or been to Pap's place, but she'd heard tales from Boot, who had accompanied Dod the one time before.

"You look really tired," said Sawny, joining the conversation. "Is everything all right?"

Dod groaned like a hippo. "I just wish people would catch Dark Hood and his helper, and The Beast, and whoever caused the fire at High Gate, and whoever's behind the trouble with the representatives, and the person who tried to poison Bonboo, and make all of the problems go away."

"That's all, huh?" joked Dilly. "Don't worry. Stuff like this has been happening for ages." Dilly was happier than usual. After dinner, Sawny had accompanied her to the boards and had calculated for her that if she won two of her six matches the following day, she was guaranteed a spot in the finals; and since one of her scheduled slots was with Buck, who wasn't dueling, she'd only need to win one. It was a huge relief off her shoulders.

"I know there are always problems," admitted Dod, sliding his pack of climbing gear to the ground, "but when you know stuff—like the strong possibility of something bad happening if you don't act—then it becomes *your* problem, not just *a* problem."

"Are you looking for the next spot that Dark Hood will strike?" asked Sawny. "We'll search with you. What do you know?"

"I wish it were that easy," confessed Dod. "I've had some awful impressions lately—"

"The weird rock quarry again?" pressed Dilly, trying to recall what she'd written in her Book of Everything.

"That, too, but most recently," said Dod, looking like he was carrying the weight of the world on his shoulders, "I've seen glimpses of something else."

"What? You can tell us," said Sawny. The hall was quiet.

"Where is everyone?" asked Dod, changing the subject. He wasn't sure if it was wise to scare the girls about his ghastly images of High Gate's destruction, especially since there wasn't much they could do to stop it; and he certainly wasn't going to tell them that he was considering taking a trip to Driaxom to visit Sirlonk.

"They all went with Boot to play a game of Bollirse," said Dilly. "Boot's feeling a bit glum about not getting a chance to go for The Golden Swot. The big game's coming up soon."

"It'll be painful to watch," sighed Sawny.

"Yeah," agreed Dod, actually feeling more concerned about whether Champion Stadium would still be around at that point. He'd already seen glimpses of it burning.

"We were going to join Boot in playing Bollirse," explained Dilly, "but our calculating took longer than we thought—"

"You made me count it out for you three times," complained Sawny, who looked like she would have preferred playing Bollirse with the others.

"I just wanted to make sure," said Dilly. "Thanks for helping me. You definitely got the brains in the family."

Sawny melted. "What are sisters for?" she beamed sweetly.

The next day, Dod stayed back when Boot and Buck joined Horsely on a hunt for The Beast's lair. He didn't tell them what he was up to. When noon rolled around, Dod finished his lunch and made his way to the old dock, expecting to find nothing. He didn't bring his climbing gear, since he was having second thoughts about Driaxom anyway. If Abbot had pulled off something miraculous and was ready to provide Dod with a way into the guarded prison, then it was meant to be and Dod would saddle up and ride. And if not, Dod planned on spending the afternoon watching Dilly and Sawny, who both had a majority of their matches left to play for the day.

Surprisingly, on the far side of the wharf, where no one ever went, something large was moving in the shade of the beachfront trees. Dod approached cautiously, listening in his mind for The Beast.

"You must be Dod," called someone from a distance away. It was reassuring to hear it was a person and not a vicious, flesh-eating creature. Dod picked up his pace and jogged out of the blazing sun, when to his astonishment, he beheld a flutter—not a giant one, though it was large enough to tear him up. Its banana-sized talons dug into the rotting dock with every step it took. Mounted on a saddle near its neck was a holoo. The little man was only two and a half feet tall, though perfectly proportioned and wearing a handsome tan riding suit.

"We've got to get hustling," said the man. "Driaxom's a decent flight from here, and their triblot barrier only comes down in the late afternoon—once a week! You're just lucky today's the day."

Dod felt uneasy. "How are they going to let me in?" he asked, putting up one of a million questions that were racing through his mind.

The man pulled a leather envelope from his satchel and handed it to Dod. "Here are your papers. I'd advise putting them back in the bag while we fly, since things may get a bit rough as we soar over the desert. The afternoon heat can cause turbulent risings."

"Okay," said Dod anxiously, handing the envelope back to the holoo without opening it up. He walked to the side of the giant bird and tried to find a way up.

"Climb on that low-hanging branch," suggested the man, pointing to a tree that was just off the dock. Dod complied like a dazed zombie, not really aware of what was happening. The circumstance was overwhelming.

Once in the air, Dod was glad that there were so many straps and buckles on the saddle. It was wild from the start, and unlike the journey he'd taken with Youk and Sammywoo, Dod didn't have anyone to hold onto since the holoo's riggings were attached near the bird's neck, leaving Dod by himself in the middle of its back. The flutter's wings were covered with rubbery black feathers; they shot out fifteen feet on each side and gave the creature enough lift to take Dod and the holoo high into the sky, though the flutter's ascent was replete with jiggles and jolts that would have sent Dod flailing to the ground if he weren't tightly fastened.

The man directed the bird to fly over part of Lake Mauj before circling up toward Driaxom, so the crowds at the dueling competition didn't see them leave.

"How do you know Abbot?" yelled Dod when the bird began to soar. The wind beat at Dod's face and took his breath away. The holoo turned to see if Dod were all right and then turned back without answering. He wore a bug-eyed pair of goggles that had a wind-blocking nose guard, making it easier for the holoo to breathe.

It didn't take long before the thrill of being in the air was outweighed by the nagging pressure to get oxygen. At that point, however, Dod discovered that if he bowed forward and put his face near the flutter's body, the bulk of the whirling air shot over him. It wasn't the most comfortable position—the bird stunk like a neglected horse stall and hugging-in blocked his view of the ground, but it worked.

What am I doing? thought Dod, clinging tightly to the leather straps as the afternoon breeze shook the flight. *What will I say to Sirlonk this time? He won't give in. I don't have anything to offer him. He's condemned to suffer and die in prison.*

Dod racked his brain until he had convinced himself that he hoped they would miss the triblot barrier's dropping, so he could return to Twistyard and forget about the whole thing. Part of him did actually want to see Sirlonk incarcerated, paying for the deeds he had done as The Dread, but as Dod approached Driaxom, that vengeful part of him sank and was swallowed up by fear.

"Let's go back," yelled Dod as the holoo made the beast glide toward a landing near one lonely pavilion. Beyond it a ghastly-looking fortress shot up out of the barren wasteland, its jagged black stones climbing hundreds of feet from the puke-green dirt. Nothing but the prison was visible for miles—no trees or bushes or plants of any kind, not even a single blade of grass. And the poisonous dirt's stench was rank as a rotten mire.

The landing was rough, testing the straps until Dod's stomach ached. Under the shade of the waiting structure, two burly, hairy men stood around a four-horse wagon, waiting for the triblot barrier to drop.

"You's late!" yelled the fatter one, his five hundred pounds of tanned flesh jiggling as he made his way to the flutter. The dirty-white shirt he wore didn't cover his midsection and was threadbare, most of his teeth were missing, and his ratty, snarled beard had globs of food stuck in it.

"I've changed my mind," said Dod. "Let's go." He no longer wanted to see the inside of Driaxom and didn't care what Sirlonk looked like. And as for his concerns about High Gate burning to the ground, they were forgotten. "I'm ready to go back to Twistyard," begged Dod.

Before the holoo could nudge the flutter to move, the trollish man had his meaty paws on the beak's harness and his partner was stripping Dod from the bird's back.

"We's been wait'n here smell'n the stretch 'til my head hurts bad," complained the man who pushed at Dod, guiding him toward the wagon. "An' they's been wait'n, too." He pointed toward the front of the formidable, guarded bastion. It looked like the devil's palace.

"Here are his papers," offered the holoo nervously, handing the larger fellow the leather envelope. Dod watched the man slip the packet into a sizable pocket.

"Give 'em the sign," bellowed the big man, nodding at his companion who held Dod by the arm. The smaller man pointed Dod to the carriage and then walked out in front of the pavilion, waving his arms in the air.

It wasn't a very technical signal, but it worked. A large bell rang, and then another, and then another, until all sides of the fortress had responded, at which point the front bell rang three times, indicating the barrier was down.

"My name's Dod," said Dod to the men driving the wagon. He sat in the back on top of a pile of crates.

"He knows his name," mocked one man to the other, not even turning to look at Dod.

"And he's a hero, too," laughed the bigger fellow. "We's got lots of hero work to do in Driaxom."

Dod's toenails curled with instant fear. Not hesitating, he jumped from the wagon and dashed as fast as he could toward the flutter that was parked in the shade of the pavilion. His legs had never moved with such purpose.

"You's gonna make me mad!" huffed the fat man, doing his best to change course. Dod hardly heard what he said; he was busy running the race of his life!

I've got to get out of here! screamed Dod in his mind. Everything about the circumstance was wrong. But to his horror, as he neared the pavilion, the holoo directed the flutter to exit.

"I'm sorry. I can't get tangled in your mess," called the holoo, leaving the ground before Dod had arrived.

And the next thing Dod knew, he felt a heavy thump across the back of his head, causing the world to spin until he blacked out.

"Wake up, wake up," said a familiar voice. "Whad are you doin' in here?"

It was Dungo! Dod recognized his stinky smell as much as his voice.

"Dungo?" coughed Dod, straining to open his eyes. The last thing he could remember was feeling the sizzling-hot ground against his cheek.

"I want his shoes!" blared a gruff voice. Dod could hear commotion, and when he opened his eyes, Dungo, the huge four-armed beast, was holding someone above his head.

"Don' douch him!" blared Dungo. It looked like Dungo was going to rip the man in half.

"All right! All right!" screamed the terrified man, his tattooed arms and legs fighting to break free. "He's all yours. Fine! Put me down!"

Dod hated what he was seeing. It was worse than any nightmare he could imagine. It was beyond belief. It was so bad that Dod closed his eyes and tried to wake up again, hoping it was just a dream.

Damp, musky air filled the dimly-lit, cave-like room. Hundreds of pitiable people paced the filthy, stone floor. Many of them were so dirty that it was difficult to tell where their ragged clothes ended and their grimy skin began. And scuffles were ensuing in multiple places without anybody seeming to care.

One wall of the confined area was a matrix of rusted iron bars, rising from the floor to the ceiling fifteen feet above. Three dull candles burned, providing limited light.

"Where am I?" groaned Dod, feeling something tickling his ear. He sat up and watched a skinny rat dash to the safety of a hole in the crumbling rock wall behind him.

"Id's block dree," said Dungo, putting out one of his four arms to help Dod to his feet. "Dis is a bad place to lay down. Da rads will chew your ears and hair." Dungo rubbed his matted, filthy beard and pulled out an inch-long bug. "And you have do wadch oud for da squigglers, doo."

No sooner had Dod stood then he yelped in pain and crumpled to the ground, grabbing at his right ankle.

"Id will hurd for a while," said Dungo sympathetically.

"What?" gasped Dod, struggling to breathe. He was having

a panic attack. The worst fate anyone could receive had been cruelly dealt to him: An Ankle Weed was implanted into his right leg, its purple stem poking just out of the skin! The guards had condemned him to a living-death sentence in Driaxom!

"Don' pull id oud!" cried Dungo as Dod pinched his fingers on the tip. "Da poison will drive you mad! Id's no use once id's in!"

"Hard work's the only way to keep it at bay," added a strong, chiseled tredder who approached from behind Dungo. He looked like Sirlonk, but sounded different.

"Don't listen to *The Dread*. His brains is full of bug dung!" taunted a scar-faced mountain of a man, bigger than all of the rest, except Dungo. "He's already lost half his senses, and he's only been smashing for nothing but a few months. I's been keeping steady for twelve years." The monstrous brute inched closer, his eyes bulging in the dim light, and added, "Wanna know my secret, little boy?"

Dod stared silently, mortified, as he watched the man smile like a mindless beast and show his bloody teeth.

"I's get my strength from eating tikes like you," he laughed, lunging at Dod hungrily.

Dungo punched the man, midair, forcing him to the ground and growled like an awful monster, "I'll rip you do pieces if you look ad him again!" Dungo flexed his muscles to prove he had the power to follow through.

The hulk of a man glared challengingly as he scooted away from Dungo and disappeared into the mobs.

Dod was shocked. He was in prison with an Ankle Weed, was nearly eaten by a lunatic who'd clearly lost his mind, and was saved by none other than Dungo.

"Thanks," choked Dod, shivering uncontrollably with fright. The setting was a nightmare.

"Id's okay," said Dungo. "He won'd dry dad again if you sday by me."

Dod glanced past Dungo in search of Sirlonk. "Um, where's The Dread?" asked Dod. A man responded, but when he got close, Dod could see that he wasn't anyone Dod knew.

"What? Where's Sirlonk?" sputtered Dod, feeling too tired to think.

"Jungo!" spat the man. "A gang of people kidnapped me and made a trade for Sirlonk, so they could torture him themselves. The world of Green is filled with barbaric scum!"

"Terro?" gasped Dod, suddenly recognizing him. They'd never met before, yet strange memories filled in the gaps for Dod.

"Yes!" declared the man, clapping his hands together joyfully. "See! I've been telling you all for months!" he said, spinning to face the crowd of people who were still watching. "I'm Terro Chantolli, Chief Noble Tredder of Raul!"

"And I'm Bonboo," mocked someone from the darkened sea of faces.

"Rabble and scum," scoffed Terro, turning back toward Dod. "And even Dungo, as good as he is, has played the coward in calling me Sirlonk."

"Bud I had do," whined Dungo.

"You're already in prison for life and joined with the roots of death—what more could they do? Please call me by my name." Terro straightened his shoulders and stood regally, like Sirlonk had always done. Nobility flowed through his veins, even while confined in the belly of an awful dungeon. No one could change who he was.

Dungo hung his head down shamefully, showing his little horns. His face looked like that of a forlorn homeless man.

"So tell me," begged Terro, seizing Dod with eager eyes. "Tell me everything Raul's done to punish Green for killing me—they've long since assumed I'm dead, haven't they? Which cities did they destroy first?"

"They're still working on the punishing—" muttered Dod, holding back his emotions.

"Break's over!" echoed throughout the crowded cavern. The orders were thundered loudly from a giant megaphone. "Time to get back to work or you're off to the lowers!"

Dod struggled to walk. His ankle felt like someone was stabbing a knife into it every time he took a step. Fortunately, Dungo and Terro steadied him.

"Where do we go from here?" choked Dod tearfully, overcome with apprehension. He wished he'd never entered Green. He wished he'd kept walking past the X-mas tree lot. He wished he'd let the medallion stay stolen. It wasn't Pap's good-luck charm—it had caused Pap's death! And now it had consigned Dod to a worse fate than poisoning!

It was a bad-luck charm. It had been a curse to his grandfather and a curse to him, and the more Dod hated it, the more he wondered what torturous thing it had done to his father. *I bet my dad came here to Green,* thought Dod, realizing for the first time that he likely had, since he'd had the charm before Pap. *No wonder he went missing! He didn't kill himself—the necklace did it!*

Dod mumbled to himself, mulling through piles of thoughts. He had spent years being angry at his father for leaving the way he had, like a coward, but now things made more sense. His father hadn't left the notes because he had planned on taking his own life—he had left them because he had suspected trouble in Green. Dod wished he had followed his dad's example and written a few words. He felt bad that his mother and Aunt and brothers would never know how much he cared.

"To the pit," sighed Terro sadly, his voice matching Dod's feelings. "It's miserable work. Many times I've wished to be done, but the idea of losing my mind is distressing. It keeps me plugging away, day after day."

"And you don' wand do be dumped in da lowers, eider," grumbled Dungo. "You wouldn'd lasd five minudes down der. Everyone's oud of der mind, and da fighding—"

"That much worse, huh?" asked Terro, his face cringing.

"Yes!" insisted Dungo. "One week of confinemend down der was doo much. I can'd dink aboud id. Dey say we all die from da weed—now or lader—bud dad's nod drue! In da lowers, da crazies kill da crazies—"

"Enough," begged Terro, looking at Dungo, then pointing with his eyes at Dod. What he was really saying was that Dungo shouldn't share the gory details in front of younger ears, especially on Dod's first day.

The pit was just as Dod had seen in his dreams: it was a large, open quarry of white rock that covered the landscape for over two miles and was completely enclosed by fortress walls; fine, powdery dust choked everyone but the watching guards, who wore gruesome facemasks made to resemble monsters; thousands of miserable workers labored with hammers and chisels to extract chunks of rock and crush them to small pebbles; and anyone who slowed their pace was whipped.

Dod did his best to hide in Dungo's shadow, avoiding the threatening sentinels and workers until the sun had set and the prisoners were escorted to their communal cells. The dismal living quarters weren't much better than block three where they'd rested, except that there weren't any rats. Food was scarce, so if the prisoners were left long enough in any one place, the vermin tended to disappear.

After eating a small scoop of nasty-tasting brew—much worse than Ingrid's stews—Dod found himself huddled in a corner behind Dungo and Terro, his body aching and his will broken. If it weren't for what happened next, Dod would have entirely given up.

CHAPTER TWENTY-THREE

SOMETIMES IT RAINS

D od closed his eyes in the darkness and wished to disappear. He wanted to go home, but was afraid to try; the stories he had been told about the tenacity of the Ankle Weed seemed to suggest that his return would be clouded by sorrow. When he had arrived on earth before, the strange bandages from Commendus's medical staff had been stripped off, and if the Ankle Weed were similarly plucked from his leg, irreparable neurological damage would immediately result, leaving his body functioning poorly and his mind trotting on a three-day course to insanity and death.

Dod was told that if he worked hard and physically exhausted himself everyday, seven days a week, the weed would sit virtually dormant and cause little damage, though it would leave a string of circular scars around his ankle. Some prisoners had lived decades with the purplish protrusion never showing any signs of its incompatibility. But eventually, the Ankle Weed always won. Its victory was subtle at first on diligent workers, breaking their minds slowly before taking over their bodies. And anyone who plucked the weed from them, or walked through certain restricted areas where high-pitched frequencies triggered an attack, felt the weed's evil effects almost instantaneously.

Dod sobbed quietly to himself. In his nightmares he had sensed that the mine's workers were in great sorrow, yet nothing had prepared him for the level of loneliness and hopelessness that filled his soul. The circumstance in Driaxom was just as Sirlonk had said—far worse than death. Dod found it ironic that Sirlonk was one of the few people who had done enough evil to truly deserve the punishment, but thanks to the countless families he had offended, he had escaped the cruel hand of Driaxom and been given a quicker death, albeit likely by torture as Terro had said.

In the blackness of the night, Dod heard a chorus of snores that was worse than Pone's room. It started with a few participants, as soon as the dim lights were trimmed, and quickly grew to a grumbling roar. The suffering men had worked hard all day and were fighting to reclaim the strength they needed in order to rise again in the morning. Dod worried about the crazy man who had tried to eat him. Would he attack in the dark? It was awful to consider. The only comfort that Dod had as he sat in the pitch-black prison was that he could smell the nasty stench of Dungo's fur.

"Are you sdill awake?" whispered Dungo in an unusually discrete voice, after Terro had drifted off to sleep.

"Yes," said Dod carefully, feeling a little embarrassed that Dungo had heard him crying.

"Where are you from?" asked Dungo, sighing as he shifted toward Dod.

"A—Twistyard?"

"No—before you came do Green," grumbled Dungo.

Dod sat in silence, speechless, suddenly bumped from his wallowing, pity party. He thought about what to say and eventually settled on the simplest answer: "A long way from here, that's for sure!"

"Me doo," grunted Dungo, "dough nod as far as you. I'm originally from Soosh—my whole family. We should have sdayed der. Dings were simpler back den."

"How old were you when you left?" asked Dod, feeling like the conversation was heading down the same path as the one he'd recently had with Boot.

"Fourdeen."

"Oh—when you were my age," said Dod. "It's probably been a while."

"Yeah," grunted Dungo, chuckling.

"Where's your family now?" asked Dod, beginning to feel like Dungo was an old friend. Dod appreciated that Dungo was being nice to him, which didn't even remotely seem like Dungo—or at least not the Dungo Dod had met before. It was like there was something magical about the darkness that peeled away the ghastly surroundings and unfortunate past they shared.

"Uh—" Dungo paused for a long time, not answering about his family. "I don' know where dey are," he finally confessed in a deflated voice, and then he turned away from Dod and went to sleep.

In the morning, a cold scoop of rotten, maggot-infested slop was dropped into Dod's hands for breakfast. He nearly threw up. Everyone else in the dimly-lit cave snarfed theirs down quickly and wished for more. Dod handed his off to Dungo and looked for water. He knew he'd be sick if he couldn't get the smell to go away. Finally, finding none, he resorted to rubbing his hands in the rock dust.

Once in the pit, Dod found his water. It was raining in torrents. All of the prisoners were soaked to the bone as soon as they stepped out from under the sheltered perimeters. It wasn't long before most of them had mud caked on their bodies and clothes.

"Sday exdra close do me doday," insisted Dungo, "because id's raining."

Dod looked at Terro questioningly as the threesome moved to their designated pounding spot.

"He's right," agreed Terro. "I'm not leaving his side—not in weather like this. The men get hopped up on the freedom that comes with the water and they stumble into fighting all day. Not to mention—well—they'll end fed."

"But what about the guards?" asked Dod, glancing back toward the covered porches that surrounded the pit. There were twice as many masked sentinels as there had been the day before, just none in the quarry. They stood watch on their dry platforms with their cruel whips and clubs in hand.

"They let it be," said Terro. "They don't care if we occasionally thin the ranks of the weaker sorts. And since the guards usually get their fill of whipping as they drift between us, the poor fools who approach cover when it rains really get a double dose. You're doomed down here and you're doomed up there—unless you're friends with Dungo."

"Right," said Dod gratefully. He didn't want to be eaten or beaten and recognized that both were more than likely outcomes if he weren't friends with Dungo; after all, Dod was one of the smallest and certainly the youngest of the people in the hideous prison, which made him an easy target.

As the rock-dust mud filled the low spots, a string of images flashed into Dod's mind. They weren't clear, but they gave him hope. A wave of relief washed over Dod. Somehow, someway, he was going to rise above the wretched circumstance he was in. He still had his gifts. And just as he had faced and defeated The Dread, he would create an exit for himself and Terro, and he would return to Twistyard and stop Dark Hood.

"Why do they post more guards when it rains?" asked Dod, wiping mud from his face. When Dungo hit the rocks with his massive sledgehammers, the rocks crumbled into the puddles and sent mud flying everywhere.

"I don't know," said Terro, shaking his head.

Dungo sat down and caught his breath while pointing at the sludge. "Dey don' like da mud," he grunted. "Da longdimers have a saying—when da rain comes down, da mud flows aroun', and da waiding, wadching prisoners make dem frown."

"Huh?" said Dod. It didn't make sense.

Terro shrugged his shoulders and went back to swinging his pick. It took a lot of exercise to keep an Ankle Weed from driving a man mad.

As Dod worked his body, he kept his mind going. He knew there was some truth to Dungo's statement because he'd seen glimpses of mud-covered men causing problems, but how the mud would help them was confusing. Perhaps the guards were allergic to it? Or maybe they hated getting dirty? Either way, a handful of mud balls weren't going to free anyone. The guards had orders to shoot arrows at mobs that approached before they were summoned, or that came to roll call with tools still in hand. All of the digging equipment stayed in the pit.

By the end of the day, Dod nearly needed to be carried back

to the cell block. He was extremely weak from exhaustion and exposure, and hunger had taken its toll, too, since he hadn't eaten breakfast and there was no such thing as lunch in Driaxom—at least not for prisoners. Guards, on the other hand, had taken turns dining on what smelled like heavenly hotdogs when the noon hour had rolled around.

Dinner came right before the candles were trimmed. Dod hurriedly gagged it down and licked his hands clean before the blackness set in. The slop was terribly disgusting, but Dod knew he needed the nutrition.

All night long Dod slept uneasily, despite his day of hard labor. His wet clothes certainly contributed to his discomfort, though that wasn't the main issue. On and off, whispers kept him awake. At first, Dod thought they were coming from men who were in the dungeon cell block with him. But by and by, he came to realize that the sounds were more in his head than they were in his ears—and the conversation kept repeating.

"Let him drag the box out," one voice would say. "When he reaches the cover, he'll drop the riggings and run."

"Why can't we kill him inside?" asked another voice.

"Because," explained the first, "he's unusual, you know. We may have inquiries about this one. And what would you tell a grand council? That he died quickly? I don't think so—not with his strength. They'd know we killed him, and they'd suspect us of a cover up. On the other hand, if he breaks orders and escapes, causing his own death—well—let's just say that it would be better to let the desert bury him and his testimony."

"But if he survives?"

"He won't!" insisted the first confidently. "We'll take the barrier down but leave the peep on. By the time he reaches the pavilion, the mark of decay will be etched on his brain, and he'll slip from reality and get lost on the flats. No one lasts more than three days in their delirium. If we ever stand to explain—he was just an ignorant beast, helping us move what our carts couldn't carry."

"Shall we wait for the regular dropping of the barrier?" asked the second voice.

"No, you fool!" chided the first. "We can't have anyone else waiting by the pavilion. We've got to do it tomorrow, in the evening."

By the third time Dod heard the whispered conversation, he was listening carefully. Someone wanted Dungo dead, and more importantly, that someone planned on having him leave Driaxom.

The rest of the night and all morning, Dod worried his mind on the matter. If they killed Dungo, things would turn wickedly wrong for Dod and Terro. During breakfast, the raving lunatic had made hungry eyes at Dod again and had only been sent packing by a second smack-down from one of Dungo's hefty fists. And at the quarry, two wandering mobs of rabble-rousers had come close to pounding Terro, claiming they were sick of his tongue, but had been routed by Dungo's ability to swing four sledgehammers at the same time.

The only thing that cheered Dod up was the rain. It kept coming down, which meant the guards would stay perched under their shelters and wouldn't be out whipping prisoners for the fun of it. Dod had told Dungo and Terro of his hunch, but they hadn't given much thought to it. Terro had quickly dismissed it as a bout of the regulars—adjustment dreams—and Dungo had only grunted "Huh." Neither one of them was interested in discussing the possibilities.

Suddenly, out of nowhere, it clicked.

"The mud," mumbled Dod happily. His eyes lit up with delight. "It's the mud! It's the mud! The answer's the mud!"

"I dold him nod do pick ad his weed," moaned Dungo, assuming Dod was slipping from reality.

"And he's the only one that calls me Terro," lamented Terro sadly, hitting a sizable outcropping of wet stone with an extra hard blow.

"I'm not crazy," said Dod, dancing around in a circle as the pouring rain washed debris from his face. "I just figured out how to free us of this place."

Terro and Dungo both stared at him.

"Really, I'm serious!" said Dod. He beamed ear-to-ear. "If we cover our Ankle Weeds with enough mud—maybe we could wrap fabric around the mud to hold it in place—then the high-pitched sounds won't trigger the weeds to attack. That's why the guards hate the rain."

"What are you talking about?" begged Terro.

"We could hide in the big box that Dungo's going to pull to the pavilion," rambled Dod, "and the noises won't bug our weeds if we've covered them with enough mud. We'll make it out alive!"

"That's ridiculous talk," scoffed Terro disappointedly. He had hoped Dod had come up with something that didn't have anything to do with the whisperings, since Terro thought the nighttime voices were nothing more than a dream, or perhaps Dod's mind splitting away.

"Da mud would prodecd us, you dink?" asked Dungo, turning strangely interested. He gave Dod a curious look of confidence.

"Yes—I'm pretty sure it would," said Dod. "I can't explain, but I feel like it would."

"Den I'm going do need someding big do hold id width," grunted Dungo, scanning the quarry.

"You don't actually think they'll drop the triblot barrier tonight just to have you pull a box to the pavilion, do you?" taunted Terro, sounding a lot like Sirlonk. "That's stupidity, you fool! It's ludicrous!"

"Bud Sirlonk—" began Dungo.

"And even if it happens just as he says," continued Terro, giving Dungo a healthy glare of disapproval, "we'd still be stuck with Ankle Weeds! There's no freedom for us!"

"I'd rather dig ditches at Twistyard than be eating maggot puke here in Driaxom," said Dod, his stomach aching for real food. "If I have to work hard to keep my mind—I'll work hard somewhere else. I'm leaving tonight with Dungo!"

A bolt of lightning flashed across the sky as the storm raged on.

"He knows whad he's dalking aboud," grumbled Dungo, standing up to Terro. "I've seen dis kid do his ding—and I don' know how he does id, bud if he says der going do come for me, den dey will!"

Terro scanned Dungo's face. "What makes you so sure?" he demanded.

"HE'S DA REASON I'M IN HERE!" fumed Dungo, losing his temper. "Dod knows dings—sees dings—he's Pap's grandson!"

A gust of wind blew the rain sideways and whipped so hard that Dod fell over.

"Are you certain he's Pap's grandson?" yelled Terro, fighting to be heard over the pounding rain. Terro looked at Dod skeptically and then offered him a hand.

"Wouldn't you like to see Sawb?" blared Dod, defying the wind and the rain. Terro slowly nodded. "Then help us work it out!"

The situation was highly unusual. Through his bursts of inspiration at High Gate, Dod had put the gears in motion which had effectually sent Dungo and Terro to Driaxom, and now Dod was working with them to break out.

As the storm increased, the guards retreated back toward the inner parts of the patios, seeking refuge. In so doing, items of all sorts were left to the buffetings of the wind. A large tarp caught the breeze and sailed through the air like a kite, finally plummeting hundreds of yards away when a downdraft pounded it into the waiting mud. Dungo, Dod, and Terro raced to retrieve it.

"Don't even think about it!" yelled a man who met the threesome at the tarp. He and his friends had brought their hammers and picks, so they were slower to arrive but better prepared.

"We're daking dis—back off!" ordered Dungo, crumpling the muddy fabric into a ball. Terro and Dod panted at his side.

"We hate the rain as much as you, beast!" shouted the lead man, raising his tool in the air. "Give us the tarp or we'll split you wide open!" Thirty men rallied behind him, chanting a war cry. They were all big and fearsome.

"And then what?" shouted Dod, stepping in front of Dungo. "You'll let Borston take it for himself and claim he's lost it?" Dod spoke from a well of impressions that instantly swirled in his mind like the wind around him.

"I knew it!" screeched the man, spinning around to face one of his own men. "You cheated us all and kept it!"

"He's speaking chicken dip!" claimed a red-faced brute, clasping his hammer tightly. "You know I wouldn't betray you."

Half of the crowd was in agreement with their leader and the other half rallied around Borston. The fight of words began to escalate as the men postured themselves for battle, which gave Dungo, Dod, and Terro plenty of time to waltz away with their prize uncontested.

"I see what Dungo means," huffed Terro, jogging beside Dod. "Are you sure you're not my brother's son?"

Dod smiled, knowing it was a compliment.

In no time, heavy layers of mud and ripped pieces of fabric were applied over Dod's Ankle Weed, then Terro's. Dungo's circumstance, however, was more problematic. He didn't have baggy pant legs to cover the trick, since his body was clothed in golden-brown hair.

"Id's no use," whined Dungo sadly. "If I hide my leg, dey'll know whad I'm doing. If I don', I'm a goner." Dungo sat in the mud puzzling, knowing that the hard rainstorm was likely to bring an early end to their stay in the pit.

"I know what to do," beamed Dod, glowing with excitement. "We've got plenty of tarp left—let's wrap both feet and ankles. We can make them look like boots. Who's going to blame you for wanting a pair of shoes? The rest of us are wearing them."

Dungo cracked a grin behind his bushy beard. "Dad mighd work," he confessed. "And if dey wand do dake dem from me, dey'll need do fighd me."

"Good," said Dod, ripping into the remaining tarp. He and Terro used sharp rock edges to guide the tears thoughtfully. And as fast as they went, they weren't a moment too soon. By the time they were wrapping the tops, mid-calf, and tying them off cleverly, swarms of prisoners were rushing for roll call, having already been summoned by the blaring bugles.

The gale and downpour made speech difficult on the patios, so the inmates were carefully directed, single file, into an inner hall to report, five hundred at a time. They were to be checked, group by group, before being sent to their cell blocks. Fortunately, Dungo's group was last, which gave Terro and Dod just enough time to complete the finishing touches on Dungo's boots, making them look presentable.

"Seventy-eight," yelled a taskmaster, peering through his spectacles at the rows of wet bodies. He waited for someone to step across the line and join the counted people, but no one did.

Dod glanced at the vaulted ceilings in the wide hall and noted the dismal chandelier-like stacks. They burned dimly and weren't smokeless. And then his eyes excitedly caught hold on something that occupied a hefty chunk of the hall, past the guards, centered below two giant double doors: It was a large wooden box, the size of six coffins. Someone was fussing beside it. Dod's heart leapt within him. He hadn't been just dreaming. He nudged Terro and nodded toward the sight.

"I said *seventy-eight*!" bellowed the taskmaster, becoming irritated. "Step forward and be whipped for noncompliance!"

"He's dead, sir," said Borston, sporting a bloody nose. He glanced angrily in Dod's direction.

"Very well, then," responded the taskmaster. "Give us the coordinates of his remains for verification—whatever's left."

Borston nodded and approached an underling guard, who listened to the directions carefully.

"He says they've got twelve men down," said the underling. "A fight broke out. Shall I go now to check?"

"The rain!" spat the roll-holding taskmaster, slapping his clipboard against a stone counter that ran parallel to the wall a few feet out. "I do hate the rain. It causes all sorts of trouble. Hold for a moment while I clear the other numbers—we've got procedures to follow—and perhaps there are more."

Dod's attention shifted back to the box. The man beside it stood up and approached a wall of shelves and cabinets that loomed behind the counter. He carried a keychain with only one key.

Oh no! thought Dod miserably, scrambling to amend his plans. He hadn't calculated that the box would be locked. Terro read the problem, too.

"Seventy-nine," yelled the man in charge. A fattish tredder wearing tattered pants and a toothy grin crossed to the other side, smugly crunching his knuckles at Borston.

Dod kept his eyes glued to the key and memorized where it was hung, fearing that even if he got a chance to snatch it, he'd grab the wrong one. The pegboard back wall of a man-sized cabinet was filled with various keys—hundreds of them—each dangling from their own numbered peg in an orderly fashion.

Terro cleared his throat obnoxiously until Borston looked over, then he rubbed his foot against the ground, as though smashing a bug. It was a taunt.

"You ready?" whispered Terro to Dod. Dungo's predetermined space in line was five people away, so he was unaware of the plan that was hatching.

Dod nodded nervously. Eight armed guards stood close by and fifty more were just a room away. Trouble would almost certainly mean swift punishment. But if the key were lost, Dod and Terro would have no way to get into the box.

Quick as the strike of a rattle snake, Terro pinched one man's shoulder and tripped his neighbor, then flailed backward, yelling, "Stop hitting me!" Dod couldn't believe how speedily the crowd erupted into punching and kicking. It was an instant brawl.

Dod scurried through the mass of moving bodies, threw himself over the stone counter, and swiped the precious key from the wall. Though once he had it, he realized how easy it would be for the guards to detect which one had been taken, which would possibly lead to a new lock, so Dod did the only thing he could think of: He pulled all of the keys off the wall, as fast as he could, and left them strewn across the floor.

Once he'd hopped back into the fray and had worked his way to the middle, he looked around and sighed. No one seemed to have noticed his deed but Dungo, who nodded at him knowingly. Dod stowed the key in his shoe and pretended to scuffle.

In the end, the plan worked perfectly—until the rule-keeping taskmaster counted keys. He didn't have time to reorganize them, nevertheless, he insisted that nobody was going anywhere if they weren't all found. And when he got to three hundred and twenty-eight, he stopped and shook his head. "Somebody's taken one," he insisted.

The bruised, wet, tired prisoners were forced to sit down on the ground, legs and arms spread apart in preparation for a dog search.

"I have canines that can smell the slightest bit of metal," huffed the reddening taskmaster. "But I'll cut you a break if you hurry and confess. Here's your choice, give me the key and my men will whip you twenty-five stripes, or wait for my puppies to find it and I'll chop your right arm off. You choose."

There was no mercy in the air, just cruelty, anger, and hatred. Dod knew for sure he would die. If he gave the key back, he'd be whipped so bad that he might not survive, plus he'd have no way to get into the escape box. If he kept the key, he'd likely get caught by the dogs and have his right arm taken. It was impossible to win. It was the end of the line. The brutal taskmaster wasn't going anywhere without seeing the key returned.

And then the most amazing thing happened—something that was so amazing, Dod knew he'd remember it for as long as he lived. When the fuming taskmaster was just signaling for his men to fetch the dogs, Dungo stood up and grunted boldly, "I dook da key, sir—and ade id."

"You did what?" raged the man, rushing at Dungo with his whip in his hand. "You ate my key?"

"I saw da key on da floor and I ade id—do make you mad."

"Well you succeeded!" spewed the man.

A hoard of guards shackled Dungo to a post, right in front of the scoffing crowd of five hundred prisoners, and began whipping him; and the men didn't stop at twenty-five stripes.

Dod couldn't watch. He hid his head in his hands and wept, though no one noticed. The calloused brutes around Dod enjoyed witnessing Dungo's punishment and were yelling for it to continue, when a well-dressed tredder came racing down the hall and made the guards cease. Dod recognized the tredder's voice. He was the one who had plotted to kill Dungo by having him pull the box to the pavilion.

As soon as the prisoners were dismissed to their cell, Dod raced to Dungo, who was still bound to the post. "Why did you do it?" whispered Dod, trying to hide his tears from the guards.

"You gave me your sandwich," mumbled Dungo, glossy-eyed with recollections. "You didn' have do—"

Dod hugged Dungo before the towering sentinels forced Dod to fall in line with the other prisoners. It was horrible for

Dod to think that something as simple as sharing a sandwich with Dungo—one Dod had been given by Tridacello and had offered to Bowlure first—was memorable enough to be a driving force in Dungo's life so many months later.

Dod walked in the midst of the crowd, feeling dazed as he blindly followed the others, though he should have been looking for a way to break ranks and hide. His plan for escape depended on it.

"Up ahead," whispered Terro, catching Dod by the arm. He pointed toward an open supply closet. Terro pretended to trip, and once on the floor, he crawled around the corner and rolled under a pile of stinky drapes. Dod was shorter than the other brutes so no one noticed when he ducked into the dark room.

Security around the halls was low. Nobody ever tried to escape. The prisoners had Ankle Weeds that would strike if they entered restricted areas, and worse still, the triblot barrier was completely impassible. As a result, when guards ushered prisoners to and from their cell blocks, they were complacent, making the slip all too easy for Dod and Terro.

Minutes passed and the bustling noises died down.

"How did Sirlonk act as a boy?" whispered Dod, wondering what motivated people like Sirlonk and Dungo to do bad things.

"I don't know," confessed Terro, poking his head out of the pile of fabric. "I was already a man, as was he, when I learned that I had a brother—well, a half-brother. So when we met for the first time, it was awkward. My mother, of course, was furious at my father for years. I guess that's why my father had Sirlonk go back to Soosh. But with his mother already dead, I can't imagine it was easy for him. When my father sent him away, it must have felt like a bitter betrayal."

"Oh," said Dod, feeling sorry for Sirlonk.

"Still, we have seen plenty of each other over the past few decades," added Terro. "He spent enough time at my palace that I can't believe he had any left for being The Dread. Do you really think he was a criminal?"

"I don't know," lied Dod, not wanting to hurt Terro's feelings. The truth was clear. Dod had heard from Sirlonk's own lips of his crimes—not the least of which was his involvement in poisoning Pap.

After a quick peek to make sure the coast was clear, Dod and Terro stole down the hall toward the big box. Dungo was no longer chained to the post, and the guards were gone.

"You can tell it's dinner time," muttered Terro sideways to Dod. "And from looking at the guards, I'd say they don't miss out too often, do they?"

When Dod and Terro reached the giant oak trunk, Dod bent down and rushed to open it with his key. Even though the halls were empty at the moment, someone could easily catch a glimpse of them and the whole plan would be foiled.

The lock clicked three times before releasing its grip. It took teamwork to swing the heavy lid open. Inside was a heaping pile of large stones.

"You weren't kidding when you said they planned on having him strain to move it," said Terro, eyeing the load. "It must weigh three or four thousand pounds. Where are we going to stash this stuff? They've packed the trunk to the top. We'll never fit."

Frantically, Dod searched the surrounding rooms for the best spot to deposit the rocks, while Terro kept an eye out for trouble. The perfect solution ended up being a strange object that Dod walked past five times before realizing what it was.

"Why not the well?" said Terro excitedly, pointing at the

statue of an angry frog. With effort, the amphibian was moved, revealing a deep shaft below it.

The rocks splashed at first, but by the time Dod threw the last stone into the hole, a thudding noise echoed back.

"Surprise!" said Terro gleefully to Dod, thinking about how frustrated the guards would be when their routine was interrupted. Each morning, fifty prisoners were compelled to draw water for five hours so the guards and their families would have an ample supply in their tank to support a pressurized system.

"I think you're right," chuckled Dod. It was two-tons worse than toilet papering, but after watching the way the men had treated Dungo, not to mention their cruelty in planting Dod with an Ankle Weed, the goodbye present was more than justified.

When the sound of Dungo and his tormentors finally entered the hall, Terro and Dod had been in the locked trunk for hours. Dod had fiddled with the inside of the latch so many times that he could unlock the lid in less than five seconds. And Terro had lost hope of success and had nearly given them both ulcers with the scenarios he'd mumbled in panic.

"And den I ged do resd?" asked Dungo as he approached.

"We's tell'n you the truth this time, boy," grunted a man whose voice made Dod shudder. He recognized that it was the fat man who'd imprisoned him.

"Sure. Jus' pull this out yonder to the pavilion and we's got plans for you to get lots of rest'n in."

Two or three men chuckled.

"Bud da driblod barrier," grumbled Dungo.

"No. It's down right now," assured the mean man. "Hows about I walk out with you just to make sure?"

"If you promise id's down, you can wadch me from here,"

agreed Dungo. The chorus of men chortled with delight, sensing Dungo was taking the bait. They were certain his mind was spinning toward freedom, since he pushed to have them stay put.

"Okay," said the mean man, opening up the double doors. "I's promise. Now get pull'n this thing."

Dod and Terro felt the box shift. They held their breath. Was the triblot field down? And were the mud wraps they'd applied thick enough to stop the Ankle Weeds from triggering insanity?

The ground beneath the trunk hissed and rumbled as Dungo started out across the barren flats. Dod was glad the guards were stupid. The hollow, nearly empty sounds that came from the oak box would have given the plan away to anyone with greater intelligence.

Ten minutes passed, and then fifteen, and then twenty. Dungo kept pulling. It was taking longer than expected. Dod and Terro started to worry. Finally the trunk came to a stop.

"I figured I'd give dem a show," grunted Dungo tiredly, watching his cargo emerge from the giant coffin. "Dey probably doughd I wend crazy since I kepd pulling da box long afder da pavilion."

Dod was glad the storm had blown over. He looked up at the starry night sky and then off in the distance to the little lights where Driaxom stood. "You pulled us all the way out here?" gasped Dod. "Thanks, Dungo! You're a real friend!"

"Id's all righd," coughed Dungo, doubling over. He slid the leather straps off his shoulders and plopped them on the ground. His feet had worn through the bottoms of both tarp boots, leaving the fabric tattered and dangling from his calves.

Dod and Terro shut the lid of the trunk and Dod locked it.

"We gave the men a little show, too," chuckled Dod. "Terro and I stuffed their well with boulders."

Dungo grunted.

The threesome walked for hours along the road to High Gate, never seeing any sign of the magnificent city in the distance, but trusting it was still there. Eventually, when the dizzying day had more than taken its toll, they stopped to rest on the stinky, damp ground for a few minutes—which turned into hours. And in the morning, Dod awoke to find his crew was down to two.

CHAPTER TWENTY-FOUR

PAYBACK

"Where's Dungo?" asked Dod, rousing from sleep at the sound of Terro's shuffling. The sun hadn't come up yet, so the chilly air prodded Terro to stand and do calisthenics.

"I don't know," said Terro, looking in every direction. Driaxom was out of sight to the east, and High Gate still loomed beyond view to the west, though the majestic Hook Mountains poked slightly above the otherwise flat horizon. "We should get walking while it's cool," continued Terro. "If we can't get help by mid-day, we'll dry out in this desert like prunes."

Dod struggled to rise. His legs were sore and he was famished. "I'd love a pile of hot pancakes right now," joked Dod.

"Would you like anything else with that order?" snapped Terro. He was on edge, trying to grasp the severity of their circumstance.

"Sure," said Dod, just happy to be out of Driaxom. But when he caught a sizzling glare from Terro, he decided not to continue his request.

Within two hours, the sun was beating down mercilessly

and the brisk morning air was gone. Waves of stench rose from the puke-green ground as it began to heat up.

"Do any *real roads* bisect this madness?" begged Terro bitterly of Dod, as though Dod were an expert since he'd lived in Green and Terro was from Raul.

"I don't know," huffed Dod, trying to keep up with Terro's big steps. At six-foot five, Terro bolted down the lane like a gazelle. "But don't worry," assured Dod, "things are going to work out. We're breathing freedom."

Terro glanced scornfully at Dod. The more bent out of shape Terro became, the more Dod couldn't help noticing how similar he was to Sirlonk.

"Freedom's a liberal term to be using right now," said Terro. "We're still stuck with these filthy things around our ankles and the desert's going to eat us before dinner—so I think you should choose your words better."

"Like what?"

Terro didn't verbally respond, he sped up until the pace caused a sharp pain in Dod's side.

"I can't go that fast," gasped Dod, slowing down. Terro kept running for a short distance, then stopped.

"How did a young human lad like you send Dungo to prison?" huffed Terro, looking down his nose at Dod. "You certainly aren't very fit. I'd have pegged you as a book-poking, momma's wippling."

Dod wished he were in better shape, though it didn't really matter. Whether they walked or ran, sweat poured from both of them and High Gate was hopelessly far away. By lunchtime, their pace had become sluggish. The pitiless sun cooked everything in the Ankle Weed Desert. It was the vegetationless terrain, with its varying dark shades of blackish-green dirt, that made it so hot, like strolling across countless miles of asphalt. And the fumes that rose from the ground made breathing difficult.

It had been over a day since either of them had slurped a meal, yet hunger had fled their minds; they were too hot and thirsty to think of anything but water. Their tongues hung in their mouths, dry and cracking, wishing it would rain as it had the past two days; unfortunately, there was not a cloud in the sky.

Then in the distance, something began to rise from the mirage that played tricks on their minds.

"I knew they'd come for me," said Dod, perking up as the spec got bigger. "Sometimes you just get a feeling—you know—that everything's going to be okay."

Terro looked skeptically at the growing image. "This road only leads to Driaxom," he muttered tiredly. "Whoever's heading there won't likely be rescuing us. They'll see our blibbin weeds, think we're escaped convicts, and with how daft everyone in Green seems to be, they'll haul us back for more punishment without believing a word we say."

"Oh," groaned Dod, not feeling nearly as confident as he'd felt just moments before.

It was pointless to run or hide. The men approaching were on horseback, and there wasn't a rise in the mud for miles that was big enough to shade a beetle.

But when the two horses got closer, Dod had to work hard to hold back tears. It was Boot and Buck.

"See!" said Boot proudly, turning to his brother. "I told you he'd be out here. We have a connection."

Buck stared with astonishment. "Terro?" he asked.

"At last!" burst Terro, turning almost giddy. "People know my name! I'm saved!"

"Your wife wants your vacation to end," added Boot, reaching into his bag and pulling out a large canteen of water.

"W-what?" stuttered Terro, his face crisscrossed with shock wrinkles. "Vacation?"

"Yeah," continued Boot, handing the container to Dod first. "What happened to you? I mean, I hate to say it, but you look dreadful." Boot enjoyed teasing Raul's Chief Noble Tredder since he was Sawb's father.

"Driaxom!" spat Terro, yanking the water from Dod's lips before he was done drinking. "The incompetent, bumbling, brainless people in Green put me in prison!" Terro thirstily gulped at the water, then paused to rant again, but this time in a garbled voice, "And thanks to the barbaric customs of this ridiculous place, I have to break my back everyday for the rest of my life — Me! — Terro! — Chief Noble Tredder of Raul!"

"He's certainly Sirlonk's brother!" laughed Boot, turning to Dod. Boot recognized he had latitude to say his mind and have fun since he was the one doing the rescuing, though he hadn't caught what Terro had said. It didn't compute. "Did the two of you visit Sirlonk?"

Dod shook his head.

"I didn't think they'd let you in," said Boot. "When Abbot told me you'd gone to see someone in Driaxom, I figured you'd be coming back disappointed. Though I must say, I'm surprised you're walking." Boot looked at Dod's face, then Terro's. Questions were whizzing through his mind.

"We were *locked* in Driaxom," said Dod, lifting his pant leg up to show his mud-and-cloth bandage over his Ankle Weed. Boot nearly fell off his horse.

"What? Why did they — " Boot began when he changed

tones. "You're kidding. It's a prank, right? Where's your wagon?"

"No, you idiot!" blared Terro. "I've just spent over three months jailed in Driaxom. A mob of jungo-hungry fools kidnapped me from High Gate and traded me for my brother, Sirlonk, so they could kill him themselves."

"Huh?" Boot still didn't believe it.

Dod bent down and unwrapped his Ankle Weed. "See?" he said. "When I went to visit Sirlonk, my ride flew away without me and the guards did this." Dod pointed at the purplish protrusion and held back tears. Displaying his life-altering injury to his best friend suddenly stirred emotions he'd suppressed.

"Wow!" said Buck, cringing as he looked away. It really bothered him to see it.

"But you've been sending letters to your son," said Boot to Terro. Boot was still holding out hope that the duo was pulling a well-planned joke.

"From Driaxom?" scoffed Terro. "Definitely not!"

"That's awful!" said Boot, once he believed their story. "No wonder your council's getting angry."

"I'd hope so," huffed Terro. "This whole mess is a real disaster. I'm not even sure if I dare enter the portal to home with this weed on my ankle. Who knows what might trigger it to drive me mad? And there's no cure! I'm stuck for life!"

Dod felt equally trapped and wanted to bawl like a baby until a glimmer of hope shot through his mind. "Maybe there's a way," said Dod, piecing things together. "I think I might know of someone who's removed one and lived."

"Abbot?" asked Boot, raising his eyebrows nervously.

Dod nodded.

"Well, if there's a doctor that knows a procedure," said Terro, looking to Dod excitedly, "then let's not waste any time. I must see this man at once. I'd give anything to get my life back." He stuck his hand up and climbed aboard Buck's horse before adding, "Of course, I don't want some crackpot like Dr. Shelderhig testing his theories on me. He's from the Grick clan in Soosh."

Dod didn't explain any more to Terro; he waited until he was riding with Boot to continue his conversation.

"Where's your horse?" asked Dod, sitting on the back of Shooter.

"I was certain *you* had him," said Boot. "Though I guess Raul Hall might be pulling a prank on me—to get me back."

"I didn't ride him," assured Dod. "Abbot set me up with a holoo and a flutter. I still don't know how he pulled it off. He said he had a friend, but who could it be?"

"A breathing friend?"

"I know," said Dod. "I thought the same thing. When he told me he could get me into Driaxom, I didn't believe him." Dod paused for a minute. "Maybe his friend's Dark Hood. When I got to the prison, two guards hauled me in like a criminal—and they had been waiting for me."

"Does it hurt?" asked Boot, turning to look at Dod sympathetically.

"It's not the pain that hurts the worst," responded Dod. "I hate knowing that it could drive me mad any minute—"

"And that's not just a myth?" choked Boot. He reached into his bag and pulled out a heavy beef stick.

"No!" said Dod adamantly.

"Are you sure?" Boot ripped the leathery jerky in half and handed Dod the bigger piece.

"I'm positive," said Dod, diving into the meat. It was the best food he'd ever tasted. Hunger and depravation had seasoned it nicely. "When I was in Driaxom," continued Dod with his mouth full, "I saw some really whacked-out people. One guy, who'd lost his marbles, tried to eat me."

"Seriously?" gasped Boot, dying to hear more.

"Yeah. I saw all sorts of crazy things in there—the kind of stuff I just want to forget about. I'm sure glad you came along. What made you decide to show up today?"

"The rain finally stopped," chuckled Boot. "I told Buck you had likely hung tight overnight with the wardens, because of the triblot barrier, and then by morning the storm was raging bad enough that you had opted to stay 'til it cleared." Boot thought for a minute and added, "I never would have guessed that you were thrown in with the prisoners. What lead them to realize they'd made a mistake?"

"They didn't. We broke out."

Boot glanced at Dod's face and read that he was telling the truth. "I can't believe it! You busted your way out of Driaxom!" Boot looked behind him and studied the distant horizon for any signs of trouble. "Do you think they'll come searching for you?"

"Probably not," said Dod. "And if they do, you better make Shooter run, because they'd haul you and Buck in for helping."

As Boot listened to Dod's tale, he took the lead and sped up the pace, not wanting to take any chances on being overcome by angry guards. And when nightfall came, they continued to ride until they had arrived at Twistyard.

Sawb was shocked to see his father in such a horrible condition, but once he heard that Dod had helped to free Terro from his treacherous imprisonment at Driaxom, the stern look on Sawb's face melted, which was about as close to a 'thank you' as Dod could hope for.

Back at Green Hall, Dilly went nuts when she saw the Ankle Weed, and Sawny looked ill. The two girls couldn't stop crying. As far as they had ever heard, it was impossible to extract the deadly plant without causing insanity. Boot read the growing look of concern on Dod's face and quickly interjected that he knew for a fact that it could be safely removed and that it wouldn't take long, either.

Whether Boot was right or not, Dod still worried all night. He wished he could slip up the inside shaft to Pap's place to speak with Abbot. The man almost certainly had been tagged with an Ankle Weed. Dod knew it. Yet a nighttime climb up the outside wall of the castle wasn't a great idea with The Beast still on the loose, so Dod waited impatiently for morning.

The next day was full of surprises. Before Dod had left his bed, Boot was beaming ear-to-ear with what he claimed was the solution to Dod's problem. He held up a large glass jar. One lonely, pickle-shaped freshwater sponge was bobbing around in the water.

"You've got to put your foot and ankle inside," said Boot eagerly. Dod was still working on opening his eyes.

"I spoke with Abbot. You were right. He said that if you keep the weed submerged for long enough, it'll choose the sponge over you and it'll come out."

"But it's barely getting light," said Dod, "when did you speak with Abbot?"

"I couldn't sleep," confessed Boot. "It was driving me crazy thinking about that thing in your leg—and it still is—just put your stupid foot in the water. It took me an hour this morning to find one of these sponges in the shallows of Lake Mauj by candlelight."

Dod pulled his pajama leg up and gently slipped his foot and ankle into the deep jar until water spilled on the floor. Nothing happened. The sponge bobbed around aimlessly.

"Did you go alone?" asked Dod, studying Boot's face.

Boot nodded.

"Weren't you afraid of running into The Beast?"

Boot smiled. "I brought my steel-tipped harpoon," he said. He reached to the side of Dod's bed and produced his weapon. "I figured that if you could find the nerve to waltz in and out of Driaxom, I could face my silly fears and climb the wall in the dark."

"They're not silly fears," countered Buck from his comfy spot in bed. He was glad to be done with his rotation on the floor.

"And you dared splash around in the water, too?" muttered Dod. He was impressed with Boot's courage.

Eventually, Dod used a sword to hold the sponge against his Ankle Weed. Many Greenlings and Coosings took turns gawking at the process as they readied themselves for breakfast. Since the violent rainstorm had landed on the last two days of the tournaments, the matches had been postponed. Dod had made it back in time for the final day. Dilly was undefeated. Her excitement was nearly to the bursting point. The only thing that dampened her enthusiasm was seeing Dod's condition.

"If only Higga were back from her study abroad," moaned Dilly, showing very little faith in Boot's remedy. "Maybe she'd know what to do. But the last letter she sent to me indicated she plans on spending at least another six months in Soosh, or more.

She's learning all sorts of things from the nomads—medical hints from the Mauj that still drift in the nomads' hocus-pocus."

"It's going to work!" insisted Boot from near Dod's side. Boot tried not to jinx the plan by staring at it.

"Oh, I hope so," muttered Sawny. "I can't stand to think about it." She wasn't the only one. Most of the girls avoided Dod.

Dod waited patiently, and then all of a sudden he felt the strangest sensation. It was like someone was pulling a knife from his leg.

"I think it's coming out," whispered Dod carefully, not daring to move a muscle. Buck and Pone joined Boot in hunching on the floor.

"Wow," said Pone excitedly. "It's slithering like a snake. Are you sure it's a weed?"

"Positive," responded Dod, motionless.

"I think it's all the way out," added Pone.

Dod still didn't move. He wanted to make sure.

"Yuck!" shrieked Donshi, glancing at Dod's bottle. She was grossed out by the blood that was darkening the water.

"Go ahead and pull your leg out," insisted Boot, "before the weed senses it's made a bad trade."

Dod quickly obeyed. He hadn't considered that possibility.

Boot wrapped Dod's leg in a towel, then applied an antiseptic balm to the wound before securing a thick bandage around his ankle.

"Do you think it all came out?" asked Sawny, looking gingerly into the murky water. She was disgusted by the sight but overcome by her drive for knowledge.

"Probably," responded Boot, drawing the sponge from the water with the sword Dod had just used. The purplish tip of the weed, which had been visible on the side of Dod's leg, had dipped into the sponge and pulled out, like a needle sewing, and was still wriggling, working it's flailing backside into the flesh of the sponge.

"Count the white lines before they disappear!" blurted Sawny. "There should be twelve."

Boot and Pone frantically obeyed. Each thread-thin tentacle was noted.

"You're right, there are twelve," said Boot with surprise.

Sawny sighed. "It's a miracle," she said. "The little creeper roots hold the poison that drives men mad—like loaded syringes. That's why no one can extract the weeds. Usually the thin roots break off and send a sharp pain up the spine to the brain—well—and then—" Sawny looked at Dod nervously. "Have you felt any zinging in your back?"

Dod was relieved beyond belief that he hadn't. The procedure was a success. But since Dod knew that he alone was certain it had worked, he couldn't help pulling a quick tease.

"What? What? What?" mumbled Dod, while rolling his eyes back into his head. It made him appear like he was going crazy.

Sawny and Dilly both gasped.

"Just kidding," said Dod, not letting the prank go very far. "I'm feeling great."

Dilly smacked Dod on the shoulder, yet beamed with relief. "Now you can come and watch me whip Sawb today," she said happily. "I'm taking first place this year."

"If you can get past Tonnis," said Pone under his breath, his eyes drifting from Dilly to Sawny and Donshi, who were both still watching Dod apprehensively, as though he were going to turn into a werewolf any moment. Tonnis was the one who had ended Pone's run.

"And Joak," added Sawny distractedly. She had been knocked out of the running by him. Dilly was the only seasoned member of Green Hall left in the tournaments. All of the rest of the level-five duelers were from Raul Hall.

"I've got it covered," explained Dilly, smirking with a secret. "I've saved a few special moves for today—stuff no one's ever seen before."

Boot smiled.

"Like disaster?" chirped Toos, coming from the hall to see what the fuss was about. Dilly cooked him lightly with her eyes, for she knew he was referring to her foul-up with The Dread, to crinkle her collar.

"It's out," announced Boot to Toos, while screwing the cap on the jar.

"I missed it?" groaned Toos, rushing over to inspect the murky water through the thick glass.

"Let's flush it!" blurted Pone. "That thing gives me the creeps."

"Not in our toilets!" spat Dilly adamantly. "I'd never be able to sit comfortably again. It could lurk in the pipes for months and wait for its moment to strike."

"I'll take care of it," said Boot, "and it won't be down our toilets." The girls all sighed with relief. "Besides," added Boot, "I promised someone I'd show it to him first." Boot slipped the large jar into his climbing backpack, secured it with three leather straps, and carried it from the room.

"Don't be leaving right now," begged Dilly. "I want you to watch my matches today." She was rubbing it in that he'd missed so many.

PAYBACK

"I wouldn't dream of skipping," responded Boot. "*All* of Green Hall will be cheering you on today." He glanced at Dod, who was the reason Boot had missed her other important rounds the day before.

"Good," beamed Dilly. Dod and Buck followed Boot to their room, where they changed and prepared for the day.

"You'll have to show Abbot the weed next time you climb the wall," remarked Boot to Dod, as he set the pack in the corner of the closet. "I promised him you would."

"Okay," said Dod happily. He was flying high, having been given his old life back. Things felt better than ever.

"And we should hurry and get another one of those pickle sponges for your honored guest. Terro's probably tapping his toes right now, waiting for a world-renowned doctor—preferably from Raul—to come and extract his leg-buddy. Besides, we wouldn't want him to miss the big matches."

Dod and Buck both smiled at the thought of saving Terro's life in time for him to see Dilly cream his son in the ring. Sawb had won first place every year for over a decade, and Terro hadn't skipped any of his son's final-day duels.

Two hours later, Sawb and Terro approached Boot, Buck, and Dod as they waited for the matches to begin. Terro wore a grin that Dod hadn't seen, and Sawb looked more sheepish than ever.

"You've done it, boys!" said Terro happily. "You've given me my life back. I still wish your doctor could have taken the time to administer the treatment himself before rushing out this morning, but it doesn't matter now. Thank him when he returns from his pressing business. It's wonderful you have such capable visitors from Raul."

Boot chuckled. Dod and Buck smiled at Boot. They knew he had gone over to deliver the priceless remedy, though when he had returned, he hadn't said a word about the details. Dilly had been busy filling the air with her pre-duel rally talk, and Boot hadn't wanted to disrupt the conversation with his gloating. He had convinced Raul's Chief Noble Tredder to allow him, an untrained Coosing, to extract the Ankle Weed under the guise that he was acting on behalf of a noteworthy doctor from Raul.

"I've got a little surprise for you, boys," added Terro in his deep, commanding voice. "I just got done spending a few moments with Commendus and his associates from High Gate and, after my son did the honorable thing and came clean about his knowledge of the billies cheating at Carsigo, the Bollirse Rules Board has decided to formally take the ill-gotten win from the Raging Billies and award it to the rightful owners. Congratulations on making it to the final Bollirse game! I'm sure you'll all make us proud as you represent the Western Hemisphere next week, and hopefully I'll get to watch you win The Golden Swot. All of Raul Hall will be rooting for you."

"What?" sputtered Boot. He thought he'd misheard.

"Sawb explained the whole story to my acquaintances," said Terro, pointing at a shaded, custom-built pavilion that was surrounded by dozens of armed guards. Commendus sat in the center with Con on one side of him and Sabbella on the other, conversing with many important-looking people, including Youk and Saluci, Neadrou, Voracio, Tridacello, Bly, Pious, General Faller, and others. The only person who was noticeably missing from the prestigious group was Bonboo.

"Oh," sighed Boot, turning to Sawb. "You told them what?"

Terro spun to face Sawb and looked expectantly.

"I just told them what I saw," responded Sawb in a dignified voice. He was his father's son, especially when he stood at his father's side. "I thought they had already weighed the treacherous acts, but to my great surprise, I discovered that they weren't aware of what the billies had done before the game."

Boot, Buck, and Dod weren't buying Sawb's look of genuine concern.

"Anyway—once they heard that those wretched humans had damaged Boot's swot—and Buck's too—and the one Dod should have been using—they all agreed that the Raging Billies didn't really win—you did!"

Boot was flabbergasted. He could hardly make his mouth say thank you. Buck was so astonished that he gazed at Terro and Sawb like a child peering at his presents on Christmas morning. And Dod was speechless with joy at the prospect of getting a chance to use the baseball skills he'd worked so hard all summer to hone.

"You're naturally welcome," responded Sawb officiously. "I'm just glad my words helped you."

Terro put his arm on his son's shoulder and together they walked back to the pavilion of elites.

"There's something I thought I'd never see," mutter Boot, still dazed as he watched the pair.

"You and Dod did just save his dad's life," said Buck, lending perspective to the moment.

"I know," gloated Boot, his chest swelling with pride, "but I still would have expected a different kind of payback." He rubbed his bruised jaw for emphasis.

"Well," recanted Buck with a sly look in his eyes, "I guess the expert doctor from Raul actually did all the hard work—"

Boot shoved Buck as Pone came strolling up with a crowd of

Greenlings. "Have they announced it yet?" asked Pone excitedly. "Dilly's up first with that thick-necked kid—"

"Harlow," plugged Toos, prancing with anticipation.

"Right—he's the one that sent Doochi to the sickbay yesterday. You should have seen him strike. If he continues to do as well today, I wouldn't be surprised if he's in the final two with Sawb."

"Then why haven't they made him a Coosing?" asked Boot.

"It's his second year as a Rauling—not that you could tell by his size—he's monstrous. Of course, Sawb makes everyone prove their devotion to him before he bows his scepter low enough to lend favors like that." Pone glanced across the ring at the crowd from Raul and let his eyes linger on Eluxa, decked in her usual black leather, but today with a bright-red belt.

"Boot knows plenty about getting special treatment from Sawb," blurted Buck, bursting to tell the great news. "Terro and Sawb told the high-ups that Sawb saw the Raging Billies break our swots before the game at Carsigo, so now the billies are out and we're heading to the final match next week against the three-year Eastern Hemisphere champs, the Lairrington Longs."

"Don't play me, Buck!" spat Toos impatiently, flattening his hair with his hand as he waited to hear more.

"I'm not," returned Buck. "It's all the truth. We'll be the ones fighting in the big game at Champion Stadium, not watching."

"I knew it!" burst Toos, jumping up and down. He excitedly pulled a wad of grayish hair from his pocket and gave the disgusting bundle a light kiss. "Ever since I started carrying this good-luck charm, things have clicked for me!"

"Oh," sighed Boot, eyeing Toos's clump of what looked like hair and dung. "Where did you get that beauty from?"

"Horsely," said Toos triumphantly. "He's been giving me pointers lately. Just this morning he told me that if I focused my positive energy, my greatest desires could come true—and what more could I hope for! He was right! My great-grandpa was a real Bollirse pro back in his day, and now I'm about to step into his shoes." Toos's eyes glazed with visions of grandeur.

"You're assuming I'll let you play," teased Boot. "What if I said that people who carry dead vermin in their pockets couldn't suit up?"

"Boot!" blared Toos, straightening his pinstriped vest with one hand, while carefully holding his trinket with the other. "It's the charm that brought us Sawb's favor!"

"No—Dod did that!" responded Boot. "He went all the way to Driaxom and busted Terro out—not to mention, he was the one who discovered how to get rid of the Ankle Weeds. That's why Sawb had a change of heart. Dod saved his dad from a gruesome, torturous death."

Toos paused for a moment, carefully turned his ball of junk over a few times, inspecting it with the eyes of a mesmerized believer, and finally concluded, "My luck charm will draw your favor to me as it did Sawb's. You just wait, Boot. By next week, you'll be begging me to play on your team with you, and you'll probably be asking Horsely for one of these." He held up his fuzzy ball and gave it a second kiss.

"Gross!" blared Dari, shoving her way closer to Dod. "*Why-o* are you holding *that-o*?" she said, squinting in Toos's direction. Her fancy shirt and stylish pants showed she was on display for the day because of the special guests, though she was horribly underdressed when compared to her sister Valerie and brother Sammywoo.

"It's my fabulous luck charm," replied Toos proudly.

"It's an owl pellet," said Sawny, joining the crowd. She had just left Dilly's side at the check-in booth.

"What?" gasped Toos.

"You were kissing owl poop!" taunted Juck, his messy short hair sticking out in every direction and his eyes desperately seeking attention. Donshi squealed with revulsion.

"Not feces," corrected Sawny, pushing light brown curls from her face. "Owls regurgitate balls of hair and bones—the non-digestible parts of the mice they eat—"

"Owl puke!" gagged Dari. "I knew it was something *gross-o*!"

Everyone laughed and stared at Toos, who looked greatly conflicted.

"I've actually been holding out on you," said Boot, quickly stepping beside Toos. He pulled a marble-sized white rock from his pocket and raised it up to the light. It sparkled beautifully. "I've used this for good luck loads of times, and it's worked wonders for me. But I really do want you to play on my team in the big Bollirse match next week, so what would you think if I gave it to you?" Boot held out the shiny stone.

"Thanks!" exclaimed Toos eagerly. The embarrassment and consternation on Toos's face melted away almost instantly. He chucked the owl pellet over his left shoulder, rubbed his hands up and down his pants, and then gingerly took the present from Boot. "Do you think it will work for me, too?"

"Of course," insisted Boot, selling it hard, "it's a remarkable roller, and it's already convinced me that I can't stand the thought of playing Bollirse without you on my team."

"Oh—right," muttered Toos gleefully.

Dod recognized the stone and remembered where Boot had gotten it from. The day before, when they'd stopped to water their horses at a stream just outside of the Ankle Weed Desert, Boot had bent down and scooped the rock from the trickling water. Dod knew Boot was a softy. Even though Boot was the first to pull a prank and loved to laugh, he couldn't stand to watch anyone get hurt.

"Take your seats," thundered Clair from one of the judges' tables. "We're ready to begin."

Dod and the other Green Coosings and Greenlings plopped onto the grass since the bleachers were filled to overflowing. Dilly entered the ring, followed by a bulldoggish boy whose wide frame hogged the space.

The second judge was Turly, a handsome-looking tredder from Commendus's palace—the chief security officer and head swordsman for the Discommo grounds. He kept smiling flirtatiously at all of the ladies.

"Perhaps Dilly's got an extra edge," whispered Dod to Pone, nodding toward Turly, who was waving to a Rauling girl that had just yelled his name.

"She would if she hadn't already cut the support beams out from under *that* encroaching bridge," responded Pone, pulling a hand of nuts from his pocket. He stuffed them in his mouth as though the two plates of breakfast he'd polished away hadn't taken the edge off his hunger.

"Yeah, no kidding," said Buck. "Poor Dilly probably wishes Turly weren't calling this match—not after what she said to him last year—or she's regretting her words."

"Well, he *is* an arrogant peacock!" snapped Sawny, defending her sister. "I think men like him are atrocious."

"Ditto," said Dari, sticking her finger in her mouth like she was gagging herself. "Anyone who's that stuck on himself is lost in patheticsville—"

When Clair hit three, Harlow struck at Dilly like a snake, though he missed and was rewarded with a jab to his shoulder. Then he did a series of vigorous plunging moves, stomping his boots as he progressed, but despite the gasps from the crowd, Dilly was light on her feet and avoided the zipping blade. Around and around Harlow chased Dilly, stabbing and swiping in her direction.

Finally, about the time Harlow was beginning to huff, Dilly turned on him and poured her strength into the art of attack. She did a string of clever jabs that drew his arms back and forth like a giant troll swatting at a gnat, until he lost track of her blade and got caught in the rhythm, at which point Dilly struck his sword with such force that she sent it flying out of the ring.

"Point for Dilly!" cheered all of Green Hall.

"Idiot!" yelled Sawb from the sideline. "Never let go of your weapon!"

Two rounds later, Eluxa battled a young Pot from Raul who did well enough that the crowd shushed to hear the judge's conclusion. It looked as much like a tie as ever a match could be. But Turly gave the not so surprising answer: "Point for Eluxa!"

Dilly battled four more matches and had four more victories, each marked by the sound of Green Hall cheering her on. She was nearly unstoppable. However, Sawb seemed similarly able in all of his duels, and Tonnis, too.

Eluxa eventually faced off against an equally good-looking girl from Raul, a hungry Rauling who was dying to show off her talent, and lost by a close margin—perhaps by the shade of her dwindling lipstick and fading perfume.

Just before dinner, the numbers revealed the top three duelers: Sawb, Tonnis, and Dilly. It wasn't entirely fair how the judges determined the next step. Since all three contestants were undefeated, Turly and Clair insisted that Sawb, as the reigning champion, sit out while Dilly and Tonnis battle for the right to fight him. Based on their selection, Sawb was automatically given a minimum of second place and a nice rest before the grand finale.

Dilly and Tonnis took their positions in the ring and waited for the countdown. Juny sat on the front row as she had before, squished between Ingrid and Horsely. The crowd went silent. Dilly was a Twistyard favorite, just as Mercy's waving sign suggested, yet Tonnis had fought every one of his matches with unparalleled skill.

On two, Ingrid yelled loudly, "Beat him, Dilly, he's a loser!" But on three, the rivals bowed courteously, then stepped back and positioned for a fair fight. Over the course of the following four and a half minutes, the duel raged back and forth. Precision jabs and swipes were equally dealt and blocked from both contenders. Dilly performed a crafty tuck and roll that landed one glance across Tonnis's leg, and Tonnis pulled off a spinning plunge that nicked the edge of Dilly's shoulder. Most of the assaults ended with magnificent clanking sounds as the spar swords forcefully struck metal against metal.

It was a tie of skills, or so it seemed. Each time Dilly rose with a new, clever trick, Tonnis would dig deeper and find a way past it. The duo was remarkable. Unlike so many of the earlier matches, the intensity was so great that the crowd remained relatively quiet, completely enthralled in the scene. Both judges were loving the duel. They no longer sat in their chairs, but stood near the line, eagerly devouring the beauty and grace of the masterful swordplay.

With only moments left on the clock, Mercy staggered to

her feet, blocking the people who were seated behind her in the stand, and yelled loudly, "YOU'RE BONBOO'S GREAT-GRANDDAUGHTER, DILLY!"

And Juny responded with equal vigor, "YOU'RE MY SON, TONNIS! YOU'RE *MY* SON!"

Dilly fought hard to take her place as the best. She drove in with great gusto but fell prey to Tonnis's clever move—he faked a slight retreat while staggering one of his long legs just enough to trip Dilly, sending her to the ground. And quick as a pouncing spider, Tonnis plopped one of his giant feet over Dilly's weapon and pointed his menacing blade at her heart. "Gotcha!" he said breathlessly.

The first sound Dod heard was the crushing of Dilly's dream, followed quickly by a thunderous roar from the crowd. Everyone had been well rewarded for their endurance through the less exciting squabbles.

Tonnis dipped his hand and, ever the gentleman, helped Dilly stand. "You bow first," he said quickly, flipping his tousled bangs from his forehead. "I was just lucky at the end."

Though moments later, as he chased Sawb around the ring, he proved luck was hardly the reason he had won. The battle between the two Chantolli cousins wasn't nearly as eventful, yet still intense. Over and over, Tonnis made his marks, while Sawb struggled to defend himself. But just before the five minutes had expired, Tonnis looked toward his mother, bowed a subtle nod, and stumbled backward out of the ring.

"HE WINS AGAIN!" shouted Terro from the special pavilion. Sawb raised his hands in the air like a champion and strutted back and forth.

"That was disappointing!" snapped Dari, starting a rumble

of conversations on the grass. "I mean, boingy-boing, why did he do it? Tonnis had him!"

"Why do you think?" said Boot rhetorically, watching Tonnis approach his mother for a hug. "If he hopes to ever return to Raul, he'll need to honor the powers that be."

"But it's not fair!" fumed Dari, giving voice to what so many other people were thinking.

"Tell me about it," sighed Boot longingly.

CHAPTER TWENTY-FIVE

TOO HOT

After dinner, Dod bumped into Tridacello and Bowlure in the Hall of The Greats. Dod was glancing at the black-and-white photo of Terro and Dungo, which really did look like Sirlonk and Dungo.

"Is it true?" asked Bowlure, looking at Dod.

"Which part," responded Dod.

"That Sirlonk's not in Driaxom."

"Yeah—he's definitely not there."

"Poor Terro," shuddered Tridacello. "Today at the matches he told me all about his incarceration. Another two weeks of that and we'd have been facing a serious war with Raul. What a lucky stroke that you happened upon him when you did." Tridacello gave Dod a suspicious smile, the kind Youk was a master at dishing.

"It wasn't luck!" blurted Bowlure, reaching with a long arm to pat Dod on the shoulder. "I've been saying it since the day we met—Dod's psychic! He's got things going on that stretch beyond the aid of regular swappers."

"Right," chuckled Dod, not sure what to say. He didn't want to get into a conversation about swappers, especially with people bustling in the halls.

"And you must have used your special powers to get in and out—" continued Bowlure, imagining the details he didn't know. "With a triblot field in place—well—how did you do it without getting plugged to an Ankle Weed?"

"I have my ways," said Dod, attempting to shorten the conversation. Everyone in Green Hall was celebrating Dilly's third-place trophy, and Dod had already taken more time than he had planned by walking the long way back from dinner.

"Did you see Dungo?" asked Bowlure. Tridacello seemed to know more, but didn't say anything.

"He was different in prison," responded Dod.

"It's a shame what happened to his family—" muttered Bowlure.

"We don't know for sure," snapped Tridacello, straightening his shoulders. His health looked every bit as solid as it had before his accident with The Beast. It was amazing to see how much stronger he was now than just a few days before.

"But Youk said that they were probably dead," argued Bowlure, disregarding Tridacello. "Bonboo's received letters from them monthly for years—ever since he helped them escape Soosh. And Dungo's roamed like a weed, so those letters were always as much for him as they ever were for Bonboo. And now that they've stopped—"

"I know, I know," rushed Tridacello, fidgeting with his pocket. His hands shook a little more than usual as he undid a button and pulled a yellowed piece of paper out. "I think Youk's being overly suspicious when he suspected that this was a forgery. Not to mention, Tinja was in the room when that conversation unfolded. Tinja's filled with murky gloom about everything pertaining to the Carsalean Sea. His history has stained his spectacles forever."

Dod reached for the note and was scowled at.

"Please," said Dod. He had a tender spot in his heart for Dungo, and something inside him pricked at his curiosity button, like an arrow pointing to a clue.

"Very well," huffed Tridacello. Dod couldn't understand what vexed the old man.

When Dod unfolded the paper and raised it to the light, the smell of jumba sap wafted into his nostrils, and he felt his gut acknowledge that Dungo's family was gone for good. It made Dod tear up. He knew if Dungo were still alive, he was trying to find them—and the quest was a lonely road to a sad conclusion.

"Poor Dungo," mumbled Dod, wiping his eyes.

"Either way, Dungo's a traitor!" ranted Tridacello insistently. "I trusted him with my life, and how did he reward me? He secretly joined Sirlonk on his evil crusade to destroy everything decent! Even if I cross paths with men who trade rounds at Driaxom, I'm not slipping so much as a word to Dungo, regardless of what Youk suggested. He's dead to me."

Dod was shocked. He was surprised to see how thick the grudge was on Tridacello's shoulders, and he couldn't believe that Terro hadn't mentioned Dungo's escape.

"Congrats," said Doochi to Dod as he passed them in the hall.

"What?" pried Bowlure, studying Dod's face. "You've got good news to share."

"Well—if Tridacello hasn't already told you, then I will: They've officially decided that Green Hall did in fact win the

Bollirse match at Carsigo, since the Raging Billies were uncovered as cheats—they broke Boot's swot, and Buck's swot, and mine too, before the game had even begun."

"No wonder!" said Bowlure. "I thought Green Hall would come out on top. Good show! You're on your way to Champion Stadium, aren't you?"

"Yup," said Dod, nodding his head. It was still settling in how big of a deal it really was.

"Then we'll probably see you tomorrow morning," added Bowlure. "We've been asked to help with some special details around Commendus's grounds—haven't we, Tridacello?"

Tridacello nodded.

"Oh—the game's not 'til next week, so we won't be going just yet."

"But you've got pre-game preparations," said Bowlure. "I'm sure the Lairrington Longs will be arriving tomorrow, so they can adjust to the larger field and do their share of publicity rounds. I doubt Commendus would be pleased if you waited. It's always about money for him."

"Huh," sighed Dod. "Maybe we are."

"Not maybe, son," huffed Ingrid, thumping her cane as she approached on Horsely's arm. "Dilly said we're leaving tomorrow—she spoke with Commendus for me as well."

Bowlure gave Dod an extra big grin when he noticed how unusually strong Ingrid smelled of her garlic brew—twice as much as normal. Dod's eyes watered once she stood near him to speak.

"I'm gonna say it because I've practically adopted you as my son," began Ingrid, shifting from Horsely's arm to Dod's shoulder. "You and your friends over in Green Hall need to take

Commendus up on his offer to spend some time away from here. It's ludicrous to sit around waiting for that *thing* to eat you. Horsely's going with me now to collect my luggage."

"It's not a bad idea," endorsed Horsely in a halfhearted voice. He looked coerced. Dod could imagine how many things Ingrid had said to him to rally his support.

"I'm sure we'll be coming back after the big game," choked Dod, tears streaming down his cheeks. His eyes were weak and couldn't tolerate the pungent odors in the air.

"I've only got one more night here," pressed Ingrid solemnly, "and you may not be able to tell, but I've taken every precaution to protect myself." Ingrid looked around and added in a hushed tone, "My stew's good luck against The Beast—the stronger the better."

"Then you're safe," choked Dod boldly, unable to see a thing. He could hear Bowlure laughing at him.

"Just consider it, foolish boy!" huffed Ingrid in frustration. "You haven't got a personal army of guards like those fancy-pants kids from Raul. If something plopped through one of their windows, they'd probably sleep right through the counterattack. But if that creeping thing pressed at your window—well—" Ingrid paused quietly. Dod wasn't sure whether to respond or not. He drenched his free sleeve with the water that spewed from his eyes and tried to read Ingrid's face.

"I just don't make friends easily," she finally confessed, sputtering with controlled emotion.

"I'll talk to the others," agreed Dod, already knowing what the answer would be. "But don't worry about us, okay? We'll be fine." He disconnected from Ingrid and made tracks for Green Hall, all the while hoping people hadn't thought he was a crybaby.

"It's about time," yelled Boot from the end of the corridor, the moment Dod strolled through the big double doors. "We've been waiting for you."

As Dod passed Pone's room, he saw everyone was busily packing their bags for the morning exodus. "So are we leaving tomorrow?" he asked, slipping into Boot's bedroom. The door was shut and locked behind him.

"Yes," said Dilly, holding her precious Book of Everything. She and Sawny were sitting on his bed. Buck stood by them with worry on his face, while Boot casually leaned against the door.

"Is everything all right?" stammered Dod, feeling the mood in the room was certainly not a celebration.

"It's nothing," rushed Boot. "They're just getting worked up over a tiny piece of paper."

"It's not the note that's ransacked my innards," blared Buck, running his fingers through his hair, "it's The Beast!"

"What?" gasped Dod, tripping over a coil of metallic line on the floor. Sneaker startled and dashed for the safety of the biggest branches in the new garden-box thicket that had been added with the renovation.

"This," said Dilly, holding up a small note. "Someone slipped it into Boot's pocket today without him noticing." She glanced at Boot with a *"Please-tell-me-you're-kidding!"* look, and then continued, "Anyway, it's bad enough to make us stew."

Dod picked himself up off the floor and read the message aloud:

I know this will sound crazy to you, Boot, but bad things are going to happen tonight. I'm really sorry. I wish it were my choice, but it's not. Your people aren't safe—not in Green Hall,

or anywhere else at Twistyard. At least
one of them will die. Maybe if you take
them away and hide them, you might
avoid it—maybe. Please don't think this
is a prank from Raul Hall. It's not.
Cheers, Boot.

Your friend,

X

"Who's X?" nagged Buck, who'd clearly already asked the
question before.

Boot shook his head. "I told you—I don't know for sure." The
wheels in Boot's brain were spinning ferociously as he clenched
one of his fists, but his face remained calm as a pleasant evening.

"Now's when you say '*just kidding*,' right?" pleaded Sawny.

"I wish," sighed Boot. "If it's a joke, it's not a funny one!"

Dod smelled the letter.

Nothing happened.

"If you really didn't write the letter," said Dilly, needling
Boot with her eyes, "then it may be someone like Sawb. After all,
your horse magically reappeared this morning, didn't it?"

"Yes," agreed Boot, "but I think this is different. We should
take it seriously." The look in Boot's eyes began to shift. "It may
be a prank—quite a good one on me—or it may be the real thing.
Either way, I'm not taking any chances with your lives—not with
a ravenous creature on the lurk. Let's be ready for anything."

"Or let's bring the note to Youk and Voracio and see if we
can get the drat troops involved," said Buck eagerly. Dilly and
Sawny nodded in agreement with Buck's logic.

"Wait!" blurted Dod. His mouth spoke before his head had finished digesting the thought that skirted the back corners of his mind. "Maybe the person who wrote the note wanted you to do that—knew that you would go straight to them."

"If they thought Boot would go running to Voracio," said Sawny, playing scenarios in her mind, "they certainly weren't much of a friend—or even an acquaintance. Everyone knows Boot thinks he's invincible—"

Boot stood a little taller and smiled.

"But he's not!" ended Sawny. She dropped the gavel of reality on Boot's pride.

"What about Commendus and his crew?" asked Dod. "A lot of important people are visiting Twistyard tonight. You saw them at the tournaments. They're the ones that have extra security detail right now. If we pull at Youk and Voracio, they might be tricked into weakening the protective safeguards on the real targets, while Dark Hood laughs at how easily we fell into his plan."

"Dark Hood," groaned Sawny nervously, running her hand up the side of a scabbard that she had placed beside her. "He's clever like The Dread. Today I ate lunch in the library with Ascertainy and she told me some horrible news—" Sawny's hand quivered as it reached the hilt of her sword.

Dilly spun to look at her sister, shocked that Sawny hadn't already rehearsed to her what she'd heard.

"I couldn't tell you earlier," explained Sawny, cringing sweetly at Dilly. "I didn't want to ruin your victory day. I had planned on waiting until tomorrow."

Dod knew what she'd learned. He could sense her thoughts.

"Ascertainy let it slip that they may be closing Twistyard down next year. There's even talk of selling all of the lands and the castle. Debt collectors are pressing Voracio—and Bonboo's been out—and the Farmer's Sackload is gone, Dilly! Dark Hood stole it—The Sparkle included! All of the Tillius's pure-sight diamonds are missing!" Sawny burst into tears.

"How did Dark Hood hear that they were being kept in the Histo Relics Building?" puzzled Dilly. Her face was clearly more angry than it was sad. "Only a few of The Greats knew where Bonboo had moved them to after last year's Central Bank incident. Once the bank's main office at High Gate was burned to the ground by plundering fools in search of the Farmer's Sackload, Bonboo hid the jewels in the secret floor safe in the Histo Relics Building. Even *we* wouldn't have known if our dad hadn't been involved in the nighttime transfer."

Boot sighed heavy and long. "I was hoping you wouldn't find out."

"You knew?" gasped Dilly, looking like she'd just been stabbed in the back.

Boot, Buck, and Dod all wore guilty faces.

"You all knew!" she stuttered. "Why didn't any of you tell us? It's the end of our family's inheritance."

"We were kinda hoping The Greats would get them back," said Buck sheepishly. "Tridacello told me they had some good leads—"

"What else?" snapped Dilly. "Out with it!"

No one said a word. Gradually, Dilly melted.

"Someone wanted Dungo dead," mumbled Dod. He was still piecing together clues in his mind.

"Not someone—everyone," corrected Boot. "That's why they call it a living-death sentence. When you're in Driaxom, you're there because people want you dead—" Boot caught Dod's eyes and staggered, "except, of course, in your case—"

"That's the strangest part," interrupted Dod, scratching at his head. "The people who were conspiring to kill Dungo—to cover up his testimony—felt like they couldn't wait for him to die on his own and had to make his death look accidental. Doesn't that seem strange to you?"

"And he's out now, right?" clarified Boot, trying to remember what Dod had discretely shared in confidence about his big escape from Driaxom.

"Sort of," responded Dod. "I don't know what happened to Dungo. He was acting weird before we took a rest, and then when Terro and I woke up, he was gone. I think his Ankle Weed may have been damaged—"

"Just as well," said Dilly curtly. "He's a criminal."

Dod wanted to defend Dungo, though his feelings were torn in both directions; Dungo had nearly smothered him and Dilly on Commendus's patio, yet had saved him and Terro in Driaxom.

"I don't know how it meshes with anything else," concluded Dod, "but the circumstance seems to fit in with those clever murders—you know—of Green's representatives—"

"That's true," said Sawny, wiping tears from her face. Her blue eyes looked at the ceiling as she calculated.

Dilly opened up her Book of Everything and began reviewing the past. Her finger paused at the dreams that had plagued Dod. "Are you any closer to knowing where the quarry might be?"

"Yup—and I'm glad that's over."

"Oh, you mean Driaxom!" blurted Dilly. Her face lit up as she scribbled away. "Is that why you went?"

"I guess you could say that," responded Dod.

Sawny sat up and looked at Dod with hopeful eyes. "You're

a lot like Pap," she said. "We'd be in serious trouble from Raul if Terro had remained hidden in the dungeons of Driaxom. No one visits there. Criminals go in and are locked up for good."

Dod felt the keys around his neck through his shirt. He had four instead of three since he'd added the one he'd gotten in Driaxom—to remember Dungo's selfless act.

"Have you had any other impressions?" asked Sawny.

Dod paused. "Well, to tell you the truth, yes. I've seen a lot of stuff burning."

"The fire at High Gate!" blurted Buck.

"Sort of."

"And the tent," said Boot, strolling over to Dilly's side. He glanced over the warning note again.

"And our bedroom," added Buck.

"Right," said Dod. "I think the billies are lighting fires—maybe they're working with Dark Hood somehow."

"With the Farmer's Sackload, he could hire all of them for years!" groaned Dilly.

"They do like flames," admitted Sawny. "Just talk with Tinja sometime. He'll tell you all about billies and their love of fire." Sawny paused, put her finger to her lip, then added, "If I'm not mistaken, jumba sap ink is used almost exclusively by billies. I bet the message we retrieved from the dead bird was sent by a noble billie."

"Commendus must be aware of their involvement," said Dilly, pulling the jumba sap letter from her book. "Remember—he's got Newmi at the palace now."

"That's all important, I'm sure," said Boot, "but the real thing to focus on right now is what to do tonight. It's nearly dark outside. We need to prepare for The Beast, or a mob of armed men, or even a wave of flaming arrows."

"I vote we take our chances with Voracio and Youk," blurted Buck squeamishly, not wanting to face trouble. "We can always suggest to them that the note may be a sneaky ploy to thin the security of the greater targets and let them make the call on what to do. Besides, there are plenty of soldiers to go around, aren't there?"

"But Buck," said Sawny anxiously, "if someone sent the jumba sap letter to Zerny—and if Zerny's still alive—he could be Dark Hood! No one's seen him for weeks—and Jibb seems completely unconcerned. If we make a fuss and secure soldiers, we may end up with a mob of traitors—brutes from the drat troops that will slit our throats while we sleep. After all, doesn't it seem odd to you that hundreds of trained men can't seem to stop one creature?"

"A Trojan horse," whispered Dod to himself.

Dilly bit her lip as she weighed the options.

"You're right," said Boot, his eyes sparkling with conviction. "Plus, if we welcome soldiers into Green Hall tonight, we'd have to hide our weapons—and I'm not willing to bet my life on a few drats' abilities, even if they're not traitors. Dilly alone could best a dozen of them with her sword skills."

Dilly liked the compliment and nodded approvingly at Boot.

"Then it's settled," said Boot, walking over to the wall where he'd propped his steel-tipped harpoon. He picked it up and began working to secure a metal line to the back loop.

Buck stared at him and boiled. "You take a few ideas and then rush back to your own muscles!" scoffed Buck in an unusual burst of venom. "People could die tonight, Boot! This isn't a game!"

Boot didn't look up. He kept working on his harpoon.

"Don't think I didn't see the look in your eye!" raged Buck, storming over to Boot. "I know what I saw!"

Boot finished securing the line to his weapon and moved on to attaching the other end of the line to a thick bolt he'd already screwed into one of the massive doorframe posts.

Sensing Buck's continued glare, Boot raised his hand in the air and called for a vote. Dod's hand shot up first, for he'd had plenty of bad experiences with soldiers and preferred taking his chances with Boot. Dilly's hand followed immediately after Dod's, and Sawny's sluggishly carried the rear.

"No wonder Bowy won't come back!" grumbled Buck, flipping the lock and exiting the bedroom door with a slam.

"He'll cool off in a few minutes," said Dilly, sliding her sword from its casing. "How should we structure our sleeping arrangements?"

"Tight," answered Boot, his voice rattled by Buck's anger.

"It's only one night," said Sawny, trying to reassure herself as much as anything. Her natural leanings were to go down the same road as Buck, which seemed logical; but with the financial affairs of Twistyard secretly unraveling and the status of the drat troops' leadership in question—not to mention Bonboo's near death from poisoning—Sawny chose Boot's radical idea: prepare to fight!

Everyone in Green Hall packed their bags for the big Bollirse game and situated them next to Green Hall's double doors. Boot didn't say why. He knew that if Dark Hood attacked with fire as he had before, they'd need to leave quickly.

Next, Boot proposed that Green Hall try an all-night preparedness drill of sorts. Buck had a hard time sitting quiet as he listened. But Boot's idea readied the Coosings and Greenlings like never before without needlessly alarming them. The strongest Coosings and Greenlings were situated with swords and bows in a line across Boot's bedroom and another line in the hall. In between them, the other Coosings and Greenlings were seated, each with their own sword. Half of the people would lay down and rest while the other half sat awake, quietly watching. The rotations were to be for two hours at a time.

If attacked, Boot was ready with three escape routes: one out his window—a rope was secured to the floor in preparation, one down the hall and out the double doors, and one through the closet up Boot's secret passage. If attacked simultaneously from the front and back, Boot would file his people into the closet and have them all magically disappear.

"I know it sounds tough," said Boot, as he finished positioning the crowd, "but we need to learn these skills. You never know when they may be needed. Remember—you're family to me." Boot raised his harpoon in the air and finished with a cry, "*Twistyard strength, Twistyard courage—though the night will be long and dark, Twistyard will prevail!*"

Dilly and Sawny struggled with their emotions. Bonboo had led men to battle with the same cry over two hundred years before and had kept Doss's troops from taking the castle. Both girls had heard the chant many times from Bonboo's own lips, yet hearing the words from Boot's as he stood to lead them was more powerful than ever before.

For the majority of the night, the arrangement was like a crowded, poorly-planned sleepover, with bodies sprawling on the floor, fully clothed and uncomfortable. True to their charges, every other person sat awake. Boot was the only exception—he didn't sleep at all!

Around four in the morning, Dod roused from slumber, only halfway into his two-hour segment of rest, and felt his heart beating against his ribs in panic. *I smell prey!* he heard The Beast say as it climbed the wall. Dod could feel its approaching presence as clearly as he could feel his own toes, and he could sense Dark Hood's controlling power over it, driving the creature to search for Dod.

"It's coming, Boot!" cried Dod in a trembling voice. Surprisingly, Boot was already standing, holding his steel-tipped harpoon and staring at the wall of windows. Boot's long, slender weapon glimmered magically in the moonlight.

"I know," said Boot. "Sneaker's been doing circles for the last thirty seconds." Boot's voice then got louder as he announced, "Everyone, carefully wake your neighbor—we might be about to witness *The Beast*."

Commotion ensued as the sleepy, make-shift militia tried to rally. They all did their best to impress Boot with their quick responses, though the moment the creature rose into view, it was clear that Boot's forces had been expecting a pretend threat.

"Fire!" shouted Boot above the tumult of screams. Pone, Voo, and Sham, who had been selected to use the bows, struggled to draw their arrows; fear made their hands go wiggly so the notches seemed impossibly small to connect and draw. The ghastly duresser filled the front of the glass wall and gazed hungrily at the scurrying bodies. Its horrible figure blocked out a majority of the moonlight that had gently lit the room before.

I SEE THEM! boomed the hairy creature, its glowing yellow eyes bulging with impatience. Drool dripped from its gaping mouth.

Go away! thought Dod, pushing back with his mind as he clenched his sword for battle. Everyone was fleeing Boot's room except Boot and The Triplets. Dilly, Sawny, and Buck had been placed on the hall's frontline, near Pone's room, so they couldn't see what was causing the flood of escapees to join the middle section near the closet.

Glass shards exploded into the air and rained down like a torrent as the car-sized brute burst through the panes. It seemed unaffected by the arrows that struck its jet-black fur. A low-pitched roar thundered from the horrendous creature's throat like a dozen angry lions on the prowl. It stretched its massive body and showed its foot-long teeth. It was so large that its head bumped the fifteen-foot peak of the vaulted ceiling.

THE BOY FIRST! roared The Beast telepathically, turning its giant glowing eyes on Dod. It instinctively discerned the desires of its master and followed blindly. Dod swung his weapon frantically at the hairy octopus-like arms that reached for him; they were thicker than Dod's thighs and capped with razor-sharp claws. Back and forth, left and right, Dod's sword whizzed through the night air—mostly on defense. Every second was filled with life-altering decisions. The monster's countless legs seemed to have minds of their own. They moved at Dod with such vigor that before long, Dod could feel the bedroom wall against his back, telling him that death was near. He had no more room to retreat and the hall was hopelessly out of reach in the opposite direction.

"HELP!" yelled Dod hysterically, wishing to disappear.

The Triplets shot arrows from the doorway until their quivers were empty, however, their efforts did little good. The Beast kept pressing ferociously as Dod scampered side to side.

Boot saw Dod's distress and tried valiantly to cut a path to him by stabbing the twisting legs with his harpoon, but the wounds only irritated the determined duresser.

Suddenly one of The Beast's claws caught hold of Dod's leather boot and slid him across the glass-littered floor to the front of the room, right next to the gaping hole in the wall of windows. Had he slid any farther, he would have plummeted to the courtyard fifty-feet below. Mud flew from the creature's wriggling, wet body as it spun and towered over Dod.

MY FOOD! it boomed loudly in Dod's head, as clearly as it had at the docks behind the castle. The creature's smell was putrid.

But before The Beast had had time to raise Dod to its mouth, Boot leapt forward, dodging legs, and plunged the harpoon into the center of the hairy creature. "DIE!" he yelled, giving all of his strength to the strike.

A swift, powerful arm whacked Boot across his back and sent him to the floor, just below The Beast. Blood from the creature's harpoon wound dripped and fell onto Boot's face as he lay motionless.

Dazed, Dod grappled to find his sword—stars were everywhere—he couldn't see straight—the only thing he knew for sure was that the stinky, swamp-loving monster was about to eat him and his best friend. Dod's hands rummaged desperately through the glass and debris.

The Beast reeled back and roared, yet above the ear-piercing sounds that it made, the words it spoke to Dod's mind were even louder: *YOU'LL PAY FOR THIS!*

Then as quick as a bolt of lightning, Dod did something that he hadn't thought through—he didn't have time to think or plan, only time to act! Dod put a death grip on the rope that his fingers had found beneath the clutter and rolled sideways off the edge.

MY PREY! fumed The Beast, following Dod into the moonlight.

The rope hissed angrily as it rubbed against the side of the hole in the wall, though it slowed Dod's fall just enough to keep him from breaking his bones when he hit the ground.

The monstrous creature lunged after him, its blur of legs beating against the castle's stone blocks as it descended to finish Dod off. But before it reached the bushes, its racing body came to a sudden halt; it was caught like a fish on a line. The steel-tipped harpoon had done its job—each barb had bent out in a claw-like fashion, clinging tightly to the flesh of The Beast. And the metal line wasn't ordinary strength, either; it was made by the Mauj and had come from Pap's plentiful supplies.

Dod didn't waste any time in jumping to his feet and scurrying backward toward the tent city of drat soldiers. "QUICK! THE BEAST! IT'S HERE!" yelled Dod as loud as he could. "ATTACK! ATTACK! ATTACK!"

Torchlight soon emerged from a number of tents, as a flow of soldiers rushed to fight the hideous creature. They approached Dod's cries just in time to hear a crashing sound billow from Boot's room. A fifteen-foot-long beam, as wide as the stump of a fifty-year old oak, came sliding through the gaping hole in the wall and followed The Beast to the ground, its blunt end landing squarely on top of the monster's head.

"He's done it!" hollered a burly drat soldier. "Dod's killed The Beast!" The throng of men, their fires licking the early morning air, could easily see that the terrifying duresser was dead.

"Three cheers for Dod!" yelled the crowd. Many soldiers set their swords and bows to the side as they danced for joy, and like a wave of the ocean, a jubilant mob burst upon Dod and hefted him high on their shoulders.

But Dod's mind was elsewhere. He couldn't enjoy the celebration—not after seeing Boot lie motionless on the floor. Was he even alive? It wrenched at Dod's gut. He had to know.

As the troops poured in to examine the massive specimen,

Dod grabbed the rope he had pulled down the wall and shot up it as fast as his arms would carry him. He couldn't wait the walk around the castle to find out the status of his friends.

At the top, Boot's hand greeted him over the lip. "I thought you were dead," huffed Boot excitedly, wiping his messy forehead with his sleeve.

"He could have been!" scolded Buck playfully, his face glowing with relief. Everyone in Green Hall had survived the attack, even Sneaker. The curious ferret sniffed at the giant breech in the wall where the large beam had ripped out. Its exit had caused the door frame to crumble and a deep gouge in the floor.

"You did it, Boot!" said Dod happily. "You're the one that killed The Beast. That silly steel-tipped harpoon and metal line really worked."

"A little differently than I had thought," admitted Boot, surveying the damaged room.

Sneaker hopped around the mess and finally settled on his favorite branch in the untouched planter box.

Within minutes, Boot had gathered everyone into his battered bunk for a victory chant. The Coosings and Greenlings followed Boot's example and raised their fists in the air, crying loudly, "*Twistyard strength, Twistyard courage—though the night will be long and dark, Twistyard will prevail!*"

Their voices carried and echoed off the barns and outbuildings across the courtyard. Dod couldn't help wondering what Dark Hood and his helper were thinking; their pet was dead and their plan to unravel Green Hall was foiled.

At breakfast, swarms of people fought to congratulate Green Hall on their victory. And at the center of the commotion, Boot sat comfortably, eating a mountainous pile of pancakes and eggs. He was nearly full when a young Sooshling girl approached him with an overflowing tray of peppers.

"Mercy said these came for you, Boot," said the girl, blushing as she spoke.

"Thanks," said Boot. He took the unusual gift and began to look for a place to set it when Dilly snapped up a note that had been wedged between two peppers.

"I think it's perfumed," teased Dilly, sniffing at the envelope.

"Then it must be for Dod," responded Boot, giving Dod a hearty shove.

"Perfume and peppers—my favorite," chimed Dod sleepily. He wondered where Boot's energy came from.

Dilly ripped at the packet and went silent. Her face did a poor job of hiding her shock. Boot took the paper and mumbled quietly:

Cheers, Boot!

X

"Peppers are part of many traditional celebrations," explained Sawny, bursting Pone's theory that someone was mocking Boot. She reached for a bright-red one, adding, "They're my favorite, even in the morning."

Boot hopped up like he'd just discovered that his pants were on fire and pulled the tray back. "These are a little *too hot*, Sawny!" he insisted, marching the vegetables back to the kitchen.

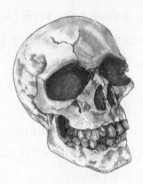

CHAPTER TWENTY-SIX

BONES

As the morning sky burst with colors of blue and orange, Dod and Buck joined Boot in riding down to Zerny's cottage to give back the steel-tipped harpoon. The metal barbs on the weapon were badly bent and needed serious work before the instrument would resemble its sleeker days; once it had been carved out of The Beast's center, it looked more like a coat rack than a spear.

"I hear ya done it," spat Skap, greeting the three as they rode up. "That's someth'n! I never'd thought ya'd be able to kill it with that thing." Skap stared at the mangled harpoon.

"Where's Joop?" asked Boot, smiling broadly.

"He's 'round back with Horsely, hear'n all 'bout yer big play this morn'n."

"Good," said Boot. "I hope it'll ease him into the idea that his stick might not look as good as it did when he lent it to me."

"Ya won it fair, Boot!" barked Skap, hopping up off the log he'd been sitting on. "If ya give it back to him—why, that's just yer way a being nice. He don't deserve noth'n—not the way he's been act'n." Skap led the group to his brother, all the while complaining about Joop.

"It's the heroes!" called Horsely the moment he saw Boot peeling back the bushes that concealed them. "I tried slapping your shoulders this morning, but I couldn't see either of you—not with all of those screaming fans."

Boot and Dod chuckled.

"Here," said Boot, doing his best to keep a straight face as he handed the destroyed harpoon to Joop. "My word's good. Thanks for lending it to me."

Horsely burst into laughter. "Don't loan things to Boot, stupid!" he choked, whacking Joop across the back. "I learned it the hard way, too."

"There's no use try'n to poke anyth'n with *this*," groaned Joop, shaking his head. "I'd make such a splash in the water—"

"Aw, you're crafty at fixing things," said Boot, grinning at Joop. "Get your hammer out and play with it for a while."

Dod's face lit up. Joop's words triggered an idea. "I think I know where The Beast's lair is," he exclaimed excitedly.

"It doesn't matter much, now," chuckled Horsely, still trying to regain his composure. Dod was amazed that Horsely was able to read his lips while laughing at the bent harpoon.

"It'd be good to check," agreed Skap. "What if the thing's laid eggs—we'd be better off mash'n a few shells then wait'n for them things to get big."

Buck's face puckered. He hadn't thought there could be more.

"Aren't you guys headed to High Gate?" asked Horsely.

"We've got an hour or so," said Boot, turning to Dod. "Is it close?"

Dod nodded. "It's just up the shoreline—the rocky outcropping where Tridacello said Dark Hood jumped into the water. Maybe The Beast was protecting Dark Hood's stolen stash."

"I'm coming," said Horsely, hobbling over to Boot's side. He put up his hand for a lift.

"Me too," added Skap and Joop. They both liked the idea of searching for stolen treasure.

"But what if there are more duressers?" groaned Buck. He was the only one who seemed hesitant, though he let Joop join him on his horse. Skap climbed aboard Shooter with Dod.

Horsely read Buck's face and broke out into more laughter. "You can use Joop's harpoon, Buck. That'll keep you safe."

"I've got one," offered Skap, pointing Dod to head for the shed. "I doubt we'll need it, but if yer nervous, we can bring it just in case."

As they reached the small clearing with the giant bird cage, Boot, Buck, and Dod all stared in astonishment. Right next to the pole-lashed edifice, Zerny was standing, hefting a couple of dead rabbits into the enclosure—the enclosure that contained four beautiful falcons.

"Zerny!" exclaimed Boot. "We've all been wondering what happened to you!"

Zerny turned and couldn't have looked more shocked. "I-I-I," stuttered Zerny, unable to speak. His face was different than Dod had ever seen it. He was clean shaven! Except for his uppity drat nose, he hardly looked like a drat. Dod had never met a clean-shaven drat. Even the little children had small white beards—girls included.

"I-it's a m-mess what's h-happened," muttered Zerny, his face turning beet red. "I-I can't b-be seen like th-this."

"He's embarrassed 'bout not hav'n his beard right now,"

explained Skap, sliding off Dod's horse to go for his harpoon. "Please keep his secret 'til he can try grow'n it back."

"B-bugs got i-in it," added Zerny, shaking his head. "T-two more weeks."

"But people think you're dead," said Boot with a furrowed brow. He couldn't understand Zerny and thought his reason sounded like a flimsy excuse. "I'll tell people you're sick—"

"No!" snapped Zerny, momentarily turning cross. "W-with Bonboo gone, Voracio w-wouldn't understand!"

"He's got a point," said Skap, returning with his steel-tipped harpoon that looked identical to the one Boot had broken. "Let him be for a few more weeks. If Voracio got word that Zerny was back, he'd be demand'n all sorts of things and wouldn't let him hide out 'til the medicine's done. It'll only be a little longer, then he can start grow'n his beard again."

"Nice birds," said Horsely, admiring the two pairs.

Zerny didn't respond. He was busy giving the boys pleading eyes.

"We'll keep it quiet," said Boot, glancing back at Dod and Buck. He was careful not to promise he wouldn't tell anyone, since he was dying to let Dilly know.

Up the shoreline, Boot quickly located the spot where Dod had referenced. The dome-shaped, rocky outcropping jutted into Lake Mauj a couple hundred yards and had a road that followed the water's edge out to the tip—a place called Fisher's Point. Because of the stone, it was impossible to tell whether anything had been sliding in and out.

"This could be it," agreed Boot, suddenly appearing less adventurous. "It's close enough to the castle and the water's really deep at the end."

Buck wouldn't let his horse enter the peninsula, so Joop hopped off and joined the others as they ventured to the tip. Dod parked his horse next to Boot's and fought butterflies in his stomach.

"I dare ya to dive in and check it out," said Joop, racing to catch up with Boot and Dod.

"That would hardly be fair, since I've already killed one duresser this morning," gloated Boot, not wanting to dip into the cool water. He was struggling to make up his mind.

"I'll let you use my harpoon," offered Skap from behind Dod, attempting to hand it to Boot.

Horsely slid off Grubber, pulled a dagger from a leather pouch around his waist, and dove into the lake as though everyone were fighting for a chance to be first.

"That boy's crazy!" muttered Skap, his eyes widening with astonishment. "He lost more than his hear'n when he was injured—lost his whole freshy-mind."

Everyone waited quietly for Horsely to surface. They were eager to know if there were any signs of The Beast's home.

A minute passed, then two, then three. By the time four minutes had expired, Boot was holding Skap's harpoon and preparing for the worst, while Dod and the others were exiting the peninsula, retreating to Buck's side.

"There's gotta be another monster," cried Skap, wearing a squeamish face. "The lug's eat'n Horsely right now—chomp'n his bones to mush. No one holds their breath for that long."

"How fast do you think they can run?" asked Buck, pale as a ghost. He nudged his horse to fall back a little more, to give him a larger head start.

Six minutes passed, then seven.

"He's dead, Boot!" yelled Buck impatiently. "Come on—let's go tell the soldiers, before we're next."

"No—that's not it," hollered Boot confidently, sliding off his horse. "I think I can see a bit of light."

Dod gingerly inched his horse back onto the peninsula and made his way to the tip. "What's he doing?" asked Dod apprehensively.

Boot looked at Dod cleverly. "Maybe he's found Dark Hood's stash—"

"Bonboo's pure-sight diamonds?" exploded Dod, thinking of how desperately Twistyard needed them.

"Could be," said Boot, glancing up and down the shoreline. "Didn't Dark Hood jump in the water with them?"

Dod nodded. "That's what Tridacello said."

"Then I'll go take a look," responded Boot, clutching the harpoon as he jumped into the water. Dod hesitantly watched Boot swim toward the faint light and disappear behind a cluster of rocks.

"He's crazy!" yelled Buck, whose face now grew less scared and more ill. Losing Horsely was one thing, but having his brother be eaten by a duresser was entirely a different kind of horrible.

Dod listened closely. He could hear the water lapping against the nooks in the rocks and the cries of a few yurflos. It was a beautiful morning.

Within a minute, Boot burst to the surface with good news. "No more pets, just an empty, underwater cave. You've got to come and take a look. The lair's truly amazing!"

"In the dark?" croaked Buck, still unconvinced that it was vacant.

"No. Horsely's got a couple of Bly's glowing rocks around his neck. You can see everything just fine."

Dod slipped into the chilly water and joined Boot, as did Joop and Skap, but Buck stayed back to keep an eye on the horses.

Twelve feet below the surface, a gaping hole opened up to an underwater cavern. Fish of all sizes swarmed the waters, feasting on the last bits of matter that clung to mountainous piles of bones. As Dod passed the eerie heaps, he felt sick. He couldn't believe the duresser had consumed enough flesh to leave the ghastly graveyard of crushed skeletons. And though many of the remains were clearly from horses and other large animals, some of the skulls, hands, and feet were undeniably human.

"What do you think?" bellowed Horsely, the moment Boot and Dod surfaced for air. Horsely stood on an island in the middle of the giant cave, his glowing rocks illuminating the scene.

"Quite a hide-out!" admitted Boot excitedly, ignoring the thirty feet of water below them, as though he hadn't noticed the labyrinth of bones. Dod didn't say a word. The grotto felt like they were in the mouth of a huge monster, with stalactite teeth looming threateningly from the vaulted ceiling and volcano-like piles of bones approaching from the watery floor.

"Any sign a eggs?" asked Skap the moment he popped up for air.

"What?" called Horsely, his voice echoing ominously off the rock walls. He couldn't see Skap's lips well enough to read them.

"He's just wondering whether you've found any eggs," said Boot, joining Horsely on the island.

"Not a one," responded Horsely.

The cave smelled like a poorly-maintained pet shop. The muggy air was wet and warm, causing large drops of water to drip from the blackened stalactites.

"I'd have never guessed this was here," marveled Boot,

gazing about the cavern. "Buck and I have fished off this point for years, and we've climbed up the dome dozens of times."

"You think you have," huffed Horsely, "this is practically in my backyard. Stallio's hold is only a stone's throw up the shore. I pass this place every day on the way to the castle barns."

"That's true," taunted Boot playfully. "There's absolutely *no* excuse for why *you* didn't know about this."

Joop was the last one to emerge from the water, dreading the circumstance like a wet cat. "Dern thing's been busy eat'n stuff, hasn't it?" he muttered, obviously bothered by the underwater display of remains. "It's no wonder we' been miss'n livestock. That duresser had an itch for flesh, didn' it?"

"I'd say!" agreed Horsely heartily. "There's quite a collection of bones in the water."

Dod walked the small island, hoping he'd find a pocket of Dark Hood's loot. But there wasn't much to see. The loose rocks had all been knocked off of the playground-sized platform, assumedly by The Beast, leaving a smooth, polished stone floor with few options for concealing anything. And water surrounded the island for hundreds of feet in every direction. If treasures were in the cave, they were submerged, hidden somewhere in the graveyard like a forgotten shipwreck.

"At least there aren't any eggs," mumbled Dod, approaching Boot.

"Nope—there's not much of anything," said Boot, and then reading the disappointment on Dod's face, added, "but there still could be a cache somewhere in here—down there." Boot pointed at the murky depths.

"Did he really expect to find the diamonds?" mocked Horsely

in a taunting sort of voice. He began to push a chuckle as he turned to Dod. "Did the monster tell you he'd put them here?"

Joop and Skap were all ears, so Horsely jumped in to explain how Dod thought he could talk with The Beast.

"Sure. I talk with critters, too," barked Joop, joining the fun. "My whip says all sorts of things to 'em—"

"It's a mayler's best friend," agreed Horsely.

Joop grinned cruelly at Boot. "Everyone knows you've got to whip hard—"

"We're leaving," said Boot curtly. "High Gate's calling. Dod and I have The Golden Swot to win." Boot didn't wait for the others to continue their ribbing. It bugged him when they teased Dod, and he didn't like Joop insinuating that he, Boot, was poor at training animals just because he didn't cruelly beat them into subjection.

As soon as the two boys made it to their horses, Boot urged them to ride away without the others. "Maybe walking back home with their shoes and clothes sloshing will teach them a bit of courtesy," said Boot, blowing steam.

"Joop and Skap?" smiled Buck, clearly glad to be going. "I doubt it—they were born jagged as the blade of a saw."

In the end, it was good they left when they did. After changing into dry clothes, they barely made it to their saddles in time to exit with the High Gate-bound procession. And unlike other times, Dilly didn't plan on bolting up Coyote Trail—not with all of Green Hall trotting with her, the younger Greenlings included. Plus, she liked socializing with the others who were leaving Twistyard. Many of them were important people. But despite Commendus's attempts to nudge her otherwise, she didn't even give the time of day to Con, who seemed perfectly entertained by a dozen swooning girls who rode near him.

At Discommo Manor, bugs were as thick as they ever were, testifying to the fact that the lake was as fishless and larva filled as before. The approach to the castle was nearly unbearable. One biting fly, as big as a thumb, took such a chunk out of Buck's arm that the wound bled for fifteen minutes. And Ingrid only survived by wearing a netting she had fortuitously begged from Youk. Dilly and Sawny both covered their heads with jackets and peeked out of small holes to see where they were going and still screamed half the way up the drive. Even Sneaker refused to ride in the open and bolted down Boot's shirt for protection.

Commendus insisted that the problem was soon to be solved—he was certain of it—but his carriage hugged the road's edge as far from the water as it could, not to mention his driver wore a Redy-Alert-Band on each wrist, which signs seemed to indicate that the diasserpentous dilemma was still an issue.

Dilly and Sawny were both emotionally rattled for hours at the palace after refreshing their memories of the blackened acres where once had stood the majestic Capitol Building—the last and greatest creation their grandfather and father had built together before their grandfather's passing.

"At least they've already started reconstruction," said Buck sympathetically, sprawling across a leather couch. "I haven't ever seen that many Huffer Elephants working on one project. People around here mean business—they'll get it back up before you know it."

"They're just tearing it out," complained Dilly.

"That's the first step," assured Boot sleepily. His night

without rest was beginning to pull him down as the afternoon limped toward dinner.

Dod had been very impressed with the hustling at the burn site. Elephants, five times the regular size of a grown bull African Elephant, were pulling and pushing all sorts of crafty machines, clearing the charred debris and digging out the ruined foundations.

"When's dinner?" interrupted Pone, throwing his weight across Buck's legs. "With all the cows Commendus had out front today, I'm expecting steak."

"I think it wouldn't hurt you to miss a meal or two," groaned Buck, squirming to free himself.

Green Hall had been given excellent accommodations on the twelfth floor—the entire spacious west wing—which included a posh recreation room and twelve separate suites.

"Didn't we just eat lunch?" asked Sawny, still full from the feast that had been waiting for them when they arrived.

"There's always room for more," chanted Pone, trying to liven the bunch. "I'm stocking up—gaining strength for the big game." He was in great spirits, and his energy was contagious enough to rouse Boot out of a near-napping state.

"Did you see the Lairrington Longs?" prodded Buck, his eyes lighting up. "They don't have any girls on their team—just big, strapping men."

"With bushy eyebrows," blurted Toos, hustling over the moment he heard any talk of Bollirse. "I bet they have to comb them down with water."

"They should shave them," added Voo, playing a round of Fifteen Rocks with Sham.

"They'll lose," sighed Boot confidently, glancing at Dilly. "No girls—no win." Dilly and Sawny both smiled.

"Like that's the reason we're heading to victory," jeered Pone playfully, rising to his feet and striking a Mr. Atlas pose.

"And where were your big muscles during the final minutes of our game against the Raging Billies?" poked Dilly.

Dod sat up straight. "Why didn't they show up today?"

"Because we won—they cheated," said Toos defensively.

"I know," agreed Dod, "but there's no way that the news could have traveled fast enough to have prevented them from coming."

"They weren't invited to the pre-game stuff," said Sawny. "There's no money in billies prepping their game. Who'd turn out to their practices? When I was talking with Dr. Shelderhig and Newmi at lunch, they said they felt bad for the messengers that were being sent to bring the billies news of the loss. Nearly all billies are being banned from High Gate for the next month as a precaution against retaliation."

"Ouch," said Buck, smiling as he thought of them being punished for ruining his match at Carsigo and destroying his favorite swot.

"As far as I can tell," added Sawny, "I think Commendus has been desperately looking for a way to keep them out—ever since the fire. Anyway, it's safe to assume that Sawb didn't have to say much before Commendus and his associates were more than willing to lend their weight in convincing the Bollirse Rules Board of our rightful win."

"Figures," said Pone. "It's not like Sawb would ever go too far to help us out."

"But we're in the game!" blurted Toos excitedly. "My dad's gonna be bragging about this for ages."

"If you play," said Boot, turning surprisingly serious. "I've waited thirty-three years at Twistyard to win The Golden Swot, so I'm planning on running the most strenuous practice days anyone's ever held—and I'm warning you now, I will choose the best-prepared eighteen players, no matter whose feelings get hurt."

"Good," choked Toos, gulping hard. "I'll prove my spot."

"Me too," said Pone, not as terrorized by the prospect. He knew he was one of the finest players Green Hall had ever seen.

"That means we get up early tomorrow," continued Boot, raising his voice so everyone could hear. "They've scheduled us in the mornings, starting at ten o'clock, but no one's going to stop us if we're there by six."

Dilly nodded in agreement, along with many of the others. Green Hall had annually watched Raul Hall do their magic and had wished to be given a shot at The Golden Swot.

"No late nights," added Boot, glancing at Pone, Voo, and Sham. "No partying, no games, and no talking after nine-thirty." Boot turned to Sawny. "And no stargazing, either. Shelderhig can show you the constellations on some other visit. We need to focus all of our attention on winning."

The following week was so filled with Bollirse that even Dod's dreams were about the game. All of Green Hall participated. And thousands of fans flocked daily to Champion Stadium and paid well to have a pre-game peek at the underdogs as they practiced. By the time Green Hall's eighteen players lined up to tip heads with the Lairrington Longs, Dod and the others were so used to the crowds that they hardly noticed the one-hundred-thousand spectators who had packed the arena to see the match.

Sammywoo had a front-row spot and waved his swot

happily, with Dari and Valerie on one side and Youk and Saluci on the other. Neadrou sat next to Sabbella, Commendus, and Con. And Bonboo came to the games with Chikada and the rest of Dilly's family. Dilly and Sawny looked like their mother, as did Dilly's two younger sisters who had come to cheer for Green Hall, and Dilly's three younger brothers looked like Chikada.

Terro was in the stands, just as he had promised, with Sawb and the others from Raul Hall surrounding him. Tonnis and Juny were sitting on the outskirts of the group, with Ingrid faithfully sticking to Juny's side.

Dod approached the towering Lairrington Longs and was grateful Bowy had made it in time to play on Twistyard's team. Bowy's creative tactics had been the critical key to fighting well against the Raging Billies at Carsigo.

Each Lairrington Long was inches and pounds more than the biggest of Green Hall's members, and their fancy uniforms flaunted that they had plenty of money behind their program.

"Good luck," repeated the men robotically as they nodded in line. And once the game began, Twistyard needed all the luck they could get. The Lairrington Longs were so expert at Bollirse that Dod quickly suspected Terro had paid them to lose for the past three years against Raul Hall.

"Hold your lines!" yelled Boot, desperately pleading with his teammates to keep their positions. The opposing squad of warriors hopped the little wall and moved upon Twistyard's turf with such force that it was impossible for anyone to keep Boot's orders. Three Coosings went up the rope ladder before the assault had ended. And a string of bots were dislodged, too, suggesting the Lairrington Longs had decided that this year was the year they weren't going home empty-handed.

Boot, Buck, and Bowy had other plans. The threesome pushed at the Lairrington Longs and managed to enter enemy territory for a few minutes before a wave of defenders drove them out.

Back and forth, back and forth—the two teams struggled for an hour to gain advantage over the other. Dod fought to make a difference. It was hard. He felt like an amateur playing against professionals. Each globe he blocked struck as though it had been shot from a gun. The best edge that the Coosings had was their ability to hide behind the wooden posts.

"I'm not waiting to get slaughtered," burst Dilly, unable to contain her frustration. Boot had placed her and Sawny in the backfield, and Dod had momentarily retreated to take a breather near them. "Our best defense of the rear would be a decent offense," groaned Dilly, noticing how many of Twistyard's bots were already down. Only a few of them remained in position on top of the thirteen-foot posts.

"But what about Boot's orders—" Sawny began to say when a globe nearly clocked her across the head.

"These Lairrington Longs are pushing our line way more than we're pushing theirs," responded Dilly. "They'll end this game soon if we don't fight back. Why doesn't anyone do something?"

Dod surveyed the scene. Bowy had begun a campaign of deep hits, hoping to dislodge all of the enemy's cone-like bots, while Boot and Buck defended him against assault and Toos ran around gathering globes for them to use. The air smelled fresh, and the late-morning sun was soft and warm. It was a perfect day to win.

"I'll fill in for you back here," offered Dod, huffing to catch his breath. "With our head-guards on, Boot won't know the difference. He'll think you're me."

Dilly liked the idea and was gone in a flash. She bolted straight for the center and hopped the three-foot wall without hesitation. But she wasn't alone; Pone, Voo, and Sham thought she was Dod and followed. The play was a powerful push that brought down two Lairrington Longs before they were driven back.

"Not bad," said Sawny, watching nervously. She knew that Boot would be mad if Dilly tanked the game after breaking orders.

Suddenly, Dod felt an opportunity. He sensed Dilly would press forward again and all eyes would be on her assault, which would leave one far side less noticed.

Up the edge Dod crept, slipping behind poles until he was positioned at the front, and then he waited patiently. He didn't throw or hit any globes; instead, he worked on becoming invisible—by taking off his bright-orange jersey. Underneath, he wore a dark-green shirt.

Technically, Bollirse regulations didn't require that teams wear uniforms of any kind, but customarily people did to keep their attacks coordinated and to identify their enemies quicker.

In time, Dilly made a risky, second press with five others and, just as Dod had suspected, everyone was so focused on repelling Dilly's approach that they didn't even notice Dod's stealthy dash into enemy territory.

The first opponent Dod passed was a burly man, fifteen feet away, whose eyes were fixed on the globes he kept hurling toward Dilly's contingent. Dod almost plunked him in the back, to send him out of the game, when a better idea emerged. He'd wait until he was deeper and try surprising two at the same time.

Eventually, Dod found himself against the back wall of the

Lairrington Longs' half of the field, completely undetected. It was remarkable. And since Bowy's aim at the distant bots was beginning to pose a real threat, the Lairrington Long rear forces had moved up as the team prepared to rush Twistyard's frontline.

Dod felt like a hidden lion, staring at his prey, preparing to strike. He greedily set his eyes on the center crew that rarely turned to look behind them. Could he take down two or more? The biggest challenge he had was figuring out how to deliver as many globes as possible before being detected. It was a tricky puzzle since Dod knew that the referees often froze the game momentarily while ejecting players, and if that happened, the rest of his opponents would have time to change their plans and redirect some of their attention to him.

"I'm all in!" muttered Dod to himself, trying to muster his courage. He quietly set his swot, shield, and jung on the ground and prepared for the ambush by loading his shirt with a pile of globes. He felt like a toddler trying to gather Easter eggs as he held the balls close with his left arm. A light breeze blew against his bare midriff. With ammunition near his throwing hand, he figured he'd be able to tag at least two before someone would turn and fire back.

When the moment came, Dod found his legs racing, his arm throwing, and his mind a blur. It all happened so quickly. Before the first globe had hit the back of one man, Dod was already launching another globe. And in the confusion, the Lairrington Longs thought they were being passed globes by their own players, so no one jumped to respond as they should have. It was wild. Dod rushed behind the line of men and nailed eight people before the referees froze the game to determine what was going on.

One referee angrily grabbed Dod by his neck padding and began dragging him from the field, for he was certain Dod was a fan who had illicitly joined the fray; but the head judge, who had watched the whole thing from above, called the ruling a sham, insisting that Dod was in fact a Green Coosing who had simply decided to take his uniform off.

The turn of events brought a rumble from the crowd that was deafening. Everyone rose to their feet and clapped as the eight players were escorted off the field and Dod was repositioned, back where he had been before.

Needless to say, the next sixty seconds of the game were the last. The moment play resumed, most of the Coosings rushed the frontline, taking advantage of the Lairrington Longs' poor arrangement, and fitly finished their opponents off. It didn't matter that six Coosing went down in the fight—plenty remained to claim victory for Twistyard!

SHE'S GONE

After the Bollirse win, Champion Stadium turned into a raging celebration party that lasted all afternoon and into the night with music, food, performances, and lots of dancing. The commemoration of the hundred-and-fiftieth Golden Swot Bollirse game being held in Champion Stadium was an event to remember, and most of the crowd was pleased to see that the local favorites came out victorious, despite their poor odds.

"I can't believe we really won," said Toos for the hundredth time as the Green Coosings and Greenlings wearily entered their special quarters in Commendus's palace. The day had been long and wonderful, and everyone was exhausted.

"Dod was marvelous," said Donshi sleepily, her eyes glazed with a growing crush. She looked at Dod, who blushed.

"Yeah, that was something," mumbled Pone, stretching his fingers. His hand ached from signing autographs.

"No one makes a peep 'til at least nine," begged Boot.

"Or noon," added Buck.

"We'll be on our way back to Twistyard before noon,"

affirmed Dilly. "Don't forget about tomorrow night's Dance Delight. A lot of people have been working hard to make the evening a memorable experience."

"Right," said Toos excitedly. He felt his value on the dance floor had gone up substantially with the win.

"Two nights in a row," said Pone, emptying his pockets and stuffing the last of his cookies into his mouth. "I love dances."

"Good," said Sawny, grinning tiredly. Then, fearing she'd said too much with her eyes, she quickly turned to Boot and added, "And where's Bowy? I expect a dance out of each of you tomorrow night."

"He's visiting some friends of ours here in High Gate," responded Boot, "but don't worry, he's planning on returning to Twistyard with us—for a stopover anyway. I'm sure you'll get your dance." Boot smiled at Sawny, knowing full well that she secretly fancied Pone.

Within a matter of minutes, the wing went silent. It was past midnight and everyone had long since spent their energy. Dod was asleep the moment his head hit his pillow, however, he didn't stay asleep. About thirty minutes into a delightful dream about being the hero who'd conquered The Beast and single-handedly taken down nearly half of the Lairrington Longs, a masked figured emerged. It was Dark Hood, and he was laughing at Dod.

"I know you!" muttered Dod, recognizing the villain. Yet once he was startled awake, he couldn't remember.

"Dod," whispered Dilly. She stood over him and was shaking his bed.

"What?" grumbled Dod. As he opened his eyes, he saw

Boot and Buck were beside her, and all three of them wore tired, worried looks.

"Sawny's gone," whispered Dilly.

Dod sat up and felt a sudden burst of panic. He instantly recalled seeing Dark Hood and his helper hefting a large gunnysack in his dream.

"Did she say anything to you?" asked Buck.

Dod shook his head, but his face gave away that he was holding back.

"Do you have any idea where she could be?" begged Dilly, knitting her eyebrows with concern. "We were just laying down—and then I thought I heard her slip out to the bathroom—and now she's gone!"

"We'll find her," assured Boot, putting his arm around Dilly. "Don't worry. She's probably so tired that she took a wrong turn."

"But Boot—the note—the one from X," sobbed Dilly. "It promised one of us would die—and since they missed their mark at Twistyard—"

"She's just sleepwalking!" insisted Boot firmly, though the muscles in his neck were tensing up and fatigue had fled his face. He looked ready to throw someone the way he'd thrown Joop.

"Dark Hood might have her," said Dod hesitantly. "I mean—I don't know—I just—"

"We'll find her!" assured Boot, rushing to slip his shoes on. Dod and Buck quickly did the same, not bothering to change out of their pajamas.

"Wake up Pone and the other Coosings," said Boot to Dilly, his tone commanding like a general. "We'll tear this place apart if we have to—but I promise you this, we will find Sawny!"

Dod, Boot, and Buck split up and began a speedy search

of logical places, while Dilly worked to rally more people for the hunt.

The first chance Dod got, he took Boot aside and whispered, "I think Dark Hood has her—he's taken her away, somewhere outside."

"What do you know?" demanded Boot firmly, his teeth on edge and his eyes narrowing. He spoke quietly, making sure no one else heard him.

"I don't know anything for sure," explained Dod. "I just had a dream—Dark Hood and his helper were outside—laughing at me—and I think they had Sawny."

"Did you talk with anyone?" asked Boot.

"Huh?"

"Did anyone mention Sawny—maybe someone from back at Twistyard—Jibb or Youk or Tonnis?" Boot's voice pressed at Dod like frantic fingers. "Did Voracio say anything? You can trust me, Dod."

"What?" choked Dod, feeling like he was suddenly on trial. "It was just a dream—"

"I know, but—" Boot trailed off, weighing things in his mind. He looked torn, as though he were unable to reach a verdict.

"Let's go outside and check for her," begged Dod, beginning to feel a crumpled knot of hot emotion building in his gut: it was a mixture of frustration, fear, and anger. Sawny was still breathing, somewhere outside in the wind—Dod could feel the wind.

"Pone thinks he knows where she is," said Dilly, breaking into their conversation with a heaping sigh of relief. "He saw her a few minutes ago, while he was coming back from the restroom. She asked him if he knew where to find a spare blanket."

"Oh," said Boot, suddenly calming. "That's good."

Dod looked around and wanted to scream. The few Coosings who had risen at Dilly's request were headed back to bed, satisfied that Sawny was going to return on her own. And none of them appeared the slightest bit concerned about Dark Hood. It was maddening.

"We've got to check outside!" urged Dod, unable to explain how pressed he felt.

"Right," said Dilly. "Let's see if we can find Sawny in the outer hall."

"No!" blared Dod, losing his cool. "Sawny's left the castle—she's in the wind—and Dark Hood's out there with his little helper—I can feel him."

"What?" gasped Dilly. Her look of alarm began to reappear before Boot settled her down.

"We'll check everywhere," said Boot, leading Dilly and Dod out of Green Hall's accommodations.

The castle corridors were dimly lit by occasional, smokeless candles. Sawny was nowhere in sight. A faint sound of laughter could be heard coming from the other side of the twelfth floor, where Sawb and his associates from Raul were spending the night—and they weren't asleep.

Dilly and Boot jogged toward the noise, hoping Sawny would be there, while Dod began his climb down the spiral staircase, trusting they'd soon follow. He didn't want to see Dark Hood on his own, and he hoped his dreams were just dreams; nevertheless, the driving, nagging, pushing feelings inside wouldn't let him slow down—not until he had smelled the night air and seen with his own two eyes that Sawny wasn't stuffed in a burlap sack and on her way to someplace bad.

The beating of Dod's feet against the ground echoed as he

entered the main-floor corridors. By the time Dod reached the mudroom, heading toward the doors that led to the barns, he was huffing and puffing. The whole circumstance seemed like a dream. The long shadows played tricks with his tired eyes, making him feel like danger was all around him.

"Maybe the Ankle Weed is going to my head," mumbled Dod. He staggered to the exit and looked out a small window. The trees were tipping steadily from a strong breeze. It wasn't a cold winter wind, like the kind he was accustomed to in Utah, but the air had a chill that sent goosebumps up his arms. Fortunately, an old leather jacket was draped over a nearby stool, and it fit nicely.

It's nothing, thought Dod, trying to calm his nerves. *I'm just going on a walk.* He grabbed for the door handle and froze. His eyes were playing tricks on him—he knew it—the sight was impossible!

Through the mudroom window, Dod saw two cloaked men dashing from the biggest barn. They were heading toward the lake. And in the glistening, soft moonlight, Dod could clearly see the burlap bag of his nightmares slung over the larger-man's shoulder, and it was weighed down with a heaping load.

No! thought Dod. *It can't be!* He wanted to run back to the stairs to make sure Dilly and Boot were on their way down, and he wanted to yell for troops to chase after the mysterious men, and he wanted to run and hide somewhere from Dark Hood's unstoppable crimson blade. But the men were running. They'd disappear into the night and no one would find where they'd gone—and worst of all, if they had Sawny, she'd be lost forever.

"I'm coming," whispered Dod, forcing himself to rush into the blustery outdoors. "Stick to the shadows. Stay hidden. I just have to follow them."

Dod muttered to himself as he chased after the cloaked men. He kept far enough back to go unnoticed and hoped they would stop at an outbuilding so he could fetch soldiers to apprehend them. Unfortunately, when they entered the front courtyard, they left the drive strip and shot toward the lake, following the tight trail that wound to the side of the enormous, rock waterfall.

Dod cringed. He didn't want to dip into the thick foliage. Dark Hood could easily ambush him—or worse still—a diasserpentous!

As though his legs had minds of their own, Dod kept running. He passed the freshly-painted benches and remembered following the old man to the crashing water—and he remembered the ominous feelings he had felt. Into the thicket he went. The sound of crickets and bugs was nearly as loud as the falls, though the deeper he pressed, the more the thunder of the splashing torrents grew. His heart beat in his chest with horrid anticipation. Confrontation was coming. He knew it. And he didn't have anything to fight with. He was completely vulnerable. No sword, no knife—not even a stick.

But his legs kept running. If the men threw Sawny into the thrashing water, she'd die in the burlap sack, and he wasn't going to let that happen—not without doing everything he could to stop it.

Finally, he burst from a tight cluster of growth and emerged at the lakeside. The men were gone. They had disappeared. Dod scanned the grassy shore for any signs of the cloaked villains, then looked to the bubbling water.

Nothing moved.

"Where is she?" demanded Dod. No one could hear. Dod couldn't even hear his own voice because of the rumbling waves. Lightning flashed across the horizon, announcing the approaching storm that would soon cover the star-lit sky with clouds. A gust of wind blew violently in Dod's face, soaking him with spray from the falls.

"WHERE IS SHE?" yelled Dod, feeling a sudden burst of vigor. He had led his team to victory against the Lairrington Longs. He had come face-to-face with The Beast and had helped Boot kill it. He had escaped Driaxom and delivered Terro with him. And he had faced The Dread and won. Why not stand against the raging wind and see the depths of Dark Hood's evil eyes? Good would prevail. After all, he was Pap's grandson!

Suddenly, Dod spun around and raced along the fake stone mountain, searching in the moonlight for a secret door. He knew there had to be one. The seasoned painter had sent his messy boys to clean up in the pump room—the very place where Dark Hood was now likely hiding. Dod studied the rocks and his feelings as he worked his way along the wall.

And there it was—a little splotch of paint—a thumb print that gave away the crooked-rock lever and the hidden entrance. Dod didn't even think before rushing in, though as the heavy stone door clicked closed behind him, a wave of concern crossed his mind. He turned and slid his hands up and down in the darkness—there had to be a handle—some way to get the passage open, so he and Sawny could escape. As his eyes adjusted to the faint light, he realized to his horror that the handle had been ripped off and that the door required a metal stick of some kind to jam into the hole in order to open the passage. He was stuck.

"You promised you would send word to me!" said a muffled voice. Dod inched his way down the stone steps, one at a time.

"I did, sir," begged another man.

"Don't lie to me, Murdore!" barked the strong, familiar voice of Dark Hood. "I gave you a chance—let you live—even after your incalculable blunder—and now look—this is how you repay me?"

Dod shivered. He couldn't believe what he was hearing—or more particularly, *who* he was hearing!

"I promise, sir," continued the gruff voice of Murdore, "I sent word by the pigeon you supplied. Fifteen men waited seven days ago at Fisher, just as you wanted. They sat with open ears and eager hands, sir. I remained with them for the papers you were to supply, so we could meet here at the big barn. It's not like they can stroll into High Gate on *their* connections—"

"Lies!" raged Dark Hood.

Dod crept a few more steps and saw how the passage opened up into a manmade cave, where water consumed most of the visible floor. An eerie, dim light filled the cavern—someone had glowing rocks.

"They're all lies! I should kill you right now!" roared Dark Hood.

"No," begged Murdore, groveling as much as he could. "I'm truthful, sir. Fifteen islands of men are docked two days out to sea—ninety-two dashers of valiant warriors. Your plan *was* working, sir. They rallied around me to join with you. They're furious about the destroyed islands. It was wise of you, and so merciful, that you chose to burn the alternates instead of us."

"And now?" asked Dark Hood. Dod could hear the clank of a sword leaving its sheath. He desperately wanted to glimpse Dark Hood and know for sure if the voice matched the man, and he wondered what Murdore looked like.

"They're angry, sir," responded Murdore. "I promised their

leaders they'd meet you, but rather than papers, they got word that the Raging Billies had been shut out of High Gate. It ruined your plan, sir! We can't attack now."

"You simple-minded fool!" scoffed Dark Hood. "Are they angry?"

"Aye," muttered Murdore.

"Do they like their brave men cast from the league as cheaters?"

"No, sir."

"Does it feel nice to have all of High Gate raise arms against you—banning your people from entry for an entire month?"

"No, sir."

"Then good! Their anger will serve me well!" Dark Hood rustled as he paced the floor, or so it sounded to Dod, who was thinking of turning the corner but didn't dare for fear of being seen. He kept listening for Sawny.

"I had no choice but to change plans," continued Dark Hood, his arrogant voice filling the damp air. "When you went silent on me, what was I to do? Your pigeon never came! So I moved a mountain, and Twistyard took your wretched team's place."

"I see—" began Murdore, catching a glimpse of Dark Hood's plan, or so he pretended in order to save his own skin.

"We'll wait a little longer, while you triple your numbers for me—"

"Triple?" gasped Murdore in shock. "I've already got over a hundred-thousand men!"

"Or I could kill you now," offered Dark Hood. "When *your* people let *my* captives go, they cost me years of work."

"I'm sorry, sir—"

"Do you know how hard it is to gain complete leverage over a representative?"

"Please, sir—"

"Twenty-two men! You made me kill twenty-two valuable men. And I had to do it quickly, too, before they got word of your incompetence. Dead family members don't keep votes in line—they create turncoat martyrs, you pathetic fool!"

"I'll work toward triple—" conceded Murdore quickly.

"And you'll take care of one more problem," said Dark Hood, breathing deeply like he was fighting to contain his anger. "Dungo must die!"

"But sir, he's in Driaxom. Have him killed there."

"He *was* in Driaxom—and we tried—but a trifle tipped things in the wrong direction. He's likely sailing the seas now, searching for his mother and sisters."

Murdore remained silent, except for a few groans. It was preposterous that anyone had escaped Driaxom.

"Would you rather I put the word out that you personally killed his family?" asked Dark Hood. "They were all he had to live for—and now that they're gone, there's no telling what he'd do to you—especially while shackled with an Ankle Weed."

"Please, sir—we'll take care of him," begged Murdore. "We billies fear nothing." His voice betrayed his bravery.

A crashing sound followed and the cave exploded with light. "Have your men prepare as much tarjuice as they can—we'll need all of it to burn High Gate to the ground."

"But wouldn't you prefer saving the buildings?" asked Murdore sheepishly. "We billies could possibly—"

"Not while The Lost City remains hidden beneath them!" growled Dark Hood. "I know it's close. I feel it! And it has something of mine—something I need before it's too late—something that's more valuable than ten High Gates filled with gold! Raise your army—have the soldiers ready in three months....And stop looking so pathetic! I'll send one of my assistants to Fisher with jewels to buy the noble billies' loyalty. But if you cross me—mark my words, Murdore—every last billie will die!"

"You're so kind and generous, sir," replied Murdore in a beaten voice.

Dod bent down and carefully peeked around the corner, eager to see his enemies and hopeful that Sawny was still alive. Unfortunately, his tired, wobbly legs slipped off the last step, and he found himself dangerously exposed.

"Dod," snapped Dark Hood, spinning around with his crimson blade in hand. A six-foot inferno rose from the stone floor, lighting the villain's surroundings like the sun at noonday. "I've been wondering when we would meet again. It's so nice to see you've dressed up for the occasion." Dark Hood grinned mockingly and pointed his weapon toward Dod's pajamas and borrowed jacket. His face was half concealed by a gruesome mask, but Dod recognized him, just as he'd recognized his voice.

"You can't fool me!" spat Dod, rising to his feet. "You're The Dread—"

"Such a smart boy," chuckled Sirlonk, taking his mask off. He threw it at Murdore, who was kneeling on the ground behind him, capeless and weaponless, his scar-pocked face glowering menacingly at Dod. "You should be the one wearing a cover, Murdore," added Sirlonk. "You scare the boy with your ugliness."

A silent, shrouded man stood behind Murdore, holding a sword. It was Dark Hood's helper—or at least one of them. He looked like he had the same build as the man who had aided Dark Hood in raiding Green Hall, and around his waist he wore Dilly's special belt from Miz—or was it Pap's? Sirlonk wore an identical belt.

"You're the ugliest one in the room," said Dod, staring at Sirlonk. "And that's to say nothing of what lies within you!"

"Very funny, *boy*," grumbled Sirlonk, taking three steps toward Dod. He put his foot on a crate, whereupon was placed Murdore's sword, and added, "Those are brave words coming from an unarmed fool."

"Do you really think I'd approach you without a weapon?" bluffed Dod, shoving his hands into his jacket pockets. They were empty except for a few clumps of gooey mud. Dod hurriedly glanced around the room for Sawny. The burlap bag was out of sight.

"I think you're as imprudent and impulsive as your grandfather," mocked Sirlonk, his evil eyes gleaming with delight. "My guess is that you couldn't keep yourself from stupidly, blindly wandering after us....We'll call it curiosity."

Dod made fists in his pockets and rammed them forward, pretending to be pointing something at the men. "I'll give you to the count of four to hand Sawny over," ordered Dod boldly. "If you don't—I'll have no choice but to unleash my secret weapon, and you'll all die!"

Sirlonk's eyes widened with curiosity. "I'm so scared," he scoffed, reading Dod's bluff. "Perhaps before you kill us, you'll let me show you my puppies." Sirlonk waved his hand in the air and his assistant moved into the corner and began laboring at a wheel. It was as if the whole stone wall were sliding open, revealing a giant hidden chamber.

FOOD! FOOD! FOOD! rumbled into Dod's mind. He could hear the chanting chorus of hundreds of creatures, their thoughts screeching into the air as The Beast had done.

"Behold my masterpiece, Dod!" shouted The Dread, waving his sword toward the opening that was flooded with cat-sized duressers. "You found my pet's lair a little too late, my boy. She's given me an army. And the lake's full of bugs, perfect feed for my hungry babies. And as you've seen, the lawns are brimming with cattle to fatten them on. Duressers grow so quickly, keeping them happy is a hard job."

"The diasserpentouses will eat them!" spat Dod defiantly, straining to contain his own mind amidst the chaos that swirled the air. *FOOD! FOOD! FOOD!* chanted the beasts, pouring out of the chamber; their claws and teeth hungered for action.

"Hardly," said Sirlonk, looking down his nose at Dod. "Who do you think planted the snakes in the lake? Miz? I don't think so. I've been protecting them while they've done their job, and now that the water is clean of trouble, I'll stop breaking the clumsy doctor's snares and let the poor chap have two trophies to brag about."

ATTACK! thought Dod, using his mind to turn the hungry mob against Sirlonk. The wriggling sea of black fur moved in The Dread's direction.

WAIT! ordered Sirlonk, shouting at the beasts with his thoughts. He waved his gloved hand in the air, like a magician, and their movements stopped. Then turning to Dod he spoke carefully, "You're Humberrone's son, aren't you?"

"What?" choked Dod, feeling a surge of emotions. His eyes had just found the burlap sac. It was lying on the floor in the chamber, covered in muck and blood and bones. He was too late!

"You've got your father's gift," said Sirlonk enviously. "You'd be wonderful with one of these around your waist." He pointed at his beautiful Soosh Mayler Belt. "We could obtain the secrets together, Dod. Think of it! You…and me…and Dilly."

Dod's blood was boiling. His glare was on the gruesome skull that occupied much of Murdore's hilt. He couldn't hear Sirlonk's words through the blur of anger that filled his mind. The Dread had killed Sawny and acted like it was nothing—he wouldn't even address it.

"You're a heartless, spineless, gutless pile of vomit!" raged Dod, his eyes tearing with frustration. And then he snapped. For a moment he hardly knew what he was doing, and he didn't care whether he lived or died.

ATTACK! yelled Dod with his mind. This time his order was so forceful that the whole floor rushed toward Sirlonk, sending some of the duressers into the flames. And in the press of the moment, Dod practically flew into the middle of the surging wave of beasts and emerged with Murdore's sword in his hand. "YOU'LL PAY FOR YOUR DEEDS!" bellowed Dod, plunging at Sirlonk.

The Dread tripped backward, flipping duressers from his cloak, but caught his balance in time to deflect Dod's blow. Meanwhile, Murdore lumbered his hulkish body out of the way.

ATTACK! thought Dod again, though the creatures pulled back from the fight as The Dread's assistant waved his gloved hands in the air and ordered them to withdraw.

But Dod's rage continued. He dove at Sirlonk with vigor and swung his rapier back and forth. The clanking of the two swords echoed off the vaulted stone ceiling. Back and forth they pushed, ignoring the frenzy of hungry creatures that surrounded their feet.

"I see you're improving," noted Sirlonk frankly, enjoying the duel. "Perhaps you were paying attention in my classes after all. I never would have guessed."

Dod stabbed inward and narrowly missed connecting with Sirlonk's ribs.

"We both know you haven't learned a thing from Clair—he hates you, doesn't he?"

Dod didn't respond with words. His pressing moves with his sword explained exactly how he felt.

"Did you enjoy your stay in Driaxom?" chuckled Sirlonk. "A place like that gives a mind perspective, now doesn't it? And to think you had consigned me to a living-death sentence. What a pity for you that it didn't fit my schedule. I'm *The Dread*, Dod. You can't outsmart *me*....You can't beat me with a sword. And you most certainly can't win, Dod! I'm the best."

Dod plunged violently, hoping to at least mark Sirlonk on one of his legs, yet missed and fell over.

"Careful now," taunted Sirlonk, "I don't want you throwing up on me, too." One of the duressers broke rank and hungrily seized Dod's leg, when Sirlonk's sword sliced it in half. "Plenty of puppies to spare," he muttered. "It's not like *that* was my family's pride and joy—some two-hundred-year-old Yonkston ferret." Sirlonk's eyes played wildly in Dod's direction.

Dod wiped blood from his nose and looked up at his nemesis, wondering how he knew so much, then glanced at his silent helper, whose face remained shrouded. Sirlonk waited smugly for Dod to rise, and when Dod didn't, he decided to give him a show: The Dread swirled around in a circle, his cape licking the air, and powerfully struck his crimson blade against a thick metal post, slicing it in half.

"Shall we get on with this, or are you done?" sneered Sirlonk, pointing his invincible weapon at Dod's throat.

Dod clutched Murdore's sword tightly, but remained on the ground. He played moves in his mind and saw that the battle was almost over. The Dread was unbeatable in a duel, just as he had so often bragged. He really was the best. If he wanted Dod dead, he could swiftly deliver a blow that would end things in an instant. And he had a whole army of vicious creatures that waited to tear Dod to pieces. The only reason Sirlonk held back was because he was amused.

"Come now—are you tired, *My Little Mouse*?"

Dod slowly rose.

"Give me my keys and let's discuss how to make Dilly reveal what she knows—there's a trick to the procedure—I'm sure of it. But don't worry about the map, I can easily take it from Commendus." Sirlonk acted like they had suddenly become friends.

Dod nodded his head, dropped Murdore's sword, and reached into his shirt. "Here," he said somberly, taking his hand out…. "Go fetch them!" Dod threw the key and ring that he'd acquired in Driaxom—the one Dungo had claimed to have eaten—right into the middle of the bustling duressers and dove backward into the water. Chaos ensued, since Dod had also thought forcefully, *FEAST ON THIS!*

The swarm of beasts hungrily piled to the center and fought to devour the morsel of metal, while Dod swam to the back wall of the cave. He knew the water connected with the lake below the falls—he could feel the pounding vibrations.

STOP! blared Sirlonk with his mind, commanding the squirming critters to cease their pursuit of the key.

Dod didn't look back. He plunged below the surface and

struggled to exit the cavern. A monstrous, two-door gate, with thick metal bars and a three-foot pole latch kept the inner pond separate from the lake. It took all of Dod's strength and breath to remove the grime-covered post from its loops, unlocking the gate. Then Dod rose to the surface, rushing to get air.

"You pathetic fool!" barked The Dread. "Do you think I don't know what my own keys look like?"

Dod coughed and sputtered and did his best to fill his lungs for another push. The water was teeming with duressers and the air whizzed with the command, *BITE HIM WHEN HE RISES TO BREATHE!*

Dod dove back to the center of the gate and pushed and pulled with all of his might. It was like trying to move a brick wall. The water around him darkened as the surface fogged with swimming monsters, blocking the bright glow of the raging fire.

GO AWAY! thought Dod in vain. They didn't respond to him. They were hungry, and their screeching cries rejoiced in the chase.

Dod's lungs burned for air and his head felt faint. Out of necessity, he launched to the surface and gulped air, fighting off the ravenous creatures with his fists.

"You're a fool, Dod—and nothing more!" barked Sirlonk. "You can't open the gate. The gears and the crank are up here. It would take a dozen swimming men to move it an inch from down there."

Dod desperately struggled to keep the attacking beasts from eating him. He hated them. Their razor sharp teeth were slicing through his leather jacket with ease, and only a few of the duressers had reached him. The rest were nearing quickly.

"Too bad we can't be friends—you seem to enjoy the

company of deceivers," mocked The Dread, beginning to laugh with delight at the scene. His bloodthirsty nature drew him to the water's edge, eager to witness Dod's demise. "Perhaps now would be a good time to use your secret weapon," he taunted cruelly. Murdore chuckled, and The Dread's helper stood silently watching.

Dod plunged below the surface and swam deep, trying to free himself from the pack of demons, and he once more dug his hands into his coat pockets, this time wishing to find a lucky knife, or anything that could help him fight the duressers. Brown mud oozed between his fingers and quickly dissipated into the murky water.

Suddenly, just on the other side of the matrix of bars, a bone-chilling pair of enormous, glossy eyes emerged from the darkness, heading straight for the gate—followed closely by a second set. Mama and Popslither bashed against the double-doors and swung them wide open; and as though they'd been starving for weeks, they began to devour the sea of squiggling duressers, working their way across the top of the water toward Sirlonk.

Dod watched the scene as he slid through the gaping hole and pushed out into the lake. The diasserpentouses were enormous. Their thick, muscular bodies trailed deep into the darkness beyond the cavern, like the twisted trunks of ancient trees.

Once in the bubbling water, Dod rushed with his might to get air. He surfaced near the edge and gasped for breath as he paddled his way onto shore. Though his energy was spent, the thoughts of what lay beneath the turbulent waves triggered his exhausted legs to dash away from the beachfront like a fresh sprinter.

In front of the castle, Dod merged with Dilly and Boot, who were accompanied by Raul Hall's thirty private guards, compliments of Terro. Dod showed them to the secret door and explained the story, excluding the part about Sawny. He dreaded telling Dilly and Boot the horrible news.

Fortunately, minutes later, Commendus's soldiers arrived, accompanied by Dr. Shelderhig, who had just left Sawny's side. They, with a number of others, had been watching a rare meteor shower from the darkened back patios, despite the uncomfortable wind.

"What are you doing in my trapping jacket?" asked the good doctor, shocked to see Dod wearing it near the lake. "There's a healthy dose of bait in those pockets. It would get you killed in an instant if you fell in the water."

"Really?" said Dod sleepily, stepping out of Boot's shadow. He was just happy that Sawny was alive. Doctor Shelderhig gasped when he saw Dod was drenched and the jacket was shredded.

Dilly and Boot laughed, already knowing the story.

CHAPTER TWENTY-EIGHT

THE PRICE

In the morning, Commendus's whole manor was buzzing with news of Dod's victory over Dark Hood, who had turned out to be none other than The Dread. Soldiers had searched the pump room and secret chamber and had found meager remains of the trapped men. The Dread and his helpers were gone for good this time—an instant death-sentence in the belly of a diasserpentous. And as a token of gratitude, Commendus awarded Dod Sirlonk's crimson sword, one of the few items that hadn't been eaten by the ravenous serpents.

Doctor Shelderhig assured Commendus that the young duressers weren't likely to leave the pond and weren't likely to survive the diasserpentouses' voracious appetites, but as a precaution, Commendus ordered a thousand guards to stand watch around the lakeside, day and night for a month, guaranteeing High Gate that the beasts would all be eradicated. And he ordered a halt on trapping the creepy pair of snakes: Diasserpentouses were bad, but duressers were far worse.

Given the fresh tales of the monstrous snakes, Ingrid changed her mind and decided to return to Twistyard with Juny, claiming Tonnis wouldn't do well without her hawkeyed supervision.

Terro returned to Raul, insisting as he left that Dod and his friends come to visit, much to the chagrin of his son, Sawb, who didn't want to host Green Coosings in his homeland, no matter how many times they conquered his corrupt uncle, Sirlonk. He was jealous that Green Hall had won The Golden Swot, and he hated the attention Dod was receiving. The look on Sawb's face, all the way back to Twistyard, was sour enough to make Dod and his friends feel like life had returned to normal.

"What do you think happened to the diamonds?" asked Dilly as the caravan turned the last bend heading into Twistyard. She was happy that her great-grandfather, Bonboo, was in the group napping in a carriage, but sad that he was returning to help settle affairs by selling off the estate and the surrounding grounds.

"They're probably hidden in The Beast's underwater graveyard," said Boot. "Maybe if enough of us search for them, we'll find the bag before it's too late."

"Not likely," said Sawny, taking a deep breath as she admired the beautiful castle. Her serenity in the face of harsh reality was a sign that she was growing up. "I'm sure Sirlonk deposited them in a private account, somewhere in one of the hundreds of banks at High Gate—and under an alias, too….It's sad, but I don't think anyone will ever see them again. I'm sure the lockbox was paid-up, so it'll be hundreds of years before questions surface and the treasure is discovered. It won't be in my lifetime."

"All of this for a bag," groaned Buck, waving his hand across the expanse of Twistyard. "It's sickening to think that the price of Twistyard—and Lake Mauj, too—"

"And the Tillius Woodlands," added Boot.

"—can be bought for a pile of stones that would comfortably fit in my hands."

"Not *any* stones," said Sawny. "The Farmer's Sackload!"

"At least The Dread's gone," said Dilly, trying to find a bright side. "And maybe Dad will let some of the Coosings come to our house in Terraboom. He's always got odd jobs around."

Boot sighed heavy and long. "It's probably time for me to stretch out anyway," he said, squinting at the beautiful sky. The storm had blown over and left nothing but sunshine and blue. "Perhaps I'll sail the oceans for a while. I've always wanted to do that. By the time Pious gets done sending the billies home and commissioning the rest of them to join him in fighting Dreaderious, the seas will be safer than ever."

"I'll come with you," offered Dod, not wanting to part with his best friend.

"Count me in," said Buck, trying to hide his melancholy tone. "Especially if we can fish every day."

"Then I better hurry and get in the dances you all promised," choked Sawny, fighting her emotions. Dilly couldn't speak; tears were streaming down her cheeks.

"Where's Bowy?" asked Dod, swallowing an apple-sized frog in his throat. He hated seeing things end.

"I thought he'd be riding with us," responded Boot, trying to ignore the atmosphere. "Something must have come up."

"Well, he should have left a note!" snapped Dilly through her tears, subtly reprimanding Sawny one more time for not informing her before slipping out to stargaze.

Inside the castle, people were bustling with preparations for the evening's Dance Delight. Bright red, yellow, and blue streamers were fastened to the ceiling and ornate decorations were situated throughout the Great Hall, making it appear like an enchanted forest.

The castle's corridors smelled more like cookies than ever before. Mercy had spent days baking thousands of them, dozens of different kinds, which melted Pone's heart. "I *love* dances," he kept mumbling to himself, sniffing the air all the way to Green Hall.

Boot's room was nearly repaired, though the floor still had a deep gouge in it, reminding the Coosings and Greenlings of the frightful confrontation they'd endured.

Within seconds of entering the bedroom, Boot and Buck were fighting over Dod's clothes, trying to decide who would get to wear his deep-blue blazer to the dance. Sneaker liked being home. He raced around the room smelling the air before scurrying up his favorite branch for a nap.

Dod gazed at his wardrobe from Pap's place and remembered about Boot's promise. "I'm heading up the wall," he said. "Do either of you want to come along?"

Boot and Buck stared for a moment.

"Don't you value your life?" choked Buck, finally speaking. "The girls take these dances very seriously. If you hope to wake up tomorrow, you'd better stay and get ready—but if you don't mind being suffocated in your sleep—"

"Or having your toes snipped off with scissors—"

"Or your eyes seared out with a hot poker—"

"I'll be back," assured Dod, ignoring their fun. "It won't take long."

"Right," said Boot, nodding his head. "I've heard that one before. Just remember that we warned you. Bad things happen when you mess with occasions like this. Go ahead and ask Pone about the time he tried to fit in a horserace before Moonlight Madness."

Dod waited.

"Let's just say he was lucky it only took three casts to bind up his broken bones," concluded Boot, jestfully serious.

"I'll probably return before the two of you get done deciding who's going to wear my blue blazer," insisted Dod, unlatching the pack to look at the freshwater sponge. It had turned gray and the water was murkier than before.

"There's not much to see," said Buck, tilting his head to catch a glimpse of the weed.

"Boot promised," sighed Dod, reassembling the load and hefting it onto his back. The water was heavy and sloshed obnoxiously.

"It was more of a suggestion, not a promise," insisted Boot. "Make sure you're quick." He followed Dod to the door and gave it a pat. His voice had changed to reflect that he was serious about the girls feeling bad if Dod missed the dancing.

Behind the castle, Dod walked across the rotting planks and smelled the Lake Mauj breeze. He wondered whether Sirlonk was right about Humberrone being his father. If he were, why hadn't Bonboo ever mentioned it? And Dod wondered how Sirlonk had known so much about what was going on at Twistyard.

The Tipper drew Dod to its base. It was the troublesome part of the cliff wall where it jut out precariously before correcting. Dod knelt down and ran his hand across the small cluster of initials that were carved into the stone. One pair read S.R. Dod smiled. "Stephen Richards," he muttered. Maybe his father had been part of the TCC and had knifed his true initials into the stone after completing the difficult climb.

"This is for you, Dad," mumbled Dod, wiping his eyes. He'd fought feelings of frustration for years over losing his father, and he'd buried them; yet magically, Sirlonk's words had reopened the wound and left him sitting on his bed, an eight-year-old boy, tears streaming down his cheeks as he stared at an envelope with his name on it.

Dod swung his first palsarflex high in the air and shot up it, then his second, then his first, then his second. He rushed the ropes until his arms burned. It was good to work through the pain. The higher Dod scaled, the more he forgot. And by the time he reached the treacherous segment, he was at peace.

"No wonder there are only five names below this one," grunted Dod, scoping the roof-like outcropping. He threw his palsarflex over and over before it cleared the lip and seemed to stick.

Dod tugged and tugged. It held, so he carefully attached himself to the rope and swung out. Hundreds of feet below him, the lonely dock was empty—not a soul in sight. Back and forth Dod swayed until his upward movement settled the line. Once he'd stowed his alternate palsarflex, he hustled in earnest, ready to be done with the freefall. It was creepy. And his stomach yelled something bad was about to happen.

Near the tip of the ledge, Dod heard a voice. At first he thought he was imaging things, but as he slowly pulled his body over the lip, he beheld a man, hopping back and forth in a shallow cave. Dod hugged the ground and watched nervously.

"Take this!" huffed the man, jumping toward the inner-most part of the nook. His back was turned to Dod. "I'll have you for lunch if you ever speak like that to me again!" raged the man. "Do you know who I am?"

Dod did, and he found the circumstance highly unusual. It was Horsely—talking to himself—and he wasn't hobbling!

Panic flooded Dod's chest, making it hard for him to breathe. He wanted to quickly escape, but the dreaded freefall was a horrible option, especially after he'd discovered that only three of his five palsarflex balls had attached correctly. The ledge surface was crumbling. It was miraculous he hadn't already died. The cliff above the cave looked fine, yet he'd need to expose himself to Horsely in order to get up to it.

And then Dod saw his salvation. Half concealed under a coil of rope near the mouth of the cave was a second sword. It was Dod's insurance. Dod sprang to his feet and dashed to the weapon, though in drawing it out he clanked the hilt against the rock wall.

Instantly, Horsely spun around ready to fight.

"You can hear," gasped Dod. His whole image of Horsely was changing by the second.

"What's it to you?" asked Horsely, dipping his blade to the ground. "I've been recovering lately. Everyone's gonna be surprised when they meet the new me."

"Yeah," said Dod hesitantly. His gut was screaming things that conflicted with his mind.

"It's nice to see I'm not the only one who's climbing the wall these days," sighed Horsely, cracking a smile. He wiped sweat from his brow and moved toward Dod. "Are you climbing as a group?"

"No," stuttered Dod, and then he wished he had said yes.

"You're brave to do it alone. I really respect that." Horsely picked up his canteen and took a swig. "Is that a palsarflex?" he asked, looking at the five red balls, three of which were pancake flat against the stone.

"Yup," said Dod, beginning to feel better. Horsely was showing no signs of aggression.

"I bet you have all sorts of neat gadgets, don't you?" said Horsely, inspecting the contraption with his eyes. He approached it and bent down to get a better look. "You're lucky to have Pap as your grandpa."

By the time Horsely rose, Dod's face gave away that the charade was over. Dod had caught a glimpse of Dilly's Soosh Mayler Belt around Horsely's waist, hidden under his shirt.

"Dod, Dod, Dod," hummed Horsely, raising his blade in the air. "It's finally time for you to make a choice."

Dod felt like he was talking with a ghost. "You're The Dread's helper!" huffed Dod, feeling winded. The shock sucked his breath.

"One of many, I'm sure," said Horsely cautiously. "Join The Order—rise to power with us! You don't have to fight it, Dod."

"But the snakes finished you off," choked Dod, backing up.

"Nearly," he responded. A big grin crossed his face. "It was every man for himself last night, wasn't it? That pair, sure as dirt, shocked the pants right off of Sirlonk and Murdore. They thought you were bluffing when you said you had a secret weapon! And snakes like *that* don't respond to belts like *this*." Horsely patted his mayler belt and chuckled.

"Is Sirlonk alive?" begged Dod, feeling horribly conflicted. The more he spoke to Horsely, the more he realized Horsely was still the same person who had helped him get his medallion despite Youk's wrath, and he was the same person who had frequently joked around with all of the Coosings, and he was the nice guy who had tricked Jibb and the soldiers into cleaning the stalls for Boot.

"I can't say," responded Horsely. "Well, it's not like I stuck around to see what became of them. I bet that male snake had a mouth as big as Bertha's."

"Bertha?"

"The Beast," said Horsely. "She was really something, wasn't she? I can't believe how much she ate."

"You knew that thing was telling me stuff—" began Dod.

"Sure—you caught me," chuckled Horsely. "And Dilly thought you were nuts after the bit about Bertha under the dock. My big gal was just waiting for dinner—"

"Those horses—" blurted Dod.

"You're quick," conceded Horsely. "I had to fatten her up or she wouldn't have laid any eggs. It's quite a chore—even for a mayler like me—to persuade a duresser to reproduce in captivity." Horsely's eyes narrowed as he added, "And thanks to your *secret weapon*, years of work just turned to boosap!"

"Sorry," said Dod instinctively. It came out before he had thought about it, the way things often do when you're joking with your friends. In truth, Dod certainly wasn't sorry he had killed the young duressers, considering he had nearly been tortured to death by them while Horsely had done nothing to stop the creatures. Not to mention, Bertha had attempted to kill people in Green Hall and had succeeded with some of the drat soldiers, whose bones lay rotting in piles at the bottom of Bertha's vacant lair!

"It's okay," said Horsely, dipping his sword down. "You've caused plenty of setbacks, but I forgive you. We don't always get it right the first time."

Dod's mind filled with memories. "When we were flying—you meant to take a detour, didn't you? Dropping that bag wasn't an accident."

"Just a little favor—"

"And when Grubber was acting up," continued Dod, putting the pieces together, "you cheated with Dilly's belt!"

Dod paused. "You've been stealing him, haven't you!"

"Borrowing," chortled Horsely. "Calm down. No harm done. He always turns up, doesn't he? Besides, when you're part of The Order, everything is yours."

"No harm done?" stuttered Dod, recalling the flaming arrow. "You nearly killed Bowy and Chikada at Carsigo—and your creature's been eating people!"

Horsely smiled and shook his head. "You're twisting things to make them sound bad. The duresser wasn't mine, and if I shot a wayward arrow, so what? You don't even know how wonderful the benefits are, Dod. It's great to be part of The Order—it's really a privilege."

Dod was speechless.

Horsely misread Dod's stupor and stuck out his hand, showing the Coosings' sign of friendship. "So," concluded Horsely, "are you ready to join?"

"About that," began Dod, feeling his face turn hotter than it already was, "I can't betray everyone...and I definitely can't betray myself. Call it what you will—I won't become like Sirlonk!"

"You don't have to," pleaded Horsely, his eyes turning gears like The Dread's. "All I ask is that you're faithful to me—you answer to me and do what I say—and as things change, Dod, you'll be part of the rising government."

"What? So I can stand silently, my face shrouded in shame, as my friends are fed to a lake of hungry beasts? I don't think so!"

"You wouldn't have died last night!" huffed Horsely, spinning away from Dod in a jealous rage. "They don't want *you* dead."

"Who?" shouted Dod.

"Our connections!" scoffed Horsely, glancing over his shoulder. It was clear he felt bitter that Dod was highly valued by the evil organization, despite Dod's rebellions against them.

"Sirlonk takes instructions, too," he continued, pacing the ledge. "Whether he's dead or alive, The Order will rule all of Green, Raul, and Soosh, and they've already got a place for you in it. You're lucky."

Dod wanted to throw up.

"It's really simple, Dod. We're friends. You sometimes do things for friends—hard things. But in return, the payback is—well—beyond your capacity to understand right now."

"You're a liar!" said Dod, feeling his backbone stiffen. He thought of how close he'd come to dying at the hands of The Beast. "Before the tournaments your pet nearly ate me," he hissed. "She was going to—I heard her thoughts, Horsely. The game's over!"

"WRONG!" shouted Horsely angrily, jumping in Dod's direction. His friendly demeanor was gone. "She was going to grab you and carry you off, so Sirlonk could convince you to see the light."

"You mean *the dark*!" spat Dod, ready to duel. He hoped he was good enough to live.

"Don't you care about your friends?" asked Horsely.

"Yes," grumbled Dod. "But your favors aren't much help—like the note you sent to Boot warning him of Bertha."

"What?" sputtered Horsely. His face looked perplexed.

"You know all about it! You cared enough to tell us she was coming to eat someone—big deal! We were ready anyway."

Horsely paused. "Boot got a note?"

"Duh!"

"Last chance," offered Horsely, his eyes glossing with a new shade of evil. "Join us or die!"

Dod felt the weight of the heavy sword in his hand and knew he wasn't leaving without a fight. He slid the pack from his back and then sprung at Horsely as he rose, hoping to catch him off guard.

Back and forth they pressed at each other, their swords gleaming in the late-afternoon sun.

"You're no match for me," taunted Horsely. "I've been well trained."

"Good!" fibbed Dod, trying to stay positive. He spun a powerful blow to the left, then a quick duck and jab to the right. It caught Horsely's shirt, but didn't draw blood."

"You've done it now!" raged Horsely, his pride tarnished. He lunged at Dod and swung his sword repeatedly, like a crazed maniac. Dod deflected the blows and stumbled out of his reach.

Eventually, their swords locked. Dod hoped to nudge Horsely near the edge, so he would become more reasonable; unfortunately, Horsely was much stronger. The plan backfired miserably. In an instant, the duel was over and Dod was clinging frantically to the end of his poorly-anchored palsarflex.

"I'm a forgiving man," huffed Horsely, catching his breath as he leaned over the edge to look at Dod. "Hear me out. If you join us, I'll let you live. And I'll go light on you. We'll chop off two of your fingers on your left hand and wound one of your legs—to prove your loyalty to me. We'll tell everyone we fought against The Dread—and we chased him off. And if you play your part well, nobody else needs to get hurt."

"What?" gasped Dod. He thought he had misunderstood him.

"If you ever betray The Order by revealing our secrets, I'll be forced to hurt people you love….Maybe Dilly, or Sawny, or Buck."

"YOU'RE AN ANIMAL, HORSELY!" yelled Dod, hoping

someone would hear him. His voice echoed off the cliff wall and trumpeted out over Lake Mauj.

"If you yell again," hissed Horsely, "your palsarflex is going to have a tragic accident." Horsely pointed the tip of his sword at the three working balls.

"Okay, okay," said Dod, feeling death approach. He had made the mistake of looking down to see if anyone was listening.

"You try to paint things black and white," continued Horsely, scowling at Dod as he attempted to justify what he'd become. "But it's all gray, Dod! Everything is painted in shades of gray! Even your wonderful grandpa knew that. Did he ever tell you about the night he gave The Dread a wicked beating? I was there, Dod! I took my share of hits alongside of Pap. I believed in him. I trusted he would fight to the death to save us — to save Green. And do you know what he did? He ran off like a coward and claimed he'd been injured."

"You don't understand," blurted Dod, wanting desperately to explain.

"No! It's you who doesn't understand! I crawled to the door when I heard Pap's knock, but there stood The Dread —"

"Pap was injured!" said Dod, starting to climb the rope.

"If you move another inch I'll send you to the ground!" ordered Horsely. He pulled away and then returned with Dod's pack.

"I didn't want to join them," continued Horsely, his face oozing regret. "But I had no choice. So to prove my loyalty to The Order, I've spent these years hobbling and reading lips. It was the price they demanded. And do you know whose fault it is? Pap's! He left me to die! He was as healthy as a spring stallion when he ran off. I know it, Dod. He visited me in the hospital two days after the fight, and I promise you, he was as solid as he ever was."

"I know," said Dod, straining to think of a way to explain their unusual circumstance—how time had stood still in Green for Pap, except for the two days he'd spent with his medallion off, while in a hospital in critical condition.

Horsely undid Dod's pack and reached in. "If you call me a traitor, then you have to throw Pap in the same pot. He was a member of The Order…"

Dod was silent. Horsely's face had become dark, for he was a murderer. Dod knew Horsely was looting his pack in preparation to throw it off the ledge with his body, so people wouldn't wonder where it had gone.

"I'd rather keep you alive, especially since you're *Pap's special grandson*," admitted Horsely. "But I can't have you tell anyone of my affiliations. That would ruin everything for me."

Horsely dug his hands into Dod's things and peered eagerly. "If you must die," he continued, distracted by his pillaging, "The Order will need to know that it was a *terrible accident*—one that *I* had nothing to do with." His remorseless eyes left Dod's bag momentarily to glance threateningly at Dod. There wasn't the slightest hint of pity or mercy. And then it happened. Horsely let out a thunderous howl. He was in excruciating pain! He raised his trembling hand and grabbed at his wrist. The Ankle Weed had decided it was done with the stagnant water and dying sponge and had attached to Horsely's probing arm.

"Aaaaa!" cried Horsely bitterly, but before he could steady himself, he passed out and tumbled off the ledge.

Dod didn't look down. He climbed back up as fast as he could. He felt sorry for Horsely and sad that the good side of him had been beaten out by the bad. And he felt sick as he thought about The Order. How much of it was true? But before he had wasted his time wallowing, he caught sight of something that lifted his spirits substantially: It was Bonboo's bag of pure-sight diamonds!

"No wonder Horsely jumped in the water so quickly," mumbled Dod, smelling the stinky sack. It reeked like The Beast's lair. "Boot was right!"

Dod excitedly rooted through Horsely's pile and found something with Pap's name sewn on the side: It was a small pouch of gold coins. "If only I could give these to my mom for Christmas," he lamented, knowing that he couldn't bring anything home with him to Earth.

At the bottom of Horsely's things, Dod found a curious treasure—an old, worn, leather map. The letters TCC were written prominently, and based on the lay of the land, to the best of Dod's ability to read it, someone had penned in ancient, frilly letters, 'The Lost City,' right where High Gate should have been noted. It was a curious find, to say the least.

With eager hands, Dod emptied his backpack and loaded it with Horsely's stash—except he stuffed the leather map in a separate pocket. He couldn't wait to give the jewels back to Bonboo, for he knew what they meant—Twistyard wouldn't be sold!

At the base of the cliff, Dod carefully approached Horsely, whose limp body was sunken into the rotten wood. "Sorry you were tricked," mumbled Dod, fighting off a wave of conflicting feelings. "Pap would have come back to save you if he could have—he tried—it wasn't his fault—"

It was pointless for Dod to explain—Horsely was dead. Nevertheless, he continued attempting while slipping Dilly's belt from Horsely's waist. Part of Dod's ramblings were coming from deep down inside. It was scary for him to consider the unfortunate circumstances that had swayed Horsely into joining The Order. What would he have done if he were thrown in the same situation? And if he were somehow tricked into their web—stuck in the matrix of evil—what would he do? Would he leave, knowing that his loved ones would be hurt?

No one heard Dod's ramblings but a few lonely yurflos. The dock was deserted as usual. And then a soft, sweet breeze blew in Dod's face. "I wouldn't do what he did," concluded Dod, eyeing the initials on the wall. "No matter where I go or who I'm around, and no matter what people call me, I'm always Cole Richards when I look in the mirror! My integrity is worth more than my life, just like it was for Pap…and just like—"

Dod bent down and ran his hand across the letters S.R. Next to them, he scratched C.R. And there it was—the peace he'd been looking for.

When Dod entered the Great Hall, Dilly's eyes caught him scoldingly. She was wearing a magnificent, flowing dress with pearls and lace, and she was dancing with Bonboo.

"Sorry I'm late," said Dod, using all of his self-control to hold back the smile that consumed the face in his mind. He approached Dilly confidently as she glanced up and down at his dirty clothes. "I had a few things to take care of."

"You're in trouble now, bro," said Pone, who was dressed in a dapper suit and dancing with Donshi.

"I tried to warn you," added Boot, wearing the blue blazer and leading Sawny closer to the pending explosion. He twirled her playfully as he moved, as though the direction they were heading had nothing to do with his desire to have a front-row spot for the fireworks.

Buck's eyes were glued to Dod, too, though he remained where he was, taking a spin with Eluxa. And Toos couldn't break free of Ingrid, no matter what—the music was still playing.

"You've already missed six!" informed Dilly. "And I must say—as a friend of course—that no one's going to dance with you so long as you're looking like *that!*"

"Dilly," said Bonboo patiently, "don't be quick to judge. Beneath every wiggling glove is a hand, and it's behind the mask where the true man lies. He has his good reasons, I'm sure: We know Dod."

Dilly surveyed Dod's face and caught a glimpse of his glee, and then she returned a curious look. Her adventurous side was kicking in. Dod had been up to real action, she could sense it. And though she *liked* dances and took them seriously, she *loved* swordplay and intrigue.

Dod swung his pack around and pulled Dilly's Soosh Mayler Belt from the top. "Here you go, my lady. Your good luck." Dod bowed like a gentleman asking her to dance.

"Sopper!" coughed Boot from a few feet away. He was wishing he had such a nice gift to offer Dilly.

"Thank you!" burst Dilly, leaving Bonboo to give Dod a big hug. "Where did you find it?"

"I've got more," added Dod, pulling the coin pouch from the pack. He handed it to Boot and looked him in the eyes. "Get your mom a place in the city."

"What?" gasped Boot, nudging the opening wider with his fingers. When he saw the gold coins, his whole face lit up. "Are you serious, Dod? This is probably all of Pap's savings! I could *buy* my mom a house for this much—and a good one!"

"Just make sure it has a bathroom," joked Dod.

Buck saw the commotion and couldn't stay put any longer, though Eluxa tried to hold him in the Raul crowd. She scowled crossly as he left her to join Boot in counting the coins. "But the song isn't over," she pouted, her bright-red lips bulging with disappointment.

And to Dod's surprise, another person joined the two brothers, having left his dance partner: It was Bowy! "Thanks Dod! I can't believe you're helping our family like this—" He put his hand up to his face and fought 'seasonal allergies.' "You don't know how much this means to us."

"Now you don't have to go to sea," said Sawny, looking at the three brothers, then glancing at Dilly.

"Or anywhere else," laughed Dod, pulling the Farmer's Sackload out of his bag. He handed it to Bonboo and watched as the old man started to cry. "I think this is rightfully yours."

Dilly and Sawny both joined their great-grandfather in hugging Dod, after which Sawny insisted on being his first dance—as soon as he was done passing out gifts.

"I have one for you, too," whispered Dod to Sawny. "But I have to give it to you later. It's a map with all sorts of tricky writing. It looks really old."

Sawny's eyes sparkled with delight. She couldn't wait to begin deciphering.

"So where did you get all of this from?" asked Bonboo, still struggling to speak. He was grateful beyond words that Twistyard wouldn't have to be sold.

"Horsely," confessed Dod in a somber tone. "He was helping The Dread, faking his injuries and everything—but he's dead now—he fell off the back wall of the castle."

Everyone looked surprised and sad, though Boot looked the most disturbed. "Did he say anything?" asked Boot.

"Not really," fibbed Dod, trying to let everyone remember the good in Horsely and hoping they'd never find out how dark he really was. "Well—he just said he felt awful about what he'd done and that he wished he hadn't ever gotten tricked into helping The Dread."

"Oh, right. He must have carried a lot of guilt," said Dilly, shaking her head. "I sure would have if I had had anything to do with them!"

Bonboo gave Dod a knowing glance before hobbling away with the jewels.

The band began to play a beautiful slow song, so Sawny snatched Dod by the hand and led him into the waltzing throng. Dod left his pack on the floor next to the three rejoicing brothers, Boot's voice rising above the other two, "We could always tell her I secretly became a doctor…"

Everything felt at peace. Even if there was trouble still lurking from The Order, their plans had been substantially derailed: their prized creature was dead, along with its spawn and one of its masters, as well as probably two more; and their plan to buy the billies with jewels was certainly hopeless, since Bonboo had the loot and Pious was headed to negotiate with the malcontents at sea; and with Zerny using his falcons to catch pigeons, messages to and from members in The Order were likely to be disrupted from time to time.

Dod enjoyed dancing. The music was peaceful, and Sawny's company was his favorite. He'd take two twirls with her over The Dread's crimson blade he'd hid in Boot's secret hiding place. And *she* had asked *him* to dance! There was hope that one day she'd start looking across the table at him the way she'd been looking at Pone.

THE PRICE

As Dod gazed happily at the colorful dresses and suits, they faded before his eyes and were replaced by darkness. A stinky, ragged chair pushed uncomfortably at Dod's face.

I'm home! he thought. His heart raced with concern as he wondered about the pirate-like people who had been ready to mash him to a pulp, right before he left Earth.

The trailer was silent, and the only light within it came from the moon, whose beams trickled through the muddy windows in dim shafts.

Dod carefully peeked around, then stood up. He was alone, and the clock on the wall said it was just past one in the morning.

"Let's see—it's Monday," mumbled Dod, calculating his time based on how long he'd left his medallion off. "That means it's…Christmas Eve!"

Dod crept out from behind the chair and turned to leave when something caught his eye. A six-inch dagger was stabbing into the center of the wobbly card table, pinning down a torn piece of fabric. It had a brief note scribbled on it in bad handwriting:

Better luck next time, Dod!

The word that surprised Dod the most was his name. How did anyone on Earth know that he was Dod? Could The Dread come and go as he did? And if so, how did time stop and start? None of it made sense. But Dod was so glad to slip out of the trailer unmashed that he didn't care. And he had just been dancing with Sawny, not to mention he had saved Twistyard from being sold.

His jubilation continued all the way to the bus stop and wasn't even hampered when a half-drunk man spilled his drink across Dod's lap on the early-morning ride from Vegas to Cedar City.

"I'm home," announced Dod, barging through the duplex door about eight-thirty. Doralee jumped from the floor, beside their meager Christmas Tree, and raced into Cole's arms.

"I'm sorry," sobbed Doralee, apologizing for pressuring Cole to visit with a shrink. "You can have all the nightmares you want. It doesn't matter—"

"No, I'm sorry, Mom," said Cole. "I shouldn't have run off the way I did."

Cole's brothers, Josh and Alex, thumped down the stairs when they heard his low voice. Alex joined the hugging twosome, while Josh raced to pick up a large present from beneath the Christmas Tree.

"I knew you'd beat 'em, Cole," said Josh, beaming ear-to-ear. "That's why I got you this!"

Book 3

THE
Adventures
OF
DOD
CODE OF THE KINGS

AVAILABLE FALL OF 2012

For more information, go to

www.TheAdventuresofDod.com

Cole's Christmas break is certainly not a rest for his mind. He's home, but something shocking drives him back to Green with a purpose! And it will take more than Sneaker's nose to reveal the rats. Increasingly, the destinies of Green, Raul, Soosh, and Earth are melting together as the present discovers the past.

With the clock ticking, Dod and his Twistyard contingent must race to gain the upper hand in the stand against The Order, whose diabolical plans are nearly unstoppable. Loyal friendships will be pushed to their limits. If you dare know the truth, follow the clues wherever they may lead!

Thanks for being part
of the adventure!

We would really love to have you come and visit us at **www.TheAdventuresofDod.com** for free downloads: free e-books, free audio-books, free maps, free comics, and more! It's the site for all things Dod related. Make sure you tell your friends that they can read book one for free if they download an e-version of it from our website. We hope everyone gets a chance to enjoy the series.

Questions for Discussion

1. Cole had the unfortunate experience of having people at his school say a lot of mean things about him. What advice did Alex give him? What about his mother, Josh, and Aunt Hilda? Which person do you think gave him the best advice? Have you ever had people say mean things about you? How did you handle it? How do you think your parents would have handled it?

2. Jack Parry told Cole, "There are only two kinds of people in the world. The kind that do stuff and the kind that always talk about doing stuff. Nobody's in between." What do you think he meant? How is he right and how is he wrong? Which of those categories would Jack Parry put you in? Why? Who can you think of that is exemplary at getting stuff done?

3. Dari and Valerie are sisters, but they are very different people. How does Dari act? How does Valerie act? When would it be good to act like Valerie, and when would it be good to act like Dari? We're all unique people. How are you similar to your friends and family members, and how are you different? If you could gain one attribute from someone else, what ability would you choose?

4. Dod had to face many fears in this book. Where do you think he got his courage from? When you've had to face hard things, what has given you courage? What advice do you think Dod would give to others who are facing challenges?

5. At one point, Sawb teased Boot about his family's poverty. What kinds of things should we never tease other people about? Have you ever had people hurt your feelings when they teased you?

Questions Continued

What did you do? What are some good ways to handle difficult situations like that?

6. Buck complained to Boot, "You take a few ideas and then rush back to your own muscles!" What do you think Buck meant? When is it better for a whole group to make a decision instead of having one person decide? Can you think of a time when a large group of people helped to make a decision? The United States of America is a democratic republic. What does that mean?

7. In speaking of the Lost City, Dark Hood says, "...it has something of mine—something I need before it's too late—something that's more valuable than ten High Gates filled with gold!" What could possibly be so important? What kinds of things are priceless to you and your family? What makes them so precious?

8. Bonboo counseled Dilly, "...don't be quick to judge. Beneath every wiggling glove is a hand, and it's behind the mask where the true man lies. He has his good reasons, I'm sure: We know Dod." What do you think Bonboo was trying to tell Dilly? How can that guidance be good advice for us, too? Have you ever thought people were doing something wrong and later you learned they had good reasons for their actions? What can we do to be less judgmental?

9. In the book it says that Ingrid would have been willing to trade all of her time riding with Toos for ten minutes with Boot. What was Boot's secret to making Ingrid feel happy? Can you think of any individuals who are good at making people want to be around them? What kinds of things do they do?

FOR MORE COMICS, GO TO

www.TheAdventuresofDod.com

"Now I know why billies like to stay at sea."

"Look who he has to come home to!"

About the Author

Thomas R. Williams grew up in Utah roaming the mountains and fields with his best friend, Kyle. He often reminded his mother that he was an outdoor boy and, therefore, had no need for books. He's since had a slight change of heart. Perhaps if *The Adventures of Dod* had been around, he would have spent a little more time inside.

His wife and twelve children enjoy trying to pry Thomas into divulging the secrets that everyone in Green is seeking, but aside from a few that he's accidentally mumbled in his sleep, the information remains safe.

To learn more about the crazy author of this seven book series, or to have a few laughs, go to www.TheAdventuresofDod.com. Also, you can email the author at Tom@TheAdventuresofDod.com.